# DEAD MEN DON'T GIVE SEMINARS

124

# DEAD MEN DON'T GIVE SEMINARS

Dorothy Sucher

## ST. MARTIN'S PRESS
### NEW YORK

*Design by Claire Counihan*

*Library of Congress Cataloging-in-Publication Data*

Sucher, Dorothy.
  Dead men don't give seminars/by Dorothy Sucher.
      p.      cm.
  ISBN 0–312–01415–5:$16.95
  I. Title.
PS3557.L353D4 1988
813'.54—dc19                                                                87–29928

First Edition

10  9  8  7  6  5  4  3  2  1

To the memory of my mother,
SHIRLEY BRYANT

# ONE

I found my boss, Sabina Swift, painting in a deck chair in the shade of a sugar maple. She was wearing a starched white smock, as she always does when she paints. I tell her it makes her look like a dentist, but that's just to tease her. Actually she looks more like chief of surgery in some big metropolitan hospital. It's something about those cool blue eyes and the authoritative way she carries her slightly top-heavy, forty-five-year-old body.

I waved. She didn't wave back and I wasn't surprised, even though I'd just driven up from Washington to Burlington, Vermont, a mere ten-hour trip, to spend the weekend with her and her husband. After all, she was painting. One thing at a time.

I came over to where she was sitting. There was a table in front of her with tubes of oil paint fanned out very neatly, a jar of tiny brushes, and a canvas that measured eight-by-ten inches. For her, that was huge. Most of her paintings are four by six. Sabina bent over and deposited a chartreuse dot on her canvas with a brush that had so few hairs—three, maybe—that it was practically bald. I said, "My God, you're painting a tree! I can see you're on vacation." At home she paints nothing but flowers, one flower per picture. Each picture takes her a month to do.

"Red spruce," she said. "They're indigenous. This seemed a good time to try an experiment. Do you want to go to the cocktail party at the Institute tonight, Vic?"

"Why not? I've never seen forty theoretical physicists in

1

one room before, not to mention two Nobel prizewinners . . . That's a lot of concentrated brainpower."

"And me without a college degree."

That's one of her vulnerable areas. She doesn't have many, or at least she doesn't often let them show. The last thing Sabina has to worry about is whether she has a college degree, because she's one of the smartest people I've ever met, and one of the best educated. Most of what she knows she's taught herself, through travel and constant reading. I could tell, though, that she was nervous about mingling with the academics. I said, "So they know more than you about physics. So what? They should, that's their field. When it comes to anything else, you can think rings around them."

A speck of blue landed on the canvas next to the chartreuse dot. At this rate the picture was going to take a long time to finish. "I assure you I'm not losing any sleep over it, Victor," she said dryly.

She always calls me Victor when I hit her a little too close to home. The rest of the time I'm Vic. "This place have a shower?" I asked.

She placed a dot of red on the canvas, swished her tiny brush around in a baby-food jar of turpentine, and placed the brush, hairs upward, in a frozen orange juice can. Then she rose, wiping her hands on her smock. Why she wipes them I don't know, they never have any paint on them—and please don't ask me how she manages to keep them so clean. The woman is compulsively neat. She claims this simply reflects a precise and methodical mind, and quotes me Zen: "What is within, surrounds us." Personally, like any self-respecting former psych major, I suspect it has more to do with how her mother toilet-trained her. Unfortunately I lack data on this vital subject and I must remember to ask Sabina about it sometime, when I'm ready to move on to a new employment situation.

She said, "Get your bags and I'll show you your room."

Two hours later, showered, shaved, and smelling hopefully of Brut, I was ready for the cocktail party. Not that I ex-

2

pected to encounter any beautiful, unattached female physicists avid for my body, but I have a right to my fantasies, like everyone else. Which usually remain just that, fantasies; for some reason the women I attract hardly ever interest me, though it's easy enough to fool around with them, while the ones I find attractive turn me into a tongue-tied idiot. I have theories about the reasons for this, which I won't go into here. Still, I like to feel I learn something from every painful encounter, and that some day . . .

Anyway, I was wearing my best jeans, a pair of white Adidas sneakers, and a brand-new blue plaid flannel shirt that I thought would be suitably rural for the occasion. I'd heard Vermont was an informal state and I didn't want to appear overdressed.

Sabina had managed to make herself look feminine, which is a trick she has when she goes out in the evenings. I guess it's cosmetics that make the difference, and stuff she does to her hair. She's not a bad-looking woman for her age. She has a heart-shaped faced with a pointed, cleft chin, a turned-up nose, and a cupid's-bow mouth that can flatten into a disapproving slit faster than you would believe possible. The skin of her jaw could be firmer, and there are lines at the corners of her pale blue eyes that add character to her face. She looks Irish. On her busty upper half she was wearing a sort of half-sweater, half-shawl thing made, she informed me, of Vermont wool, over a tight knee-length skirt of gray mohair. Her body has thickened some around the waist, but she still has very good legs with delicate ankles and she's proud of them, judging from the fact that she always wears extremely sheer stockings and expensive shoes with high, needle-thin heels. Tonight the stockings were tinted pale gray, with faint silvery flecks in them, and the shoes were black suede. There were twisted silver loops hanging from her ears. She looked elegant.

I was proud to escort her to my van, and opened the door on the passenger side with a flourish. She stuck her head inside and said, "How can you drive such a filthy car? It looks like Tobacco Road on wheels."

Stung, I said, "You wouldn't understand, because of the

3

generation gap." My car is a nine-year-old Volkswagen Microbus, which happens to be one of the finest, roomiest, most durable vehicles ever made. Also one of the cheapest, no small plus on the salary Sabina pays me. I see no reason not to keep a lot of stuff in it, otherwise all that space just goes to waste.

"We'll take the Mercedes," she said, and added, to appease me, "You can drive it."

I chauffeured her to the Champlain Valley Physics Institute. It was set on a hill overlooking Lake Champlain, which we could see below us, flecked with sailboats and sparkling in the late-afternoon sun. On the far shore, range after range of blue and purple mountains retreated into upstate New York.

"Quite a view," I said, as we bumped up a long gravel driveway to the administration building. "Physicists know how to live. Do these guys actually do any work, or do they just come up here on their grants and go sailing?"

"They exchange ideas, Vic."

"Doesn't sound too exhausting. I wouldn't mind doing that for a month."

Her eyebrows rose. "Don't be too sure. It isn't easy to exchange their kind of ideas. When I ask Bruno questions about his work I find his answers hard to follow."

"You too, huh? That's a help."

We were approaching a big white clapboard house with a porch running around three sides. Sabina said, "That's the administration building, which used to be a farmhouse. This whole area was once a farm, or rather several. The seminars are held in the barn, which is also where the cocktail party is going to take place in about an hour. That small building over there, which used to be a one-room schoolhouse, is the Institute's library, and there are a number of other buildings that are used for offices and VIP housing."

"How come you didn't get one of those?"

She shook her head. "Victor, you have to remember that this is a community where status depends on only one thing—achievement in physics. These people are intensely competitive. The sort of work *I* do may be a matter of some curiosity

4

to the physicists—in fact, it is—but what really matters here is that Bruno is not really a world-class physicist, even though he's quite good. Pull up here."

I parked next to a big spruce. There were a lot of cars in the driveway, most of them with stickers from car-rental agencies on the rear bumpers. The participants in the Institute had flown in from all over the world. "I have to run up to Bruno's office. I'll meet you in the barn in an hour," Sabina said. We got out of the car and she turned and started heading up a hill toward a long, low yellow building that looked as if it might have started life as a chicken barn. Her stiletto heels sank into the earth with every step, and I wondered if she'd brought any sneakers with her. She was going to need a pair.

I'd been working for Sabina Swift for—God, was it possible?—almost five years, ever since I'd gotten fed up with being a used car salesman. Before that I'd been a psychiatric aide in one of the chronic wards at the state hospital in Crownsville, Maryland—not that that job had been fantastic either, in terms of my duties or my paycheck, but at least it had some logical connection, minimal though it seemed at times, to what I'd learned as a psychology major at the University of Maryland. I'd been warned more than once during my student years that I shouldn't expect to find any great jobs in the field of psychology with only a bachelors degree, but I was sick of taking exams and figured that my advisers had failed to take into account the fact that a dynamic, energetic, creative prospective job seeker such as myself simply had to have a brilliant future. Such is the arrogance of youth, as I learned in the months that followed my graduation. Finally I became so hungry and demoralized that when Crownsville offered me a job at barely more than the minimum wage, I was actually eager to take it, even though I'd sworn I'd never work in a state hospital.

But the job only lasted a year—a year of shock treatments, wet packs and other restraining devices, cleaning up feces, and playing an occasional game of Ping Pong with the healthier patients. Therapy? Forget it—these people were too sick; despite which the state, following the enlightened policy

5

of "deinstitutionalization," forced many of them to leave the hospital and scrounge a living on the streets where they could be beaten and robbed, or worse. I can get emotional on this topic so maybe I'd better just drop it. Anyway, as the patients were discharged, so was the staff—last hired, first fired. That's how I'd found myself singing the praises of second-hand Mazdas.

Maybe if my father had still been alive he'd have given me some sage advice, like "Go to graduate school"—maybe even offered to pay some of my tuition. But he'd died when I was twenty, after raising me for the thirteen or so years since the death of my mother; so that was out. He'd left me the house in Bowie, which is a big, sprawling, suburban Levittown—I may have been the only student at the University of Maryland who owned his own home. Renting out some of the rooms helped pay my expenses and kept me from feeling too lonely, but I'd rather have had my old man around. I missed him a lot.

Anyway, he wasn't there any more the day I happened to see Sabina's ad in the *Washington Post:* "Wanted: resourceful, hardworking, intelligent, average-looking person in search of varied and interesting work. Irregular hours, occasional danger." The ad intrigued me, even though on the score of looks I was probably overqualified. But I could always skip shaving for a day or two and muss up my hair. Dad would have vetoed the whole idea right away—danger, even if only occasional, for his precious Victor? Please! But since I was on my own, I answered the ad. And now here I was, a licensed private investigator—though sometimes I still had thoughts of going to graduate school and becoming a shrink, when I tired of a life of crime.

I watched Sabina climb the hill in her high-heeled shoes, leaving me with an hour to kill. I decided to take a walk around the grounds of the Institute, which—judging from the length of the fence along which I'd just been driving—seemed to consist of several hundred acres of Vermont real estate. I strolled up the driveway, noting that most of the parked cars were unlocked; in some the keys had been left in the ignition.

Automatically I thought, "Mistake, they'll be stolen." Then I told myself to forget about crime, this wasn't Washington, D.C., but Vermont, which had the third-lowest crime rate of the fifty states. Refreshing idea—and so was the thought that Abby Rademacher was back home, minding the agency and sweating out Washington's annual record heat wave, instead of me. I'd have to remember to call Abby—she was keeping an eye on a couple of my cases—and when I did I might just happen to mention that the temperature up here was sixty-eight degrees, with a slightly chilly breeze from the lake, and that once the sun went down a fire would be nice.

I was smiling as I rounded a big spruce tree, and I got an answering smile from a good-looking, black-haired woman with Slavic cheekbones who was sitting in a wooden chair on the lawn, writing in a notebook—physics, presumably. I wondered who she was as I climbed the granite steps to the front porch of the administration building, figuring this would be the place to pick up a few maps.

The wooden screen door slammed behind me. I was in a large lobby lined with bulletin boards covered by announcements of physics talks, whitewater rafting trips, and hikes into the neighboring mountains. The reception desk was empty.

"Anybody home?" I called. Nobody answered. There was a coffee machine and a tray of doughnuts on a table. I had taken two bites out of a cruller when I heard a female voice behind me say severely, "Those are intended for participants in the Institute, if you don't mind."

"Uh-oh, caught in the act," I said, and turned around. Whoever this lady was, I could tell right away that public relations wasn't her forte. She was a diminutive, spike-thin, fiftyish woman with a tight, razor-sharp jaw, a mass of dyed red hair that was bound into a hairnet that made her look as if she were wearing a cheap wig, and cold little eyes that glared at me as if she'd caught me stealing the plans for the H-bomb. Her narrow feet gripped the floor like the paws of a small but fierce animal defending its territory.

I gave her a winning smile and said, "Hello, I'm Victor Newman." Her face didn't change, so I added, "I'm a guest

7

of Professor Bruno Herschel." That didn't captivate her either. Professors, her expression seemed to say, were one of the lower life-forms, and she preferred to have as little to do with them as possible. Ignoring her body language, I inquired, "Do you work here?"

"I'm Judith Wiley." Apparently that was supposed to take care of my question as well as any others I might have, because she turned away, making it clear that, as far as she was concerned, the conversation was over.

I didn't know what her problem was, but she had a big one. The woman oozed hostility. I didn't feel like hanging around to plumb her depths, so I said politely, "Do you happen to have any maps of the Burlington area?"

She snapped, "A map of Vermont, a street map of Burlington, and a map of the Institute grounds are included in the packet every participant receives upon arrival."

"Could you possibly spare some copies?"

"We cannot be expected to provide maps for guests of the participants." Her voice was harsh, her enunciation sharp, and her voice lingered over the word "guests" as if they were a species of household pest. She walked away. I was dismissed.

I raised my voice a notch. "Oh, really? Why not?" She was getting to me.

A wiry man with big glasses and pale, thinning hair appeared from the hallway and buzzed past us on a beeline for the reception desk, stooping as if to make himself a smaller target to possible enemy attackers.

Judith Wiley whirled on him. "Where were *you?*" she demanded. "Why weren't you at your desk?"

His pale face reddened and he threw a glance in my direction. "Well, I just stepped away for a *minute,* Judith."

"And what time did you get here this morning?"

"Judith, really. I was on time. I had to go to the little boys' room, do you *mind?*"

The nostrils of Judith's small, sharp nose distended and she crossed her arms over her narrow chest. "I said, *what time?*"

I interrupted this inquisition. "You know, I really don't see why you can't spare a map. Is the Institute on the verge of bankruptcy, or what?"

She snapped, "Mr. Newman, I'm busy today. You'll have to come back some other time." She turned on her heel and her skinny, black-clad back disappeared down the hall.

My eyes met those of the little man. "Charming lady," I said, loud enough for her to hear if she cared to listen. He threw me a look of agreement but didn't reply. I leaned on his desk and said in a lower voice, "Is she always like this? What's eating her?"

He darted a glance over his shoulder. Down the hall where Judith had gone there was the sound of a door closing, and the little man drew a breath of relief. "Vanished into her lair," he said. "At least for now. Listen, I'll give you a map but please don't tell anyone. She's on this screwball economy kick lately. I mean, what's the cost of a Xerox copy compared to the budget of the Institute?" He opened a drawer and started taking out papers. "Okay, maps. Here's a list of the participants and their addresses. Restaurants. Tourist attractions. . . ."

"Is she your boss? Don't you ever get an urge to strangle her?"

"All the time. But I happen to need this job." He leaned toward me and said in a conspiratorial tone, "Listen, if you want anything in the future, ask me. Off the record. Don't ask her. I'm Gerald Ainsworth."

"I'm Vic Newman."

"I didn't see your name on the list."

"I'm not a physicist. I'm a guest of Professor Herschel and his wife. She's my boss."

A calculating look came into his eyes, which were magnified by his round, thick-lensed glasses. "Isn't she Sabina Swift, the detective?" I nodded, and he surveyed me with more interest than before. "And you're a detective, too. Hm." He bent his head closer to me. "Something going on up here they haven't told me yet?"

"Not that I know of, Gerald."

"Come on," he wheedled. "I gave you a map."

9

"No, really. I'm just here to get some relief from the Washington heat wave."

"Well—" He peered at me, unconvinced, and then shrugged. "Anyway, I bet your work must be fascinating. I've often thought I might have a flair for it, actually." He paused, his head cocked, looking up at me—I was half a head taller— as if hoping I might offer him a job on the spot so he could escape his present boss. When I didn't, he sighed and sat down at his desk.

The intercom gave a loud buzz. "Drat," he said, and flicked a switch.

"Come in here, Gerald," Judith's rasping voice said. "Immediately."

He stuck out his tongue at the intercom box and said, "Be right there." Standing up, he shrugged and muttered, "We who are about to die salute you." He scuttled away down the hall.

# TWO

Outside, a big gray cloud that had blown up out of nowhere had covered the sun, and the breeze from the lake was more than chilly, it was cold. My encounter with the abominable Judith and her disgruntled assistant had piqued my curiosity. I sat down on the wicker porch swing and looked through the information sheets Gerald had given me. Judith Wiley was listed as "Administrative Associate" and Gerald Ainsworth as "Secretarial Assistant." I didn't know for sure what an Administrative Associate was, but I guessed that Judith might at one time have been the Institute's secretary and been given a fancier title as the place expanded.

At the bottom of a sheet of miscellaneous information were the words "If you need any additional information or assistance, call Judith." Right. Like if you needed a map. I wondered why she had been promoted, and how she managed to keep her job, with a chip on her shoulder the size of a two by four. Who was her boss? I shuffled through papers. Apparently it was one Florian Gawthrop, Ph.D., the director of the Institute, who was listed as Dean of Students at a New England college I'd never heard of. It was hard to believe Florian Gawthrop would find Judith a pleasure to work with.

An angry male voice broke through my thoughts. "You are going to listen to me!" Whoever had spoken had a strong French accent.

A female voice, also with an accent, though this one sounded Middle European, replied in shrill tones, "I am not, Jean-Paul. We have nothing left to talk about."

Under the sugar maple, the young woman who had smiled

11

at me earlier tossed back her dark hair angrily and then wrote something in her notebook, pointedly ignoring the man who stood over her. He was a short, dark, Mediterranean type of guy, about thirty, with powerful shoulders and a face that might have been handsome if it hadn't been distorted with rage. "I still have much to say, Magda. And you will listen! No woman is going to dismiss me as if I am a child of five. I am a man, and no one trifles with my honor!"

She shrugged. "Your honor! Who cares about such things? Your ideas are medieval, they bore me. We are not on your ridiculous little island."

*"Putain!"* He snatched the pen from her hand and stood with it poised above her, his arm lifted, so that for a moment he seemed about to stab her with it. Then he flung it down on the grass.

"How dare you!" She jumped to her feet and slapped his face. "You're interfering with my work, I have a seminar to prepare." She turned her back on him and began to walk away, clutching her notebook to her body.

He grabbed her arm. "Your work! Always your work! When Magda Tenofska gives a seminar, the whole world is supposed to kneel in the dirt!" He seized the notebook from her hand and began to tear pages from it. The wind snatched them up and blew them across the gravel driveway. "I don't give *that* for your work!" He snapped his fingers in her face. She tried to claw the notebook out of his grip, and with an ugly laugh he raised it above his head beyond her grasp. "Jump!" he cried, as she tried to reach it. "Jump, bitch!"

She grew very still, except that her breast was heaving. In a quiet, deadly voice she said, "Everyone knows how you feel about my work, Jean-Paul. So jealous you are sick with it— because you could not find an academic position."

"It is the system here, it is not my fault," he said in an injured voice. "America is corrupt, it is materialistic. It is not moral, the women run everything, now there are quotas for them in the university. This is ridiculous! For a man there is nothing."

"So go back home! Maybe there you can raise pigs in your

village!" Her eyes flashed. "No, not you—you would rather make war toys for the Pentagon. This is not physics, this is engineering!" She shrugged and said scathingly, "For a Corsican you are a pretty good physicist. That is not saying much." She turned away.

His face darkened and he grabbed her arm and whirled her around to face him. Then he struck her in the face. I could hear the blow land, though I was twenty yards away. Her knees buckled and she went down under the impact.

"Hey!" I yelled, and sprinted across the gravel toward them as she tried to roll out of range of his feet, which were kicking at her furiously. "Hey, folks, what's up?" I said, and pulled him away from her.

He turned, his face a mask of blind fury, and swung at me wildly. I gripped both of his shoulders in my hands and held him at arm's length. I was half a foot taller than he and my arms were longer. "Calm down!" I said loudly. "Jean-Paul! Get a hold on yourself!" The sound of his name got through to him, which is why I'd used it, and I could see him focus on me for the first time. A look of uncertainty crossed his face, even though he kept waving his fists. I said loudly and clearly, "You don't want to get in a brawl, Jean-Paul. This is a physics conference. You want to calm down. You want to go wash your face and start thinking rationally. Isn't that right?" I'd learned how to quiet an agitated patient while I was at Crownsville. It was a skill that still came in handy.

Jean-Paul's hands fell to his sides and the rage drained out of his face. I could see him taking in the situation and realizing he wasn't exactly distinguishing himself. I let go of him and he whirled and ran off down the driveway, tossing away the notebook. It lay on the gravel with its pages flapping. I was glad to see him go. I don't like unnecessary violence.

Magda was struggling to her hands and knees. On one of her cheeks was a dark-red blotch. I helped her up. "Are you all right?"

"That pig, that scum, I'd like to kill him!" She wriggled out of my grasp and started limping down the driveway, fast.

13

Damned if she didn't want to go after him! I figured she couldn't be hurt all that badly.

I grabbed her arm and said, "Hey, Magda. You calm down, too."

"Did you see what he did to my manuscript? Let go of me!" She tried to shake me off.

"I will if you cool down. How about it?"

"I—" Her eyes took me in. I couldn't decide whether she was attractive or not. The eyes were huge, dark, and deepset, with tawny flecks. Her skin was creamy, except for the reddening patch on her cheek where Jean-Paul had hit her, and she had thick, coarse black hair that fell below her shoulders. But her eyebrows were too heavy, almost mannish, the ridge of her frontal bone was massive for a woman, and her nose was slightly flattened. In fact, in profile she was borderline ugly; but full face, as I saw her now, she was a strikingly good-looking woman, and obviously no creampuff. She was about twenty-five. She shrugged, and a tiny smile twitched at her lips. "I am cool. You will let go of me and we will pick up my manuscript. Yes?"

"Yes. You're all right?"

"So-so." She laid a hand on one trim buttock. "He kicked me here, not too serious. This?" She touched her cheek and worked her jaw experimentally, wincing. "Not wonderful. And the knees. I think that is all." She raised the front of the embroidered peasant skirt she was wearing and inspected her knees. They were scraped and bleeding, and smeared with gravel from the driveway. Otherwise I couldn't see a thing wrong with them. She shrugged again. "It is not important, I will live." She picked up her notebook and we walked down the driveway while I picked up the scattered pages. I glanced at them before I handed them to her—they were covered with long equations that conveyed nothing to me—and she noticed and said, "I was preparing a seminar for Tuesday. I am working now on supersymmetry."

"Supersymmetry?" It wasn't a word I recognized, if it was a word.

She nodded. "I have been calculating condensates in super-symmetric gauge theories."

"Sounds fascinating."

"I thought I had found a simpler way of renormalizing, but now there seems to be a problem."

"That's a shame."

"You must come to my seminar on Tuesday."

"There's nothing I'd like better, only I won't be here Tuesday. I'm just up for the weekend."

She raised her heavy eyebrows at that. "You are not a physicist?"

"Afraid not. Is that essential?"

"Essential?" She gave me a blank look. No sense of humor or a problem with English? I wasn't sure which, though aside from her accent she seemed to have a good command of the language. She said, "I thought I had not seen you before. I am Magda Tenofska. You?"

"Vic Newman."

She shook my hand in the automatic way of Europeans. She had a strong grip. "I thank you for assisting me." She didn't seem particularly upset, considering the treatment she'd just received from Jean-Paul, and I wondered whether she might be used to it. I said, "What was your friend so excited about, if you don't mind my asking?"

"Jean-Paul?" She shrugged. "We used to live together, but then we broke up. He does not want to accept this. Also his career is not going well, and mine is. Probably that is what is really bothering him."

"Are you a better physicist than he is?"

She gave a proud, abrupt toss of her head. "Some people think so."

"And are they right?"

She gave her half smile and then winced and put her hand to her cheek. "Yes, certainly. I think maybe I put some ice on this. I go now to my house. And I must change for the cock-tail party."

I started walking her home on a path that led through a

15

patch of woods. After a few moments I said, "You said Jean-Paul works for the Pentagon. I didn't think foreigners could get that kind of security clearance."

"He has been in this country for seven years, he did his graduate work here. And the Pentagon is not really his boss. He works for a firm near Boston that has many defense contracts, especially in high-altitude photography, but I am not sure how sensitive his position is. I think he only works in the theory division." The path narrowed. I could hear the rushing of water, and after a few minutes a stream came into sight. We walked along it for a short distance and then crossed it on a couple of weathered wooden planks that had been nailed together. When we reached the other side, Magda said, "I don't know what to do about Jean-Paul." She shook her head with a puzzled look as if not knowing something was a new experience for her. "This persecution is intolerable." She gave her characteristic little shrug. "If I had known—but how could I? We met in graduate school and we were both foreigners. That is how it began. But his ideas about women are not at all progressive."

"I noticed."

"We were together for a while and then I left. He behaved very stupidly. Well, you saw. He is not a bad person, but he is stubborn. He does not give up easily."

She said this with a hint of satisfaction that made me wonder whether her relationship with Jean-Paul was really finished, as she claimed. Pursuing my ongoing research project into female psychology, I inquired, "Are you in love with him?" This was easy for me to ask because I'd decided Magda didn't attract me. Too literal-minded, too serious—anyway, too something.

"Oh, in love," she said with impatience. "*He* talks of love. What does that mean, though? A right to make very many demands?" A shadow crossed her face. "Was it for this I left Poland? And my mother. . . ."

"You're Polish? How long have you been in this country?"

"Four years."

16

"Your English is very good. Are you planning to stay permanently?"

"Oh, one has so many plans. And choices—sometimes one has them, sometimes not. . . ."

The path curved and emerged from the woods. Ahead of us on a rise there was a small but gorgeous Vermont farmhouse surrounded by flowers. The place had weathered silver gray, and the door was painted blue, with shutters to match. This looked like one of the VIP cottages Sabina had mentioned, and I wondered what a twenty-five-year-old physicist like Magda had done to rate such classy housing.

# THREE

On the porch of the silver-gray cottage, Magda shook my hand again. She did it with formality instead of the heartfelt appreciation I'd have expected from a damsel I'd just rescued from distress. "It is really too bad you cannot come to my seminar," she said, and opened the door.

A voice from within called, "Maggie, is that you?" A moment later a large-boned woman in a dowdy yet expensive-looking print silk dress appeared in the doorway. She had gray-blond hair cut short in a "sensible" style, and her scrubbed face devoid of makeup had a vaguely youthful look, though she must have been over forty. Worry lines were engraved on her forehead. "Where have you been?" she cried when she saw Magda. She ignored me. "You'll be late for the cocktail party if you don't change— Oh!" She stepped out on the porch. "*What* has happened to your *face?*" She grabbed Magda's chin and turned it so that the light fell on her cheek. "Was it—" She seemed to notice me for the first time and broke off, but in her eyes as she examined Magda's bruise flickered anguish and something like despair. "Animal!" she whispered. Then she sighed. "I don't know what Moore-Gann is going to say when he hears about this."

I'd been about to leave but the name caught my attention. Hervé Moore-Gann was one of the two Nobel prizewinners at the conference. What was Magda's connection with him?

"And your legs—there's blood on them!" The older woman leaned forward and hiked up Magda's skirt. "Look at your knees! You fell!" she said accusingly. She had a fussy,

18

motherly manner, like a housewife who has spent her life taking care of the petty details others prefer to forget.

"It's nothing, Theresa," said Magda in a bored voice, but she didn't draw back and seemed to like having the older woman make a fuss over her, perhaps even to enjoy upsetting her.

Theresa turned to me and demanded, "Can you imagine not even washing these knees?"

I felt like a medic caught napping on the job, not that Magda's knees were my responsibility. Theresa seemed to have a talent for laying guilt trips. I said, "Theresa, I don't believe we've met. I'm Vic Newman."

At once she switched on a gracious, social manner. I couldn't tell whether it was something that came naturally, but I had the feeling that she'd had so much practice at it that she could turn it on for public consumption at a moment's notice, regardless of how she might be feeling. She said, "How do you do, I'm Theresa Moore-Gann, so nice to meet you," and gave me a smile that looked warm but was completely impersonal.

So this was the wife of Hervé Moore-Gann. I'd seen his picture in the paper plenty of times, and I'd roomed once with a physics major who'd had a poster of Moore-Gann hanging over his desk. It showed the great man, his bald head gleaming, chewing on a pencil and gazing into space as if lost in thought. You could even buy T-shirts with Moore-Gann's picture on them—the height of fame.

According to the list of conference participants I'd studied on the porch of the administration building, Theresa Moore-Gann was a physicist, too; she was scheduled to give a couple of talks. I wondered how it was for her, living in the shadow of her famous husband.

She put her arm around Magda's waist and said with another smile, this one more real, maybe because I could see pain in it, "This young lady happens to be my husband's prize student. We're all expecting great things from her." Her arm tightened around Magda and she moved her toward the door.

Magda docilely allowed herself to be led. I didn't budge, and after an instant Theresa said to me with resigned politeness, "Do please come in."

We went into the kitchen and she sat Magda in a chair while she bustled over to the sink for a bowl of water and a clean towel. Briskly she washed the scraped knees with soap and water, saying, "This may sting a little, dear."

Magda drew in her breath and said, "That hurts," in a petulant tone. She'd been a lot more stoical, I reflected, when her boyfriend—former boyfriend, whatever he was—had been knocking her around.

Theresa said firmly, "Just hold still. If you get an infection, you know Moore-Gann will find some reason to blame it on me. Have you been at the Institute before, Dr.—I'm sorry, what did you say your name is?"

"Vic Newman." I wondered how many hundreds of strangers she'd had to be gracious to, in the years she'd been the wife of Hervé Moore-Gann. "Not 'Doctor,' just plain Vic. I'm not a physicist. I'm staying with Professor Herschel and his wife for the weekend." Theresa's smile brightened and her faded blue eyes, which were slightly prominent and very intelligent, now inspected me as if she were actually seeing me. "Oh, Bruno is an *old* friend. He used to come to our Sunday brunches for the graduate students quite often. Will he be at the cocktail party?"

"I think so, Mrs. Moore-Gann."

"Call me Theresa. Well, you certainly picked a good year to come to the Institute, Vic. You ought to try to attend some of the lectures, even if you find them a bit hard to follow. Everybody is going to be talking about string theory and supersymmetry, and it ought to be quite exciting. These are new and rather revolutionary ideas, and you're going to be reading about them in the press before long." She smiled at me. "You'll be able to say you heard them from the horse's mouth. Did you know the Institute is celebrating its twentieth anniversary this year? In fact that's why—well, never mind."

"She means, that's why Moore-Gann and Sachs are both here at the same time," said Magda with an abrupt laugh.

"Now, Maggie," said Theresa, and turning to me went on, "I'm quite sentimental about the Institute. My husband and I were here the year it began and we were married only a few months later." Her lips curved in a secret little smile and for a moment she looked handsome and young. "But we've never been back."

"Why not, if you like it so much?" said Magda.

"Oh, reasons," said Theresa vaguely. "Hervé gets so many invitations." To me she added, "It's lovely here, but I prefer mountains that are a little more rugged. My husband and I like to climb." In her silk print dress, Theresa didn't look much like a mountain climber, but now that she'd mentioned it I could see that her bare arms were strong and her movements were limber. She squatted easily on her haunches, bathing Magda's knees, and as she shifted position to reach for a towel the muscles knotted smoothly in her calves. "There! That's clean. I'll just run and see if I can find some mercurochrome somewhere. I know there isn't any in the house. Wait here, Maggie."

She left the room and we heard the front door slam. Magda jumped up. "I'll see you at the cocktail party," she said. "I'll get dressed now and go."

"Aren't you going to wait for Theresa to come back?"

"Theresa is kind, but a little too—" She shrugged. "I'm certainly not going to let her paint my knees red. She should have had children, she is too much the frustrated mama. It gets tiresome at times."

I left. I was looking forward to the cocktail party. It would be interesting to meet Hervé Moore-Gann and his fellow laureate Saul Sachs, not to mention seeing the two of them in the same room. Twenty years earlier they had been collaborators and eventually shared the Nobel prize; but according to Bruno they had had a falling out and were no longer on speaking terms. Sachs had refused for years to make an appearance at any event where Moore-Gann would be present, and nobody seemed to know why he had decided to come to the Champlain Valley Physics Institute's twentieth-anniversary session, where he would have to encounter his former collaborator.

I headed for the barn. In the west the sun was low in the sky and the mountains on the New York side of Lake Champlain were purple and hazy. The temperature had dropped ten degrees in the last three-quarters of an hour.

As I came around the big spruce tree I almost tripped over a naked giant with his foot on a shovel. To be technical, he had on sandals and wore a skimpy pair of sweat-soaked nylon shorts over his muscular body. He had a mane of shoulder-length red hair that stood out in a bush and a face that was handsome but blank, as if not too much was going on behind it. "Whoops!" I said, as I gracefully recovered my footing in time to avoid falling into a trench the giant was filling with manure. A bunch of shrubs with their roots wrapped in burlap were standing around waiting to be planted.

"Hi," he said, and turned over a spadeful of dirt. Then he rested his arms on his shovel and gave me a big smile. The sun flashed on his perfect teeth.

"Hi," I replied. "You the gardener?"

"Yep." He continued smiling. "You one of the professors at the conference?"

"No, I'm just a guest."

"Guest. Oh." It was a long time since I'd made anyone as happy as I was apparently making this guy. He was still smiling. He said, "They're smart. Real smart."

"I guess they are. Well, nice to have met you."

"I'm Jordan," he said. "I'm planting. Bushes."

"I see that."

"What's *your* name?"

"Vic."

"I like the name Vic, Vic."

"Thanks." Jordan might look like a male model, but he obviously didn't have much upstairs. I decided not to worry about the fact that I didn't care for the way he was staring at me. "Got to go now," I said, and went.

He stood watching me as I climbed the hill to the barn, and when I looked back he was still smiling.

# FOUR

There were at least a hundred people in the barn, physicists and their spouses and friends, as well as employees of the Institute. Also there was a motley collection of chairs, tables, and blackboards scattered around, and an assortment of lamps that didn't do much to dispel the darkness of the big, windowless, high-raftered room. On the wall opposite the double barn doors, which were about ten feet high and sagged on their hinges so that they scraped the cement floor when you pushed them open, a fire was burning in a big fieldstone fireplace. I gravitated toward it. Plastic cups and pitchers of Bloody Marys had been laid out on a table. I helped myself. The first swig sent my taste buds into shock, and by the second they had begun to vibrate as if about to do the samba. I tore open a bag of Doritos and grabbed a handful. It wasn't a formal atmosphere.

I surveyed the party. It was a peculiar shape. There was a tight crowd of people at either end of the barn, a few wandering drifters, and a No-Man's-Land in the middle. A bipolar party, as a physicist might say. I assumed that each of the laureates was holding court in his own group. And never the twain shall meet.

I wandered in the direction of a long table where a team of women were setting out a buffet supper. I had had little food since I'd left Washington, and I needed more ballast to discourage the Bloody Marys from eating through the lining of my stomach. As I got closer I could see that one of the workers was the abominable Judith, though all she seemed to be doing at the moment was drilling into a bowl of dip with a

23

stalk of broccoli. She was saying something I couldn't hear to the buffet crew, who without actually being rude more or less ignored her.

The Bloody Mary had mellowed me, and of course I'm a nice guy to begin with; so thinking sympathetically that poor Judith must suffer from the rejections that would naturally result from her hostile, obnoxious manner, I hailed her in friendly fashion. "Hi, Judith, nice party."

But I was a nonperson as far as she was concerned. She looked right through me, bit the head off her broccoli, and walked away.

It shook me. What was bugging the woman? Or had I broken some unwritten law of the Institute when I'd asked for a map?

"Don't pay any attention to Judith," said a woman behind the table, a sleek person of indeterminate age, with a short cap of shiny black hair and long, dangling earrings. I took a closer look at her and saw she was no kid, though her figure in a tight yellow sheath dress was fairly sensational. She had one of those leathery but handsome faces you see in women who've spent a lot of time sunning themselves in Florida or riding the range in Texas or sailing on the Chesapeake Bay; this woman looked as if she'd done all these things and more. Her eyes glittered at me, or was it the layer of silver she'd painted skillfully on her eyelids so that they matched her earrings and the heavy turquoise-and-silver necklace she was wearing? Her dark skin and arched nose made her look like an Indian priestess. She let out a bubbling, throaty laugh and gave me a satirical look. Bobbing her head toward Judith's retreating back she added, "She's probably suffering from severe sexual frustration."

"It's an interesting theory. Tell me more," I said.

"Where would you like me to begin?" said the priestess. She offered me a platter of fried chicken. "Do you like legs? Breasts?"

The priestess's assistant, who was young and blond and wore a fluffy pink dress, shook her head and said, "Judith's a sick person really." She gave me a smile that was comforting in a professional sort of way, as if she was a nursery school teacher. She had a southern accent. "Don't feel bad, that's how she treats *everyone*. Do you know what she said to Gerald Ainsworth, the male receptionist? I could hardly believe my ears—"

Gerald picked that moment to stagger up to the table with an enormous wheel of Cheddar in his arms, so I didn't get to hear what Judith had said to him. I helped him settle the cheese on a platter. The blonde opened a box of sesame seed crackers and dumped them in a basket. I helped myself to a few.

Gerald thanked me and asked if I was enjoying the party.

"It's great. Who mixes up your Bloody Marys?"

"I do," he said with pride, brushing crumbs of cheese rind from his tie.

"Old family recipe?"

"No, I just keep throwing ingredients into a *huge* barrel— actually it's a plastic garbage pail, new of course, but don't tell a soul—and I keep *tasting* it and *tasting* it till I think it's right."

I could see he'd tasted it quite a bit. "Well, it's fine," I said.

"Strong enough?"

"I'd say yes."

Gerald leaned toward the buffet crew. "Have you ladies met Vic Newman? He's a detective, so you'd better be careful what you tell him." Had he overheard the blonde mentioning his name? "Actually, he works for Sabina Swift, the detective. She's married to Professor Herschel."

"Really?" said the blonde, and I knew what her next words would be. "How fascinating!" She fluttered her eyelashes at me in a southern sort of way. "I'm Charlene. A friend of mine in Arlington lost her pearls at the Italian Embassy once under *very* embarrassing circumstances, and Sabina Swift got them back for her."

"I remember that case," I said. Charlene's friend had lost her pearls in the bed of the ambassador's sixteen-year-old son, with whom she'd been getting better acquainted while her husband had been downstairs attending a reception honoring a delegation of industrialists from Milan. There was a pitcher of Bloody Marys on the buffet table and I refilled my glass.

Charlene leaned toward me and said coaxingly, "What *really* happened? I know what Millicent told me but I always had a feeling there was more to it."

I shook my head. "Sorry, my lips are sealed. Professional ethics."

Charlene gave a solemn nod. "I understand perfectly, I'm a nurse. Confidentiality." She giggled. "If you get a headache, I'll be just delighted to give you two aspirin."

"And can I call you in the morning?"

"Better not, my husband's a *terrible* old grouch in the morning."

The priestess held out her glass and said, "If I may disturb this medical consultation, I'm Vita Sachs, Vic. Anything left in that pitcher, perchance?" I refilled her glass. So this was the wife of Saul Sachs, the other laureate. She wasn't my idea of a Nobel prizewinner's wife, not the way Theresa Moore-Gann had been. Vita was more the theatrical type; her gestures and facial expressions were all a bit larger than life, as if she were playing to an invisible balcony. "So you're staying with Bruno," she said. "I'd heard he was going to be here." Her eyes strayed over my shoulder as if she were searching for him, and for a moment I thought the silver eyelids looked scheming and anxious. When she caught sight of him she waved, mouthing "Bruno!" and threw him a kiss with both hands, her face lighting up in a smile so brilliant that it made me wonder if I'd imagined the look of strain.

"With Bruno and Sabina, yes."

"I adore Bruno. We're old, old friends." Indifferently she added, "I don't really know Sabina."

A group of physics wives arrived with casseroles and began bombarding her with questions about chafing dishes, and she gave my arm a caressing pat of dismissal. "I seem to be in charge of the eats at this shindig. Don't ask me how they managed to rope me in." She shrugged and turned to the newcomers. "You can put that stuff here temporarily. Didn't

I see a box of Sterno somewhere?" She bent over and began hunting under the table, the yellow sheath dress molding so tightly to her shapely rear that I could make out the outline of her skimpy bikini panties.

Pleasantly stimulated, I moseyed on over to Bruno, who I could see near the fireplace, standing on tiptoe and waving his arms in the air to attract my attention. Sabina and Magda were near him. They were all holding Bloody Marys.

"Hey, Vic!" said Bruno when I got there, and gave me a bear hug. The top of his head barely reached my shoulder. He's a guy who always needs a haircut, and his shaggy, pepper-and-salt beard is generally lopsided, as if he started out to trim it with good intentions and then thought of a theorem or something and rushed off to write it down. He was wearing one of his shaggiest Harris tweed jackets, and baggy pants with chalk on the front and a shiny patch in back (theoretical physicists sit a lot). The pants were held up by an old leather belt with three worn holes. Bruno's waistline has a tendency to expand, and every few months he takes off fifteen pounds that start creeping back immediately. If there's one thing Sabina believes, it's that neatness counts; still, she tolerates Bruno's messy ways with only minor crabbing. Why? I suspect because he keeps her human and she knows it.

Bruno wanted information from me about exactly how long it had taken me to drive to Vermont, which route I'd used, why I'd chosen it over the one he'd tried to talk me into taking, and what kind of gas mileage I'd managed to get. I obliged, giving full details.

Meanwhile, Sabina was grilling Magda about string theory. "You say these theories can't be made to work in a world with the usual four space-time dimensions," she was saying, sounding perturbed and frowning the way she does when she doesn't understand something. "That would seem to be a very serious problem, since we live in a world of four dimensions."

"Only as far as we're aware," Magda pointed out. "There may be more dimensions than we are capable of perceiving."

"I'm not used to thinking in these terms," said Sabina. She was determined to grasp string theory, apparently. "Perhaps you can give me an example?" She knocked back what was left of her Bloody Mary in one gulp. I didn't blame her.

Magda furrowed her brow. She was looking fantastic in the dim light of the barn, in a simple, high-necked white knit dress that clung to her curves. Her long, coarse black hair framed her face, which she had made up heavily to cover the bruise on her cheek. Her white face with its slash of scarlet mouth, angular cheekbones, and straight, dark brows was like the mask of a Kabuki dancer.

Thinking maybe I should reconsider the question of whether she attracted me, I blurted, "Magda, you're looking terrific."

She shrugged me aside. I was distracting her. "Conceive of a beetle," she said to Sabina, "crawling along the beach. To that beetle, the world might seem a flat plane. He can understand, shall we say, the notion of length and width—he can go forward and back, he can go sideways—and perhaps the notion of time. But the notion of *height* is beyond him, though it is obvious to us." I made a mental note to add to my female psychology file: "Never compliment a female physicist when she's been asked to give an example."

Sabina nodded. "So there may be other dimensions of which we as humans are unaware."

"Yes," said Magda. "One fascinating question for me is whether it will ever be possible to detect the existence of these other dimensions. But these theories are all so *beautiful,* with such nice mathematical properties, that there must be some truth to them."

"And you say that the theory operates in a *ten*-dimensional universe? How do you decide on the number ten?" Sabina was still game, but I could tell from the peek she sneaked at her empty glass that she was starting to feel the strain. I figured I'd better get her a refill.

"Be right back," I said, taking the glass from her hand.

I slipped away through the crowd. Behind my back I could hear Bruno getting into the act. "Personally, I don't think beauty is such a reliable criterion, to say the least. In my opinion—"

When I reached the drinks table I bumped into Charlene, the blond nurse. Vita wasn't in sight—I wouldn't have minded running into her again. So what if she was old enough to be my mother? Charlene said, "What's your sign, detective man?" and I told her "Pisces." Turned out she was a Virgo. People complain about mindless chatter at cocktail parties, but I think there's a lot to be said for it, at least compared to physics. Charlene had made quite a study of astrology, but I had to excuse myself before learning all the conclusions she'd come to. I was on a mission of mercy.

By the time I got back with Sabina's refill, the topic had changed to "What Motivates Theoretical Physicists?" and Hervé Moore-Gann had joined the group. I recognized him right away, though he was a lot shorter than he looked in his photographs—five-three at most. The famous bald cranium with the bulging frontal lobes gleamed in the light from the fireplace. His eyes were huge and alert in his narrow face and his expression didn't change when he spoke, as if his face had been set in plaster. At the moment he was listening intently as Sabina said, "I would think it must be curiosity that motivates you primarily—the desire to uncover hidden truths that lie underneath the surface of appearances."

I handed her her drink. She took it, her eyes on Moore-Gann.

He said, "Is that what motivates *you*, my dear? I believe I've heard you're a detective."

She hesitated. She hates being called "my dear," but I could see her deciding to let him get away with it because she wanted to hear what he had to say. "Certainly," she said briskly. "Also craftsmanship."

He nodded once. "Naturally. The satisfaction of a job well done. I would say theoretical physicists are motivated by the same factors, but I would also emphasize the role of ambition. It's commonly overlooked in discussions such as this because it doesn't seem high-minded enough. Curiosity, craftsmanship, originality, keen insights, persistence—all these are nothing without ambition. A man's first duty is to be am-

29

bitious. I don't know about a woman's." The corners of his lips flickered for a second. Had the great man made a joke? Apparently, for there were a few chuckles from the audience—not from Sabina or Magda, I noticed, though Theresa managed a wifely smile. "The noblest ambition is that of leaving something of permanent value behind—an impossible goal for the vast majority of mankind, needless to say. But for a few . . ." He pushed his lower jaw forward thoughtfully. He had five-o'clock shadow. He was wearing skin-tight designer jeans and a red nylon shirt that was open almost to the waist and showed his black chest hairs and a gold neck chain. The clothes and the head didn't match at all. He was over sixty, but he had the body of a much younger man and he wanted the world to know it. "Ambition has been the motivation behind most of the world's best work. The desire for reputation and position, even for power and money, are motives of which no one need be ashamed. When a physicist tells me that the driving force behind his research is a desire to add to the sum of the world's knowledge, I don't believe him."

During this speech, Sabina hadn't moved. Her cool blue eyes kept taking him in and her face was serious. She hadn't touched the drink I'd brought her. "There's truth in what you say, of course. But when ambition is unbridled it can lead to the blunting of scruples. Don't you agree?"

His face remained impassive. "Many so-called scruples are merely the tag-ends of outworn superstitions whose origins lie in attempts by primitive man to control natural forces of which he had no real understanding. The greater the understanding of the laws of nature, the less the need for such taboos."

"That can become a dangerous doctrine if carried to extremes. Very dangerous, Professor Moore-Gann." She almost seemed to be giving him a warning.

He took a sip from the glass he was holding, which looked as if it contained club soda. Theresa took a step closer to her husband, and Magda said to Sabina, "Power corrupts—is that what you mean?"

30

"*Knowledge* can corrupt, when it focuses too much on power and ambition."

There was a sudden silence. In it, the harsh voice of the abominable Judith was heard, coming from somewhere in the middle of the room. "Saul Sachs has cancer, he's going to die. As far as I'm concerned, it's good riddance."

There were gasps, and heads turned. I caught sight of Judith's red hair near the buffet table. She was talking to a woman I hadn't met. Nearby, a tall, distinguished-looking man in a handmade Norwegian sweater jerked his chin upward, and his face flushed. He hurried toward her, saying in a low voice, "Judith, really."

She put her hands on her hips and stared at him defiantly. "It's a free country, Professor Gawthrop. I'll say whatever I please." Her boss, Florian Gawthrop, the director of the Institute.

"Now, Judith," he murmured. He raised his hand and after a momentary hesitation laid it on her arm. "We're about to start the welcoming ceremony, let's not have a scene."

I glanced at Moore-Gann. He was staring at Judith and there was a faint flicker in his oversize dark eyes, like a computer scanning a disk very thoroughly and very fast. Theresa was beside him with one hand on his shoulder; next to her stood Magda. The three of them looked like a family group waiting to be photographed.

Suddenly Moore-Gann shook off his wife's hand. Then he began to walk forward. The two women followed in his wake. Smoothly, almost mechanically, he crossed the floor and I heard someone gasp. "My God, he's going over to Sachs." The crowd on our side of the barn surged after him, the group around Sachs parted to make way for him. I saw an emaciated, gray-faced man lying back against the cushions of a sofa. Next to him, tensed as if to spring, sat Vita, with a look of total fury on her face.

Moore-Gann came to a stop in front of Sachs. Vita made a swift, protective gesture and seemed about to speak; then she changed her mind.

The eyes of the two men locked. Moore-Gann's face was as

expressionless as ever, Sachs's showed only exhaustion. He didn't try to sit up, didn't even seem to see the other man. Abruptly, Moore-Gann knelt in front of the sofa and held out his hand. After a pause that seemed to go on forever, Sachs took it in a limp grip.

A prickling ran up my spine. The crowd started to clap and while that was happening the two men exchanged a few words. People started milling around. Jean-Paul appeared carrying a pitcher of Bloody Marys and a stack of plastic cups, and drinks were handed around. Suddenly it was New Year's Eve.

I was on my fourth drink when I saw the abominable Judith come up and say something to the two laureates. They ignored her. She raised her arms above her head and clapped her hands together a few times. The room grew quiet. "May I have your attention?" she said in her loud, harsh voice. "Professor Gawthrop would like to say a few words."

# FIVE

Florian Gawthrop had a patrician look that seemed to be unusual for a theoretical physicist. Most of them, at least the ones I'd met through Bruno, were small, dark men with chalk on their coats—Mediterranean and Middle European types, Jews, Orientals, and Indians. I hate to sound prejudiced, but I found myself wondering if Gawthrop could be any good. I asked Bruno.

"Not very," he said. "But he's found a niche, he's a dean at some small New England college and in the summers he runs the Institute. Makes up the deficit, too, I understand, from his personal funds. He comes from a wealthy Boston family. Up until a few years ago he edited the *American Physicist.*"

On the podium, Gawthrop smoothed back his straight blond hair and gave the crowd a chilly smile. He stuck his hands in the pockets of his designer jeans. Beside him and slightly to the rear of the platform, Judith had stationed herself. In the audience I noticed Jean-Paul, his eyes fastened on Magda, his expression heavy and brooding. Next to him, a massive man in a heavy tweed suit glanced from Magda to Jean-Paul and poked him with his elbow, saying something with a grin that revealed a gold tooth. The Corsican didn't smile. Magda appeared to be ignoring Jean-Paul, but I could tell from the too-animated way she was talking to a handsome young man that she was aware he was watching her. After a moment I recognized the young man as my friend Jordan, the naked giant, now all dressed up in slacks and a pullover. Jean-Paul's eyes burned as he stared at them.

Gawthrop cleared his throat and said, "First of all, I want to welcome you to the Champlain Valley Physics Institute. For one month you'll have a chance to eat, sleep, and breathe physics twenty-four hours a day, which is the thing theoretical physicists like to do best—even if their wives aren't quite as enthusiastic." There was laughter from the audience. "As you know, our theme this year is 'Superstrings and Supersymmetry.' There will be a full schedule of seminars and colloquia, as well as ample opportunity to exchange thoughts on an informal basis with colleagues from all over the world. Not that there won't be time to enjoy the beauty of the Champlain Valley and the Green Mountains, as well. Judith tells me she has arranged a program of outings for participants and their families, including hiking trips along the Appalachian Trail and up Camel's Hump, and a moonlight party on the lake. I trust you'll plan to take advantage of them.

"As most of you are aware, this is a very special session." I perked up at the words, though I hate speeches and there's something about the word "special" that makes my eyelids want to droop. I was wondering how, or rather if, Gawthrop was going to deal with the encounter that had just taken place between Moore-Gann and Sachs. "This year we are celebrating the twentieth anniversary of the founding of the Champlain Valley Physics Institute. I know that quite a few of us remember the old tent in which our first seminars were held, especially those who sat under the leaks in the roof." He paused for laughter. "Everyone who was present that first year was invited to return this summer, and as I look around I am gratified to see that a number of you have done so, among them our gracious alumna Theresa Moore-Gann." His eyes sought her in the audience and when they found her his pompous manner dissolved for an instant as he gave her a nod and a smile. She flushed, looking pleased but flustered at being singled out.

"Actually, the idea of a Champlain Valley Institute was the brainchild of Saul Sachs, who has fathered more good ideas than any one man could possibly bring to maturity. This particular one I adopted, and I have been nurturing it to the best of my modest ability ever since. Er—with, of course, the invaluable assistance of Judith Wiley." Was it my imagination or did I detect a note of sarcasm in his tone? "Judith, as many of you know, was my secretary twenty years ago and is now administrative associate of the Institute. Without her dedicated attention to the day-to-day details of what has become a rather complex operation, who knows where we would be today?" He paused as if to invite applause but nobody clapped. Behind him, Judith stood impassive.

"At that first session, in addition to Saul Sachs and myself, we had the great good fortune to count among our number Hervé Moore-Gann. A fruitful collaboration between Sachs and Moore-Gann began that summer, which as you all know climaxed in the winning of the Nobel prize. Now"—there was a hush, and as I looked around I saw Moore-Gann draining a Bloody Mary—"they have both returned to the place where it all began. And if that very moving scene we witnessed a few moments ago is any indication, perhaps we can look forward to a new Sachs–Moore-Gann theory in the future." The audience applauded with enthusiasm.

It didn't seem likely, from what I'd heard, that the collaboration between Moore-Gann and Sachs would resume; according to Bruno it was common knowledge that Sachs was dying of cancer and that Moore-Gann's interests had become increasingly political; there were rumors that he was about to be named ambassador to one of the NATO countries.

Gawthrop went on, "At this time I would like to propose a round of applause for, in alphabetical order"—a laugh ran around the room—"our two Nobel prizewinners. First, Hervé Moore-Gann." The crowd turned toward the pint-sized laureate, who bowed his head slightly and raised a hand to acknowledge the applause. The crowd parted in front of him, and he set down his glass and began to move toward the podium. Then he seemed to stumble. He paused, as if he had just remembered something, and looked over his shoulder toward his wife. Taking another step, he threw out his arms and his body began to shake.

"Hervé!" cried Theresa, and ran toward him. "Hervé! He's ill!"

Moore-Gann crumpled and fell to the ground. He twitched spasmodically.

"Oh, call a doctor, call a doctor!" Theresa cried, and threw herself down beside him. "Hervé! Hervé!" She gathered him into her arms, exclaiming, "Can't somebody help him?"

Gerald Ainsworth ran from the room calling, "I'll get an ambulance."

All around me people were pressing forward, and I could hear them saying, "What's happening? Has he had a heart attack? Has he had a stroke?"

Florian Gawthrop jumped down from the podium exclaiming, "Theresa!" In four strides of his long legs he was beside her. She looked up at him wordlessly, and he dropped to his knees and pressed his ear to Moore-Gann's heart.

Charlene, the nurse with the southern accent, pushed her way through the crowd and began to give Moore-Gann mouth-to-mouth resuscitation.

Everyone was milling around. Magda was standing as if paralyzed, staring at Moore-Gann and Theresa in horror.

I caught sight of Jordan, who for once was not smiling. He was standing by the podium plucking at Judith's sleeve and whimpering, "Why are they on the ground, why are they on the ground?" She was staring down at him from the platform with a despairing look. Seeing them together like that I couldn't help noticing a resemblance between the hostile, middle-aged woman and the handsome, dull-witted young giant; they had the same sharply etched profiles, the same pale skin and flaming red hair. They looked to me like mother and son.

After a while I looked around for Moore-Gann's glass. I'd seen him put it down on a small bamboo table when he'd headed toward the podium. The packed crowd shifted, and I caught a glimpse of the table. There was nothing on it. The glass had disappeared.

# SIX

"Take it easy," said Sabina as we headed home.

I was surprised, for she isn't usually a backseat driver. "How come?"

She was sitting next to me in the passenger seat, her back straight and her trim knees together. In her lap she was clutching her pocketbook and a lace-edged handkerchief. "Because I don't want to spill any of this."

I took another look at the handkerchief. There was something underneath it. "So it was you who took the glass," I said. "I should have known."

"What glass?" said Bruno. He was sitting behind us.

Sabina turned around and said, "The glass Moore-Gann had been drinking from."

"You took it? Why?"

She pursed her cupid's bow lips. "I thought it might be a good idea, Bruno."

The ambulance had taken Moore-Gann to the hospital ten minutes earlier. Theresa and Magda had gone with him, the older woman leaning heavily against the younger as the stretcher-bearers preceded them out of the barn. Florian, too, had gone to the hospital, following the ambulance in his car.

"You think something's fishy?" I said.

"Maybe. It won't hurt to have the dregs analyzed."

"I'll dust the glass for prints and take some pictures when we get back to the house."

Bruno objected. "I don't see why. What makes you think Moore-Gann didn't simply have a heart attack or a stroke? He's sixty-two, after all. I know he's supposed to be one of

37

these fitness fanatics, but there are plenty of joggers who drop dead while they're running—you see articles in the newspaper all the time."

Sabina's pale blue eyes registered annoyance. "I'm well aware of it, you read most of them aloud." For years she's been trying to get him to take up tennis or golf, and he's been on a countercampaign to prove to her that exercise is bad for your health. The only form of exercise I've ever known him to engage in was picking up a piece of chalk and writing on the blackboard.

Bruno shook his head. "You've got crime on the brain, Sabina. You've been working too hard. Remember, this is supposed to be a vacation."

"If I have crime on the brain," she said tartly, "it's because there's a lot of it around."

I said, "I agree with Sabina, Bruno. There are some peculiar things about the setup here."

"For example?" he said in a skeptical tone.

"Well, Judith." I described my encounter with her and Gerald in the administration building, plus our brief run-in at the buffet table; I also quoted what Vita and Charlene had said about her. "Here's a woman who's nasty to everyone, who says tasteless, outrageous things—you heard her say 'good riddance' about Saul Sachs's cancer—yet Florian Gawthrop lets her get away with it. Why? Why didn't he fire her long ago?"

"I suppose she's indispensable," said Bruno. "She arranges all the housing, does the scheduling, does the bookkeeping—Gawthrop's pretty vague about details, and she's been here forever."

"Nonsense," said Sabina. "She's not indispensable, there are plenty of people who could do her job. Gerald Ainsworth could probably step into her shoes without the slightest difficulty. I agree with Vic, it is odd."

"Another thing. Why did Saul Sachs and Hervé Moore-Gann both show up this summer when they've done their best to avoid each other for years? Why the sudden reconciliation, followed by Moore-Gann's keeling over just a few minutes later? The timing is too pat, I don't like it. I can't believe the shock was so great that it gave him a heart attack—he didn't seem like the emotional type." It was getting foggy and I slowed down.

"He isn't," Bruno admitted reluctantly, threatened as usual by what he thinks of as my tendency, and Sabina's, to over-dramatize things. Bruno likes to believe he lives in an orderly, rational universe.

We drove for a while in silence. Finally Bruno said, "Let's hope Moore-Gann pulls through. I wonder how good the hospitals are up here."

Sabina said, "You don't really like Moore-Gann though, do you, Bruno?"

"Well—not too much, not personally, no." It's hard for Bruno to admit he doesn't like somebody. "There's something about him— I'm fond of Theresa, though. They used to hold open house every Sunday when I was a graduate student, and she really made the students feel welcome. I went to their home quite often. Moore-Gann himself always struck me as a cold fish."

I said, "Another thing I don't understand is the relationship between Magda and the Moore-Ganns. Apparently she's living with them." I told them about the fight I'd broken up between Magda and Jean-Paul, and the way Theresa had reacted when I'd brought Magda home.

"Magda is Moore-Gann's protegée," explained Bruno. "She's one of the top-notch younger physicists. She's supposed to be the best student he's ever had, and he's had some good ones. Including his wife, by the way."

"Theresa was his student?" said Sabina. "I didn't know that. And she was good, you say. I wonder where Theresa fits in, as far as Magda is concerned. From Vic's description, the three of them really sound like a family."

"Well, they are, sort of. Magda moved in about five months ago, when she left Jean-Paul Brocchiu. Supposedly he was abusing her. I don't know if it's true or not, these things get exaggerated, but he does have a reputation for being hot-tempered, even vindictive. I've heard he was involved with a group of student radicals at the University of Grenoble that supposedly planted a bomb on campus that did some damage, though fortunately no one was hurt. Basically they were just idealistic young people, and I've been told Jean-Paul had nothing to do with it personally; he was quite young then." Bruno hesitated. "However, when one of the administrators accused him, he threatened the man with a knife." He shook his head, looking distressed. "It seems very hard to believe. It's true though, I have it from a reliable source—he was thrown out of the university because of the incident. Then he came to the States and he and Magda got together. Unfortunately for her, apparently."

"Maybe for both of them." I was thinking of the look I'd seen on his face at the cocktail party as he stared at her. Whatever he'd done in the past, he was really suffering now— of that there was no doubt.

Sabina said, "It still seems strange to me that Magda has remained with the Moore-Ganns for such a length of time."

"The story I heard is that she turned up at their house in Cambridge in the middle of the night, covered with bruises. Moore-Gann was in Japan at a meeting but Theresa took her to the hospital. By the time Moore-Gann got home she'd practically adopted Magda. She treats her like the daughter she never had, that sort of thing."

"I think the feeling's mutual," I said. "You know the way adolescent girls treat their mothers sometimes, bitchy and clingy at the same time? That's how Magda was with Theresa."

"We defer to your greater knowledge of adolescent girls," said Sabina. Bruno put his hand on her shoulder and she removed it, but nicely. She doesn't go in for public displays of affection. "Right, Bruno?"

They laughed, and I felt dumb. They both have grown-up daughters by previous marriages. Bruno said, "I think *post*adolescent girls are really Vic's field of expertise." Bruno seems to think that because I'm a bachelor I have a vast knowledge of women—or maybe it's because he got married when he was twenty.

"You flatter me." I slowed down as we came to another patch of fog.

Bruno said, "Magda doesn't have much family of her own, and those that are left are in Poland. Her father's dead and her mother was imprisoned for Solidarity activities."

Sabina said, "Watch out!"

The Mercedes swerved as I slammed on the brakes. The figure that had loomed up in the roadway ran toward us.

"Idiot!" said Sabina, referring not to me but to the guy on the road. "I almost spilled this."

Bruno said, "It's Leo Pesnik." He opened the back door. "Get in, Leo. What are you doing on the road?"

"Walking. Isn't it obvious?"

Leo Pesnik was a gaunt man in his forties with wild, unkempt hair and a beard on which the fog had left droplets of water. He was wearing a backpack full of books over an old quilted down jacket with a hood. He climbed into the backseat next to Bruno and slipped the pack off his shoulders.

Bruno said, "Did your car break down?"

"Why do you assume I have a car?" Pesnik's tone was self-righteous.

I restarted the Mercedes and said to our new passenger, "We're heading toward Burlington, is that where you want to go?"

"That's where the road leads, isn't it?" His dark, sunken eyes in the rear-view mirror had the withdrawn, angry look of a loner with a grievance.

"It leads a lot of places." People who answer a question with a question annoy me.

Bruno said, "How do you get back and forth without a car, Leo?"

"I manage. I like to walk. Do you know what the probabilities are that you'll have an accident if you own a car? It's a lot more likely than a plane crash." He poked me on the shoulder. "How many miles a year do you drive?"

"I have no idea."

"You must have a rough idea. Make an estimate. Do you take many long trips?" Great, he was going to tell me my chances of becoming a highway fatality. Probably had the statistics at his fingertips. "Let's say it's ten thousand miles, that's an average figure."

Bruno said, "Leo, I don't think you've met my wife, Sabina. And that's Vic."

Leo said to Sabina, "Is he your son?" Meaning me. The man was full of social graces.

I said, "No, we're much closer than that." His eyes flickered uncertainly in my direction, rested on my chin for an instant and then slid away.

Sabina said, "How did you get here so fast if you were walking?"

"Obviously I left before you did." His tone implied she'd asked a stupid question. He turned to Bruno. "Did you see Sachs shake that bastard's hand? Could you believe it? I couldn't, it turned my stomach. I thought Sachs at least had a few principles left, but apparently that's too much to expect." He gave a short, bitter laugh. "Did I miss much? Did they embrace? Nothing would surprise me after that touching scene." His eyes flickered at Bruno and at me in the mirror, and then he turned his head and stared out the window.

Bruno said, "You mean you don't know what happened? Moore-Gann collapsed, he's been taken to the hospital."

For a moment I thought I saw a smile on Pesnik's lips and then it was gone. "You don't say. What a tragedy. Maybe his conscience caught up with him."

"What did he have on his conscience?" said Sabina.

Pesnik hesitated. "You're not talking to an unbiased party. Let's not speak ill of the dead."

"He's not dead. He was alive when they took him to the hospital," said Sabina.

There was an uncomfortable silence. Leo broke it, finally. "I did see an ambulance go by. So that was Moore-Gann! And he's still alive—well, well. All we can do is hope." It was pretty clear what he was hoping for.

I said, "Sounds as if you don't like him."

"Why should I like him? He stole one of my ideas. Moore-Gann!" He spat the words out. "The name's as phony as the

42

man. Don't get me started on this, I don't like to talk about it. I'm not supposed to talk about it, anyway." He turned to Bruno. "Apparently if I say anything, Moore-Gann could sue me. Can you imagine? He steals my idea and *he* gets to sue *me!* It's unbelievable, but that's what Gawthrop told me." He laughed again. He was getting excited. "Listen, you won't say I said anything, will you?"

"No," said Bruno. "Calm down, Leo."

"Not that it matters. Not that everyone doesn't know about it. They laugh at me behind my back."

"Nobody laughs at you," said Bruno, who is very tender-hearted.

"Sure they do! Leo the sap, Leo the dope, Leo the crazy—"

I switched the radio on. Loud rock.

After a couple of minutes Pesnik said, "Do you ever listen to the *words* of that stuff?"

The rest of the way back to Burlington he lectured us on the filthiness of rock lyrics. Quoted plenty of examples, too.

I wasn't too taken with Leo Pesnik, he struck me as a bitter, paranoid guy with a frustrated craving to be the center of attention. If Moore-Gann had really stolen his idea, I couldn't get too excited about it.

# SEVEN

While I poured the dregs of the Bloody Mary into a small bottle and dusted the glass for prints, Sabina and Bruno went through their usual nighttime ritual. First she put the kettle on the stove in the tiny kitchen. Then with hot water she rinsed out the pale green porcelain teapot she'd brought back from Japan, and opened the leather carrying case that held two teacups in a gizmo that looked like a brassiere, and a row of tin cannisters of different kinds of tea. Now came the earthshaking decision: oolong or lapsang? Darjeeling, jasmine, or Earl Grey? Sabina stood in her stocking feet (she'd slipped off her spike-heeled shoes, as always, as soon as she'd walked through the door), holding her pointed chin in her hand and pondering with total concentration. Finally she said, "Darjeeling." I've never figured out on what basis she makes these choices. There isn't any simple rule, such as going down the row and then starting over when she comes to the end. She just stands there communing with the tea until inspiration strikes. For a couple of weeks she'd been on a Darjeeling kick, but it could end at any time.

She pried open the cannister and began spooning tea into the pot. She didn't believe in teabags. I was convinced that if you blindfolded her, she wouldn't be able to tell tea made with teabags from any other kind. She claimed she could but didn't seem eager to make the experiment, and I didn't care to push her.

Meanwhile, Bruno had disappeared. Now he came back carrying a crumpled white paper bag that contained his secret cookie stash. His lips were sealed and his jaws weren't moving, but I could tell by his innocent look and the crumbs on his beard that he'd already munched one or two.

"What's *that?*" said Sabina, when she saw the bag.

"Nothing."

"I thought we were each going to lose five pounds."

"We will, we will." He put the bag on the table.

She poured tea into the two cups. "At least put them on a plate. Where'd they come from, anyway?"

"I have my sources." He dumped them in a bowl, breaking several in the process and showering the table with large crumbs, which he picked up and ate before I had a chance to do so.

I said, "Don't you ever get tired of chocolate chip?"

"Not really, do you?"

"I guess not." I helped myself to a glass of milk.

Sabina said, "When are you going to stop drinking milk, Vic? Do you know what it's doing to the inside of your blood vessels?"

I knew she had my best interests at heart—she'd told me often enough—but I was irked. Sabina can be too bossy. I know she's my boss, but what I eat is none of her business. "I guess I'm just a growing boy," I said. I sat down at the table and took a handful of cookies before Bruno could eat them all.

"You're almost thirty. Can't you at least drink skim milk?"

I said, "No. It's blue. And for your information, tea contains more caffeine than coffee. If you keep drinking it you'll have insomnia and become a nervous wreck."

Sabina said severely, "Tea is a drink for civilized adults. I have no trouble sleeping and I'm perfectly calm. Bruno, now that you've produced those cookies, would you kindly leave one or two for me?"

"Sorry, dear. I wasn't thinking." He gave her a couple from the pile in front of him.

Sabina said, "About Leo Pesnik. Did Moore-Gann really steal his idea?"

Bruno said, "I don't know for sure. Pesnik's a bright guy but you have to take what he says with a grain of salt."

"He seems paranoid to me," I said. "Has he ever had a breakdown?"

"Two, as a matter of fact. Both times he was hospitalized briefly."

Sabina turned to me. "So you don't think there's any truth to it?"

"I wouldn't say that."

Bruno said, "All this happened years ago, when Pesnik was still a young assistant professor." He washed down a cookie with a swig of tea. "Pesnik claims that at one time he discussed an idea he'd had with Moore-Gann, and Moore-Gann quickly wrote a paper about it. Pesnik's a very slow worker, he checks things out a hundred times before he decides to publish."

"Like you."

"Oh, no. Compared to him I'm a speed demon, believe me. Pesnik has done some good work, but he's also written a few papers that seem screwball to me. Or maybe they're so deep I can't understand them. Anyway, he mulled this thing over for five years or so, which is just what Pesnik would do, and then wrote a letter to the *American Physicist* accusing Moore-Gann of plagiarism. Florian Gawthrop was the editor at that time, and I gather he persuaded Pesnik not to publish the letter. But people heard about it, these things get around."

"Did Moore-Gann win the Nobel for the idea Pesnik claimed was his?"

"Oh, no, no, no. Nothing like that, that *would* have been a scandal. No, it was a separate paper on a different topic."

Sabina poured herself another cup of tea, draining the pot. "And what was that about Moore-Gann suing *him?*"

Bruno shook his head. "I don't really know. I suppose Moore-Gann may have gotten tired of the rumors—which would be understandable—after all, there's no proof whatsoever, it's simply an assertion on Pesnik's part—and threatened to sue Pesnik for slander if he didn't stop talking about it."

Sabina said, "Assuming Moore-Gann did it, his motive

wouldn't have been money. This idea of Pesnik's wasn't a concrete thing like an invention, was it?"

"Oh, no. It was purely theoretical."

I said, "*I* think his motive would have been ambition, pure and simple. Reputation, fame, whatever. You heard what he said tonight."

"That's right," said Sabina. She rose and began to clear the table. "I'm going to bed."

I said, "In case you're interested, there are three sets of prints on that glass."

"Three," she repeated. "One must be Moore-Gann's, of course. One would belong to whoever gave him the Bloody Mary. Jean-Paul Brocchiu was handing out drinks after Moore-Gann and Sachs shook hands, so they're probably his. I wonder who the third set belongs to."

"Want me to start collecting prints? There are only forty physicists at the conference, plus their spouses and a few guests and the employees of the Institute. Of course I'd have to stay in Vermont a little longer instead of going back to Washington, but I'm prepared to make the sacrifice if you insist."

She ignored me. "Bruno, you said Moore-Gann was a fitness fanatic. It seems surprising that he'd have drunk alcohol."

Bruno replied, "As a matter of fact, you're right. He said at lunch today that he'd stopped drinking because alcohol kills brain cells." Bruno looked worried. "Do you think it really does?"

I said, "If you'll forgive my curiosity, what are you planning to do with the dregs?"

"Send them down to the lab in Washington. You can drop them off at the post office tomorrow morning."

"Fine. And now if you'll excuse me, I'm going to photograph those prints. No rest for the weary."

"Good night," said Sabina. She picked up her shoes and left the room. Bruno followed, shedding crumbs as he went.

47

# EIGHT

The next morning, which was Saturday, I went to the post office and mailed the dregs of the Bloody Mary to the lab in D.C. Then I drove to the Institute to meet Bruno and Sabina. A subdued crowd was milling around on the lawn below the administration building, waiting for news. A table had been set up with doughnuts and coffee, and behind it Gerald Ainsworth was filling a sugar bowl. I went up to him.

"Hello, Vic. Isn't this a terrible thing?" he said avidly. "Have some coffee." Gerald struck me as one of nature's voyeurs, and I didn't think he missed much as he peered out at the world from behind his round spectacles.

I took a cup. "Have you heard how Moore-Gann is doing?"

He shook his head. "It doesn't look good, even though the doctor says he has *tremendous* vitality. Well, you could see it, couldn't you? The *shape* that man was in, at sixty-two." He slapped his own waist, which was flabby. "They say even if he does survive he's almost sure to suffer brain damage." Behind the thick lenses his eyes gleamed. "He could turn into a vegetable, imagine."

"Have you heard why he collapsed?"

A mask of not-too-convincing discretion settled over his face. "I really couldn't say."

"Come on, Gerald. It's sure to get around sooner or later."

"Well—" Pursing his lips, he gave a rapid glance over each shoulder and then whispered, "Since you're a detective, I guess I can tell you. He was *poisoned.*"

48

"Well, well. Who would want to poison the great Moore-Gann?"

"I never laid eyes on the man before yesterday, so I really wouldn't know. Of course, darling Judith absolutely hated his guts."

"She did? Why?"

"Well, they *say* she was an episode in his past. Or vice versa."

"A recent episode?" I wondered whether Theresa was aware of it, that is if what Gerald said was true.

"Oh no, we're talking ancient history, Vic. I mean look at the woman, she's a hag."

Judith was standing on the porch of the administration building not far from us, and it was true the years had not been kind to her. Maybe once she could have been cute and petite, but now she was skinny and sticklike and her skin had begun to sag; her face was so sour and angry that it took an effort to realize she might have been pretty when she was young.

"I wouldn't call twenty years ago recent," Gerald said. "Not that Judith is the type to forgive and forget."

A couple of physicists came up to the table and asked Gerald for coffee. I took my cup and went over to Sabina and Bruno, who were talking to the dark, massive man I'd noticed at the cocktail party next to Jean-Paul. He had a Ghengis Khan mustache and eyes that patrolled the room as if he'd learned the hard way the importance of being alert. He was wearing a thick woolen suit that weighed easily eight pounds and had a fly fastened with buttons instead of a zipper. Foreign. I take pride in noticing little details like that.

Sabina took the coffee I handed her and said, "Moore-Gann is in a coma."

The thickset man shook his head. "Is terrible thing, coma."

Bruno said, "I had a professor, back in my pre-med days, who used to say 'coma, period.' Why do things like that always stick in my mind?"

49

Puzzlement appeared on the face of the big man. "Excuse, what is this 'coma, period'?"

"What I meant—" Bruno began.

"It's a pun," Sabina said. "A play on words. Never mind."

Enlightenment dawned and the thickset man grinned, showing his gold tooth. "Very good! I, too, make play with the words in my own language. But my English is not enough good. Some day!" He gave a loud laugh and wagged his finger at Sabina. Several people gave him disapproving looks, to which he was oblivious.

Bruno said, "Vic, this is Andrzej Modzalewski."

I recognized the name, which wasn't one you encountered every day, because I'd seen an article about him in the *Washington Post*. A Polish physicist who'd been arrested as a leader of the Solidarity underground in Wroclav, he had served a year in prison and then been given a pass to visit his family. Somehow he'd managed to flee the country. Bruno had received a call from Saul Sachs half a year earlier, asking whether he might happen to know of a position for Modzalewski.

"I've heard about you," I said.

He took my hand in two hairy fists and compressed it, his quick little eyes fastened on my face. "Good! Good!" he said, grinning. He squeezed harder.

"I'd like my hand back, if you don't mind."

"I hurt you? No! Not big man like you." The booming laugh was repeated as he released my hand. After a few seconds I was able to spread the fingers.

Bruno said to him, "Have you heard how Theresa is taking it?"

Gloom descended on the face of Andrzej immediately. He appeared to be a man of rapid mood swings. "Is tragedy for wife. Coma, very bad." He tapped his temple with a thick forefinger. "Who knows what will be up here?" Shaking his head, he drifted away.

The door of the Institute headquarters opened, and Florian Gawthrop appeared on the porch accompanied by a police officer in uniform. The crowd moved uneasily in their direction. Florian held his hands up in the air and a silence fell, in which Leo Pesnik was heard to say, "I never touch doughnuts. Don't you know sugar is poison?"

Poison was on my mind, too, and I knew it was on Sabina's. And also on the mind of somebody else in the group, if what Gerald had said was true. But who? I looked around. Jean-Paul Brocchiu was standing by the big spruce tree. He hadn't shaved, and he looked as if he hadn't slept. Nearby, Jordan was wolfing a jelly doughnut. The powdered sugar fell on his bare chest. It was a chilly morning, but all he wore was his nylon shorts. What was keeping him warm? Hormones, I decided.

Vita Sachs, her brown hands clasping a Styrofoam cup, her profile in daylight even more like that of an Indian squaw, was standing next to her husband. He stood upright, seeming less frail than yesterday, but his skin was a bad color—yellowish, as if he had a touch of jaundice. He said a few words to her. Looking impatient, she took a pack of cigarettes from the breast pocket of her red silk shirt and lit one without replying. He said something more, and she tossed her sleek black head as a stream of smoke issued from her nostrils. Theresa and Magda, nowhere in sight, were presumably still at the hospital with Moore-Gann.

Florian Gawthrop moved to the edge of the porch. "I am glad to be able to tell you," he said, "that Professor Moore-Gann has survived the night. However"—he shook his head—"his condition is far from good. If anything—well." He fell silent, as if uncertain how much to say. "Where there's life there's hope, of course. Although even if he survives, there is a possibility that his mental functioning may not be quite what it was previously." A profounder silence fell, as if everyone in the group was holding his breath. These people lived by and for their intellects, and to them the idea of brain damage was the ultimate obscenity. Saul Sachs muttered, "Son of a bitch."

Florian took a deep breath. This morning his long, patrician face seemed drawn and pale, and a nerve jumped in his cheek below one eye. "There is something else I must tell you, much as I regret the necessity. It has been determined beyond any doubt that Professor Moore-Gann's collapse was caused by the ingestion of a chemical substance. In other words, some sort of poison."

There was a gasp, and a buzz of rapid words in the crowd. People eyed their neighbors covertly.

"I am unable as yet to tell you the nature of the poison, or precisely when he swallowed it. However, there will have to be an investigation. Captain Wayne Eaken of the Burlington Police Department is in charge, and I trust you will give him your fullest cooperation. He and his colleagues will need to talk to each of us, but he particularly requests that anyone with information about what Professor Moore-Gann ate and drank yesterday inform him as soon as possible. Needless to say, no one is to leave Burlington until further notice.

"There is one more thing. Mrs. Moore-Gann has expressed a desire that the conference should continue with as little disruption as possible, since she feels that is what her husband would wish. Therefore, we have decided to proceed with our normal activities despite the investigation. Captain Eaken will be using the library as his headquarters, but if you need to take out books the librarian will be happy to obtain them for you.

"I would like to remind you that Tuesday's seminar will be given by Dr. Tenofska on the topic, 'New Tests of Supersymmetry.'"

I looked around and saw Magda standing by the big spruce tree. I hadn't noticed her arrival. She hadn't bothered putting on makeup, and the bruise on her cheek was plainly visible, as were the dark circles under her eyes. Not far away, Jean-Paul was standing with Andrzej Modzalewski. Both men were watching her, Jean-Paul with misery and the Pole with an intense stare that made me wonder how well he knew her. Had they met in Poland? Modzalewski had been a big Solidarity hero, and hadn't Bruno said something about Magda's mother being arrested for political reasons? They'd been on the same side so they might have moved in the same circles; anyway, how many Polish theoretical physicists could there be?

Jean-Paul shook his head with a discouraged look, and Andrzej placed a hairy, sympathetic hand on the Corsican's shoulder, then bent and spoke in his ear.

Florian Gawthrop disappeared into the administration building, followed by Judith and Captain Eaken.

I took a step closer to Sabina and said in an undertone, "Captain Eaken particularly requests that anyone with information about what Professor Moore-Gann ate or drank yesterday inform him as soon as possible."

Bruno, on her other side, said, "Listen, Sabina, about that glass. You'd better tell the police."

She pressed her lips together and said to him testily, "I thought you said I had crime on the brain and needed a vacation." It was petty of her to rub it in, but she hates to be told what to do, and anyway they're married. Marriage, I've noticed, makes people more petty—one of many good reasons I have for avoiding the married state. It is *not* true that I have a fear of commitment, as Abby Rademacher claims.

"I admit you were right," Bruno hissed.

"Aha!" she said.

"But did I or did I not tell you to *wait* before you mailed that specimen to the lab, until you heard how Moore-Gann was doing? I don't know what your rush was. Now you'll have to explain to the police why you don't have it any more."

"They can get it," she muttered. "In a couple of days." He was right and she knew it. In an attempt to cloud the issue she added, "Anyway, *nobody* would have it if I hadn't picked up the glass." She strode off in a huff and I followed her. I didn't feel the need to point out that her statement was false. If she hadn't picked up Moore-Gann's glass, I'd have done so.

# NINE

We found Captain Wayne Eaken in the old one-room school-house that served as the library. He was sitting beside a uniformed sergeant at a long conference table in the center of the big, booklined room, reviewing a list of participants in the Institute. Eaken was a tall, well-built man of middle age who looked as if he'd spent most of his life outdoors, maybe on a farm. He had alert, rather cool gray eyes with laugh wrinkles in the corners, and a long, taut-skinned jaw he was stroking with his index finger.

"How do you do, Captain Eaken," said Sabina briskly. "I'm Sabina Swift and this is Victor Newman. We have some information we'd like to pass on to you."

He rose politely, glancing at the list. "Thank you, ma'am. You're here with—uh, Bruno Herschel, right?"

"I'm his wife."

"Okay, Mrs. Herschel."

"My name is Sabina Swift."

He looked confused. "You don't call yourself Herschel?"

"No."

"But you are married."

"Yes. Captain Eaken, let's get on with this."

"Common law?"

I could see he was determined to get it straight. "Married," I said. "Liberated woman."

"Oh." I think he appreciated my contribution, because after that he addressed himself mostly to me, to Sabina's annoyance. "Now, Mr. Newman, I don't see your name on this list."

"I'm a guest of Professor Herschel and Ms. Swift."

"Make a note of that, Lovely," he said, and to us he added, "This here's Sergeant Lovely."

Sergeant Lovely, who appeared to be barely in his twenties and had a round baby face and short, silver-blond curls, nodded and said, "Got my notebook right here."

Sabina said, "I'm a private investigator in Washington, D.C., and Mr. Newman is my employee." She fished in her handbag and handed him her license. I gave him mine as well.

Captain Eaken studied them and passed them to Sergeant Lovely, who copied the information into his notebook. Eaken said, "Well, I be dang. Detectives. You on a case?"

Because he was addressing me, I said, "No. Just a vacation while Professor Herschel is attending the conference."

He stroked his jaw with his finger and narrowed his cool gray eyes. "That so? Well, let's hear what kind of a statement you wanted to make."

Sabina told him that after Hervé Moore-Gann's collapse she'd picked up his glass and we'd taken it home with us.

He looked at me suspiciously. "And this was *before* any suggestion had been made that we were dealing with anything but a natural death here. Excuse me, occurrence—the man's still alive." We nodded. "Now—how come you thought of picking up the glass? Something make you suspicious?"

"Nothing specific," Sabina said. "I just thought it couldn't hurt."

"Okay, female intuition, like." I sneaked a look at Sabina's face. It was turning purple, but she held her tongue. What was really bugging her was that Eaken had never heard of her. That seldom happens in Washington, and she's spoiled. Eaken said, "Where's the glass now?"

"At our apartment in Burlington. Mr. Newman dusted it for prints."

"Okay, save us a job. You didn't wipe it off?"

"Please," I said.

"Just asking, nothing personal."

"One thing you should know," said Sabina. "I sent the

contents down to a lab in Washington for analysis. I'm sorry to inconvenience you."

He took a deep breath. "Yes'm. Yes, ma'am, I guess that'll inconvenience us, all right. Might I ask the name of the lab?" He'd have liked to blast her, but she hadn't broken any laws. We'd had no knowledge Moore-Gann had been poisoned when I'd mailed the specimen.

I gave him the name and address of the lab.

"You haven't gotten any results back yet, I take it."

She said, "Naturally not, I just sent it off this morning. It's in the mail."

"Which post office? Maybe we can catch it."

I told him which one it had been.

"I don't think you can intercept it," said Sabina. "Isn't that against federal law?"

He looked at her. "Vermont's kind of a small place, ma'am. Backward, you might say. Get the postmaster on the line for me, will you, Lovely?"

We sat in silence while Lovely dialed and got the postmaster. Then Eaken took the phone. "Nate, how you been? Good. Good. Looks like you got some of our evidence over to your place. Yep, could turn into a murder." He paused. "Over to the Institute, one of them big mucky-mucks, Nobel prizewinner and all. Keep it under your hat." They talked awhile longer and then Eaken hung up. "Says he'll look around, it should be there."

"Great," I said. I could see Eaken had his methods.

He sat regarding us for a while, pensively. "Private detectives, eh? We don't have too many of those around here, not much to detect. Probably starve to death. I imagine in Washington, D.C., now, you get plenty of crime." Was there a note of wistfulness in his voice?

"Lots," said Sabina, rubbing it in.

"Crooked politicians, spies, all that?"

"Oh, of course," she agreed. "And the embassies, Congress, the White House, the Pentagon—" He should never have brought up the subject of feminine intuition. "Some-

56

times, of course, our cases bring us into contact with the CIA . . ."

Eaken sighed. "Well, Vermont's got its points, 'specially if you like fishing. Happens I like it. Right, Lovely?"

"Yep."

Sabina and Sergeant Lovely went into Burlington in a squad car to pick up the glass, but I turned down their offer to take me along. I was getting very curious about the fingerprints, but I knew the police would find out whose they were a lot sooner than I could. It was the kind of thing they were good at.

I decided to give Abby Rademacher a call and see how things were going back at the office, which I'd left only a day and a half earlier. It seemed longer, though not long enough. I was supposed to go home the next day and I didn't feel ready for it. I liked Vermont.

"What's up, kid?" I said, when I got Abby on the line. She's only a year or two younger than I am, but she still looks like a coed at the University of Maryland—short, a little on the dumpy side, chubby cheeks and wire-rimmed granny glasses, usually wears jeans and, in the summer, sandals and wrinkled cotton blouses from India. She's good at tailing, blends right into the crowd.

"The air conditioner's on the blink again," she said. "I'm waiting for the repairman. He was here yesterday but it still isn't working right. It's ninety-eight degrees, supposed to go up to one hundred tomorrow. How's the weather in Vermont?"

"Are you sure you want to know?"

"Go ahead and tell me. I'm a masochist, you'll make my day."

I told her.

She said, "I hate you, Vic."

"I know. How's business?"

"Slow. Everyone with money is out of town. There was a call from Georgetown Hospital. Drugs have been disappearing, not just pilferage but really massive amounts. They said it could wait until Monday when you get back. You'll be wearing a white coat for this one, dear, and they'll teach you how to test urine specimens."

"That'll look good on my résumé."

"I thought so. Mort tailed your guy from Quantas up to Baltimore yesterday, but he lost him at the Inner Harbor. Meanwhile I left a bug in his apartment."

"Thanks. Up here we have a poisoned Nobel laureate." I told her about it.

• She said, sounding hostile, "Does this mean you won't be home tomorrow night?"

"I wish it did. Unfortunately, the case is being handled by the police." We talked awhile longer but I didn't really pay attention, she'd given me an idea. By the time I hung up I'd decided to run over to the hospital where Moore-Gann was a patient. You could call it ambulance chasing if you like, but it seemed at least possible that if I dropped a few hints to Mrs. Moore-Gann she might decide to hire us to find out who'd poisoned her husband. Then I could stay in Vermont until the heat wave back home was over.

# TEN

※

At the hospital I was told that Professor Moore-Gann was in intensive care and visitors were not allowed. This didn't surprise me. I looked around and soon found Theresa in a waiting room, sitting on a plastic sofa with Florian Gawthrop. He was patting her hand and saying, "My dear, I wish you'd let me take you home to rest awhile."

The two of them looked up as I came in. Theresa still had on the print silk dress she'd worn at the cocktail party. It was soiled and creased and so was she. The faint lines I'd seen on her face the day before had all been gone over with an engraver's needle. Someone had draped a white cotton hospital blanket over her shoulders, and she was holding a pen and an open notebook in her lap. As I came nearer I could see equations on the page. Damned if she hadn't been doing physics, they can do it anywhere.

Gawthrop let go of her hand and she gave me what was probably meant to be a smile. It was a nice try, under the circumstances. "Hello, you're—let's see, it's Mr. Newman, isn't it? Bruno's guest."

"Vic," I said, sitting down next to her. "Actually it was his wife who invited me up. Sabina Swift, the detective. She's my boss. Do you know her?"

I don't think the information registered, because she was having trouble keeping her eyes open; it was obvious she hadn't gotten a whole lot of sleep on that plastic couch during the night, despite the fact that someone had brought her a couple of pillows. She introduced me to Florian, who acknowledged me absently but kept his eyes on Theresa. He had the harassed look of a man who is trying to be in two places at the same time.

"How is your husband?" I said to Theresa in a low, respectful tone.

She closed her eyes for a moment. "Not good." She shook her head. "I don't know how it happened, I can't understand it. There must have been some kind of mistake." She took a long, sighing breath. "Hervé was always so strong, so young for his age, it's impossible to imagine him sick, maybe even—" Her speech was slurred, as if she'd been given a tranquilizer. She shook her head again and repeated, "I don't know how it happened."

Florian Gawthrop said, "There's hope, Theresa. There's a good chance he'll recover."

"Not a good chance."

He didn't contradict her. After a moment he rose. "My dear, I'm so sorry but I must get back to the Institute." He took her hand and pressed it. "I have responsibilities, you know how it is. Forgive me?" He seemed to feel he needed her permission before he could leave.

"Of course." She was using her gracious manner but there was a cool edge to it.

"Won't you let me take you home for a rest? There's nothing you can do here."

"I'd rather stay."

"Well—" He pressed his lips together as if annoyed that she wouldn't do as he suggested. "I'll come back then as soon as I can."

"Please don't," she said. "I understand you have work to do. Anyway, Magda's coming. And Vic's here now. Sit down, Vic." She patted the plastic cushion beside her. I sat.

"Well—" After a moment he bent and kissed her on the cheek. She didn't seem to notice. He hesitated as if about to say something, but didn't. He left.

Theresa turned to me. "They let me see my husband at the end of every hour, for five minutes. Of course he isn't conscious but I wouldn't feel right if I left, Florian knows that. Though I do wish I could get some sleep, I was up all night.

Have you seen Magda? I wonder what's become of her. I thought surely she'd be back by now." Anxiously she added, "She's all right, isn't she?"

"I saw her at the Institute and she seemed fine."

"I couldn't bear it if both of them—" She fell silent, then demanded in a fretful tone, "Where is she, then?" I said nothing, and after a moment she went on, "I'm glad you're here, I hate to be alone. But I was worrying about Florian because of *course* he has to be at the Institute, I *told* him to leave." Suddenly she leaned toward me and placed her hand on my wrist. Her fingers were icy. "No one could really want to harm Hervé, isn't that true, Mr. Newman? Vic? It must have been an accident. He was a national treasure, I don't think that's an exaggeration—did you know he was going to be named ambassador to Norway? That shows you how he was thought of in the highest places. Oh, heaven help me!" She snatched her hand away from mine and pressed it against her mouth. "I'm talking about him as if he were dead, I'm using the past tense."

"Don't give up hope."

She shook her head. "I have to face the facts, don't I? The doctor says that even if he recovers there'll be brain damage. My God, a brain like his!" She put her hands over her face and began to rock back and forth. "It's worse, it's worse!" I thought she was crying, but when she looked up her eyes were dry. I felt she'd have been better off if she could have let herself go, let herself cry—even scream and have hysterics if she needed to, not that she was the type. She fluffed up her gray-blond hair automatically and closed the notebook in her lap.

I said, "What's that you're working on?"

"This?" she looked at the notebook. "What is it?—oh, yes. I'm supposed to give a seminar on Friday."

"Surely you won't give it now."

She tossed her head. "Surely I *will*. Why shouldn't I?" Her blue eyes turned steely. "I have to do *something*. Do you expect me to sit still with my hands folded? Why *not* go on with my work?"

She had a point. Before I could reply, a man in a white coat with a stethoscope in his pocket entered the room. "Mrs. Moore-Gann?"

She jumped to her feet, the muscles knotting in her calves, and glanced at her watch. "But it's not an hour yet," she said uncertainly. Her notebook fell to the floor and I picked it up.

The doctor cleared his throat. "Mrs. Moore-Gann, I'm terribly sorry to have to tell you this. We did everything we could, but I'm afraid—your husband has just passed away."

I drove her back to the silver-gray VIP cottage in my VW. She lay back with her head against the seat and her eyes closed for such a long time that I figured she was asleep, but after a while she stated in a flat voice, "The doctor said Hervé was poisoned."

"I heard," I said. "Theresa, do you have any idea who might have wanted to kill your husband?"

"No one!" she cried. "It was a mistake, it had to be. I should have watched him more closely, I should have taken better care of him." She spoke as if Moore-Gann had been a child she'd been responsible for.

"Did he have any enemies that you know of?"

"Oh, enemies," she said, with a wave of her hand. "Naturally he had enemies, in his position. It's envy—there are plenty of sick, jealous people in the scientific community, just like anywhere else. Did you know envy can become a sickness?" She stared out the window. "Saul Sachs hated my husband. He and Vita both—they absolutely loathed him, not that poor Hervé ever harmed them."

"Why did they hate him, then?"

"Envy," she repeated impatiently. "I told you. Saul thought Hervé got too much credit for the work they'd done together. He actually resented the fact that Hervé's name came first on their papers, even though they'd agreed to use alphabetical order, because people might think it meant Hervé was the senior author. Can you imagine anything more absurd, more childish? And Vita! I don't know, maybe I'm

6 2

the one who's being petty, as a rule I don't believe in gossip. But Vita's said some *vicious* things about us."

"Why did *she* hate your husband?"

Theresa hesitated, and her gaze strayed out the window. "I don't know," she said uncertainly. "Maybe she didn't hate him, exactly. Certainly there was a time when she absolutely threw herself at him, it was disgusting; he didn't pay any attention and maybe that's why—" She hesitated, then blurted, "Anything in pants—well, never mind. At one time I thought she was my friend." She shook her head. "I was naive. Maybe she didn't hate Hervé, maybe she did. But envy? She was eaten up with it, especially once he became a sort of—oh, unofficial government representative, you might say. He was always being asked to go abroad and serve on commissions and that sort of thing. And there was the publicity, the television interviews. That's what she wanted for Saul but he wasn't the type. He has a filthy mouth, he drinks too much, he doesn't know what it means to be diplomatic—all of which she ignores, naturally. Vita used to be an actress in her younger days, not a very successful one I believe, and she couldn't stand seeing Hervé in the spotlight instead of Saul. With herself by his side, of course. Loaded down with jewelry like the Queen of the Gypsies!"

"You don't like her."

"I have good reason not to like her."

"But you say she was once your friend. What happened?"

"You're asking a lot of questions. And I'm talking much too much."

"Why, what harm can it do?"

She didn't answer, and we drove down the highway in silence.

"What about Leo Pesnik?" I said after a while. "He has a grudge against your husband."

"Why are you asking me all these questions, Mr. Newman? Are you investigating my husband's death? You're a detective—like Bruno's wife."

The information had registered, then. "Yes. She's my boss."

"I don't know her."

"She's good. She's the best."

"I don't know her," she repeated shortly. "I knew Bruno's first wife when they were in graduate school."

That was the wife who'd been addicted to morphine, who according to what I'd heard had been well known in every emergency room and detox ward in Washington, D.C. Maybe Theresa didn't know about that, but I had a feeling she'd heard that Bruno had moved in with Sabina before his divorce, and she disapproved. Theresa Moore-Gann seemed to be a lady of the old school.

"Anyway," Theresa said with finality, "as far as Leo Pesnik is concerned, the man's completely crazy." She lay back again and closed her eyes.

We got to the house and she climbed out of the van and stumbled up the steps to the front door. It was unlocked. We entered, and she called, "Magda? Magda, are you here?" There was no answer.

I said, "I'll be going now."

"No," she said, and her fingertips brushed my arm. "Would you mind very much staying with me a few minutes longer? I can't understand where Magda is, she was supposed to have come to the hospital." I saw worry in her blue eyes.

"Maybe she's upstairs sleeping. Or at the Institute." Or with Jean-Paul, I thought, remembering the way he had looked at her while Florian Gawthrop had been making his announcements that morning. Was that what Theresa was worried about?

"Please don't leave me alone, I don't want to be alone. Do you think that's selfish?"

"Of course not," I said in a soothing voice. Why didn't the woman let herself cry? She was wound up so tight that I felt she would twang if anyone brushed against her.

We went upstairs together. The door to Magda's room was open and she was lying on the bed sleeping. She was fully dressed and had her shoes on, as if she'd just stretched out for a moment and fallen instantly asleep.

Theresa stepped quietly inside the room, tiptoed over to the bed, and bent over the girl, peering at the pale, bruised face, half covered by the mass of dark hair. After a moment she took a folded blanket from the foot of the bed. With a trace of a smile on her lips, she spread the blanket over Magda and then left the room. She whispered, "Poor child, she must be exhausted."

I took Theresa's arm. "You could use some sleep yourself."

She let me lead her to her room, and while I drew the shades she took off her shoes and lay down in one of the twin beds, pulling the covers up around her shoulders. By the time I left the room I could tell from her quiet breathing that she was asleep.

I went noiselessly down the hall to the bathroom, locked the door behind me, and opened the medicine cabinet. All it contained was a dozen or so bottles of different kinds of vitamins, with brightly colored labels—Moore-Gann's, probably. If he'd hoped to buy immortality at the health store they'd come from, he definitely hadn't gotten his money's worth.

The only other personal things in the bathroom were three toiletries bags lying on a shelf; I reminded myself that these were rented quarters in which the Moore-Ganns and Magda could only have been living for a few days. Quickly I went through the bags. More vitamins in Moore-Gann's. A bottle of Valium tablets in Theresa's, with her name on the label— her emotions weren't as totally controlled as they appeared on the surface, then. In Magda's there was nothing remarkable except for eye shadow in six different colors, including Gold Dust.

I flushed the toilet, just in case Theresa wasn't really asleep, and went downstairs. There was a room lined with bookcases they must have been planning to use as a study, judging from the books and papers that had been dumped there. I wondered whether the two desks were to have been allocated to Moore-Gann and Theresa or to Moore-Gann and Magda. I opened the drawers with the tips of my fingernails. Empty. Not very optimistically I shuffled through some of the piles of papers, which seemed to consist mainly of physics. There were lecture notes and preprints of articles, and books with titles like *Gauge Theory of Weak and Electromagnetic Interactions.* There were novels, too—*War and Peace, Heart of Darkness, The Good Soldier,* a few others of that ilk. One of the members of the household had been planning on doing some heavy-duty summer reading.

I heard footsteps outside. People were coming up the stairs to the porch. I looked up quickly and a sheet of grayish paper sticking out from under one of the piles caught my eye. On it I glimpsed the words "It is almost too terrible . . ."

Didn't sound like physics. I grabbed it and slipped it inside my shirt, hoping it wouldn't crackle. There was a knock on the door. I went out into the hall. Captain Eaken and Sergeant Lovely were standing on the porch. I could see them through the glass panel. I let them in.

Captain Eaken said, "Mr. Newman. Well, well." His eyes slipped past me to the open door of the study. "Mind if I ask what you're doing here?"

"I just brought Mrs. Moore-Gann home from the hospital. I guess you heard that her husband died."

"We heard."

"She's sleeping, so if you came here to talk to her I think you should wait."

"Listen, buddy," he said, and his gray eyes were cold. "You may be hot shit down in Washington, D.C., but up here we don't appreciate suspects telling us how to conduct our investigations."

"So I'm a suspect?" I'd been trying to decide whether to hand over the paper I'd just picked up. Now I decided not to. Anyway I wanted to read it first and make a Xerox.

"Everybody who was at that cocktail party is a suspect, and don't you forget it."

"I won't. I promise."

I brushed past him and out the door. He didn't try to stop me, and the paper I'd stuck in my shirt didn't rustle.

When I got in the microbus I drove half a mile down the road and then pulled off on the shoulder. The paper I'd found was the recycled type, gray with a greenish cast, with tiny brown flecks and hair-fine threads embedded in the blotterlike surface, which was too soft to hold fingerprints. It was unusual paper, the kind that would be a breeze to identify, if I ever happened to see another sample somewhere.

The paragraph had been typed in the center of the page.

> It is almost too terrible, the picture of that judgment, as it appears to me sometimes, at nights. It is probably the suggestion of some picture that I have seen somewhere. But upon an immense plain, suspended in mid-air, I seem to see three figures, two of them clasped close in an intense embrace, and one intolerably solitary. It is in black and white, my picture of that judgment, an etching, perhaps; only I cannot tell an etching from a photographic reproduction. And the immense plain is the hand of God, stretching out for miles and miles, with great spaces above it and below it.

I read it twice. The thing gave me a weird feeling. I didn't have the faintest idea what it was about, but the desperation of whoever had written it was obvious. Had it been Moore-Gann? Was this what had been going on behind that impassive face, those unwavering eyes? Maybe Theresa had written it, or Magda.

Yeah, I told myself as I stuck the paper back inside my shirt, and maybe it was written by the previous tenant of the cottage. I shifted gears and got back on the road heading toward Burlington.

# ELEVEN

It was midafternoon by the time I got back to the house in Burlington. Sabina, in her starched white smock, was sitting out on the lawn with her art gear, depositing specks of paint on her eight-by-ten canvas, working as usual from left to right. Bruno was snoring on the porch swing, a physics book across his chest and a pair of reading glasses perched on his nose.

"What a peaceful scene," I said as I came up to her. "You'd never know there'd been a murder around here."

After a moment she said, "You're standing in my light."

"Well, excuse me." I moved about a foot away. "Have you ever tried Painting by Numbers? You'd be good at it." She didn't deign to answer. "I've had some interesting experiences since last we met. Care to hear about them?"

"Later. When the sun goes down."

"Okay, if that's how you feel. You did hear that Moore-Gann's dead?"

"Of digitalis poisoning. Yes." She was working on the sky now, using two small brushes: one for white and the other for blue.

"So it was digitalis." I unbuttoned my shirt and reached inside. Her brush hand faltered.

"What *are* you doing, Victor?"

"You wouldn't be interested." I took out the paper, rustling it a little.

A cloud passed over the sun and Sabina flung her brushes into the baby-food jar. She sighed. "Victor. This is not our case. I happen to be on vacation. As far as we're concerned,

68

Moore-Gann's death is an interesting and, presumably, tragic event. Period. And you *are* going back to Washington tomorrow. Not that Bruno and I wouldn't enjoy having you stay longer, but we're shorthanded back at the agency, as you're aware."

"Abby says business is slow."

"What else did she say?"

I delivered a full report.

"You see? You'll have to cover that drug theft at Georgetown Hospital. What is that piece of paper you keep rattling?"

"Just a little something I picked up in Moore-Gann's study when I took Theresa home from the hospital."

She glanced up at the sky. A second cloud had appeared— a small one. "The light seems to be going," she said. "All right, Victor. Let's see that paper."

She stuck out her hand and I gave her the paper. She read it through slowly, saying "Hm" once or twice. Then she said, "What do you make of this?"

"I'd say whoever wrote it was in a lot of pain."

"That's fairly obvious. But isn't there something about it that strikes you as odd?"

"Odd?"

"Yes." She started to read it again, leaving me to wonder what she'd meant by "odd."

A light-green Saab pulled into our driveway. We looked up and saw that Florian Gawthrop was at the wheel.

I said, "Business?"

"Could be." She laid the sheet of paper face-down on her painting table and anchored it with a tube of paint so it wouldn't blow away. "Please go and wake Bruno, Victor. That snoring sounds unprofessional."

Bruno's a fantastic napper, and I've had occasion to awaken him before. It's easy, you just nudge him and he opens his eyes and sits up and pretends he's been awake the whole time. Which he did this time, too.

"Looks like Sabina may have a client," I told him, as Florian's car came to a halt. I jumped down off the porch and sauntered over to the driveway in time to greet the director of the Institute as he emerged from his car. "Hi!" I told him. "We meet again."

"So it seems, Mr. Newman. Vic, isn't it? Actually, I came to consult Sabina."

I led him over to the table where Sabina was pretending to be immersed in her art. "Sabina, Professor Gawthrop would like to consult you about something."

"Certainly," she said. "How are you, Florian? Vic, perhaps a chair?" I brought over a couple, and he took one and I took the other. Bruno had vanished into the house. When it comes to agency business, Sabina has trained him well.

Florian cleared his throat. "Sabina, as you've probably surmised, I'm here because of Moore-Gann's death. His— murder, I suppose I should say." He shook his narrow blond head. "Hard to believe. A frightful thing! I've been in constant touch with the board of trustees and we are all deeply distressed. Deeply! I don't wish to impugn the competence of the Vermont police, in fact I've known Wayne Eaken for years and he's a splendid fellow, but there's no doubt, none whatsoever, that he has never had occasion to investigate the murder of someone of Moore-Gann's international stature. And it goes without saying that the world of theoretical physics is *terra incognita* to him. Whereas you, on the other hand, are not only widely known as a private investigator but, perhaps equally important, are the wife of a physicist." He smiled briefly. "As the young people say, you know the turf. Sabina, we want you to find out who murdered Hervé Moore-Gann, and to do so as quickly as possible, to minimize the destructive effect that this is bound to have on the physics community as a whole. As for your fee, let me assure you that will not be a problem."

Swishing her brush in the turpentine jar, she thought it over for at least five seconds. Vacations are threatening to workaholics like Sabina, the prospect of having to fill all that unstructured time drives them crazy. Florian didn't know what a favor he was doing her, not to mention me. "All right,

I'll take the case. My fee will also include the services of my assistant, Mr. Newman, if that's agreeable to you."

Aha. I did my best to look modest, stalwart, and indispensable. Florian said, "Fine. Whatever you need to get the job done."

She said, "Vic, please ask Bruno to join us."

I stood up and as I went into the house I heard her say, "Since he knows the people and their backgrounds . . ."

I found Bruno at the kitchen table, drinking coffee and eating cookies out of a paper bag. I said, "Your wife has just been hired to investigate Moore-Gann's death, and you are summoned."

"Really? She wants me?" He looked pleased. Usually she keeps him firmly in his place when it comes to her cases. Bruno's one of the sweetest guys in the world, but when he forms a theory he turns into a terrible nag if you don't happen to agree with him.

I brought an extra chair down from the porch for him, and the four of us sat facing each other. Sabina said to Florian, "Please tell me as much as you can about Hervé Moore-Gann. How long have you known him?"

"Twenty years this summer. I met him for the first time, right here at the Institute. Saul Sachs and I had decided to try and start some sort of an advanced summer school for physicists in New England—there were several in other parts of the country that were quite successful—and we chose Burlington because I knew the area well, in fact I'd spent all my summers here since I was a boy. My family owned land that had some unoccupied buildings on it, and although they needed repair they were usable. It was Saul who suggested we invite Hervé. They had gone to the same high school in New York City, and each had subsequently gone on to become a distinguished theoretical physicist, Sachs at Yale and Moore-Gann at M.I.T."

"Were they already collaborators by then?" asked Sabina.

"No. Their collaboration started here."

71

"By the way, do you happen to know why they stopped speaking to each other after they had won the Nobel prize?"

Florian shook his head. "No, I do not. Neither Sachs nor Moore-Gann ever told anyone, as far as I'm aware."

"Not even their wives?"

"They may have told their wives, of course. I really wouldn't know. If so, the ladies kept it to themselves."

"All right. Go on."

"As I was saying, Sachs invited Moore-Gann to become a member of the board of trustees, and we were delighted when he agreed to come to Vermont as soon as the spring semester ended and help us plan the first session. Moore-Gann was then in his forties and quite well known, although not as famous as he later became. He brought a graduate student with him—Theresa, whom he married the following winter. She was one of the most promising students of her year, as I recall."

"In his forties," mused Sabina. "Had he been married before?"

"Oh, no. In fact—" Florian paused abruptly, as if he'd changed his mind about something he'd been going to say. The thought occurred to me that Florian himself was now in his forties and apparently unmarried. I wondered why.

"In fact, what?" said Sabina. "I'm sure you realize how important it is for you to tell me everything you know about Moore-Gann."

Florian passed one narrow hand over his lank, blond hair, and a pained look flitted across his good-looking but rather bland face, the face of a man who has trained himself to be discreet. "I was going to say I was rather shocked when I learned that Hervé had married Theresa. He had a reputation as something of a ladies' man and had evaded quite a few matrimonial traps in his day. Not really the type you expect to marry."

I said, "Maybe he felt it was time to settle down." I've thought more than once that *I* might settle down when I'm about forty.

Florian looked at me in surprise, as if he had been expecting Sabina to do all the talking. "It's possible."

Sabina said, "And do any of these women he was involved with happen to be here at the Institute this summer?"

Florian didn't answer immediately, and Bruno said, "Someone once told me he'd had a fling with Vita Sachs. I've even heard it was the reason Saul stopped speaking to him. I don't know if it's true or not."

Florian shook his head. "Oh, I'm sure that's just a rumor. Vita never liked Hervé, and she's the sort of person who lets her feelings be known."

Personally, I didn't think that meant Hervé and Vita couldn't have had an affair. Some men think women who can't stand them are an irresistible challenge, and some women pretend to dislike men they secretly feel attracted to.

Florian cleared his throat. "Of course—ah—there's Judith. My secretary. Hervé was here all summer that first year and they had a romance. Well, actually—an affair." He cleared his throat again and looked unhappy at having divulged this piece of ancient gossip. "She was quite an attractive girl at one time. Peppy, vivacious, quick on the uptake. Judith was born in Burlington—her father used to repair our furnace and do other odd jobs around my parents' place. She was very intelligent and efficient and she'd taken a secretarial course while she was in high school. I needed a secretary when the Institute was in the planning stages, and I—ah—preferred having a person who would be here year-round." He appeared uncomfortable. "I think she believed Moore-Gann was going to marry her. And maybe he would have."

"If it hadn't been for Theresa, you mean?"

"Oh, no. Theresa was a student of his, but at that stage there was nothing between them as far as I'm aware."

I said, "Judith isn't the pleasantest person in the world—in fact, it's common knowledge that she makes a habit of being rude to visitors. Why does she get away with it? How come she hasn't been fired?"

Florian replied with urbanity, "Oh, I think you exaggerate.

It's just her manner, no one takes her seriously. She's remarkably efficient and we'd be lost without her. Why, she's been making all the arrangements for twenty years. The housing—you have no idea how complicated it can get." He flapped his hands in the air to indicate an enormous problem. "But as for her affair with Moore-Gann—" He shook his head. "The breakup affected her deeply, I'm afraid. She was pregnant, though Hervé insisted he wasn't the father—and there were circumstances which made it possible he was right—and he refused to take any responsibility for the child. Judith went away to have her baby, and when she came back she told people that she'd married a soldier who was killed shortly afterward in Vietnam. I don't know how many people believed her, but they more or less accepted it." Florian shook his head. "It was a messy situation. Pathetic, really, especially since Judith's son turned out to be mildly retarded. Perhaps you've seen him around the Institute; he helps our caretaker with the grounds. Nice-looking lad, you'd never guess there was anything wrong with him, to see him." He shook his head. "Moore-Gann never contributed anything to his support, although I believe Theresa sent Judith some money from time to time."

Sabina said, "This story doesn't show Moore-Gann in a very sympathetic light."

Florian hesitated, and a nerve jumped in his lean cheek. "You have to understand what sort of man he was. He wasn't likable in the usual sense, although he inspired respect and even awe in a great many people. He had tremendous powers of concentration. In a certain sense he had a one-track mind. Of course that quality was a great asset to him as a physicist, for once he got hold of an idea or made a decision, he moved forward undeviatingly and with total dedication. It was almost as if everything else in the world became unreal to him until his obsession—I don't think that's too strong a word for it—ran its course. And in some ways that quality showed up in his personal life, as well. I think once he made up his mind that he couldn't be certain he was the father of Judith's child, she simply ceased to exist for him. Some people called him cold. I've heard it said that he used people, although I've had no experience of it, personally." He hesitated. "Well, there was the Pesnik business."

"I understand Pesnik accused him of stealing one of his ideas," said Sabina.

"His best idea, actually. Oh, so you've heard about that."

"How did you get involved with it? I gather you did."

"I had no choice," said Florian with distaste. "At that time I was the editor of the *American Physicist,* rather a thankless job, I might add. Pesnik wrote a letter to the editor accusing Moore-Gann of plagiarism. His language was intemperate in the extreme, and our lawyer thought it was libelous. On the other hand, I couldn't simply ignore it. It was a serious charge. Pesnik was a bona fide physicist, an assistant professor at Brandeis who'd done some good work even though he'd also had serious emotional problems and had been hospitalized briefly for shock treatments. On the advice of our lawyer I arranged to meet with Pesnik to discuss the matter. He claimed that about six years earlier he'd happened to meet Hervé at a conference in Sweden and had told him about an idea he was working on. A short time later Hervé published a paper based on the same idea and didn't give Pesnik any credit. I asked Pesnik why he'd waited so long to say anything about it and he gave me some vague reasons. I gathered he'd been brooding about it for years. He showed me a letter Moore-Gann had written him, thanking him for the 'very stimulating conversation' they'd had in Sweden and suggesting that he give a talk at M.I.T.—which he never did. But the letter didn't mention the specific topic the two of them had talked about. I confronted Moore-Gann with Pesnik's letter to the editor and he was absolutely furious, denied the whole thing and threatened to sue the magazine if we printed it. When I suggested that we might print the letter together with a reply to be written by Moore-Gann, he wouldn't hear of it. As for the letter he'd written to Pesnik thanking him for the 'stimulating conversation,' Hervé claimed it referred to some work of Pesnik's for which he *had* given him credit, in a footnote to a second paper he'd published not too long after the conference in Sweden. Moore-Gann was very prolific, he was always publishing papers, and Pesnik was just the reverse. He would check his results endlessly before making them public. I think this increased his bitterness. I can remember his saying 'The rich get richer!'"

Sabina said, "So you persuaded him to withdraw his letter."

Florian looked uncomfortable. "Oh, you've heard about that, too." He leaned forward in his chair. "But there was nothing to be done, there was absolutely no proof! Pesnik was up for tenure, and Moore-Gann made it clear that he would try to block his promotion if he didn't back down. Moore-Gann had won the Nobel prize by then and he was a very powerful and influential figure."

Sabina said, "Do you think Moore-Gann stole Pesnik's idea?"

Florian paused. "That's an extremely difficult question to answer. Theoretical physics is such an abstract thing. It's people's thoughts—ideas, notions, concepts, words—not tangible things like experiments that can be replicated or inventions that can be manufactured and sold. Ideas are all we have to base a career on. Physicists talk to each other and exchange ideas constantly, and sometimes it's hard to be certain exactly who said what first. And especially between junior and senior people, a professor and his student or post-doc, the professor may feel he really has a right to be co-author of a paper, or to get credit for an idea, because without his help and suggestions the student could never have worked the thing out in all its details. And the student may not see it that way."

"But don't you think that, after all, an idea originates with one person?"

"Not always. Sometimes two people come up with the same idea independently—it's happened many times in physics—and they may both publish papers without having any knowledge of each other's work." He interlaced his fingers and propped his chin on them. "In Pesnik's case, I don't know. Moore-Gann had a superb intellect and there is certainly no doubt that he's made major contributions to theoretical physics. But a mind such as his can be like a powerful vacuum cleaner, sucking up every idea that comes its way. And when you combine it with an enormous ego—and he certainly had that, no one who knew him would dispute it— well, he *wanted* to get credit, he *wanted* to be right and come up with dazzling ideas, and astonish everyone with his brilliance. That's the way theoretical physicists are. So he might have—deluded himself, convinced himself an idea was really his when perhaps it wasn't."

"Or he might have known it wasn't."

He nodded. "That's of course possible, too. But in the case of Pesnik there was simply nothing to be done, whatever the truth may have been. He claimed Moore-Gann stole his idea, and Moore-Gann said he hadn't. Years had passed, there was no proof of any kind, and Pesnik had nothing to gain and a good deal to lose by making a public accusation. So I persuaded him not to. I still think I gave him the best advice possible, under the circumstances."

Sabina said, "I understand. Yet I'm still curious about the personal opinion you formed after speaking to both men. You must have had an opinion."

"My personal opinion?" Florian crossed his long, thin legs and smoothed the cloth of his immaculate jeans over his knees. He darted a glance around our little circle from under his pale-blond eyebrows. "Personally, I believe Hervé did exactly what Pesnik accused him of. I think he knocked out a paper as fast as he could, knowing Pesnik's reputation for painstaking slowness, so he could scoop him. And he succeeded. But I'd rather you didn't quote me."

"Even now that Moore-Gann is dead?"

"I don't want to make things harder on Theresa. She has enough to cope with."

"You seem to be fond of her."

"Why—I respect her, of course. Theresa Moore-Gann is a very fine woman, extraordinarily bright, a person of the highest quality. Why shouldn't I be fond of her? When I was an instructor at Boston University and Moore-Gann was at M.I.T. she was kindness itself." A flush had stained his long thin neck, with its prominent Adam's apple. "But if you're suggesting—" He gave a short laugh. "Everyone knows Theresa was devoted to Hervé. Caesar's wife, you know." He stood up. "Now if you'll excuse me, I have to get back to the Institute." He held out a limp hand toward Sabina. She rose and shook it. "If I can be of any further help, feel free to consult me."

"I will," said Sabina. "You can rest assured I'll do my best to find Moore-Gann's murderer—no matter who it may be."

# TWELVE

We watched Florian drive off in his light green Saab. I said,
"Would a woman scorned have a motive for murder, twenty
years after she'd been scorned?"

"What a frightening idea, Vic," said Bruno.

Sabina said, "Worried about your past catching up with
you, darling?"

"My life is an open book."

"Good. As for your question, Vic. No, I don't think that
would be enough of a motive, if the woman were normal and
the circumstances fairly ordinary. But from what you've said
about Judith, she doesn't sound normal. And there's the
child. Raising a retarded child alone can't be easy."

I said, "So maybe every time she had a problem with her
son she thought about Moore-Gann and how he'd abandoned
her, and got enraged all over again, and then finally met up
with him again and—bingo. How about that?"

"Possibly. Though according to Florian, Moore-Gann may
not have been the father."

"I've met Judith's son," I said, and described my encounter
with him.

"I've noticed him working in the garden," said Sabina. "He
doesn't resemble Moore-Gann, but that doesn't prove anything."

I said, "By the way, when I went to the hospital, Florian was
sitting in the waiting room with Theresa and holding her hand."

Bruno shook his head emphatically. "If you think there's
anything going on between the two of them, I must say I
doubt it. Theresa's a lovely person but certainly no sexpot,

and Florian's a confirmed bachelor. In fact, I've heard rumors that he's gay."

"Anything specific?" I asked.

"No, but the rumors seem a little too persistent to just be speculation, the sort of thing people say about men his age who've never married. Personally, I've always thought of him as rather asexual, if anything."

Sabina picked up the sheet of gray paper that had been lying facedown on her painting table. "Bruno, I'd like your opinion on something."

He stroked his beard in a gratified manner. "Certainly, my dear. What is it?"

"What do you think of this?" She handed him the paper. He read it through and then said, "Who wrote it?"

"That's what we don't know. Vic found it in Moore-Gann's house. You knew the three people who were living there. Do you think any of them might have written it?"

I'd been reading over Bruno's shoulder, and I pointed out, "Whoever wrote it seems to have been having trouble sleeping, which is a prime symptom of depression. If it was Moore-Gann, could he possibly have committed suicide?"

Sabina frowned, "Under the circumstances it seems far-fetched. If he wanted to kill himself, why not do it in private? Anyway, Moore-Gann didn't strike me as depressed—did you think he was?"

"Well—no," I had to admit.

We reread the passage:

It is almost too terrible, the picture of that judgment, as it appears to me sometimes, at nights. It is probably the suggestion of some picture that I have seen somewhere. But upon an immense plain, suspended in mid-air, I seem to see three figures, two of them clasped close in an intense embrace, and one intolerably solitary. It is in black and white, my picture of that judgment, an etching, perhaps; only I cannot tell an etching from a photographic reproduction. And the immense plain is the hand of God, stretching out for miles and miles, with great spaces above it and below it.

Bruno said, "You know, it really doesn't sound to me like any of them. Magda—I doubt that her English is that good.

It couldn't be Theresa; as a beginning graduate student she used to work as a bubble-chamber scanner and they spend hours and hours poring over films. She could certainly tell an etching from a photographic reproduction, no doubt about that."

Sabina said, "Why couldn't it have been written by Moore-Gann, then?"

Bruno shook his head. "He was a confirmed atheist. I can't see him referring to the hand of God."

"Maybe he meant it metaphorically."

"I doubt he'd choose that metaphor."

I said, "Well, somebody wrote it."

He shrugged. "I just don't know. Maybe it has nothing to do with Moore-Gann's murder."

That was possible, yet I had the feeling that the paragraph was important.

Sabina crossed her long, slim legs. "Bruno, how well did you know Moore-Gann as a person, not just a physicist?"

"Not well at all. Basically we had a student-teacher relationship, and although I met him a number of times at meetings after I'd left graduate school, we never talked about anything but physics." He paused. "Maybe that was why I didn't really like the man, he seemed like a machine for doing physics instead of a whole person. I never had the faintest idea how he felt about anything. He didn't seem to *have* feelings, he handled everything in a totally logical, intellectual way. Sachs was different. He used to get angry or sarcastic, or hug people if he was in a good mood. The two of them were complete opposites and it always amazed me that they could collaborate so successfully. Though maybe the contrast between them was a strength, at least for a while. By the way, speaking of Sachs, Vita invited us over to their house for drinks this evening. Nine o'clock."

"Excellent," said Sabina.

"Maybe I should call and make sure the party hasn't been cancelled because of Moore-Gann's death."

"No," she said. "Don't call." She turned toward me. "All

right, Vic. I want to hear about everything you've done and seen at the Institute since you got here."

I settled back in my chair and gave her a full report. When I had finished she was looking thoughtful. She sat for a couple of minutes in silence—and a couple of minutes is a long time—and then she said, "I'd like you to talk to Gerald Ainsworth and ask him again whether he has any ideas about why Judith hasn't been fired. Be persistent."

"I'll stick like a tick."

"In the meantime"—she stood up and began stashing her paints in their box, and I don't mean she *threw* them in, I mean she slipped each tube into its elastic band, arranging them in the order of the colors of the spectrum—"I think I'll take the Mercedes and pay Judith a visit." She glanced at her watch. "And don't forget, we're due at the Sachses' at nine."

# THIRTEEN

I found Gerald at his desk in the reception area, looking harassed. Long strands of his dark, thinning hair, which he usually wore combed neatly across his bald spot, had slipped out of place and hung down in strings. He was shuffling papers furiously.

"Hi, Gerald, we meet again," I said, and perched on the edge of his desk.

He gave me an unhappy smile, his hands full of papers. "Oh, hello, Victor."

"Got a minute?"

He touched the switch of the intercom to make sure it was turned off and said, "Well, no, I'm sorry but actually I haven't. Unless it's something that really won't take but a minute."

"I don't know whether you've heard yet, but the board of trustees has hired my boss to investigate Moore-Gann's death."

"Oh," he said. "Nobody bothered to tell *me*. God!" He flung a handful of papers on the desk. "I don't know why I'm doing this!"

"What are you doing?"

"Rescheduling. Changing the times of all the physics talks to cover the days when Professor and Mrs. Moore-Gann were supposed to give their seminars. *We're* not supposed to do that, that's the *physicists'* job." He cast a quick, uneasy glance over his shoulder in the direction of Judith's office and lowered his voice. "But *she* insisted, she just wouldn't listen! They're going to get into a major snit over this, wait and see."

"I don't know about that," I said. "But I'm pretty sure Theresa Moore-Gann is still planning to give her talks. At least that's what she said when I spoke to her at the hospital."

"Oh, my God, it'll be World War Three around here." Gerald cocked his head as though a thought had just occurred to him. "You know, I bet that's why Judith is doing it. She absolutely *hates* Mrs. Moore-Gann."

"Does she." It wasn't hard to guess why; Judith had wanted Moore-Gann and he had married Theresa instead.

The intercom crackled, and Judith's voice cut through our conversation like a buzz-saw. "Well? Are you done yet?"

Gerald flicked a switch. "Not quite. But Judith, listen—"

"Never mind, just bring the schedules in here. I want to see what you've done so far."

"Okay, be right there." He turned off the intercom and began gathering papers together. "Ours is not to question why. Sometimes I think the woman is actually, certifiably cuckoo."

I said, "Look, I see you're busy, but I really need to ask you a few questions. How about later? When do you get off?"

"Should be fairly soon. I hope." He darted a quick look over his shoulder. "Frankly, I'd rather talk to you someplace else."

"Fine. You name the place."

He touched the tip of his tongue to his upper lip, musing. Then he said, "How about my house? I live in West Bolton, on a ridge with a fabulous view. You can come to dinner, if you're not fussy. Say six-thirty?" The intercom gave a warning squawk.

I had no idea where West Bolton was, but it couldn't be far if Gerald commuted every day. I should be able to spend some time there and still make the Sachses' party. "Great," I said. "But I'll have to eat and run."

Gerald gave me directions. Then he scuttled down the hall toward Judith's office.

I left the administration building. Outside I saw Magda Tenofska standing on the lawn as if she were waiting for someone. Apparently I was the someone, for as soon as she saw me she headed in my direction, the thick black hair that framed her face bobbing up and down as she walked. She'd taken the time to apply makeup and you could hardly see the outline of the bruise on her cheek, but the cosmetics didn't conceal her tense, worried expression; the jeans and cotton sweater she was wearing made her look younger and more American. She took my arm. "I must speak to you," she said.

"I have that effect on women," I said. "I can't seem to help it."

Frowning, she dropped my arm. "This is not a time for stupid jokes. Let us go to the pond, no one will see us there." I followed her down a path that led away from the administration building, wondering if there was ever a time for jokes in Magda's life. She seemed completely lacking in humor. She had plenty of brains, obviously. A capacity for passion, maybe—of a heavy, brooding, masochistic kind. But no humor. A fatal flaw.

She was also one of the most tense people I had ever met, I decided as she strode down the path, her movements taut and abrupt. I couldn't tell whether this was a basic characteristic or whether it had to do with some strain she was continually under—maybe the stress of trying to excel as a woman in a field dominated by men.

The path we were following had been mowed through a field of wildflowers and long thorny canes of wild blackberry, which formed a solid wall on either side of us. It was late afternoon and the air was cool, but the field we were crossing was cup-shaped and seemed to catch the heat of the sun and concentrate it. Bugs were buzzing. I started feeling carefree and relaxed and had to remind myself that I was supposed to be investigating a murder.

I said, "What did you want to talk to me about, Magda?"

She studied me, biting her lip, her expression doubtful. "Is it true what I have heard, that you are a detective?"

"Absolutely."

She hesitated, then said, "Very well, I wish to hire you." She took a navy-blue plastic billfold from the back pocket of her jeans. "You take travelers' checks?"

That stopped me. *Did* I take travelers' checks? No one had ever asked me before. "Sure. Why not?"

"I can give you three hundred dollars in travelers' checks now and more later." She opened the billfold and took out a pen.

"Wait a minute, before you start signing checks why don't you tell me what this is about?"

"The police, they think I killed Moore-Gann."

"Did they say so?"

There was a silence. Then she muttered, "No, they did not say so."

She tossed her hair back over her shoulder and we resumed walking. The path curved around the edge of the woods and soon we came to a pond as big as a city block. At the far end, a wooden footbridge arched over a cement spillway. We sat down on a bench.

Magda said, "I did a stupid thing. I lied to the police."

"What about?"

She threw me a glance, then turned away to stare at the pond. She seemed to be avoiding my eyes, avoiding any kind of contact, as if she hated asking for help and was trying to do it at arm's length if possible. In a dry, unemotional voice she recited the facts. "They asked me about Moore-Gann's drink, who gave it to him and when, and so on. I said I didn't know."

"And that wasn't true?"

"No. I thought he was not so intelligent, that policeman, a simple countryman. Anyway, how could he find out? Everything was thrown out after the cocktail party, all the glasses, so I assumed—falsely, it seems. For the policeman told me he had Moore-Gann's glass and there was poison in it. And—my fingerprints were on it. I told the police I did not know how they got there. But I do know." For a moment her composure wavered and she said pleadingly, "You will help me? Truly?"

"If I can. Why were your fingerprints on Moore-Gann's glass?"

"Because it was my drink." She ran her fingers through her loose, dark hair. "After Moore-Gann and Sachs shook hands, everybody applauded and started moving around the room, you remember? Suddenly Jean-Paul was standing in front of me, holding a Bloody Mary. He started talking to me, begging me to come back to him, saying he was sorry for"—she touched her hand to her cheek—"this." He seemed sincere but I was still angry and said I did not want to speak to him. He said"—she frowned as she tried to remember his exact words—"'people get what they deserve, that is called judgment.' Then he handed me the glass he was holding and went away."

"And did you drink it?"

"No."

"Why not?"

Her mouth turned down in disapproval. "I do not take much alcohol, it makes one stupid. I had had a drink earlier that evening, for me it was enough. Then that young man came over, I do not know his name, he is very handsome but foolish. I did not really listen to what he was saying but I was looking at his face and wondering where I had seen him, he looked familiar. I was upset, you understand. People kept coming and going. I put down my glass on the table; later I may have picked it up again. Moore-Gann came over. There was a strange look on his face. He said, 'Magda, I need a drink.' I said, 'Take mine, I have not touched it.' And I handed it to him." She shrugged. "That was all."

I said, "When you handed the glass to him, had you been holding it or was it still on the table?"

She pondered. "I am not sure. I think—maybe it was still on the table."

"Did Moore-Gann drink it right away?"

"Some of it."

"Did he say anything indicating that it didn't taste right?"

"No."

"I didn't think so but I thought I would ask."

"Bloody Marys are strong drinks, they have a nasty taste. I do not care for them."

"So he drank some of it. How much, would you say?"

"Oh—maybe a quarter of the glass, I am not sure."

"And then?"

She shrugged. "I moved away, I went to look for—someone."

"Who?"

"It does not matter."

She seemed calmer now that she had spoken. There were dark smudges in the hollows under her eyes, above the high Slavic cheekbones. The dark eyes under her heavy brows had a slightly Oriental slant at the corners, as if some distant ancestor had ridden out of China, heading west across the steppes.

I took out the spiral notebook I carry in my pocket. "Tell me again what Jean-Paul said to you when he handed you the glass."

"He said, 'People get what they deserve, that is called judgment.' I know what you are thinking, Vic."

I wrote down Jean-Paul's words. "What am I thinking?"

"You are thinking that the poison was meant for me, am I not right?"

The thought had occurred to me. Though if Magda was telling the truth, the poison might also have been dropped into Moore-Gann's drink after she had left him. It would have been far less easy to do, though, than to drop something into a glass she had left on a table for several minutes while "people kept coming and going." Of course the easiest thing of all would have been for Jean-Paul to have poisoned the drink before he gave it to her. I said, "Is that what you believe, that the poison was meant for you?"

She nodded. "I think maybe someone wants to kill me, yes."

"You don't sound very upset about it."

She said scornfully, "You think I should act like hysterical woman, you think this is the first time my life is in danger?" Her accent became more pronounced as her voice rose.

"It isn't?"

"You Americans, your lives are so secure, you don't know what it is to be afraid of a knock on the door in the middle of the night. My mother is in a Polish prison—that is, if she is still alive. Without the help of friends I could have ended up the same way. That is why I can never go back, as long as the communists are in power."

There was a silence. Then I said, "Magda, do you think Jean-Paul tried to poison you?"

"No!" she exclaimed. Again she pushed her strong fingers through her hair. "No, I do not really believe he would harm me. This"—she touched her cheek again—"is something different, this he did in the heat of anger but to plan my death, coldly and deliberately—" She shook her head. "I know him, that he would not do." She seemed anxious to convince me. Or possibly herself.

I said, "Magda, I'm sorry but I can't work for you. I already work for Sabina Swift."

"You do not need to tell her everything you do."

"Just listen. Sabina has been hired by the Institute to investigate Moore-Gann's death, and I'm assisting her. So we're going to be looking into the case anyway, and you can hang on to your travelers' checks."

"That is not the same!" I could see she was angry, wishing she hadn't told me so much. "I want you to look after *my* interests!"

"I'll try. I'll do the best I can. I'll give you some free advice—go to Captain Eaken and tell him what you've told me."

"But he will arrest me! Because I lied to him, he will think I killed Moore-Gann!"

"He'd need more evidence than that; people lie for all kinds of reasons."

Stubbornly she shook her head. "No, I do not trust the police. You, Vic—you will discover what happened. You and Sabina Swift."

"But what if we find that it was Jean-Paul who poisoned the drink?"

She shook her head again. "You will not, because he did not do it. I am sure of that."

I said, "Is there anyone else who might want to harm you?"

She thought the question over carefully, obviously aware that if the answer was no, Jean-Paul would appear a more likely candidate. Finally, reluctantly, she shook her head. "There is no one."

"I see. And do you have any ideas about who might have wanted to kill Moore-Gann?"

She shook her head again. "No. To kill? No."

"Who disliked him, then?"

She rose from the bench where we were sitting and began to walk in the direction of the wooden bridge. I got up and followed her. We were close to the edge of the pond, where cattails grew in the shallows and scarlet dragonflies swooped and darted. At our feet, tiny frogs the color of the mud hopped away and plinked into the water.

Magda said, "I do not mean to accuse, you understand. But everyone knows about Moore-Gann and Sachs, their feud. And Pesnik hated Moore-Gann. Judith, too, I think— that horrible woman. I do not know why she hated him, one would not think they—how you say?—moved in the same circles."

"Could she have had any reason for hating *you?*"

"Me?" She stared at me. "Certainly not. Although she was very rude to me, for no reason. I misplaced a sheet from my packet and I asked her for another. First she pretended not to hear me and then, if you can believe, she refused to give it."

I could believe. "What did she say?"

Magda turned her head away sharply. "I would rather not repeat it."

"I'd like to know, though."

There was a stubborn set to her jaw. "I do not remember."

"Magda, I'm trying to investigate a murder and I have to ask questions, some of them unpleasant. You're a scientist— when you do your work, don't *you* have to ask all sorts of questions, some of which don't pay off?"

She smiled briefly. "*Most* of which don't pay off."

We had reached the end of the pond and we walked out on the rickety wooden bridge, our footsteps echoing. There was no handrail. "They should repair this bridge, it is dangerous," said Magda, picking her way with care around a couple of planks that were splintered and rotten. Below us, the cold green water surged toward a concrete spillway with a heavy steel gate set in the center. Over this the water plunged into a streambed that vanished into the woods. We could feel a damp chill rising around us.

Magda said, "Judith told me I would have to borrow Professor Moore-Gann's copy and Xerox it. She said, 'You're his latest floozy, aren't you?'" Her eyes darkened. "My English is not perfect but it so happens I know that word."

That sounded like Judith. I said, "She was implying that there was something more between you and Moore-Gann than a professional relationship?"

"Obviously."

"And was there?"

She stared at me, her face expressionless. Then she said, "I have never had sexual relations with Professor Moore-Gann. Anyone who says I have is a liar." She turned her back on me and walked away. I let her go.

# FOURTEEN

The road to West Bolton, where Gerald Ainsworth lived, was pretty good for the first fifteen miles and then became a gravel track that wound through woods, passing a clearing with a house in it every half mile or so. In between the clearings the forest was dense and clogged with boulders and fallen trees. The road was as corrugated as the top of a xylophone, but the noises the microbus made as it jounced along were far from being musical. Every clonk gave me a pang.

Eventually the road came to the West Bolton general store and began a steep upward climb, turning into a rocky track that looked like a dry streambed. There didn't seem to be room for two cars to pass; luckily I didn't meet anyone. The microbus skidded from side to side as the road twisted around the switchbacks and I shifted into my lowest gear, my respect for Gerald growing with every mile at the thought that he drove this route five days a week, and for what? To work under Judith. It seemed more than a man should have to bear.

Finally the road straightened out as if preparing for a new surprise, and a few hundred yards farther it burst out of the woods and into the open. I was on a high ridge, where the road was bordered by meadows on which black and white cows grazed peacefully; up ahead I could see a barn, silo, and farmhouse. To my left the land sloped down to a deep valley containing a long, narrow lake, on the far shore of which mountains rose, their slopes covered with trees. Except for the farm, not a house was to be seen. I took a deep breath.

The air smelled of manure, of which there was an enormous pile outside the barn. Chickens scratched at its base and wandered across the road. They seemed surprised to see me, and not impressed. I gave them the right of way.

Once past the chickens the car leaped into high gear and I was able to speed along at a daredevil 35 mph. Five minutes later I reached the red mailbox that marked the foot of Gerald's driveway. It bore his name, "Ainsworth," and next to it "Ruane," and above them both, "Flowers."

There were a couple of battered pickup trucks in the driveway. I parked next to one of them, got out of the microbus, and followed a series of broad, deep, terracelike steps that led to the house, which was a log cabin with a large clapboard addition on one side. Alongside the steps there were raised beds filled with lilies in every imaginable color. The impact of that mass of color, after all the green and brown miles of woods I'd just covered, was pretty spectacular.

On the porch of the cabin, watching me approach, an elderly man sat in a straight-backed chair. He hauled himself to his feet with the aid of a cane and said, "Did you want flowers?" as he shuffled toward me. "I'll have to call the boy to dig them up."

"No, I didn't come for flowers. Is Gerald Ainsworth here?"

"He's at work." He blinked and then said, "Oh, are you the fellow who's coming to supper? Have any trouble finding the place?"

"Not a bit."

"How'd you like the road?" Slowly, as if it took an effort, a grin appeared on his face. I could see he had once been a handsome man. He had a narrow, well-shaped nose, finely modeled temples, and deep-set gray eyes that were studying me with a hint of mockery. I could also see that he was younger than I'd thought at first. Fifty at most, maybe less. And he was ill. The skin of his face was reddened in a butterfly-shaped patch that contained many small blisters. His arms and hands were reddened, too, and there were purplish spots on his skin, as if the blood vessels beneath had ruptured and the blood had pooled. I hoped whatever he had wasn't catching.

"That road's quite an experience," I said in answer to his question.

"We think so. Gerald should be home any minute. I'm Brad Ruane. Gerald said you were a detective."

"That's right. Vic Newman's the name." I wondered who was in charge of the garden. There wasn't a weed in sight.

Brad said, "Would you like to see the flowers?"

"Are there more?"

"About two acres. In back." He shook his head, and a gloomy look settled over him. "Pretty neglected, I'm afraid." Cautiously he negotiated the step down from the porch, steadying himself with his cane. "I don't know what I'm going to do with this place, wish I could find a buyer. You like flowers?"

"Sure."

"Want to buy a house?" Slowly he edged his way down to the terrace below the one I was standing on. "Come on."

"Are you sure you—"

"Come on," he repeated impatiently. "I can walk, just don't expect any bursts of speed out of me. In case you're wondering what I've got, it's called lupus. Know what that is?"

I caught up with him. "Something to do with the connective tissues, isn't it?"

"That's right," he said. He didn't seem like my idea of a farmer, or even a gardener; he had an ironic, Ivy League manner that seemed out of place in a cabin in the woods. "Lupus," he repeated as if naming his enemy. "Most people have never heard of it. *I* never had. Nice if I'd never had to. Well—*c'est la vie.*"

We rounded the corner of the house and followed a path between a double row of apple trees. At my feet something slithered through the grass and vanished with a flash of silver-gray.

"Snake," Brad said. "You afraid of them?"

"Not if they aren't poisonous."

"They aren't. I like them. Phallic symbols," he added unexpectedly, and laughed.

"I see you're a Freudian."

"Not me. Just a gardener. There it is"—he waved his hand—"the wreck of the Hesperus."

The two acres of flowers looked more than all right to me, even though only some of them were in bloom. But as we got closer I could see that a blight had shriveled the leaves and stained the blossoms of many of the plants. Weeds were everywhere.

Brad turned to me and demanded, raising his voice a little, "Would you please tell me what I'm supposed to do with these? Gerald doesn't know a lily from a lilac. Some of these varieties happen to be very rare. Look at this one." He laid his hand lightly on a tall bushy lily plant with flowers that had deeply curved, creamy petals and dark pink throats. The touch of the plant seemed to calm him a little. "You never saw that one before."

"I'm hardly an expert—" I began.

He ignored me. "I know you haven't, because I bred it myself. Hybrid." He nipped off a branch with half a dozen blooms and handed it to me. It had a fragrance that was heavy and sweet. "Oh, the hell with it. Let's go back to the house. This depresses me."

We turned. A young man pushing a wheelbarrow appeared from a shed. He was naked to the waist, and I recognized Jordan. He recognized me too, and smiled. "Hi, Vic, this isn't the Institute."

"That's right, Jordan."

Brad said, "You two know each other?"

"Oh, yes, we're old friends," I said.

A frightened look passed over Jordan's handsome face. "He was there when they fell on the floor."

I said "It's okay" the way you might soothe a horse that was about to shy, and added carefully, "Jordan, I wanted to ask you something. You know Magda?"

Confusion muddied his eyes and he frowned in concentration. Then his expression cleared. "She's pretty," he said triumphantly.

"That's right. Very pretty. Remember, you were talking to her when Professor Moore-Gann came over. You were, weren't you? Before he fell down?"

He smiled broadly. "'I need a drink,'" he agreed.

"Is that what he said, 'I need a drink'? You heard him?" He nodded. Score one for Magda's version of what had happened. I said, "What about the glass? Try to remember. Was it in Magda's hand, was she holding it? Or was it on the table?"

"On the table—" he responded, and then seemed to recall something and stood with his mouth half open, looking frightened again. He shook his head violently and kept shaking it. "No, no, no. He said, 'I need a drink.' I didn't see anything. I didn't see anything on the table! I have to go now. Nothing happened, I didn't see anything." He dropped the handles of the wheelbarrow as if they had suddenly become hot.

Brad looked taken aback. "But you've only worked an hour—" A car door slammed in the driveway and he said automatically, "Gerald's home. Wait, Jordan—"

Jordan was no longer with us, he was already halfway to the driveway. I supposed one of the pickup trucks must be his. He ran well, the muscles rippling in his back and his arms swinging.

"He didn't even put the wheelbarrow away." Brad turned toward me accusingly. "You scared him. I hope you're not planning on scaring *me,* I can't run like that anymore."

We went back to the house.

The three of us ate dinner out on the porch. Below us the lilies stretched away, their colors fading as darkness fell, a few persistent bees still buzzing over them. In the distance we could see an enormous panorama of the Green Mountains, range upon range of hills receding toward Canada.

I said, "Gerald, why doesn't Florian fire Judith?"

"One of life's little mysteries," said Gerald. "More wine?"
I shook my head. "I wish you'd tell me why he puts up with
her. I think you know. I think you know more about what
goes on at the Institute than most people."

"Gerald doesn't miss much," said Brad dryly.

"*If* that's a compliment, thanks." There was a tension between the two men, as if they'd had an unresolved quarrel
that morning, or as if they were struggling with some more
basic issue. Like what to do about the flowers, the house,
Brad's illness, possibly his death?

I said, "What does Judith have on Florian? There has to be
something."

Gerald shook his head. "Well—I don't see how I could
know *that*. They would hardly tell me."

"But you don't deny there is something."

"Vic, I'd like to help, honestly. But—"

"I've heard a rumor that Florian is gay."

Gerald and Brad exchanged a look. Then Gerald shrugged
and said, "If so he's *deeply* closeted. *I* have no way to be
sure."

I said, "On the other hand, he does seem rather fond of
Theresa."

"He adores her," Gerald agreed. "I've noticed that."

Brad gave a short, scornful laugh. "*Adores* her. At a distance, maybe. That's all."

"I didn't realize you knew them."

"I know him." Brad looked at Gerald. "Might as well tell
him, he's heard anyway. What the hell, in this day and age—"

Gerald said, "I suppose so." To me he said, "All right,
Florian is probably gay. But I don't see what that has to do
with Moore-Gann's death."

"*Probably* gay!" said Brad scornfully.

I turned to him. "You seem more sure of it than Gerald is.
How come?"

"I knew him—very well at one time. We're the same age.
He used to come up every summer with his family and we
were friendly, even though I went to the local high school and

he was a student at some fancy prep school down near Boston. Burlington is a small place and it was even smaller then. All the young people knew each other." Brad's wineglass was empty and he picked it up. He said to Gerald, "Can't I have some more of this stuff?"

"The doctor said just one."

"Screw the doctor." But he put down his glass. "I knew I was gay when I was in high school, I've always known, from a very early age. Not that there was much I could do about it at that time. When I met Florian I had a hunch he was like me, only he didn't know it. We did a little experimenting one summer."

Gerald clasped his hands together under his chin and fluttered his eyelashes. "Brad's first romance."

"What do you know about it?" said Brad without heat. "You were still in diapers."

"A mere tiny tot."

"Florian felt very guilty afterward and didn't want to accept the implications—what it meant about himself. He claimed he wasn't really gay, though I don't think we used that word back then. Actually I think it would have been a good experience for both of us except for something that happened. There was a big splash party and picnic down by the lake one evening. I forget who organized it—I think one of the churches. A lot of the kids went. Florian and I wandered off into the bushes and were seen by one of the girls in a rather compromising situation. She turned a flashlight on us, actually. Florian was absolutely terrified that his father would find out. He left Burlington the next day, and after that when he came up for summers he went out of his way to avoid me."

Gerald leaned forward. "And *guess* who that sweet girl was!"

I recalled that Florian had said Judith was a Burlington girl. "You mean Judith?"

Brad looked surprised that I'd guessed correctly. "That's right. She and I were classmates, I've known her since the seventh grade. She's had a very rough life, which explains to some extent why she's so awful, but I must say I never *could* stand her. She used to call me 'Sissy-boy.' She seems to have had a natural talent for going for the jugular."

"Still does," I said.

"*That's* putting it mildly," agreed Gerald.

"She had a crush on Florian, though. Quite a few of the girls did, I guess he seemed glamorous, a change from the local yokels, not to mention that his family was rich. And he was good-looking."

Gerald said, "Brad never could resist a pretty face," and fluttered his eyelashes again.

"Don't flatter yourself."

I said, "So Judith had a crush on Florian in high school and then she saw the two of you together. Must have been a shock for her."

Gerald said, "My dear, hell hath no *fury!*"

"What did she do?"

"She must have said something to the other kids, because I was pretty much ostracized for the rest of my time in high school." He grimaced. In the dusk the rash on his face was only a shadow and he was strikingly handsome. "Not that I'd ever been popular, but I'd been tolerated. I never heard a word about Florian, though, so I think Judith kept that part to herself."

"Saving it for a tiny spot of blackmail," said Gerald.

"Do you know that for a fact?" I said.

"Florian got her a secretarial job at Vermont College, where his father was on the board of trustees," said Brad. "I doubt that he did it out of the goodness of his heart."

We sat for a while in silence. Although the sky was not completely dark yet, a pale round moon was floating above the mountain range and one or two stars had made their appearance. So Judith, Florian, and Brad had all known each other as children. A thought occurred to me. "What about the policeman, Captain Eaken?" I said. "Did you all know him, too?"

"Sure, Wayne was in our class," said Brad. "He was on the football team. Always very macho, Wayne."

"You don't say." It was all interesting, but nothing I'd learned from Gerald and his lover really explained why Florian was afraid to fire Judith. I said, "I can't believe Florian is still putting up with Judith, thirty years later, because of a youthful indiscretion. I could see that it would have upset him at the time, but surely it couldn't hurt him now."

"Don't kid yourself," said Brad. "There's still plenty of prejudice against homosexuals, and lots of gays are still in the closet."

Gerald shook his head. "I don't think that's it. *I* think Judith knows something else about Florian, something that could really damage him. Don't forget, he's Dean of Students at that college where he works, and anyone who deals with students has to be as pure as Vermont maple syrup."

I said, "But you don't know what it could be."

"No. But if you find out I'll be dying to hear." His eyes gleamed in the candlelight.

I waited, but no one said any more. I stood up. "Well, I have to be going. Thanks for everything. Thank you both."

"Come again," said Brad. "You won't mind if I don't get up. Give him some lilies to take along, Gerald."

"Oh, lilies, of course." Gerald dashed into the house.

Brad said, "Frankly, I don't think it showed much character on Florian's part to drop me the way he did after Judith turned up with her little flashlight. After all, I had feelings, too. I wrote to him, but he never answered any of my letters." I couldn't read his face in the dimness. "Florian is weak, I imagine he wouldn't be too hard to blackmail. Well, none of it matters anymore. Not to me, anyway. All I care about is what's going to happen to my damn lilies. If only Gerald took an interest in the place—" Gerald chose to appear at this moment with a scissors in his hand, and Brad exclaimed. "*Not* a scissors, I've told you a hundred times never to cut flowers with a scissors. Get a knife!"

"I'm tired," Gerald protested. "What difference does it

make? I worked all day, I made supper, I'm tired." There was a note of martyrdom in his voice.

"Oh, all right, you do everything and I do nothing. I just sit here. Well, it's not my fault. *Cut* them with scissors, I don't care."

I said, "Don't bother about the flowers, it doesn't matter. I really have to go."

Gerald said, "If it's such a big issue I'll get a knife." He turned and went back in the house.

We waited in silence until we heard Gerald returning. Then Brad said to me in a low voice, "I have friends in Boston who tell me that Florian is partial to young boys. *Very* young. I don't know if it's true, but that's what I've heard. You might want to check it out."

# FIFTEEN

The Sachses owned a summer house on the shore of Lake Champlain, down a dirt road complete with the usual Vermont potholes; I was beginning to get used to them. The road branched off from the highway and led down toward the water through woodland. A cloud of dust was hanging above the road as I turned into it, as if a car had passed that way not long before me. I speeded up and soon caught sight of Sabina and Bruno in the Mercedes. I honked, and she gave me a wave in the rear-view mirror; she was driving. I was curious to know what, if anything, she'd managed to learn from talking to Judith, because I was starting to like the idea of Judith as the murderer, on grounds that were personal and illogical— the woman was a pain. Unfortunately I was also aware, as Sabina still wasn't, that the intended victim might have been Magda. And why should Judith have wanted to poison Magda, when the two of them had met for the first time only a few days earlier?

The Mercedes turned into a driveway that led to a clearing and I followed. Several cars were parked there already. We walked down to the house together over the pine needles that lay thickly on the ground. The house was unpretentious, an overgrown cabin painted barn red and deeply shaded by a grove of pine trees. Baskets of fuchsias hung from the roof of the porch. Vita Sachs stood below them wearing a low-cut purple jumpsuit that clung to her trim but shapely body, and a heavy silver necklace that almost reached her waist. She waved at us with both hands, saying, "Hello! Hello! So glad you came, we didn't really know who to expect once we heard the news about Moore-Gann. Not that we wept bitter tears, but there *are* certain boring conventions, and we wondered for about two seconds whether we should cancel the party. We decided not to." She stepped down from the porch. "It's not *really* a party, just a few friends dropping in for a drink." She laughed nervously. "And some days you need one, don't you?" She kept darting her head from side to side, watching our reactions like an actor gauging the temper of an audience. Laying her hand with its long red nails on Bruno's arm, she said, "I'd better warn you, Saul's not in great shape today. I was hoping—" Her sigh was a little larger than life. "Oh, well, what can you do? Maybe it's the shock of Hervé's death. After all, Saul's known him practically forever, they went to high school together. *Something's* making him act strangely. I don't know if it's that or what. I hope it's that—" The gush of words ended as if a dial had been switched off.

Bruno patted her hand and said, "Try not to worry so much. We understand."

She tickled his chin, under the beard, and leaned her head against his shoulder. "You're such a sweetie. Sabina, mind if I borrow your husband for a minute? I need a hug."

Sabina's eyes narrowed but all she said was "Be my guest."

Bruno put his arms around Vita, who said to the rest of us, "This man is one of the great, world-class huggers. Saul used to be one too, but not anymore, alas. Ooch! Bruno, don't squeeze me to pieces!"

When the hug was concluded—I figured Sabina had decided she could spare one, not that she'd had much choice— Bruno stepped up on the porch while Vita gave Sabina a kiss, the kind where two women brush their cheeks together and kiss the air.

There were four men in the living room. Sachs, dwarfed by a black leather Eames chair, was lying with his emaciated legs propped on a footstool, staring into a half-empty glass. There was a flush on his sharp cheekbones, as if he'd had a good deal to drink, and the tip of his big fleshy nose was red. He raised the glass as we entered, said, "Cheers," and downed the contents. It surprised me that he was allowed to drink, considering the shape he was in.

Leo Pesnik, Jean-Paul Brocchiu, and Andrzej Modzalewski were standing together near a big plate-glass window overlooking the lake, as if they had just been admiring the view. The full moon was hanging over the mountains and there were silver reflections in the ripples on the water.

Bruno said, "Hello, Saul, good to see you. You've met my wife, Sabina, and this is Vic Newman."

He raised his glass to us, said, *"L'chaim,"* and then to his wife, "Nothing in this damn glass, Vita. Let's have some more of that Scotch. This is very special Scotch," he said to Bruno. "Take my word and try some. Got it from this little guy in green tweeds when we were in Glasgow; they only make ten bottles a year or some crap like that." He shrugged. "Who knows? Who cares? Your wife can drink something else, *schnapps* like this is wasted on women."

Vita said, "Saul, that's not nice." After a momentary hesitation she took the glass from his hand and refilled it.

"Why? What, me not nice? Honey, did I hurt your feelings?" Without waiting for Sabina to reply he went on, "Listen, open a bottle of decent champagne, give her that. Veuve Cliquot, the good stuff. It's not a question of money, sweetheart, it's the principle." He eyed Sabina as if waiting for her to react, but she kept her mouth shut and her eyes steadily on his, and after a minute he looked uneasily away.

Jean-Paul, standing by the window, remarked, "This view reminds me of Corsica, some of our lakes up in the mountains. Only our mountains, they are much more rocky and tall. Corsica is very beautiful."

Vita said, "Poor Jean-Paul misses Corsica. Don't you, lovey?" Playfully she mussed his thick dark hair. He stared at her and then gave her a knowing little smile, the first smile I'd seen on his face.

"Crap," said Saul. "What's to miss? Thorns on all the bushes, the world's worst roads, pigs all over the place, and a bunch of ignorant peasants."

104

"That is not all there is to Corsica and you know it," protested Jean-Paul.

"Uh-oh, I better watch out," said Saul. He gave a short bark of laughter. "Brocchiu believes in the vendetta."

Jean-Paul's face darkened. "I am modern, I am a scientist. I thought you liked Corsica, Saul." He sounded hurt.

"I like it, I like it." To me he said, behind his hand, "Better I should like it than find a knife in my back, right? Corsica is gorgeous country, no joke." Jean-Paul looked slightly mollified.

Vita said, "Saul brought Jean-Paul back with him from the physics institute on Corsica."

"Oy, was that a mistake. I thought he was good," said Saul.

"Now, Saul," said Vita. "Oh, Sabina, have you and Bruno ever been to one of those summer sessions?"

The conversation quickly became general, about conferences they'd been to in different parts of the world—standard chitchat that reminded me of the parties Sabina threw occasionally for Bruno's colleagues back in Washington. Theoretical physicists have two main topics of conversation: physics and the places they go to *do* physics.

I found myself standing next to Andrzej Modzalewski, who was staring into a glass of vodka with great concentration. He looked up and saw me, raised his glass and said *"Prosit,"* and knocked it back in one gulp. Then he flashed his gold tooth at me in a smile and clapped me on the back with a heavy hand. He seemed to be in a good mood. "How you like so much physicists?" he said heartily. "Is too much technical talk, no?"

"I don't mind it."

He looked surprised. "But you not physicist. What you do for living?"

"I'm a detective." I wasn't sure he'd know the word.

He did. He seemed taken aback, and a wary look came into his eyes. "Police?" I shook my head. After a moment he gave a roar of laughter. "We have in my country, too, detectives. Only nobody know who is and who isn't. Or least they don't tell."

I said, "I don't work for the government, if that's what you mean." I sipped the drink Vita had given me. "Are there many Polish physicists in this country?"

He shook his head. "Not much. Me, I leave or they put me in prison. For Solidarity, you hear of that?"

I nodded. "I saw the article about you in the *Washington Post.*"

He gave me a delighted grin. "Is good, no? Is bi-i-i-g article." He showed me with his hands how big it had been. "With two pictures." Then he looked sad. "But I cannot send my family because of censor. Too dangerous."

"You miss your family."

He nodded heavily. "Here I have no one. Professor Sachs is kind, but—" His massive shoulders rose and fell in a sigh. He turned to the table where the drinks were laid out and poured himself another shot of vodka. He seemed to have lost interest in our conversation and a moment later had merged into a physics discussion that had been taking place behind us.

For some time, nobody mentioned Moore-Gann's death. Finally, during a lull in the conversation, Saul brought it up. "So he's dead, that poor schmuck," he announced, to nobody in particular.

There was a silence.

Andrzej spoke. "Saul, is all right if I ask? No, maybe is not my business."

"Ask, ask. I probably won't be able to understand your English anyway."

"I have terrible accent," agreed Andrzej humbly. "Saul, what did he say to you? You understand, is historic moment—two great men, first time they speak in much year."

"*Many* years, *many* years, Andrzej. You really want to know, huh?" He fell silent. "Tell you what *I* said to *him*. I said, 'Harvey, you're still a crook as far as I'm concerned.'"

"You said that?" said Pesnik excitedly. "You said that to Moore-Gann?"

Saul said, "Oh, don't give me that 'Moore-Gann' shit.

Moore-Gann my ass. Hervé, no less. He was plain Harvey Morgan when I first met him at Erasmus Hall High School. His family lived over a delicatessen on Flatbush Avenue and their apartment always smelled of pickled herring and so did he. Maybe that's why none of the girls would give him the time of day." Pesnik was listening intently, vindication in his sunken eyes. "I don't know who he thought he was kidding when he changed his name. As far as I was concerned, he was still the same pipsqueak." Pesnik nodded, his lips drawn back over his teeth.

Sabina said, "And what did *he* say to *you* when you shook hands?"

Saul gave her a quizzical look. "That's for me to know and you to find out."

Pesnik said, "But how could you shake his hand, Saul?" His tone was belligerent yet plaintive. "You said you never would!"

Saul looked at him with indifference. "I'm dying," he said bleakly. "So I shook his hand, so what? I'm dying, what the hell difference does it make?"

"There he goes again," said Vita. "Will you please stop saying you're dying? You're not dying."

"I am, baby. I'm a dead man. Today, tomorrow—"

"Stop saying that!" she cried. "You had chemotherapy, you're getting better."

He gave her a pitying look and shook his head. "Oy, Vi-tavitavitavitavita."

Her eyes blazing, she said, "Don't give me Vitavitavita. You're *not dying*. The doctor said you have a good chance."

"Doctors, what do they know? A *fighting* chance, he said."

"All right! All right! So fight!"

His gaze turning inward, he shook his head again. "It's no good, baby, I'm—"

"Don't say it, I don't want to hear it!"

"All right. For you I'll make a special effort, okay?"

"That's better."

There was a silence. Then Saul said in a conversational tone, "So you see what it is to have a wife. I'm dying and she doesn't want to hear it. Take my advice, stay single." To Bruno he said, "For you of course it's too late. My condolences. She's not bad-looking, but maybe a little long in the tooth. You couldn't find somebody younger? I see she's starting to get mad. Don't, doll, I'm an old dying fool. Don't waste your energies. Oy, such eyes she has. She's smart, this one." He turned to Bruno. "You always had good taste, that's important for a physicist. Good taste, nice calculations, but you could have used a few more ideas."

I could see Bruno swallow as the shaft hit home. The sick man was playing sadistic games. He was angry at life, at death, and he was taking out his anger on any target that came within range. But what do you say to a dying Nobel laureate? Nothing. So nobody said anything, except for Vita. "Behave yourself!" she commanded sharply.

He ignored her. "Of course *you're* single, Pesnik. That was one good idea you had. Bruno, you should try to be more like Pesnik. He had another good idea, too. Well, we know what happened to that one. Pesnik! Did you see him get down on his knees, that pint-sized *goniff?* He knew I knew, oh yes he did."

Abruptly Pesnik turned his back.

"Oy, these crazies. At least you, Jean-Paul, you're single, you're independent. You don't know how lucky you are that bitch Magda threw you out." Jean-Paul turned pale and I saw his fists clench. Saul did too. "Maybe you should've roughed her up a little more. With a bitch like that, a smart bitch, you have to beat her brains out or you end up feeling like a dummy. Am I right or am I right? Now with Vita I never had that problem, fortunately."

Vita bit her lip. "Saul," she whispered. "It's enough. Saul, stop." He ignored her.

"Modzalewski is single, aren't you, Andzej? Our big Solidarity hero, or was it the other side you were on? I forget."

Andzej Modzalewski said coldly, "I have wife in Poland. I have not hear from her long time."

"So okay, that's almost as good as not having one. Next best thing."

Vita got up and left the room.

There was a long, flat silence. Bruno was staring at Saul, who was huddled in the Eames chair as if the spurt of malign energy that had possessed him had vanished when Vita left the room. I don't think I've ever seen Bruno look sadder. Shaking his head, he turned and went after Vita.

Sabina's eyebrows rose.

"Vita?" said Saul. "Where'd that woman go? Did you see a woman leave this room?"

I'd had a bellyful. I left. There was no sign of Bruno in the hall. Upstairs I could hear Vita sobbing, and I figured Bruno was with her. I went to the lavatory and opened the medicine cabinet. It was crammed with medications. Among them was a bottle of Digoxin, about two-thirds full.

# SIXTEEN

We drove back to the apartment in our separate cars. Nobody said much when we got there. Sabina kicked off her shoes, communed with her traveling tea case for a while until she settled on Lapsang Souchong, and put up the kettle to boil. Bruno sat down on the couch and stared into space, looking depressed.

I plunked down beside him. After a while I said, "That bad, huh?"

He heaved a sigh that came all the way up from his round-toed Space Shoes. "I wish you could have met him before he got like this, Vic. He always was kind of a teaser, but in a good-natured way, basically. Nothing like this, nothing like tonight." He shook his head. "He was deliberately trying to hurt everyone in sight, especially Vita. Didn't you think so? He seemed evil." He paused. He dislikes melodrama. "Maybe that's too strong a word."

"Could it be his illness?"

"That's what Vita said."

Sabina took down a teapot from the cupboard. "While you were comforting her?"

"Yes, while I was comforting her. I've known the woman for years, Sabina."

"I'm aware of that."

He said, "She thinks the cancer is spreading to his brain. The doctor warned her his behavior might start to become erratic. It's possible, brain damage *can* cause personality changes." Bruno used to be a medical student, before he

110

switched to physics. "Hardly a pleasant thought, but at least it seems better than—"

"Evil?" Sabina said, and he nodded. She took a teaspoon from the silverware drawer and laid it on the table at Bruno's place; he takes sugar in his tea despite her best efforts to convince him this ruins it. Although I happen to agree with her, I try to stay out of their discussions on the subject. She said, "Bruno, do you think it's plausible that Sachs might have hated Moore-Gann so much that he'd want to kill him? From what you know of him, could *that* be the reason Sachs agreed to come to the Institute this summer, when he knew Moore-Gann was going to be here and he'd avoided him for years?"

I said, "I think I should tell you—"

Bruno said, "You mean, even though he knew he was dying? He wanted to make sure that Moore-Gann died first, something like that?"

"Possibly."

Bruno pondered. "It seems fantastic. Certainly they've been feuding for years and nobody knows why, but physicists don't poison each other over scientific feuds." He shook his head. "At one time I'd have sworn Saul wouldn't kill a fly, but if his brain is going and he's becoming unbalanced, who can say?"

Sabina said, "Saul called Moore-Gann a *goniff*. That's a Yiddish word, isn't it?"

Bruno nodded and I said, "It means 'thief.'"

Sabina was standing in her stocking feet by the sink. Absentmindedly she rinsed out the pale green teapot with hot water from the tap, over and over. At this rate it was going to be the best-rinsed teapot west of the British Isles. "Saul called Moore-Gann a thief when the two of them shook hands," she said. "I suppose he could have been referring to the Pesnik business, but I can't believe that's what was on his mind when he was about to speak to Moore-Gann for the first time in years. It must have been something closer to home, something that concerned the two of them. Bruno, could Moore-

Gann have stolen an idea of Sachs's? Could that have caused the feud?"

"It certainly could have—*if* anything like that ever happened. But if it did, why didn't Saul complain publicly?"

"And he didn't? There weren't any rumors?"

Bruno shook his head. "None that I ever heard about."

I said, "Still, something like that could explain why Moore-Gann got down on his knees in front of Saul."

Bruno said, "Oh, I think he just wanted to be on Saul's level. Saul was sort of lying back on that low couch, remember?"

Sabina shook her head. "No, it was definitely a symbolic gesture. Saul referred to it tonight, if you recall."

"Well—I guess so," Bruno admitted reluctantly. As I said before, he hates melodrama. Sometimes this makes him really dense, brainy though he is.

The tea was ready and we sat down at the table. Bruno produced a bag of peanut butter cookies and we shared them. They seemed to cheer him up a bit.

Sabina said to me, "Vic, what was it you started to say before, about something you should tell me?"

"There are quite a few things I haven't had a chance to tell you. For one, Saul takes Digoxin. There was a bottle in the medicine cabinet in his house."

Bruno looked interested. "Digoxin! That's digitalis. It's a heart stimulant—I didn't know there was anything wrong with Saul's heart. It's a useful drug, but the correct dosage is vital because it's highly toxic in large quantities. So that's where the digitalis came from that killed Moore-Gann."

"Possibly," said Sabina. "And any of those people who were there tonight had access to it. Saul and Vita, naturally. And the other three are close members of Saul's circle who may have been in the house before."

"They have been," said Bruno. "Jean-Paul stayed with the Sachses for a week before the Institute started, and Pesnik and Modzalewski joined him there on the weekend. Jean-Paul was a protégé of Saul's, and so was Modzalewski—Sachs found them both teaching jobs when they came to this country. And he's gone out of his way to help Pesnik, used to visit him when he was in the psychiatric ward and supported him strongly when he came up for tenure. Saul always took the lame ducks under his wing." A spasm of distress crossed his big, good-natured face and he added, "Before he got like this."

Sabina said, "Do you know much about Modzalewski? All I recall from that article in the *Washington Post* is that he was an imprisoned Solidarity leader who somehow managed to flee the country."

Bruno said, "I don't know any more than that. He's from Wroclaw, which is really the only place in Poland where they're doing anything in theoretical physics nowadays, except for Warsaw."

"Isn't Wroclaw Warsaw?" Sabina's ideas about geography are vague.

I said, "No, it's Breslau. Warsaw's Varsovie. That's where Magda's from. And speaking of Magda—"

Sabina ignored me. "Saul hinted that Modzalewski wasn't really on the side of Solidarity."

"Of course he was!" Bruno protested. "Saul was just lashing out irrationally."

"Was he?" said Sabina. "Most of the things he said were quite true—that was what made them cutting. Think about it. Jean-Paul Brocchiu really *isn't* a first-rate physicist, and he does resent Magda Tenofska's brilliance, judging from that scene Vic intervened in yesterday. Vita's *not* a great brain, I'm no longer young—"

"And I certainly wish I had more ideas; I've always known that was my weakness as a physicist," Bruno admitted.

I said, "Suppose I call Washington tomorrow and make a few inquiries about Modzalewski." I have a friend in the CIA who used to be my classmate at the University of Maryland. He majored in classical languages, which was about as much help to him in finding a job as my bachelors in psychology was to me.

"Good," said Sabina. "Now what was that about Magda?" One thing I'll say for Sabina, when she interrupts you, which she does frequently, she at least has the decency to remember you were trying to say something.

I said, "She tried to hire me. I told her I was working for you, and you'd already been hired by the board of trustees, but she didn't see any reason why I shouldn't do a little moonlighting on the side. Maybe that's how they make ends meet in Poland. On my salary, I was tempted."

"The salaries I pay are competitive," Sabina said stiffly. "Also you get medical insurance."

"It's nice to know I can always get sick." Her salaries *are* competitive, not that that's saying much, but I think it's a good idea for the working classes to gripe whenever an opportunity comes along. This keeps the bosses on their toes and sometimes results in a raise.

"Why did she want to hire you?"

"She thinks somebody's trying to kill her, and Moore-Gann was poisoned by mistake."

"Really. Details?"

I gave her a full report of what Magda had said, and then told her about my visit to Gerald's house in West Bolton and what Brad had said about Florian.

When I'd finished she was silent and thoughtful, staring into the dregs of her tea like a gypsy fortune-teller as she absentmindedly swirled the cup in her hands. Wisps of hair had escaped from the bun at the back of her neck and the hairpins were starting to slip out. One hit the floor with a tiny clink. I picked it up and handed it to her and she stuck it back in automatically, saying "Interesting. Things are starting to open up. If Magda was the intended victim, Jean-Paul is the obvious suspect with the obvious motive—a twisted but typically male desire to annihilate the woman who has rejected him."

"Hey, wait a minute, I object to 'typically male'—"

She ignored me. "Would you repeat what he said to Magda when he handed her the Bloody Mary?"

I took out my notebook and read: "People get what they deserve, that is called judgment."

Bruno said, "Sabina, I know what you're thinking but

you're wrong—Jean-Paul wouldn't kill anyone. Not like this, with premeditation. What he must have meant by 'judgment' is that he knew he shouldn't have hit Magda, and when she refused to have anything more to do with him he was getting just what he deserved." He looked around to see if anyone agreed with him, and when Sabina and I said nothing he seemed disappointed. "I admit that in the heat of an argument he might lose control and conceivably even kill someone, not that I think it's likely. But he couldn't possibly plan such a thing in cold blood."

Sabina rested her elbows on the table and pressed her hands together, propping her pointed chin on the joined tips of her fingers as if she were praying. "What you say may be true, Bruno. Or you may be wrong about him. Personally I'm not convinced that Jean-Paul could only kill in a fit of rage. Don't forget that he's a Corsican, and according to Saul he believes in the vendetta—an ancient code in which men and entire families concoct elaborate plots to murder for revenge. Jean-Paul may have felt he had a right or even a duty to kill Magda, to punish her for leaving him against his wishes."

Bruno frowned. "Really, Sabina. Jean-Paul's an educated man, a theoretical physicist, a man who's lived in this country for years, and I can't imagine that he subscribes to such a primitive code of conduct, or that he ever did. Even in Corsica the vendetta is just a historical curiosity. It's been illegal for decades."

"True, but every year a certain number of killings still occur for which no one is ever punished." She turned to me. "At this point we really don't know whether the murderer intended to kill Moore-Gann or Magda, so we'll have to proceed on both fronts and keep an open mind. It's too soon to be sure of anything—even the source of the digitalis. There happens to be a magnificent border of foxgloves right in front of Judith's house. I saw it when I visited her."

"Is that so? You think she might have brewed up a little potion?"

"We don't know enough yet to rule it out."

I said, "So you bearded the abominable Judith in her den. Aren't you going to tell us what happened?"

Sabina poured herself another cup of tea. "I went to her house, which is about a ten-minute walk from the Institute, and rang the bell. She was expecting Jordan, because when she opened the door she said, 'Why can't you remember to take your key?' before she realized who I was. Then she tried to close the door in my face, but I inserted myself rather quickly and started talking."

"What did you say?"

"I'm afraid I told quite a few lies."

"I'm shocked, Sabina," I said. Duplicity is something you have to get used to in this business. When I think of the idealistic kid I was only a few short years ago it makes me uncomfortable, frankly, so I try not to think about it. I said, "What was your story?"

"I told her I had a retarded nephew and I wanted to ask her where Jordan had learned to be a gardener, because my sister was looking for a school for her son. So she invited me in."

Bruno said disapprovingly, "Really, Sabina. Couldn't you have thought of something a little less—"

"Such as?"

He pondered for a while but nothing came to him. Sabina then suggested that since it was late he might like to go to bed rather than hear more about her morally offensive activities, but he didn't take her up on it.

She went on. "The living room was tiny and the colors clashed. There were too many patterns. Pictures of kittens and puppies on the walls." She shuddered. "No wonder Judith seems irrational at times—living in a room like that could drive anyone mad. I sat in a chair that had been upholstered in clear plastic over some sort of huge floral print." She shook her head as if to clear it of the horrible image; the poor woman is hypersensitive to decor. "Although people who like clear plastic upholstery obviously lack certain basic human instincts, I tried not to let this sway me."

"It must have been tough."

"It was. However, I will admit that the room, although cluttered with vulgar knickknacks, was clean and neat—extremely so, in fact. I wondered how it was possible to keep it that way in a household consisting of a nineteen-year-old boy with at best borderline IQ and a working mother. She must rule with an iron fist."

I thought, "It takes one to know one."

"She asked how old my nephew was and when I said he was thirteen she warned me there was no time to lose. Jordan was ten when she sent him to the special school he attended in Connecticut. It was very expensive. She stressed that. It seems Jordan went to a public school at first, but the authorities didn't want to keep him, and Judith made quite a fuss, insisted she paid her taxes just like everybody else, and so on. Finally they gave in, and he stayed until he finished the sixth grade. The teachers passed him, although he really couldn't do the work. But now she wasn't sure she'd done the right thing, thought perhaps she should have sent him to a special school sooner. She said she'd found motherhood very difficult because she'd had to raise the boy alone and had never had anyone to consult." Sabina poured herself some cold tea from the pot and took a swig to moisten her throat.

"Up to this point she was perfectly pleasant. I had the feeling she liked talking about her son, that it was an opportunity that didn't often come her way. A relief, possibly. She struck me as a woman who had no friends and didn't want any—too proud, perhaps, to risk making a friend who might pity her. A very lonely woman. But then I made one or two innocuous comments about the boy's father, and immediately she became guarded. She told me the story about having married a soldier who'd been killed in Vietnam, but she didn't seem to have the faintest idea *where* in Vietnam he'd died and it was obvious she was lying. I didn't pursue the topic. Jordan still hadn't come home, and she started complaining that now that he could drive she never knew where he was and she was worried about his coming under 'bad influences.' She didn't specify what they were."

I said, "Maybe she meant Gerald and Brad. He seems to

spend a lot of time there working in their garden. Maybe she's afraid he's gay."

"That thought crossed my mind. Anyway, she was eager to go on talking about him, although she was careful about what she said. She told me what a beautiful baby he'd been, and that she hadn't grasped the fact that there was anything really wrong with him until after he'd started school. She finally took him to a doctor who advised her to put him in an institution. She was still very angry about that and said she would never allow it to happen, but I could see that she worried continually about the boy's future. 'He can earn money,' she said, 'but he fritters it away unless I watch him every minute. He just doesn't have good judgment.' She hinted that she had some financial resources, but didn't say what they were. I asked whether Jordan's father's family helped her out at all, and she said, 'Occasionally. They could do more.' She laughed when she said it, not very pleasantly."

I said, "Did Jordan turn up while you were there?"

She shook her head. "He hadn't come home by seven-thirty, when I left. What time was it that Jordan ran off, after you spoke to him at Gerald's house?"

"I'd say six o'clock. And it only takes half an hour to get to Burlington from West Bolton. Obviously he didn't go straight home."

Sabina rubbed her brow in a worried way. It was getting late and she looked tired. "I'm beginning to wonder where he went. And why he was so frightened."

# SEVENTEEN

I was the first one up the following morning. I made coffee in
the electric percolator and mixed up a bowl of buckwheat
pancake batter. I made a stack of pancakes, spread them with
unsalted butter from the Cabot Creamery, and poured on
plenty of Vermont Fancy Grade maple syrup that had been
made, according to the label, by "the Dunn's of High Ridge
Farm." The only thing missing was the *Washington Post*. I
thought of Abby Rademacher back in Washington, D.C., and
wondered whether the air conditioner in the office had been
fixed yet. Outside my window the thermometer said fifty degrees and the sun was trying to burn its way through the mist.
I was wearing a sweater and it felt just right.

After I'd had my second cup of coffee and washed the
dishes I made two telephone calls. One was to my old classmate Mort Goldman of the CIA at his apartment in Crystal
City. He recognized the name of Andrzej Modzalewski but
didn't know much about him and promised to get back to me
when he'd had a chance to look him up.

The other was to a police officer in Boston who'd once
been on the D.C. force. Her name was Betsy Fiorentino and
she was the only cop I'd ever kissed. Later she'd had the bad
taste to marry a guy who did something with computers in
Cambridge, Massachusetts, and she'd left the Washington
area for good.

Betsy sounded glad to hear from me, and we talked about
this and that for a while before I got down to business and
asked her to find out whether Florian Gawthrop had ever
been arrested in Boston, possibly for impairing the morals of

119

a minor or a related offense. She said she'd ask around and let me know. She also said she'd been trying to get pregnant, so far without any success, and I told her I'd always be glad to help an old friend in any way possible.

Bruno appeared, looking like Santa Claus in red flannel pajamas. He helped himself to coffee. "Oh, there are pancakes," he said, taking in the bowl of batter next to the stove and the maple syrup on the table.

"There are if you make them." I knew what was coming.

He looked helpless. "Have I ever made pancakes? I don't remember. What do you do first?"

"You take out a frying pan."

"Any frying pan? There seem to be three of them. What size?"

"Large."

"With straight sides or rounded?"

"Forget it," I said. "I'll make you pancakes."

"I don't mind doing it."

"I know. I'm just not sure my heart can stand the strain." I hate to call a sweet guy like Bruno manipulative, but he has ways of getting out of things he doesn't want to do.

Sabina appeared in a peach satin negligee trimmed with lace. She's the only woman I've ever known to actually wear things like that and she looks great in them; they tend to make my mind wander to thoughts of what she might be like as a woman rather than a boss, something I think about occasionally but not too often. I guess that's what the manufacturers had in mind. Which goes to show we're basically nothing but bundles of conditioned reflexes, myself included.

I made pancakes for Bruno and Sabina. Instead of being grateful, Bruno said, "Don't you think you'd better give that paper you found to the police, Vic?"

He was right, it was evidence, and I knew Captain Eaken wasn't going to be thrilled with me for holding on to it as long as I had. We discussed how to deal with it. Sabina decided the best strategy would be for the two of us to go to the police together, instead of waiting until they got around to questioning us. They were questioning everyone who'd been present when Moore-Gann collapsed.

We went to the Institute in separate cars. About a mile before I got to the entrance I saw Theresa Moore-Gann striding uphill along the side of the road, carrying a walking stick and wearing hiking boots and a windbreaker. It was the first time I'd seen her since I'd taken her home from the hospital.

I pulled up next to her. "Want a lift?"

She looked up at me, shielding her eyes against the sunlight. In the hollows of her face the shadows were like bruises. "Vic? Yes—yes, I think I do, if you're going to the Institute." She was out of breath, and the exercise had stained her cheeks a feverish pink. I opened the door and she pulled herself wearily into the passenger seat. "I don't usually get so tired," she said and leaned back against the seat, her stick between her knees. It was made of a glossy reddish wood, with a round brass knob on top and a shaft carved to look like a twisted rope.

I said, gesturing toward it, "That's unusual."

She touched the brass knob. "My alpenstock? Hervé gave it to me in Switzerland, the year we climbed Monte Rosa." She fell silent and stared out the window.

I drove for a while and then said, "Mind if I ask you something?"

"What?"

"Have you ever seen this before?" I handed her the paper I'd found in her house. "Do you know anything about it?"

I could only see her profile, but from the way she hesitated and then seemed to force herself to take it I could tell she'd recognized it immediately.

After a moment she laid it down on the seat between us. "The answer to your question is 'yes and no.' I don't know anything about it, but I have seen it before. Hervé found it in his packet. You know, each participant gets a packet of information when he arrives at the Institute. This"—she touched the sheet of gray-green paper—"was in Hervé's when he re-

121

ceived it. He showed it to me and asked me what I thought it meant. I told him I had no idea. He said he was going to ask someone about it—Florian or Judith, I suppose. I don't know whether he ever did or not."

This was unexpected. I said, "You mean it was part of the packet? Everybody got one?" As soon as the words were out, I knew they couldn't be true. Bruno hadn't gotten one, or he'd have said so. Anyway, it was obvious the paragraph had nothing to do with physics.

"*I* didn't get one," she said.

"You and your husband each had a separate packet?"

"Certainly. We were both registered."

"How did you pick up your packets? What was the procedure?"

Theresa paused, her expression courteous but strained, as if she found conversation an effort. "It was very simple. As soon as we arrived, we went to the administration building to check in. There was a pile of packets lying on a table in the reception hall, and we went through them and each took the one that had our name on it. Hervé's packet also contained the key to the cottage. We drove there immediately and brought the luggage inside. Then we sat down in the living room and looked through our packets. That was when Hervé found—*that.*"

"Was Magda with you?"

"No, she drove up from Cambridge a few days later."

"Was anyone in the reception hall when you arrived? Gerald?"

"No. It was empty."

"So anybody could have gone through the packets, just as you and your husband did, and inserted an extra sheet in one of them."

She nodded. "I suppose so. But why? What does it mean?"

I turned into the driveway of the Institute. "I wish I knew, Theresa."

She gave a slight shudder. "I don't like it. That paper gave me a bad feeling the first time I saw it. It seemed so odd, so—meaningless."

I said, "Do you think it was as meaningless to your husband as to you?"

She took her time thinking it over. Finally she said, "I'm not sure. Possibly it—meant something to him."

"What?"

"I don't know. I have no idea."

"And how about Magda—did he show it to her?"

"I don't know," she said again. "They didn't speak of it in my presence. Really, we had more important things to think about, we all had seminars to prepare."

I parked next to the big spruce tree and Theresa and I went into the administration building. She began to look over the piles of handouts on the table—announcements and reprints of papers and such. There were quite a few physicists in the lobby, milling around. Bruno was there, using the Xerox machine, and Sabina was studying a wall map of the Champlain Valley that was tacked up on a bulletin board. I edged over to her, passing the reception desk where Gerald, Florian Gawthrop, and the abominable Judith were in some kind of a huddle. Judith's skin was sallow and she looked red-eyed and grim. Was it the death of her former lover, the man who'd apparently been the father of her child, that was affecting her to this extent? Or maybe she was worried about something— about being charged with his murder, for instance?

I overheard Florian saying in an agitated voice, "But you know perfectly well it's up to the physicists to decide when they want to give their talks—" His handsome face was flushed with annoyance.

There was a loud bang, and people's heads jerked. Theresa Moore-Gann, her expression furious, had slammed the tip of her walking stick down on the wooden floor. She looked around for a moment and then bore down on the threesome at the desk, waving a sheet of paper. "Florian! What's the meaning of this?"

They looked up. Gerald saw me and rolled his eyes as if to say, "Here comes World War Three!"

It was Judith who replied, taking a step forward and folding her thin arms across her chest. "Do you have some problem,

Mrs. Moore-Gann?" she demanded. I don't know what the proper tone would be for addressing the newly bereaved widow of a Nobel prizewinner, but this definitely wasn't it.

Theresa was taken aback, but she rallied fast. "Why—I certainly do. Who made these changes in the schedule?"

"I did," Judith snapped, staring up at Theresa, who was half a head taller than she.

"Who authorized it? Who told you to cancel my talks? Florian, did you know about this?"

Florian looked as if he would have liked to leave the two women to battle it out on their own. However, there was no escape. He said, "Theresa, my dear, are you really sure you ought to be here? After the shock of Hervé's death—"

She tossed her short, gray-blond curls and said, "I'll handle the shock in my own way, thank you very much. *Did* you know about these changes?"

"I just found out." Wretchedly Florian glanced at Judith. "It's all a mistake."

"What do you mean by a 'mistake'?" said Judith. "I cancelled Moore-Gann's talks because he's dead. Dead men don't give seminars. As for *hers*—" She stabbed a finger through the air in Theresa's direction. "Nobody really wants to hear them anyway." To Theresa she added, "Aren't you even planning to bury your husband? Won't that keep you busy for a while? Or don't you want to be bothered?"

Theresa gasped and burst into tears. Florian came forward and put his arm around her, patting her shoulder as he protested, "Judith, really—how can you—"

Judith turned her back on them and began to fiddle with the papers on the desk. Gerald looked at me and raised his eyebrows. The physicists in the crowded lobby were listening in horrified silence.

Theresa pushed Florian away. "For your information," she said in a shrill voice, suppressing a sob, "I intend to give both of my talks. I also intend to give my husband's, in his place." She paused, and when she spoke again she'd gotten herself under control. Placing her hands on her hips, she said, "Preparing those talks was Hervé's final contribution to physics,

124

and I intend to see they are delivered, just as he planned. I am thoroughly familiar with his work, and if necessary Magda can assist me. I trust I've made myself clear. Florian?"

"Oh, this is a farce!" Judith exclaimed, and stormed out of the room.

"You can also inform your secretary, since she seems to be so interested," Theresa said to Florian, "that my husband will be cremated privately, according to his wishes, as soon as the police give their permission. A memorial service will be held in September in Cambridge." She stalked to the door and paused on the threshhold. "I shall look forward to receiving a notice stating that the revised schedule has been cancelled."

She swept from the room, and after a moment Florian followed, his face now pale, a nerve jumping in his cheek.

For a minute or two nobody spoke and then there was a hubbub of voices. Gerald sidled over to me and said, "I do believe dear Judith has met her match. Oh, hello, Sabina. I heard that you're investigating the murder. Can't you try to pin it on Judith? Don't quote me."

I said, "We'll do our best. Could I ask you one or two questions?"

"Of course."

"Do you happen to know anything about an extra document that was included in Professor Moore-Gann's packet?"

Gerald looked blank. Sabina's eyebrows rose. Gerald said, "An extra document?"

"This." I handed him the piece of gray-green paper.

He took one look at it and shook his head. "Nothing like this would have been included in the packet. All the packets were identical, except of course for the addresses of accommodations and the keys."

"I see. Did you prepare the packets?"

"Yes."

Sabina said, "And how long did the completed packets remain here in the reception hall before being picked up?"

"Depends when the participants arrived. Several days, usually."

I thanked him, and then Sabina said, "We'd like to speak to Captain Eaken, Gerald. Is he around, do you know?"

"He's interviewing people in the library. Let's see." He picked up a piece of paper from the untidy pile on his desk. "He has back-to-back appointments. Right now he's questioning Magda Tenofska for the second time. I must say I'm curious to know why she rates so much attention."

"Could you please call him for us and say that Mr. Newman and I would like to meet with him at his earliest convenience?"

He picked up the phone and after a brief conversation informed us, "Captain Eaken will see you at twelve noon in the library."

We separated, Sabina to find Jean-Paul and question him, yours truly with instructions to circulate among the physicists and learn whatever I could.

As I headed toward a group at a bulletin board, a soft hand grabbed my arm from behind, and I smelled gardenias. I turned around. It was Charlene, the nurse *cum* physics wife I'd met at the cocktail party, the one who'd done postgraduate work in astrology. By daylight I could see that her platinum-blond hair was natural and her skin was flawlessly smooth. Fortunately I'm hardly ever attracted to blondes, I prefer brunettes; so I knew I'd have no trouble handling whatever it was she wanted from me. It was clear she wanted something. She was dressed as if about to apply for a job, in a tailored gray suit, a white blouse with a pussycat bow, and black heels. She had shell-pink fingernails, lipstick to match, and panic in her eyes. She came right to the point.

"I need to talk to you."

"Fine. Where?"

"Your car?"

"Let's go."

The microbus was parked on the driveway next to the big spruce. We got in and I said, "Nice to see you again, Charlene. What can I do for you?"

Immediately she burst out crying. Since she was the second

woman I'd seen cry in the last half hour I couldn't help comparing her style with Theresa's. Charlene was a loud crier who let it all hang out, while I'd describe Theresa as a controlled crier, someone who got a grip on herself after one or two sobs.

I handed Charlene some Kleenex from the glove compartment, said "There, there," patted her on her padded shoulders every now and then, and waited. Finally she simmered down and said, "Are you really a detective?"

"Yes, I really am."

"Then you have to tell me what to do."

"About what, Charlene?"

"First swear you won't tell anyone." She pressed her hands together pleadingly, so hard that her fingertips reddened around the shell-pink nails.

I just couldn't believe Charlene was a murderer about to make a confession, so I said, "Okay. I swear, except for Sabina."

"Well, I guess that's okay." She paused. "You probably don't remember I'm a nurse." I didn't bother to tell her she was underestimating me. "Actually, I'm the Institute nurse this summer; maybe you saw my name in the packet. I just got my degree in June, but when they asked me if I'd do it I said I would, because they're taking fifty percent off our housing costs. Ralph is still a graduate student and fifty percent is quite a lot. I thought it would, you know, give me something to do and I'd meet some people, and there'd be nothing more serious than cleaning scrapes and handing out aspirin and, oh, maybe the worst thing would be a fracture and I'd have to take somebody to the hospital. I never imagined anything like *this!*"

"You mean Moore-Gann's death."

"Yes." She straightened her shoulders and folded her hands in her lap as if about to deliver her three-o'clock report.

"If you know something, I think you should tell me." Actually I thought she should tell the police, but that was obvious, and so was the fact that for some reason she didn't want to.

Her blue eyes opened wide. "I think I know where the poison came from, I'm almost sure." The shell-pink lips began to tremble again. "And it's *my fault!*"

"Charlene, get a grip on yourself."

Obediently she took a deep, sighing breath and said, "Okay. It was this way. Ralph and I arrived on Friday at noon and picked up our packet at the administration building. I'd talked to Gerald Ainsworth beforehand on the telephone, so when I told him who I was he showed me where the medical supplies were kept. Frankly, when I saw the setup I was horrified. First of all they didn't have a regular infirmary, just a dusty old file room with some ancient furniture in it that he said I could use. I figured I could live with that once I'd cleaned it up, the kind of nursing I'd be doing. But what really bothered me was the supplies. Most of them, bandages and so forth, were kept on open shelves in a sort of closet without a door where the coffee things are stored. It's down at the end of the hall near the bathrooms, maybe you've noticed it."

"What about medicines?"

"Well, that's the thing. At least there was a medicine cabinet, but it didn't have a lock. And inside! You never saw such a collection of old junk in your life, it looked like every aspirin, every bottle of mercurochrome or tube of ointment anyone had left behind since the Institute was founded had ended up in that cabinet. I took a quick peek and knew I'd have to come back and do a real job on it—throw away the stuff that was outdated, make a list of basic supplies to purchase, install a lock—" She leaned forward and said intensely, "I've been well *trained,* Vic, not that you'd know it from the way I acted. My supervisor, Mrs. Hodges at St. Catherine's, would absolutely flay me! Because"—she looked at me tragically—"I figured it could wait till the next day. We'd just arrived and I wanted to get settled, drive around the lake a little because it's so gorgeous here, we live in Pittsburgh and I don't have to tell you the difference— But I *did* buy a padlock for the medicine cabinet, I made my husband take me to a hardware store that very day." She began to twist her hands together. "Oh, if only I'd gone straight back to the Institute and installed it, maybe Professor Moore-Gann wouldn't have died! Because I'm *positive* I saw a bottle of Digoxin in that cabinet when I arrived, and the next day it was gone."

This was interesting. I said, "You're sure you saw it?"

"Yes, because I remember thinking, 'now what on earth is *that* doing there?' "

"What time did you see it?"

"I'd say about twelve-thirty on Friday."

"And when did you notice it was missing?"

"Saturday—yesterday—about ten in the morning. I brought the padlock and some cleaning supplies with me when I drove Ralph to the Institute. I was planning to get everything in shape. Professor Gawthrop was making a statement about Professor Moore-Gann's condition when we got there, and as soon as he said the word 'poison' I thought of the Digoxin in the medicine cabinet and the most awful feeling went through me. I just *knew,* it was like a premonition. Really I guess that Digoxin had been bothering me subconsciously. As soon as I could I went and looked in the medicine cabinet, and sure enough it was gone. I didn't tell anyone, not even Ralph. I've been going through absolute hell ever since." Her clasped hands writhed in her lap. "I thought of calling Mrs. Hodges my supervisor and asking her what to do, I even thought yesterday—and this I'm really ashamed to tell you—of putting the lock on the cabinet and pretending I'd installed it the day before and never even *mentioning* I'd seen Digoxin." Again the blue eyes brimmed with tears. "I'm just terrified I won't get my license because of this! You don't know how strict they are! I've worked so hard, and we really didn't have enough money for my tuition but my sister loaned it to me and she really couldn't afford it either—"

"Okay," I said. "Don't overreact. Now, did you put the lock on the medicine cabinet or didn't you, finally?"

She shook her head. "No, I didn't."

"Good. And did you call your supervisor at St. Catherine's and tell her about it?"

"No."

"Well, don't."

129

"But don't you think—"

"No, I don't. Now listen to me, Charlene. You must go to the police and tell them you saw Digoxin in the medicine cabinet at twelve-thirty on Friday, and at ten o'clock Saturday you noticed it was gone, and today when you heard Moore-Gann had died of digitalis poisoning you remembered about the Digoxin and thought you'd better let them know. And that's *all* you have to tell them. All this soul-searching you've been going through is strictly your own business, so keep it to yourself."

"But it was my fault! I was careless! I was slipshod! If I'd installed the lock right away—"

I shook my head. "You're going to make a terrific nurse when you get a little more experience. That's the kind of attitude I'd want in a nurse who was taking care of *me*. But Charlene, Moore-Gann's death was not your fault. It wasn't an impulsive act. Whoever did it planned it in advance and if he hadn't found the Digoxin he'd have used something else. That is, *if* he used the Digoxin."

"He did."

Privately, I agreed with her. She was not stupid and she was certainly conscientious—if anything too much so, that was her problem. I sympathized; I knew that awful feeling of guilt that came when you'd overlooked something and someone died—not exactly *because* you'd overlooked it, but maybe if you hadn't, they wouldn't have. "The thing you have to get through your head is that you are not responsible, and don't go around telling people you are or some of them might start believing you and, who knows, you *might* have trouble with your license. The medicine cabinet has been like that for years, maybe decades. It makes no sense to blame yourself for it, you might as well blame everybody else who was responsible for it and didn't put a lock on it before you ever took this job. You'd just arrived."

"You really don't think it's my fault?"

"I really don't."

"I'd still feel better if I could talk to Mrs. Hodges."

"Don't. Find some other way to feel better."

She took a deep breath and relaxed against the back of the seat. "God, I'm glad I told you. I feel relieved. I don't know how to thank you. I guess sometimes things get blown out of proportion. I'll go back to the Institute and talk to the police." She picked up her black calf handbag. It matched her shoes. "How much do I owe you for the consultation?"

"No charge. But there's one question I'd like to ask you, out of curiosity. What did Judith say to Gerald?"

"What did—" She had opened the door and was halfway out of the van, but she slid back onto the seat.

"When you were setting up the buffet at the cocktail party you said that Judith had said something terrible to Gerald."

Her face changed. "Oh, that. Oh, it was awful. I was in the supply closet and she didn't see me. She started yelling at Gerald, she was upset about something. She said, 'If I catch him going over there again, you're fired.' Then she said—I could hardly believe it—'that faggot has AIDS and I bet you'll get it, too, if you don't have it already. And you'll die. You'll both die. And you know something? I'll be glad. If I had any sense I'd fire you right now.'"

"What did Gerald say?"

"He started to cry. He said, 'He doesn't have AIDS, he has lupus. He has lupus!' Then Judith went into her room and slammed the door. I felt *so embarrassed!* I sort of slunk out. Gerald had his head on his desk and he must have known I was there and I'd heard everything, but he just kept his head down. And I left."

# EIGHTEEN

It wasn't yet noon. I wandered across the lawn that sloped uphill in the direction of the library, passing wooden deck chairs that had been arranged into groups by physicists discussing their theories al fresco the day before. The chairs were empty today, except for Jean-Paul and Andrzej sitting together on a bench under a maple tree, talking. They were absorbed in their conversation and didn't notice me, although I waved at them from across the lawn; they seemed to be friends—or maybe they were collaborating on a research project. Was that likely? I wondered idly. Jean-Paul, I recalled, worked at a consulting firm near Boston; I didn't know whether Andrzej, too, worked in industry or whether Sachs had managed to find him a university position. Andrzej was well over forty, and it must be tough at his age to start over, in a new country and with a strange language, despite the fact that physics was an international community.

It was Sunday. All but the most diehard researchers had been dragged off on outings by their families. I looked up at the sky, which was cloudy and becoming grayer by the minute, and wondered whether all those holiday-making physics families were destined to be rained on.

The trench that Jordan had been filling with manure was still half empty, and there was rust on the spade that had been left thrust into the earth. Shrubs were still standing around waiting to be planted, and a couple of them had been toppled by the wind. Something about the way they lay on the ground with their roots shriveling made me uneasy. Why didn't Jordan come back to finish the job? What was he scared of?

As I climbed the hill to the library the wind grew colder and the air felt damp. I could see Bruno sitting on the steps talking to Vita Sachs, but there was no sign of Sabina, although it was now five to twelve. I turned and looked behind me toward the administration building. No Sabina. Had she found Jean-Paul? My uneasiness increased. Of all the people at the Institute, Jean-Paul was the only one with a known history of violent behavior, and if Magda had been the intended victim, he was the most obvious suspect. I remembered the mask of blind fury that had been his face when he'd swung at me on Friday, and wished I'd managed to talk Sabina into letting me be the one to question him. She'd figured he was the kind of macho guy who might respond better to a sneaky (that wasn't her word) approach by a female than to a direct confrontation by a male, especially one who'd broken up a brawl of his two days before, and this had made sense; but I was sorry now I'd agreed to it.

Bruno and Vita waved at me and Vita said, "Well, hello. Bruno tells me you and Sabina are investigating the murder." She wriggled her shoulders in an exaggerated shudder. "Br-r-r! Murder! It's really quite exciting in a way. I mean, physicists are such dull people, which is sort of amazing when you think they can blow us all up, but maybe it's compensation. They're always intellectualizing, sometimes I could scream." She tossed back her sleek head of close-cropped black hair and laughed, throwing out her arms. "Raw emotion for a change— I love it!"

Bruno said, "Vita, really, don't you think you're being a bit—"

"Stuffy old teddy bear," she said, playfully tweaking his beard. Her eyes sought mine as if inviting me to share her amusement. Her eyes were narrow, darting, silver-lidden ovals in her deeply tanned face. Although it was weather-beaten and lined, the skin of her arms and legs was satin smooth. Maybe to show them off she was wearing a one-piece white playsuit with the cuffs turned up high on her shoulders and thighs, although the day was chilly. A wide, shiny red belt drew attention to her waistline. She saw me looking at it and said, "Oh, please don't look! I'm so fat I could die." She spread her hands in front of her belt buckle. "It's these damn cocktail parties every night. Too many hors d'oeuvres and *far* too many Bloody Marys. Alcohol is *insidious* when you're on a diet." If she was overweight I couldn't see where.

Bruno said, "We're waiting for Saul. The police are interviewing him."

"And I can't imagine what's taking them so long." Vita looked at her watch. "I hope they don't tire him out."

I said, "Have you been questioned yet?"

"My God, have I! I thought they'd never stop. Apparently Moore-Gann may have been poisoned with one of Saul's medicines, isn't that sinister? That seems to make us suspects." She grimaced.

Bruno said uncomfortably, "I guess we're all suspects."

"Saul and I have enough to worry about without running around murdering people."

The library door opened and Saul emerged. Vita jumped to her feet. "Saul, finally! Are you all right?"

In fact, he looked surprisingly peppy, as if his meeting with the police had energized him. His wife grabbed his arm but he brushed her away, saying "Please, Vita, stop with the Florence Nightingale act already. Hi, Bruno. Hi, Vic. You know, it's interesting the way these guys work, they're very systematic. I was impressed. Now I gotta go home and count my Digoxin capsules. Looks like that's how Harvey got bumped off." He gave us an impish grin, like a kid who can't wait to try the detective kit that just came in the mail. When I was nine years old I sent away a quarter for one of those kits, but all I got in return was a stamp pad for taking fingerprints and a blurry magnifying glass. Disappointing.

Vita said, "What good will it do to count them *now?*"

He looked at her. "Oy, the great brain. You read the label, you do a little calculation, maybe you can call the drugstore— Come on, babe, I'm going home. Walk me to the car."

The Sachses departed. A sprinkling of raindrops fell, and Bruno and I retreated under the roof that projected over the door to the library.

I said to Bruno, "Have you seen Sabina?"

"There she is."

I looked, and saw her struggling up the hill in her stiletto heels.

Bruno shook his head disapprovingly. "I told her to take an umbrella," he said, clutching the top of his own folding umbrella, which was sticking out of the canvas shopping bag he carried instead of a briefcase. "But she just wouldn't listen."

She was out of breath and damp by the time she reached the top of the hill and climbed up on the porch beside us. She lifted first one foot and then the other and wiped the loam off her shoes with a Kleenex.

Bruno cleared his throat. "Uh—Sabina." He looked deeply guilty. Bruno would make a lousy poker player.

She gave him a sharp glance. "What is it? Something bothering you?"

"Bothering me?"

She was going to have to worm it out of him so that it would end up looking as if she was really the one who was bothered, not him. Why Sabina plays this game I don't know; I consider it one of the many mysteries of the married state. Another one is why they don't play it behind closed doors. Since they don't, I do my best to fade into the woodwork.

They alternated saying "I know something's bothering you," "No, nothing's bothering me," a couple of times until finally Bruno came out with it: "Would you mind very much if I had lunch with Vita Sachs?"

"Vita and Saul?"

"No, just Vita."

"Just you, not both of us?"

He nodded, looking guiltier.

I could see her thinking, "Hm. Bruno and Vita. Well, why not?" She said, "Okay."

"She *is* an old friend of mine and she's going through a rough time. Sometimes Saul is hard to take. I mean, we saw how he was last night. She just needs to talk to someone, get things off her chest. So if you really don't mind—"

"I already said okay."

"Yes, but I had the feeling you didn't like the idea."

"Bruno, I *said okay*. What is this with you and Vita? Were you in love with her once or something?"

"Oh—" He blushed. "I wouldn't say in love."

"A crush, maybe? A crush on an older woman? I'm sure she was attractive."

He nodded. "But there was never anything *between* us."

"You just worshipped her from afar?" He nodded. "Okay, as long as you keep it afar I have no objection." He looked a little disappointed. Sometimes I think he wants her to inject more drama into their relationship, but she gets all the drama she needs from her work. "And Bruno—" He looked apprehensive. "If you get a chance, see if you can find out what Moore-Gann said to Sachs when they shook hands. I think Vita must have heard, she was sitting right next to her husband."

The door to the library opened. Sergeant Lovely appeared. His beard hadn't sprouted yet and he looked about sixteen years old. The heavy responsibility of being the one to summon us into the presence of the great Captain Eaken had made him blush in pink blotches all over his peaches-and-cream complexion. "You can come in if you want to," he said.

He held the door open and Sabina and I entered, while Bruno opened his umbrella and ambled off down the hill to his rendezvous with Vita. It was hardly raining at all, but Bruno thinks you catch cold from getting wet, even though as a scientist he ought to believe in the germ theory.

Captain Eaken was seated at the big table in the center of the library, finishing off a ham sandwich. "Have a seat, folks. Understand you wanted to see me." He smiled at Sabina. He didn't bother smiling at me.

Sabina said, "I've heard that the fingerprints on the glass, aside from Moore-Gann's, belonged to Jean-Paul Brocchiu and Magda Tenofska." We'd decided it wold be a good idea to mention the glass right away, sort of remind Eaken we'd done him a favor.

His cool gray eyes looked tired, as if he hadn't had much

sleep the night before. "The news travels fast." There was a pale stubble on his jaw. He rubbed it with his forefinger, looked surprised, and said, "Danged if I didn't forget to shave this morning."

Sabina said, "I've also heard Moore-Gann died of digitalis poisoning, so I assume you've found digitalis in the remains of the Bloody Mary."

He hesitated, then nodded. "I don't see any harm in telling you that we have. Course we had to find out without the benefit of a lab in Washington, D.C., but we managed."

She gave him a charming smile. "I'm sure your facilities are excellent, Captain."

He looked gratified. "We try. And now, mind if I ask why you're here? I don't figure you came just so you could ask me questions, now did you?"

"Mr. Newman found this paper," said Sabina, handing it over. Her fingers brushed his. "I felt you should have it." The general idea was that she was the compliant female, eager to cooperate with the police, while I was the maverick. No point in having him riled up at both of us.

He glanced at the paper and then at me, and his eyebrows rose. He read it. Then he looked up and asked me, "Where'd you get this?"

"In Hervé Moore-Gann's study. I was looking for something to read and I happened to pick it up. Then you and Sergeant Lovely dropped in and it slipped my mind."

"Slipped your mind my Aunt Tilly. Funny I didn't see it in your hand." He leaned forward and growled, "This here paper is evidence, Mr. Newman. You've interfered with evidence in a murder case. I don't know how the police feel about that in Washington, D.C., but up here in Vermont we don't care for it one bit." The gray eyes had turned icy and seemed to have grown smaller. "You get my message, sonny?" He turned to Sabina. "This here feller is your employee, right, ma'am?" She nodded. "Well, keep him in line! That's a warning. Next time—well, there better not be a next time." He bent over the paper and read it slowly, several times. Then he read the first words aloud: "'It is almost too terrible, the picture of that judgment. . . .' Wonder what judgment he meant. You think he was involved with the law in some way, maybe a court case?"

"Moore-Gann, you mean? I haven't heard of anything like that," said Sabina. "But it seems doubtful this was written by Moore-Gann; he was a confirmed atheist and he probably wouldn't have referred to the hand of God." Eaken looked interested, and she went on to tell him what Bruno had said about Magda's English not being this good and about Theresa's having been a scanner at one time.

This flow of information seemed to have mollified Eaken, but now he frowned. "What's a scanner?"

I said, "They run these charged particles—electrons, I think—through these big machines and a camera keeps taking pictures to see if they can catch the particles doing something or other that gives information about the nature of matter. That seems to be the general idea. Anyway, the scanners study the pictures looking for anything interesting that might turn up."

"You don't say." He looked confused. "Anyway, if Mrs. Moore-Gann was one of them—what'd you say they're called? Scanners?—it stands to reason she'd know what a photograph looked like, all righty. I guess I don't need to know any more about it than that." He seemed relieved at the thought. "So nobody wrote it, that what you're telling me?"

I shook my head. "Actually, Mrs. Moore-Gann said her husband found it in his packet when he got here."

"That so?" He made a note. "Well, the paper's unusual, maybe we can trace it." He read the paragraph again, shaking his head. "These here people sure are smart, sounds just like something in a book." He paused, as if trying to make up his mind, and then said confidentially to Sabina, "Tell you the truth, I don't think this paper's gonna turn out to be important. We're working on kind of a different tack. May be making an arrest before long." He leaned back to see how we would take his little bombshell.

Sabina said, "Really? Whom are you planning to arrest?"

He shook his head. "Don't know as I can tell you, ma'am. But I'll say this—he has a record."

Sabina said, "For assault and battery?"

"Well—yes."

"So you've decided Jean-Paul Brocchiu intended to poison Magda Tenofska, and Moore-Gann was killed by accident."

Eaken gave her a long, thoughtful look and scraped the stubble on his jaw. "I hear the trustees of the Institute have hired you to investigate the murder, Mrs. Herschel. Looks like you've been keeping yourself busy."

"I've been hired, that's true. I trust you have no objection."

He waved his hand in the air. "No, no. It's their money if they want to waste it. No offense, ma'am, but they pay their taxes and they're entitled to the best efforts of Burlington's law enforcement agencies, without charge, and that's exactly what they're gonna get. However—" He shrugged. "It's their business, they can do what they want." He hesitated, and then leaned forward. "Strictly between us, looks like we'll be taking Jean-Paul Brocchiu into custody tonight, soon as we hear from the California police. What do you think about that?" I got the impression he really wanted to know, because he wasn't completely happy with his case and wondered what we'd found out. He'd be happier when I told him, as I knew I'd have to, about the fight that had taken place between Jean-Paul and Magda only a few hours before Moore-Gann's death. Or had he heard about it already?

Sabina said, "What makes you so sure Jean-Paul is guilty?"

"Stands to reason. He threatened the Tenofska woman more than once, I understand. According to Theresa Moore-Gann, he used to call the girl all the time at the Moore-Ganns' house in Cambridge, and once Mrs. Moore-Gann happened to pick up an extension and overhear him saying that he'd kill her if she didn't come back to him."

I wondered whether Theresa had made a habit of listening in on Magda's telephone calls. It was a disturbing idea, the sort of thing the mother of a teenager might do—a mother

139

who was meddlesome, or worried sick. It was also something a jealous lover might do. . . . For the first time I wondered how deep Theresa's feelings for Magda went and exactly what kind of a relationship the two women would have now that Moore-Gann was dead. Would Magda go on living with Theresa when the stay at the Institute ended?

Eaken was saying "He's had a couple of previous arrests for assault, once in Boston and maybe once in California. In Boston it was a fist fight in a bar, fellow said something he didn't care for. The other time, from what we heard, sounded more serious: guy cut him off while he was driving and at the next red light Brocchiu jumped out and threatened him with a knife, maybe gave him a couple of cuts. We're checking into it."

"Still, that's quite a different matter than poisoning someone."

Eaken frowned at Sabina. "I see you don't think he did it. Got any evidence?"

She shook her head. "If he ever killed someone, I don't think he'd use poison. Neither does Magda."

"Let me tell you something I've learned," said Eaken good-naturedly. "These women who live with men who beat them always think that, deep down, they're not such bad fellers. They figure if they keep trying long enough, they'll reform 'em. I guess that's why they keep going back. And they do go back. I've seen it more times than I can count. *You* wouldn't go back, *I* wouldn't, but *they* do. I figure they've gotta have some kind of a kink. A matching kink, you might say, not that I'm a psychologist. Anyway, I don't take what they say about these fellers too seriously, what they would and wouldn't do." He shook his head. "I know Magda's a smart woman, least that's what everybody says, but not about Brocchiu."

"But she did leave him," Sabina pointed out.

"They all do. Then they go back." He pushed back his chair. "Anyway, that young lady didn't exactly tell us the truth, the whole truth, and nothing but the truth. I'm planning on having another conversation with her, real soon."

The telephone rang. He picked up the receiver. "Professor Sachs? Yep. Yep. You don't say." He listened. I could make out Saul's voice. Captain Eaken was shaking his head and there was a look of confusion, or maybe it was exasperation, on his face. After a while he said, "Now let me get this straight. You say the only Digoxin missing is the bottle your wife left in the medicine cabinet at the Institute. When was that?" He listened. After a while he nodded. "Okay. And it was so you'd have it handy in case you needed it. Why didn't you carry some with you?" There was a pause. "I see. Absent-minded professor, like. Oh, that's what your *wife* thinks." There was a notebook on the table in front of Eaken. He took a ballpoint pen out of his breast pocket and made a note. "Yep, thanks for calling." He hung up. We sat in silence for a moment. I wondered whether Charlene was going to take my advice and let Eaken know when the Digoxin had disappeared. If she didn't, I supposed I might have to tell him myself. Eaken said, "Okay, now we know where Brocchiu got the digitalis. Wasn't no Digoxin in the medicine cabinet when we checked it over. Lovely, you see any Digoxin in that medicine cabinet?"

"Nope."

"Didn't think so."

Eaken cleared his throat. "Well, that brings us back to Mr. Brocchiu." He began to enumerate on his fingers. "Number one, he's got a motive. Magda walked out on him, he begged her to come back and she wouldn't, he threatened her. Number two, he's a hot-tempered feller with a violent background, comes from one of these Mafia places over in Italy."

"You're thinking of Sicily," I said. "Jean-Paul's from Corsica, which is part of France."

"It's close, anyway. Number three, he had the opportunity, he handed the glass to Magda. We're sure the glass Moore-Gann drank the poisoned Bloody Mary from was hers, even though she denies it. It has her fingerprints on it, and Brocchiu's, too. And now number four: means! All he had to do was help himself to the bottle of Digoxin Mrs. Sachs left in the medicine cabinet for her husband. Right?"

He was watching Sabina carefully to see if he was convincing her, and I felt again that he had doubts about the case he was making.

"The medicine cabinet is near the bathrooms," she said. "People went in and out all the time. Anyone could have taken the Digoxin."

"We can still try to place him on the scene, narrow the time down. Judith Wiley or Gerald Ainsworth may have seen him, they're usually in the building." He gave us a challenging look. "He's our man, take my word for it."

"Speaking of Judith and Gerald," I said. "Did you hear what she said to him about his friend Brad?"

"Yep," said Eaken, and added unexpectedly, "I went to high school with Bradley. We were in different crowds, though."

I said, "I didn't think Brad *had* a crowd."

"Come to think of it, he didn't." He gave me a thoughtful look. "Been doing a little detecting, have you?"

"A little."

"Found anything out?"

"Not much so far. By the way, does Brad have AIDS?"

"Nope. According to his doctor, he's got lupus. It's serious, but it's nothing anybody can catch. We haven't had much AIDS in Vermont so far, and that's fine with us."

There was a knock at the door. Captain Eaken called, "Come in!"

The door opened, and Charlene stuck her head in. "Captain Eaken, I have some information," she began, and then caught sight of Sabina and me. "Oh, I beg your pardon."

He rose. "That's quite all right, ma'am. How about in half an hour?"

"I'll wait outside," she said. "Hi, Vic."

The door closed. Eaken sat down again. "Well, folks," he said. "Long as I've got you here, we might as well go through your movements on the day of the crime. Lovely, you got your notebook?" Sergeant Lovely leaned forward, his pencil poised. "Let's start with you, Newman. And don't leave anything out."

I gave him a complete rundown, holding nothing back that had happened up to the time of the murder. He was very interested in the fight between Magda and Jean-Paul and made me go over it twice. When he was done with me, he questioned Sabina.

# NINETEEN

It was raining steadily when we left the library. Charlene was on the porch in a plastic poncho, waiting to see Eaken. "Hi again," she said to us, and to me she added, "I'm taking your advice."

"Good for you," I said. She went inside.

We paused on the porch, hoping the rain would let up. Sabina said, "What did she mean?"

I told her about my conversation with Charlene in the microbus.

"Excellent," she said. "If the Digoxin disappeared some time after twelve-thirty on Friday, and Moore-Gann was poisoned around seven-thirty that night, it narrows things down quite a bit. Possibly Gerald Ainsworth may be able to recall who came into the building on Friday afternoon. Or Judith— her office is right next to the supply cupboard and she may have seen or heard something."

"Or she may have taken the poison herself."

"As you say."

I said, "Tell me, what do you think of the idea that Jean-Paul is the murderer?" Sabina looked skeptical but said nothing. "Eaken could be right. I hate to admit it, but sometimes the police do catch criminals. If it's one of those times, this isn't going to end up as our most distinguished case."

She waved my words aside, her face thoughtful. "Eaken has a tendency to jump to conclusions, but he's not a stupid man, by any means. In fact, he just made an extremely intelligent remark that throws light on something I've been worrying about."

This was news to me, but I wasn't going to give her the satisfaction of knowing that I didn't have the faintest idea what she was talking about. Mentally I began reviewing the conversation we'd just had in the library.

Sabina said, "I don't think the rain is going to stop. We might as well start walking down the hill. It shouldn't be too wet under the trees." We started out. The trees did give some shelter, but the sloping path was muddy. She said, "About Jean-Paul, I talked to him. He's a complex man, intelligent of course and more politically aware than many physicists; he was talking about the proliferation of nuclear power plants. He thinks they're hazardous and he's very worried about the waste products. I found him more likable than I'd expected. Still, under the surface—and not very far under, at that—you can sense the violence and anger in the man. We walked down to the pond together, where you questioned Magda. It's a beautiful spot but rather lonely, and once or twice I must say I felt uneasy with him."

"I wish you'd be more careful," I said, trying to keep the irritation out of my voice. "Or if you won't, at least learn karate. My *sensei* says he's willing to teach you, not that he knows what he'd be getting into. For God's sake take him up on it if you can't stay out of risky situations. You could have sat down under a tree near the administration building to talk to him. Nobody would have overheard you, but there'd at least have been people around."

"I will not take karate. I'm not the physical type, and I'm too old. And I thought Jean-Paul would talk more freely if we weren't where people could see us."

I knew this made sense, yet I said, "I still don't think you should question male suspects in lonely places. Why look for trouble?"

She smiled. "Vic, you're sweet. You were worried about me. But you needn't have been, Jean-Paul didn't try to harm me. On the contrary, once I'd told him I was investigating the case he was eager to cooperate. He knows the police suspect him because his fingerprints were on the glass, which he said was stupid of them because he'd poured drinks for many people and they hadn't all died. He does have a point. He seemed unaware of the possibility that Magda had been the intended victim, said he thought that the police might suspect he'd wanted to kill Moore-Gann because he thought Magda was in love with him. That was ridiculous, he told me. How could she be in love with Moore-Gann when he was an old man, no matter how young he tried to look?"

I said, "That's not too bright. Plenty of young women have fallen for older men, even without the Nobel prize. Father fixations are pretty common."

"Of course." The wind was blowing the fine gray-brown hairs out of Sabina's bun. Absently she tucked them back, pushing in the hairpins that had loosened. "Vic, why don't you see if you can get Magda to tell you more about her relationship with Moore-Gann. Even if she was telling the truth when she said they'd never had sex, there may have been more between them than we're aware of. Oops!" We were heading downhill on a steep part of the path and she stumbled and grabbed my arm. "These damn shoes!"

"I'll talk to her. When are you going to get yourself a pair of sneakers, Sabina? This is the country."

She made a face. The truth is, she's too vain to wear sneakers, though she claims she doesn't find them comfortable because she's been wearing high heels all her life. Reluctantly she said, "I may possibly buy myself a pair. I'm going into Burlington later anyway."

I wondered why, but I didn't ask. "Good. Do yourself a favor. What else did Jean-Paul have to say?"

"He claims he doesn't believe in the vendetta, called it stupid and a waste. His father and brother were killed when he was a child because of a family feud that had been going on so long that no one could remember what had started it. After they died, his mother sent him to France to be educated, and he's spent most of his life abroad. He mentioned that his family comes from Sartène." Sabina paused, her blue eyes thoughtful. "Bruno and I visited Sartène when we were in Corsica, and I remember it well because it's an extraordinary place—an ancient town with steep, narrow streets and gray stone houses built like fortresses that cling to the hills. It's beautiful in an austere sort of way, and the men you see in the square look exactly like bandits. In fact, for centuries Sartène has had the reputation of being a refuge for bandits—which in Corsica generally means men who have killed someone because of a vendetta and have had to flee to avoid the police."

I said, "So do you think he believes in the vendetta or not?"

"I'm not sure. Perhaps he's not sure himself. Part of him is a modern man and a scientist. But the other part?" She shrugged.

We walked for a while in silence. I said, "I suppose you asked him about his movements during the cocktail party."

"Naturally. He said that when Moore-Gann and Sachs shook hands he happened to be standing near a table with drinks on it. Everyone started applauding, and he picked up a pitcher of Bloody Marys and a stack of plastic glasses because he wanted to offer each of them a drink for a toast, to mark the occasion. But as he moved through the crowd, people started to snatch the glasses out of his hands and he found himself pouring everybody drinks. Then he saw Magda. There was still one drink and some ice left in the pitcher, and he pushed his way through the crowd to her side and poured the drink into a glass and gave it to her. He told her he was sorry he had hit her and promised he would never do it again, he said that even though he felt she'd provoked him he knew that was not a good excuse. But she wouldn't listen. I asked him, did you say to her, 'People get what they deserve, that is called judgment'? He was somewhat taken aback but admitted he'd said it. I asked him what he'd meant by it and he answered rather guardedly, 'I meant that I deserved her anger because of the way I had treated her. Of course.' And that was the gist of our conversation."

I said, "Well, what do you think? Is he our man?"

"I doubt it. But it's too soon to be sure."

"Eaken doesn't seem to think so."

Sabina stopped and turned to face me. "Victor, you're young and impatient and you jump to conclusions. It's your single greatest flaw as an investigator, as I've told you before. There's a great deal we still don't know about this case. That paper you found is important, in fact it may turn out to be crucial. If only I could remember—" She bit her lip and frowned, as if trying to recall a memory that kept slipping away.

We had reached the driveway and she got into the driver's seat of the Mercedes. "Get in," she said. "I want you to tell me again, in as much as detail as possible, exactly what you saw and did in Moore-Gann's study when you found that paper."

There was a sudden clap of thunder and then the rain came pouring down. I jumped inside, and slammed the door shut. The windows began to steam up inside. Sabina blotted her hair with Kleenex while I went over in detail my finding of the paper in Moore-Gann's study.

When I was finished she made no comment. After all, why should she share her thoughts with the hired help? She put the key in the ignition and looked at her watch. "I have to go to Burlington," she said. There were two umbrellas on the backseat and she handed me one.

I was dismissed. Outside it was pouring. Before I opened the door I said, "Do you mind if I ask why you're going to Burlington?"

"Not at all." She turned on the motor. "I have to get to the public library before it closes. I need something to read."

Served me right for asking.

# TWENTY

The reception hall in the administration building was empty. Through an open window, gusts of damp air flogged the bulletin boards, making the maps of the Champlain Valley and the announcements of upcoming seminars flap as if they were trying to escape from their thumbtacks. Across Gerald's desk, a long strip of computer printout paper had been draped, and on it was scrawled in red Magic Marker: "It is two o'clock Sunday afternoon and I am GOING HOME!!" The building was quiet and seemed deserted. I closed the open window and turned on a light. The fluorescent fixture cast a bluish glare on the waxed linoleum floor, where papers lay scattered by the wind. Taking a Styrofoam cup, I helped myself to bitter coffee from the coffee machine.

On one of the bulletin boards there was a sealed envelope with my name on it. I opened it and found a note from Magda: *Victor—I must speak to you. Please call me as soon as possible.* Her telephone number was scrawled on the bottom. I called her from Gerald's desk.

"Magda, this is Vic. I got your note."

"Vic!" Her voice was urgent. "I need to talk to you. Please." There was a silence on the line. Then she said, "Last time—I was not so nice, I walked away. You are angry? I see now I was wrong to do that."

"No, I'm not angry. What's up, has something happened?"

"We cannot talk on the phone." I wondered if Magda thought Theresa was listening. I hadn't heard the click of another extension, but maybe Magda was aware the older woman eavesdropped on her conversations. "Where are you?"

I said, "At the administration building."

"Stay there, I will come."

She hung up. Fine, I thought. Sabina had wanted me to question her about Moore-Gann anyway. I headed down the hall toward the supply cupboard, wondering what Magda wanted. The police had questioned her that morning for the second time; did she know Eaken was planning to arrest Jean-Paul?

As I neared the closed door of Judith's office I heard the murmur of voices; I wasn't alone in the building, as I had thought. I paused to listen, but it was impossible to tell who was speaking or what was being said.

Ten feet past Judith's door was the cupboard. I moved toward it noiselessly and slipped inside. It wouldn't have been hard for someone to have done the same on Friday afternoon, and if that someone had been Judith it would only have taken her a couple of seconds to leave her office and dart down the hall. Even if Gerald had been at his desk, he sat with his back to the hall and would have seen nothing.

The cupboard was a deep, doorless niche in the wall, lined with shelves from floor to ceiling. There were stationery supplies, filter papers for the coffee machine, packages of Styrofoam cups and plastic spoons. The medicine cabinet hung from the wall at eye level, and my face looked back at me from the cloudy mirror as I opened the cabinet door. Inside were yellowing boxes of Band-Aids, dusty aspirin bottles containing a tablet or two, half-empty bottles of disinfectant, twisted tubes of ointment without caps—a bunch of old junk, as Charlene had said, all jammed together except for a gap on the second shelf. Someone—Judith?—had taken the bottle of Digoxin from the shelf, leaving that gap. And then? Broken the capsules open, probably, and mixed their contents with water—not much, just enough to dissolve them. Once the digitalis was dissolved it could be dumped into a drink, quickly and easily.

I moved down the hall and went into one of the restrooms.

I was still carrying the Styrofoam cup of coffee; I emptied it into the sink. There were plenty of cups just like this in the supply cupboard, and the murderer could have filled one with water in the restroom. Then he—or let's say she—could have gone back to her office, dissolved the capsules, and transferred the solution to a bottle small enough to conceal in her hand. Judith would have known that Bloody Marys—perfect for concealing the taste of the Digoxin—were going to be served at the cocktail party, and she'd have been unaware that Moore-Gann had given up alcohol since apparently she'd had no direct contact with him for years.

It could have happened that way. Something like it *had* happened—but had the poisoner been Judith?

I heard a door opening. Theresa came out of Judith's office, her arms filled with papers, her face in profile tense and pale. "I'll let you know," she said over her shoulder.

Judith replied but I couldn't hear the words. I was surprised to find the two women together after their bitter confrontation over the schedule earlier that day. Theresa looked up and caught sight of me, and gave me a smile that cost her an effort. "Vic," she said. "How are you?"

She looked terrible, and I thought, "This woman should be home in bed." Not that rest would solve her problems, bring her husband back to life, just that it didn't seem natural for her to be carrying on with her work after the calamity that had devastated her life. There was a lot to be said, I reflected, for the Jewish custom of sitting *shivah,* as I'd seen it practiced by my grandmother and one of my aunts after their husbands had died. For a week they'd sat in their stocking feet on low stools, mourning, while a parade of friends and relatives came by to console them and bring them food. Only when the week was up did they try to go on with their lives.

Obviously that wasn't Theresa's style. I went up to her and said, "Hello, Theresa. Do you think you'd have some time this afternoon to talk to me, answer a few questions? The board of trustees has hired my boss to investigate the case." Over her shoulder I could see Judith at her desk, watching us in silence.

151

Theresa hesitated. "Well—I hate to say no, Vic, but I'm terribly busy. Hervé was to have presented the opening seminar tomorrow morning, and since I'm giving it instead"— there was a flicker of a glance in Judith's direction—"I have a lot of preparation to do. Judith and I have been getting the handouts ready." She sighed. "Oh, well, I'll have to take a break sooner or later, around suppertime I suppose. I haven't eaten all day. Why don't you come to the house at seven?"

I said I would and she left, plodding wearily down the hall.

I entered the office. Behind the large metal desk, Judith's narrow frame seemed even thinner, as if she had shrunk since yesterday. She didn't greet me. I took a chair, saying "Mind if I sit down?"

"I suppose it never occurred to you to wait for an invitation before you walk into someone's office." Her manner was as hostile as ever but her heart wasn't in it; she seemed anxious about something. I sat down and she snapped, "Well?"

"I suppose you know by now that the board of trustees—"

"Yes, yes," she said with a wave of her hand. "They've hired Sabina Swift to investigate Moore-Gann's death." She pressed her lips together and then blurted, "She doesn't really have a retarded nephew, does she? She doesn't, she was lying. Snooping."

"She was investigating the case."

"She has a rotten way of doing it, if you're interested in my opinion."

"I'm sorry you feel that way."

"I feel exactly that way." Her mouth twisted with disappointment, and something else—satisfaction, maybe. Her low opinion of human nature had been reconfirmed and she could add another injury to her collection. "I thought she seemed decent, only no decent person would take advantage of a thing like that. *You* wouldn't understand, being a man. But a woman should know . . . should be able to imagine. . . ." She jumped up and went to the window where she stood, her arms folded, watching the rain slashing down the panes. Abruptly she whirled and said, as if unwillingly, "Have you seen Jordan? My son?"

"I've met him, yes."

"No, have you *seen* him? Today, yesterday—"

"No."

"Neither have I." She hesitated. "I'm worried sick." The words came out in a rush, involuntarily. "Not that you give a damn."

"He hasn't come home in two days?" She shook her head. "Has he ever done anything like this before?"

"Well—sort of," she admitted. "Once or twice, when I've had to—discipline him."

I wondered what form of discipline she used. "Did you discipline him recently?"

"I don't see where that's any of your business. Anyway, you didn't come here to talk about my son." She wheeled and returned to her chair behind the desk. "What do you want?"

"Do you have any idea where he might be?"

"I told you, it's none of your business. Maybe I do and maybe I don't. Why don't you get to the point?"

"All right, I will. Can you tell me who was in this building on Friday afternoon, starting about twelve-thirty?"

"I doubt it. I was here, of course, and Gerald. And Dr. Gawthrop—his office is upstairs. A number of participants in the Institute arrived on Friday and picked up their packets. Gerald has a list and he should have checked off their names and noted the day of their arrival. *You* were here. And I suppose people were dropping in all day to pick up their mail and check the bulletin boards and use the restrooms and complain about one thing or another. They think we have nothing better to do than get them apartments with better kitchens, and babysitters, and plane reservations. *I've* no idea who was here that day or what they wanted. I keep my door closed. Otherwise I wouldn't get any work done."

"I thought that was your work."

"I don't need you to tell me what my work is."

I leaned forward and said in a hard voice, "The digitalis that killed Hervé Moore-Gann came from the medicine cabinet right next door to your office, Judith. Saul Sachs kept a bottle of Digoxin there, and it disappeared some time after

153

twelve-thirty Friday afternoon. We want to know who took it. Because of the location of your office, you're in a better position than anyone else to have seen or heard something." She was watching me, impassive. "Or maybe you took it yourself."

She gave a mirthless laugh. "You think *I* killed Moore-Gann? That's ridiculous! I didn't shed any tears over his demise," she said sarcastically. "But what does that prove? Mr. Newman, I don't think much of the human race, I've good reason not to; but that man was the lowest of the low, I don't care if they gave him *ten* Nobel prizes!"

"He treated you badly?"

She placed her hands flat on the desk and pushed her chair back. It rolled on wheels that squeaked a little. "Look. I didn't kill Moore-Gann, somebody else was kind enough to do it. And nobody's going to fasten it on me. I've picked up enough pieces in my lifetime."

"You mean like raising Moore-Gann's child without any acknowledgment from him?"

Her face became stony. "What do you mean? Jordan's father was killed in Vietnam before he was born, not that it's any of your business."

"Then why did Moore-Gann send you money?"

"Money? *He* never sent me money, not a cent!" she flared. "That cheap bastard!"

"Well, maybe he didn't. Theresa did—doesn't it come to the same thing?"

"Of course not! It—" She faltered and fell silent. Then she demanded, "Who told you Theresa sent me money? Did she? I bet she did, she probably gets a thrill from bragging about it." She laughed harshly. "She had the nerve to send me a five-dollar bill for Jordan's birthday. Five dollars! I let her know what I thought of her; she found a special little note of welcome when she opened her packet." She gave a venomous little smile. "Lady Bountiful!"

She stood up again. "I don't care to answer any more of your nosy questions, Mr. Newman. I'll talk to Gerald and see

154

if we can come up with a list of people who were in the build-ing on Friday afternoon."

"You're going to have to answer questions, if not from me, from the police."

"Fine. I prefer the police."

I remembered that Eaken had gone to school with her. "Captain Eaken a friend of yours?"

"Good-bye, Mr. Newman," she said again, and folded her arms over her chest. "I have nothing further to say."

"I'm employed by the trustees of the Institute, and you're an Institute employee. I'm sure Professor Gawthrop expects you to cooperate with the investigation."

She stared at me defiantly and didn't answer. I left. She shut the door behind me.

# TWENTY-ONE

I waited for Magda in the lobby of the administration building, reading the notices on the bulletin board. After a couple of minutes Judith came out of her office in a raincoat. She ignored me as she passed through the lobby and left the building. From the window I saw her get into her car and drive away.

The room was cold and I zipped up my windbreaker. I kept thinking about the dead man, trying to figure him out. He seemed a mass of contradictions, a man who had been a genius, world famous, but "not likable in the usual sense," according to Florian, and a "cold fish," according to Bruno. Judith had called him "the lowest of the low"; Theresa thought of him as a national treasure and had been devoted to him, although according to Florian he'd been a womanizer.

The one and only time I'd seen him, what had struck me most had been the contrast between his powerful, intellectual head—and his reputation, of course—and the skin-tight jeans and gold neck chain he'd been wearing. He'd impressed me as a man who was keenly, maybe painfully, aware of his aging sexuality; a man who might be torn between the conflicting demands of mind and body. Bruno had said Moore-Gann never showed his feelings, yet he must have had them, like other men; if any one had really known what they were it would be Theresa, who had lived with him for twenty years. Maybe when I saw her that evening she'd say something that would help me understand what kind of a person he'd really been.

Magda appeared, with a dripping umbrella in her hands

156

that she propped against the wall. "It's pouring," she said. "I was stupid, I should have taken the car." She was wearing a belted black raincoat and a shiny black rainhat with a brim that shadowed her face. She took off her hat and looked at me; there was something abject in her eyes, as if she didn't trust me but was prepared to plead with me anyway. But for what?

She said tensely, "Vic, tell me what you've found out—please. Do you know yet who killed Moore-Gann?"

"No."

Her shoulders jerked with disappointment. "I saw the police, they have discovered it was my glass that Moore-Gann drank from. Vic—they are going to arrest Jean-Paul. Maybe they have done so already."

I said, "I thought everything was over between the two of you. Isn't that what you said? It sure doesn't sound that way."

Her hands gripped each other, the fingers knotting together. "You sound like Theresa," she said. "She hates Jean-Paul." I was sitting at Gerald's desk, and she dropped into a chair alongside it, looking away from me so that I saw the bold outline of her profile, the nose with its broad nostril, the strong bones of her brow, and one deep-set eye. "Vic," she said with an effort. "I owe you apology. The other day you asked me questions. I did not answer, I was not polite. Now I see I must tell you everything even if I do not think it matters, even if I do not see how it can help Jean-Paul. I know he did not try to poison me."

"I don't see how you can be so sure."

"I know him," she said simply. "No one knows him as well as I." She took a deep breath. "On Saturday you asked if there was anything between me and Hervé and I said no. That was the truth, but not the whole truth."

I remembered Captain Eaken saying "That young lady hasn't exactly told us the truth, the whole truth, and nothing but the truth." I said, "What did you leave out?"

She didn't answer at once. Finally she said, "I came to Cambridge to work with Hervé last September. It will be one year next month. Jean-Paul came, too. We had been together

157

in California and when I got a position at M.I.T. he was able to find work nearby in a consulting firm that has many government contracts. I was very excited about working with Moore-Gann, naturally. At first I was in awe of him and overwhelmed by the honor. Although I had had other job offers, you understand." She shrugged. "I am good in my work and now everyone looks to hire a woman, the government has certain rules. But after a few months there were things I began to notice, things I did not like."

"Such as?"

"Moore-Gann, he was aloof, he was very intellectual always—this I expected and found natural. But then he changed. We start to work later in the evening, after the secretaries are gone, and he starts to touch me here, touch me there. I did not like it. By then I had heard talk about his affairs with women." She threw me a veiled glance. "You have heard?"

"Yes."

"Good." Her mouth twisted with distaste. "I do not care to repeat such things."

"Did you ever hear that he'd had a *serious* affair?"

"Serious? No, never. It was said these were passing things. And I did not care to be one of his conquests, it would become known and be bad for my reputation as a physicist. This I would never risk, you understand. Anyway, I was not attracted to him, I was involved with Jean-Paul and although we had our difficulties we were still living together. I did not know what to do, I could confide in no one. Jean-Paul is very jealous and I could not tell him, and aside from him I had no real friends." She looked around the barn and then at me, but I said nothing. After a moment she went on. "Something else happened, too. It concerned my work."

"What was it?"

She hesitated. "Do you know much physics?" I shook my head. "Well, perhaps you are aware that those in the forefront are all working now on something called supersymmetry. For some time we arrange the elementary particles, like electrons and protons and quarks, into groups we call multiplets that have a common spin. And now we try to group these multiplets into larger units, which allows us to form theories that are mathematically sounder than the ones we had before. Of course all this is theory, it has nothing to do with nature—yet. But if our theories are correct, in ten or twenty years they will lead to an understanding of the forces of nature that is more fundamental than anything we have ever known. You see?"

"Go on. You said something happened concerning your work. What was it?"

"Soon after I arrived at M.I.T. I came up with a new idea for arranging particles into supermultiplets. This I discussed with Hervé and he said it seemed promising. I went ahead with it and kept him informed of the progress I was making. Then he went away for a few days to a conference in Mexico City where he gave a seminar that was very well received. Only I learned from colleagues who were there that he had presented the work *I* was doing, but my name had not been mentioned. You can imagine my feelings—or perhaps you cannot."

"What did you do when you found out?"

"For a week I did nothing. Figure to yourself my position, he is a world-famous professor, a Nobel prizewinner, and I am a post-doc only. But one evening we were working late and he leaned over me as I was at my desk and put his arm around me and his hand—here." She touched her breast. "I jumped up and shouted at him to stop. There was no one to hear, we were alone on the floor. And I said everything I had been holding back—that he had used my work and not given me credit, and this could not happen again in the future. And that I did not wish to flirt, that I respected and revered him as a colleague and a teacher, but never could he be anything else to me. That it would damage my career. Oh, he was very angry! He said something nasty about my relationship with Jean-Paul. And what did I think I was, to be so proud?" She tossed back her hair, and her eyes flashed angrily. "He used a word I will not repeat, and I slapped his face. Yes, the great Moore-Gann!" She crossed her arms over her breast and stared moodily into the fire. "For weeks he did not speak to me. I barely saw him except in the halls, and when we passed each other he ignored me. I worked alone and felt very isolated. I started to think I would have to look for another position.

"Then one day he came to me in my office. He apologized, he told me he respected me for standing up to him. He said that when he had given the talk in Mexico he had meant to give me credit and had forgotten because there were many questions from the audience and he ran out of time. He promised to give me credit in the future. And he did, or I would not have continued to work with him. About the other business, it was not mentioned again, but he treated me afterward with the greatest respect. In fact, the whole episode brought us closer. He became a true friend to me, almost like a father. My own father died when I was eleven years old. There was no longer formality between Hervé and myself, I could talk to him about anything and I could even tease him a little. He liked it, I think. Most people treated him with awe, and it bored him. He helped me in many ways and was trying in the last few months to get me an immigration visa. If he had lived I am sure he would have succeeded. Now that he is dead I do not know what will happen. I cannot go back to Poland!"

"Why not, Magda?"

"I might be arrested. If not that, certainly I would not be allowed to teach in a university. You see, my mother was very active in the Solidarity movement. She is an intellectual, a teacher and poet, and she has"—she swallowed—"*had* a small press. She began to write certain antigovernment pamphlets and distribute them to the workers in the factories. I helped her, we set them in type together. It was secret, naturally. Then I had an opportunity to do graduate work in America, I won a fellowship. We talked for a long time about whether I should go, whether she could manage without me. You understand, I, too, felt the work we were doing was very important. She urged me not to lose my opportunity." She pressed her lips together and turned her head aside. "I do not know what happened after that. Someone must have betrayed her, that much I know. I got word that she was in prison. After that—nothing. I do not even know if she is still alive. Sometimes I fear—"

"Who could have betrayed her?"

She shook her head. "I do not know that either. Many people were aware she had a press, for she had published the work of poets—others, not her own work only. But only a few friends knew about the political literature, and we thought they were all reliable." In her lap, her hands closed into fists. "If I ever find out—"

She turned to face me, tears in her hazel-flecked eyes. "Hervé was a good friend," she said. "He was trying to discover where she is, he said he might be able to arrange for amnesty to be granted, even for her to leave the country. He knew many people high up in the American government."

Still another Moore-Gann, I reflected; this one an altruist, a wielder of influence on behalf of the underdog.

She took a handkerchief from her pocket and dabbed at her eyes, then gave a halfhearted little smile. "We used to joke he would find me a rich American husband so I could become citizen."

"Would you marry an American just to solve your visa problems?" After all, the immigration authorities made exceptions, and everyone seemed to agree that she was an outstanding young scientist.

She shook her head. "You are an American, you cannot imagine that some people do not have so many choices as you do. You have never been in that position. I refused to marry Jean-Paul, though he asked me many times, partly because I thought that I might *have* to marry an American so I would not be deported. It would not have to be a real marriage. It could be a sham, a facade for the world, and one could later get a divorce." She shrugged. "Well, poor Hervé is gone. Theresa will do what she can with the immigration authorities, I am sure. She, too, has powerful friends. But what will happen?" She spread her hands and said fatalistically, "Who can say?"

161

"Magda, how much does Theresa know about what happened between you and Hervé?"

She looked startled. "Nothing—unless he told her. She has never said a word to me about it."

"Would he have told her?"

She thought about it. "I don't know," she said slowly. "I was very close to both of them, they have been my American family. But I have never understood their marriage." She shook her head, and wiped her eyes with the handkerchief. "I still cannot believe that Hervé is gone forever! I do not think Theresa has really taken it in either. When she does she will need someone to lean on, and maybe I will have to be that person."

I said, "I've often wondered how you feel about Theresa."

"I admire her. She is good physicist, we have many discussions. She has an intuition that amazes at times. I think she was a great help to Hervé."

"And personally?"

She hesitated, and her mouth twisted into a gesture of distaste, as if the personal were something she preferred not to acknowledge. She shrugged. "She is very kind and patient. Very strong. Sometimes a little—I do not know how to say it in English. Intense, too intense?"

"Did she know about Moore-Gann's affairs?"

"Oh, those." She made a gesture of dismissal. "She never mentioned them, but she knew. I am sure she knew. But she did not consider them important. Perhaps they were not. Theresa speaks often of rising above petty things. But she can be petty, too, even though she does not think so."

"How?"

"Oh—she fusses. It is nothing, really. Vic—" She turned toward me and gripped my hand in hers. "I am very worried for Jean-Paul, I am afraid they will put him in prison. Tell me the truth, do *you* think he is guilty?"

It was a hard question to answer. "I don't know yet," I said slowly. "There are other possibilities. Maybe this crime goes back many years into the past, and if that's true, it has nothing to do with Jean-Paul."

"And you will find out, you and Sabina Swift?"

"We're trying, Magda. We'll do our best." I stood up. "I'm going to your house," I said. "To talk to Theresa. Can I give you a lift?"

"No. I must make a telephone call, I will stay here."

# TWENTY-TWO

The rain was still coming down, and I took the microbus to Theresa's house, although she lived not far away. A thread of smoke was rising from the chimney of the silver-gray cottage when I got there. Theresa's and Magda's cars stood in the driveway, and I pulled up behind them and jumped out into a puddle, feeling the water slosh over my ankles. I made a dash for the front porch and knocked on the door. Nobody answered. After a while I opened the door, and the wind grabbed it out of my hand and slammed it behind me, shaking the old walls. Theresa's voice called, "Maggie, is that you?"

I found Theresa in the kitchen, standing beside a black iron woodstove that radiated heat. She looked like a farm wife, in a flannel shirt and baggy corduroy pants, with an apron tied around her waist. "Oh, it's you, Vic," she said when she saw me. "I thought it was Maggie, coming home for dinner." I had an idea Magda might have made other plans but I didn't say so. Theresa looked at my feet. "You're wet, why don't you take your shoes off?" Her eyes were concerned, despite the exhaustion that seemed to have settled in them permanently.

I looked around the kitchen. At one end there was a long table covered with papers and books, where she had obviously been preparing her talk for the following day. At the other, near the wood stove, stood a smaller table covered with a red cloth. On it were a bottle of wine in a sloping basket, a loaf of bread on a board, and a pair of flickering candles. The table was set for two.

I took off my soaked sneakers and refused her offer of dry socks. She went and got some anyway, with a towel, and gave me a lecture on the importance of dry feet. I found myself thinking of my mother, the little I remembered of her, and enjoying being fussed over by Theresa. She had a definite maternal quality, despite her childlessness. Were these little attentions the kind of thing she'd done for Moore-Gann, part of the bond between them, maybe even the reason he'd always come home after his extramarital affairs?

She cleared a space at the table where the books were, pulled out a chair for me, and brought over a bowl of beaten eggs and a plate of breadcrumbs. "I'm making wiener schnitzel," she said. "Breaded veal cutlets—it's Magda's favorite dish. I should really work on my seminar, but cooking relaxes me. I'll finish my talk tonight—I can't sleep anyway." She brought over some slices of veal in a piece of waxed paper, sat down, and began to dip the veal in the eggs and then the crumbs, carefully and thoroughly, making sure the surface was evenly coated. She said, "I should have had a big family to cook for."

"It's too bad you didn't," I said.

"You're wondering why, aren't you? People generally do, but they're too polite to ask." The circles under her eyes were so dark her blue eyes looked faded. "I simply couldn't," she said, and turned her hands palm upward. "Fortunately my husband didn't mind, his work was always the most important thing to him."

Asking myself why she wanted me to know these things, I said, "I wish you'd tell me about him, Theresa. That's really why I'm here. You knew him better than anyone."

"Did I?"

"Didn't you?"

"I suppose so. What would you like to know?"

"You won't mind if I ask you personal questions?"

"Well—that depends. Of course I realize you have to ask questions, now that you're investigating his death."

I said, "Since you brought the matter up, I wonder why

you and your husband never adopted a child. You must have thought about it."

The shadow of an ancient hurt showed in her eyes as she shook her head, but her voice was matter-of-fact. "*I* did, yes. My husband, though, felt strongly that he didn't want to be responsible for someone else's child."

"Is that why he refused to have anything to do with Jordan?"

Her eyebrows rose. "I see you've been listening to gossip. Well, it's not a secret, many people know that my husband and Judith were once . . . *intimate.*" She handled the word with precision yet aloofness, like soiled bedding she was dropping into a washing machine with rubber-gloved fingertips. "It was a long time ago, and it wasn't very serious."

"I heard it was serious."

"Not to him," she said sharply. "He never believed the child was his. Judith tried to put pressure on him, and of course then he wouldn't have anything to do with her at all." She shook her head, a ghost of a smile on her lips. "She made a great mistake, my husband couldn't be pressured; it only made him stubborn. If you want to know what he was like, that's one trait he had." She turned her head aside. "He could be like a stone. You had to manage him."

"How did you manage him, Theresa?"

She lifted her chin. "Vic, don't you think it's important to keep one's perspective and overlook certain things in this life? I do. I always made a point of being pleasant and polite to Hervé, and I suppose you might say I deferred to him. I put my career aside so I could travel with him. Oh, I did a little teaching, of course. But I gave up research. I know that sort of thing is considered very old-fashioned nowadays, but it so happens that husbands like it—Hervé did, anyway. I didn't mind. Why should I? He gave me so much in return."

"Such as?"

"You do ask personal questions. Isn't the answer obvious? We had a certain position in the world." She fell silent, her gaze inward, leaving me to imagine the embassy receptions,

166

the dinners at the White House, and the day he'd received the Nobel prize in Stockholm. I could picture her beside him on the platform, basking in his triumph; maybe she'd earned the right.

"Would you call him a happy man?"

"Certainly! Certainly he was happy, who says he wasn't?" There was a sharpness in her tone and her eyes were guarded.

"I just wondered. You'd have known if he wasn't?"

"Absolutely. He told me everything, he shared every aspect of his life with me."

"Even his affairs?"

"Why—" She gave me a haughty look and I could see her struggling with the decision she seemed to have made earlier to answer my questions frankly. "I see you've been listening to a *great* deal of gossip," she said finally. "As a matter of fact we *did* talk about his little flings, though that may surprise you. My husband worked very hard, with total concentration, and every now and then he needed a—mindless diversion. That's all it amounted to. We had a wonderful marriage," she said with emphasis. "Not everyone might have thought so, but *I* did. And since it was *my* marriage, that's what mattered to me. We had a marvelous intellectual companionship, we talked about physics, we talked about everything."

"Did you talk about the pass he made at Magda?"

She sucked in her breath. "I told you we talked about everything!" She stood up and carried the breaded veal slices to the stove, turning on the burner. A blue flame flared up. She slid a pan over it and waited, her back to me. "But you have to realize that was something that happened before she came to live with us. It was an isolated incident. And once we were all together we really became like a family, truly we did, it was wonderful." She leaned toward me in her eagerness to make sure I understood how she saw it. "That's what I mean by overlooking things that don't really matter. Magda is like a daughter to me now, the daughter I never had."

I said, "Maybe I'm naive, but I can't understand how you

could treat her like a daughter when you knew what had happened between her and your husband."

"But *nothing* happened!" She arranged the slices of veal in the pan; they sizzled as they touched the hot surface. "I'm extremely attached to Magda!" My incomprehension seemed to irritate her. "Don't you see? She's like my younger self, only wiser and stronger. She'll go far, she may win the Nobel prize herself some day, it's not impossible. She's very good." She glanced at me over her shoulder, the shadows of her thoughts crossing her pale eyes too fast for me to read them. "Please don't tell Maggie I said this, but the best thing that could happen to her would be for Jean-Paul Brocchiu to be convicted of my husband's murder. The best thing in the world! That may seem a strange thing to say, but I mean it. He's bad for her." She shook her head. "Terribly, terribly bad, but I'm afraid he still has a hold over her."

"Do you think he did it?"

"Captain Eaken seems to think he wanted to kill Magda, and somehow my poor husband died by—mistake." Her voice broke on the word. "I believe Jean-Paul to be capable of anything! I have reason to!" There was a shrill edge to her voice. "Magda's attachment to that man is simply disastrous. It's hard to believe she could still care for him—but there's no logic to love, how well I know it!" She shook her head. "Have you heard that she appeared at our house in Cambridge in the middle of winter at three in the morning, after that brute had beaten her up? He drinks, you know. My husband was out of town and I've never slept well when he was away. I had insomnia that night—fortunately, as it turned out. Otherwise I'd never have heard her knocking. I found her lying on our doorstep. She could have died of exposure! Imagine what a loss that would have been—to physics, to us! I literally carried her to the car and took her straight to the emergency room. She was bruised from head to foot." Theresa's voice shook with indignation. "When she was able to leave the hospital I took her home with me, and she's lived with us ever since."

She turned the veal and lowered the flame under the pan. Then she picked up a corkscrew, went over to the table set for two, and opened the bottle of wine. She filled the two glasses. She drank from one, and when she took it from her lips it was half empty. The other she brought to me. The wine was dark in the lamplight.

I said, "You think she'll go back to him."

She lifted her glass and drained it. Bitterly she said, "Wouldn't you think a brilliant girl like that would have more sense?" In the silence that followed this question, the telephone began to ring in the next room. Theresa went to answer it. I heard the murmur of her voice and a moment later, after a pause, "But I've made wiener schnitzel!" There was a long silence, followed by the sharp exclamation, "He's bad for you!"

When she came back to the kitchen, her expression was distraught. "Magda isn't coming home," she said. "She's with him." Her eyes flickered toward the table with the red cloth and the two place settings. "Vic, wouldn't you like to join me for dinner?"

"No thanks, Theresa. I'll have to be going." I'd had a feeling this question was coming and I didn't want to eat with her.

"Oh, surely you're not in that big a hurry." The smile she gave me was forced and vulnerable.

I shook my head, feeling a twinge of guilt, and said, "By the way, I was surprised to see you coming out of Judith's office this afternoon, after the argument about the schedule."

She shrugged, and the vulnerable look vanished from her face. "We have to learn to rise above these things," she said briskly. "Judith is the secretary of the Institute, and I needed her help to prepare the handouts for my seminar." She hesitated. "Have you talked to her yet, have you asked her about my husband's death?"

"Yes. Why, do you think she knows something?"

"I didn't mean that. I wondered what she said about Hervé, whether she talked about their—relationship." Her words were coming faster now, as if she didn't want me to leave. "I'm surprised she even let you question her; Judith can be so brusque."

"She didn't say much." I stood up. "She talked quite a bit to Sabina about Jordan."

She looked surprised. "Jordan? What about him?"

"Oh—that his schooling cost a lot of money. You sent her money, didn't you?"

"Occasionally. I thought, you see—if he *was* Moore-Gann's son—it would be right to do something for him. Still, it amazes me that she mentioned it. It was really Hervé she wanted money from, not me, of course; but he wouldn't even allow me to mention the subject."

I walked to the door and she followed. I said, "You were generous—not many women in your position would have sent her anything. Did she at least thank you?"

She gave a wry little smile. "Oh, I'd hardly say *that*. In fact she even—well, never mind," she said in a tone of dismissal. "I'm sorry for the poor creature. As far as I'm concerned, she's pathetic." I suddenly saw why Judith might have hated Theresa Moore-Gann, Theresa who had everything Judith wanted, who was so secure in her position that she could afford to be charitable to a former rival. "Don't make me out to be better than I am," Theresa said. "The boy was no threat to me. My husband could never have cared for a retarded child—never! Even if there'd been no doubt about his paternity."

We had reached the front door. "It's still raining," she said. "I won't be able to go for my walk. I take a walk around the pond every night after dinner. I find I get quite restless when I don't have enough exercise." She peered up at the sky. "Do you think it might stop?"

I opened the door. "Theresa, let me ask you something. Do you think Judith could have hated your husband so much because of what happened twenty years ago that she'd have held a grudge all these years and finally killed him?"

"Killed him? Judith?" Theresa looked surprised and then thoughtful. "The idea never occurred to me," she said slowly.

170

"It seems far-fetched, but not impossible." She was silent for a moment. "I suppose Hervé could have become some sort of an obsession with her, but she would have had to be a rather warped person to begin with, don't you think? Though perhaps she was." Her hand grasped my arm. "You're absolutely sure you won't stay for dinner?"

"I can't, but thanks anyway."

I closed the door behind me, leaving her to return to her warm kitchen, her table set for two, and her loneliness.

# TWENTY-THREE

When I got back to Burlington I found Sabina reading on the living-room couch. She greeted me, took a sip from the cup of tea she was holding, and resumed reading.

"I just talked to Theresa," I said as I took off my dripping windbreaker. "And before that to Magda and Judith."

"Mmm-hmm. Hang that in the bathtub, please."

"What's the plan for dinner?" I hadn't eaten since morning and I was hungry.

"Help yourself from the refrigerator." She turned a page.

"You're not eating? What about Bruno?"

"He's at the cocktail party." Was I imagining things, or had a marital tiff taken place?

"What about you?"

She turned another page and after a moment murmured, "I'd rather read."

"Maybe I should go to the cocktail party. At least they'll have food." I wasn't really in the mood for a party, all I wanted to do was change into dry clothes and report. After all, we had a case, didn't we? And hadn't Florian, our client, specifically asked us to try and get quick results?

Sabina didn't respond. I said, "That must be an interesting book."

Without looking up she said, "It is."

When she acts like that you can't do anything with her, so I wandered toward the kitchen, saying "I can see your trip to the library was a big success." I got no answer. What was bugging her?

I changed into dry clothes and heated up a can of soup.

While it was coming to a boil I made myself a grilled cheese sandwich.

I was eating and reading the sports page of the *Burlington Free Press* when Sabina came into the kitchen to make herself a fresh pot of tea. English Breakfast, which she has explained to me can be drunk at any hour of the day. Since she was standing there anyway, I gave her a report on what I'd been up to—not that she asked, but at least she stuck around while I kept talking. She didn't comment. This gets on my nerves, because I have a need for positive reinforcement. All she said when I was done was "So Magda would consider marrying an American to solve her visa problems. I wonder what the immigration status is of Andrzej Modzalewski. Have you heard from Mort Goldman about him yet?"

"Not yet."

"Why don't you follow up on it?"

Carrying her tea, she went back to the living room and her book and I called Mort at his apartment in Crystal City. He was apologetic for not having gotten back to me. "We've been busy," he said. "Car bomb exploded outside the Mexican Embassy this morning and three people were killed, including the ambassador. Do you have any idea how many Mexican nationals there are in Washington, D.C., not to mention the suburbs? Legal *and* illegal?" I said I didn't, and he said they really didn't either, which was part of the problem.

"As for our friend Modzalewski," he said. "He seems to be exactly what he claims. He's a fairly well-known Polish physicist who was a professor at the University of Wroclaw, married, no children. Wife's still in Poland. He definitely was arrested and tried for antigovernment activities in connection with the Solidarity movement, mostly for being involved with a strike of factory workers in the Wroclaw area—he's supposed to be quite a good orator and made speeches at meetings and that sort of thing. After his conviction he served eight months in prison, we know that for a fact. He was given a weekend pass on humanitarian grounds to visit his sick father, and with the help of a couple of old Solidarity pals he was smuggled out of the country in a carpenter's van that had a false floor." He hesitated as if about to add something, then said, "All kosher, apparently. When he got to this country he contacted Saul Sachs through mutual friends and stayed at the Sachs home for a while. Sachs and his family were Hungarian Jews who were refugees during World War Two, and Sachs has gone out of his way to help a number of scientists who were political emigrés. He pretty much supported Modzalewski until he managed to find him a position at City College in New York. And that's it, Vic. What do *you* know about Modzalewski?"

"Not much. His English could be better. He's a big guy with a bone-crushing handshake. Obviously part of the Sachs circle, seems to be close to Sachs and to a couple of physicists named Leo Pesnik and Jean-Paul Brocchiu. Brocchiu's a Corsican who the police are about to arrest for Hervé Moore-Gann's murder. Sabina doesn't think he did it. There's another Polish physicist here, Magda Tenofska, but they don't pal around together—in fact I've never seen them speak to each other. She's a lot younger than he is, still in her twenties."

"Magda Tenofska," he said thoughtfully. "Where have I heard that name?"

"Her mother's in a Polish jail. Solidarity activities—she had a press and printed antigovernment pamphlets. Magda used to help her."

Mort said, "Sounds vaguely familiar. You know anything else about Modzalewski?"

"He's got buttons on his pants instead of a zipper."

He laughed. "Thanks, I'll make a note of it. Well, sorry I couldn't be of more help, Vic."

"By the way, what's his visa status?"

"He has a visitor's visa. He's trying to get a permanent one, apparently. That could take years."

We talked for a while about other things, including Moore-Gann's murder. Mort was interested in the idea that Magda might have been the real target of the poisoner, and asked me to contact him if I learned anything about either Modzalewski or Magda that I thought he'd like to know. I said I would, and hung up.

I went into the living room and told Sabina what he'd said, but she just nodded absentmindedly and returned to her book. That made twice in a row she'd given me the brushoff; I went and took a long, hot bath, which helped a little but not much.

Bruno appeared at ten o'clock with an extra-large pizza and a guilty expression. "Anyone hungry?" he cried cheerily. "Sabina?"

She turned a page, ignoring him. This was not normal—usually she says hello.

I said, "I could eat. What kind is it?"

"Mushroom and sausage." Her favorite. He opened the top of the box and steam eddied into the air. I saw her eyes swivel slightly in his direction and wondered how long she'd hold out.

I stood up. "I'll get plates and some beer." I headed for the kitchen.

When I returned he was saying "I had no intention of spending the whole afternoon with her, Sabina. It just sort of happened." He spread his hands helplessly, and I gathered the lunch with Vita had escalated. "She wanted to visit the Shelburne Museum. It seemed pretty close, so I said 'Fine.' How was I supposed to know there was only one road you could take, and they were doing construction? Traffic was totally tied up coming and going. Was that my fault?"

Sabina said, "You could have called." She took a wedge of pizza and reached for a napkin as I put down the tray on the coffee table.

He said, "Well, I'm sorry. By the way, Vita told me about some of Moore-Gann's affairs." He dangled the tidbit, like a dead mouse before a cat.

"And?" she said coolly.

"She said he made a pass at her one time, wanted them to have an affair, and she refused."

"Probably it was the other way around," Sabina said caustically. "I can't see her saying no to anything in pants. What else did you and your . . . museum piece talk about?"

175

Bruno looked pained. "Sabina, she's an old friend. Her husband has cancer, she's going through a rough time." He took a plate and selected the largest slice of pizza. I took the next biggest. We started eating. "She also told me Moore-Gann had an affair with a stenographer at a two-week conference in Finland, and another in New York with a Eurasian woman who was a tour guide for a group of Chinese physicists at a weekend meeting—that was the type of thing he went in for. Brief and not serious."

I said, "So maybe Theresa was right to ignore it, in a way."

"You think she knew about them?" Bruno reached for a can of beer.

"I know she did, she told me so. I don't mean she knew about those two in particular, though she may have. She claims Moore-Gann told her everything—and I think he really did, judging from the fact that she even knew he'd made a pass at Magda."

Bruno looked surprised. "Magda? Really?"

"Yes. Apparently she spurned him, and after that they were just good friends. So Magda claims, anyway."

He mulled that over as he took another slice. Tomato sauce had spattered on his tie, and a string of cheese decorated his beard. I'd collected a few crumbs on my knees, which I brushed off carefully. Sabina, taking dainty but remorseless bites, was well into her second slice and still immaculate. She wasn't talking, but I could tell she was paying attention. Bruno said, "Vita doesn't believe there was anything between Moore-Gann and Magda, even though she's heard some speculation. The women he had affairs with were never intellectuals, so Magda isn't his usual type."

"Theresa's an intellectual," Sabina pointed out.

"Well—of course, but he *married* her. Vita also thinks Magda is too ambitious to do anything that might give other physicists the idea she was getting credit for work that wasn't completely her own. The general impression about Magda is that she intends to win the Nobel prize. As Vita put it: 'What she wants is a prize, not a prizewinner.'"

"Unlike Vita herself," said Sabina.

"Wouldn't most women like to be married to a Nobel prizewinner? Wouldn't you? Not that you should get your hopes up."

"I haven't thought about it," said Sabina. "Vicarious achievements don't interest me."

"You really don't care?"

"Not at all."

"That's good." He actually sounded relieved. Theoretical physicists never get over the feeling that they ought to win the Nobel prize. "By the way, I did find out one thing that may interest you."

After a moment Sabina said, "Vita told you what Moore-Gann said to Sachs when they shook hands."

"Oh, you guessed. Well, you're right, but I can't see that it's helpful. What he told Saul was, quote, 'I was sorry to hear you've been ill. I've learned what it means to suffer.' Unquote."

"That's it? That's all?"

Bruno nodded.

Sabina looked thoughtful. "'I was sorry to hear you've been ill. I've learned what it means to suffer.' Yes, I believe he had. Yes, certainly."

She knew something, and I had no idea what it was. This irked me. I said, "According to Theresa, he was happy." We sat in silence, mulling things over. Finally I said, "Frankly, I don't see that what he said to Sachs tells us much."

The pizza was gone. Sabina said, "Did Vita say anything else?"

"Only that she knew for a fact that Moore-Gann was going to be named ambassador to one of the Scandinavian countries very soon. She thought it was ludicrous, that's the word she used. I'm not quite sure why."

It was getting late and I was tired. Bruno produced a bag of mint-flavored Oreos but I decided to go straight to bed. I said good night and left Bruno and Sabina to divvy up the Oreos without me.

At 3 A.M. a thunderclap awakened me. I went to the bathroom and saw that the light was on in the living room, so

177

I went downstairs and found Sabina curled up under a blanket on the sofa, still reading.

"Hi," I said. "You're going to be sorry tomorrow."

"Oh, hello, Vic." She stifled a yawn and sat up, placing the open book facedown on her lap. I was getting curious about what she was reading and I circled around behind her, where I could see the title: *The Good Soldier*. The name rang a bell but I couldn't place it. It wasn't anything I'd ever read.

"Good book?" I said.

"It's a horrifying book. Horrifying and marvelous—about the destructive undercurrents beneath the surface of lives that seem to be eminently civilized." She placed a finger on the cover of the book. "It also told me who killed Hervé Moore-Gann."

"You don't say. Care to let me in on it?"

She shook her head. "So far there's no proof—not a shred. And I'm worried. Vic, how long is it since anyone has seen Jordan?"

"I saw him late Saturday afternoon, at Gerald and Brad's house."

"Where he was so frightened that he ran away. And when you spoke to Judith twenty-four hours later she still hadn't seen him and didn't know where he was."

"She seemed concerned about it, too. But maybe he came home tonight. For all we know, he's asleep in his bed."

"I wish I were sure of that. I have an idea Jordan knows something about the murder, that he saw or heard something, even if he doesn't understand the implications."

"Then why should he be scared?"

"I don't know, Vic. That's what puzzles me. Unless he told someone who *did* understand the implications."

"And maybe that someone was the murderer?"

She shook her head. "We don't know, it's all speculation—but I want to speak to him. In the morning I'd like you to find him and bring him to me—try Judith's house first and then Gerald's place in West Bolton or wherever else you think he might be."

I remembered the trench Jordan had been digging on the

Institute grounds, the rusty spade and the abandoned shrubs. "You don't think anything's happened to him, do you?"

There was a worried crease between her eyebrows when her eyes met mine. "I hope not." She opened the book again. "Why don't you go back to bed, Vic?"

"What about you? It's three in the morning, you're not going to be good for much tomorrow if you don't get some sleep."

"Soon," she said. "Good night, Vic."

# TWENTY-FOUR

Early the next morning I parked in front of Judith's bungalow. It was small and cheaply built, sheathed in buff-colored, aluminum siding, one of a row of ten houses that were identical except that some had attached garages and others didn't. Judith's house had a garage.

It was a cold, damp, cloudy morning, and woodsmoke was trailing from the chimneys of nine of the ten houses; every house but Judith's. Did that mean she wasn't up yet, or didn't she bother to make a fire before going to work? Maybe she didn't have a woodstove.

I got out of the car. As I started up the asphalt driveway, a stout, white-haired woman in a plaid wool jacket and rubber boots popped up from behind the bushes on the far side of a chain-link fence that separated Judith's property from the house next door.

"Morning," she said. There was a trowel in her hand. "Visiting Mrs. Wiley?"

"And her son," I said. "That's right."

"I haven't seen that boy of hers around for a couple of days. They reach a certain age, they start to roam. Know what I mean?" She had a pudgy, good-humored face that was red from bending over. "You a friend of theirs?"

"In a way."

"They don't have too many visitors, not that it's any of my business. I don't believe in butting in where I'm not wanted. Folks want to keep to themselves, I say let them." Her eyes flickered toward Judith's house, where there was still no sign of life. No smoke in the chimney, no twitch of a curtain in a

180

window, no sound of a radio. On the weatherbeaten forehead of Judith's neighbor, worry lines had appeared. "Quiet this morning. Course, they're usually pretty quiet."

I said, "Have you and the Wileys been neighbors for a long time?"

"Ten—twelve years. Can't say I know them much better today than the day they moved in. But they're quiet, mostly. Except for last night." The worry lines reappeared.

"Oh? What happened last night?"

"I didn't say anything happened. Just the car woke me up around midnight."

"Somebody coming home?"

"I thought so. Now I don't know. I woke up again around one and I could still hear the car. Woke up again and the motor was still running. Funny. Then it stopped, so I went back to sleep."

I looked around. "I don't see any car now."

"No. Well, you wouldn't. Most times she parks it in the garage. Guess I better not keep you from your business." Trowel in hand, the white-haired neighbor moved off down the chain-link fence and bent over a flowerbed.

I hurried up the driveway, turned down a narrow cement path that led to the front door, and rang the bell. There was no answer. I rang some more and then tried the door. It opened. Over my shoulder I could see Judith's neighbor watching me. When she saw me looking at her, she bent down and resumed her gardening. I went inside.

"Hello!" I called, but no one answered. I looked around the house, which didn't take long; there were only five rooms—living room, dining room, kitchen, and two small bedrooms, all empty. Both beds were made. Neither Judith nor her son had slept in the house that night, or else they'd made their beds and left early. I looked at my watch. It was a few minutes before eight o'clock.

There was only one place left to look.

I opened the door that led from the kitchen to the garage. It was dark but I could make out the shape of the car; there was a strong smell of exhaust and oil. I flicked on the light, saw that someone was slumped behind the wheel, and slammed the garage door shut and retreated into the kitchen where I took a couple of deep breaths. Then I threw the windows open. After a minute or two I filled my lungs with air, held my breath, opened the door again, dashed into the garage and yanked the car door open. The someone behind the wheel, as I'd known it would be, was Judith, and she'd been dead for hours; when I touched her body it was cold and stiff. Her face was cherry red, the classic sign of carbon monoxide poisoning. I went back into the kitchen, stuck my head out the window, and took a few good deep breaths. Then I returned to the garage. This time I found a note, lying beside her on the front seat: *"Spare me your sympathy, I have no regrets. Judith Wiley."*

That was all. She'd written it on a torn-off scrap of paper. For a while I sat in the living room feeling dizzy and wondering whether I'd inhaled more carbon monoxide than I'd thought. Then I called Sabina. I could tell from her voice that I'd awakened her; she must still have been asleep on the living-room couch where I'd seen her when I'd tiptoed out of the house in Burlington less than an hour earlier. I told her what I'd found.

"Dead?" she said, sounding groggy. She's not a morning person. "Judith? Suicide?"

"It sure looks that way."

"I don't believe it! You're sure she's dead?"

"She's been dead for hours."

There was a silence. "I should have realized . . . maybe if I'd said something to Eaken. . . ." She was awake now, and she wasn't happy. "Is Jordan there?"

"No sign of him, and his bed hasn't been slept in."

Another silence. "You'd better notify the police and wait for them to arrive—the neighbor saw you go in. I doubt they'll keep you long. When they let you go, try to find Jordan."

"Then we're still working? You don't think Judith killed Moore-Gann and committed suicide? Because it sure looks that way."

182

She snapped, "Certainly we're still working. Suicide makes no sense, none at all. Judith would never have left her son to fend for himself, it's totally out of character."

I called the police, and while I waited for them to arrive I searched the house. There was a desk in Judith's bedroom, but it contained no papers of any interest, aside from the deed to the house, which Judith and Jordan owned jointly, and a life insurance policy for fifty thousand dollars naming Jordan as beneficiary. I didn't think fifty thousand dollars would last long in his hands—that is, if he ever saw any of it. Whether he would or not was questionable, considering the way his mother seemed to have died—which was another reason for doubting the "suicide." If Judith had wanted to kill herself, wouldn't she have tried to make it look like an accident so her son could collect the insurance money?

There was a remarkable absence of souvenirs, keepsakes, old letters, clippings—not so much as a recipe torn from a magazine. Clearly the dead woman hadn't been the sentimental type, or else there was nothing in her past she cared to be reminded of. The only thing of interest that turned up, unless you count a half-finished pink-and-green afghan that Judith had been crocheting—I found it hard to imagine her crocheting—was a bundle of old checkbooks in a shoebox in the closet. I skimmed through them and found that in addition to her biweekly salary checks she'd made unexplained deposits for varying amounts ranging from $200 to $1,500 at irregular intervals over the years. It's amazing how many people who are careful to throw out everything else hang on to their old check stubs forever. I think this is because everybody in the United States expects to be audited by the Internal Revenue Service eventually.

Captain Eaken and his men arrived. They aired out the garage with a couple of big fans and then the photographer started snapping pictures of the car and the body and the note and the crumpled newspaper that had been stuffed into the cracks around the garage door. While this was going on, Captain Eaken questioned me in the living room in a manner that was almost friendly. Despite having informed me and Sabina only yesterday that Jean-Paul was the murderer, he now seemed convinced that Judith's death was a suicide motivated by remorse over having killed Hervé Moore-Gann. He seemed relieved, in fact. Probably he'd been plenty worried that he'd never get enough evidence for a conviction in the case, which had to be the most sensational of his career.

"So," he said. "You just happened to drop by at seven forty-five and discovered the body. Mind if I ask how come this early-morning visit?"

"Investigating," I said politely. "Just wanted to ask Judith a few questions about Professor Moore-Gann. It seems they had an affair at one time." I didn't mention Jordan.

He gave me a pitying look. "I could have told you that, and so could a lot of other people in Burlington. You just find out?" He shrugged. "Well, we're none of us perfect. Hell, I took Jean-Paul Brocchiu into custody last night. Now I'll have to let him go. By the way, the Tenofska woman was with him in his room when we picked him up—what'd I tell you?" He gave a self-satisfied smile. "Anyway, all this lets him out. Lets everybody out, I figure." He shook his head, frowning. "Poor old Judith. I've known her all my life, you might say. Wouldn't have believed she'd end up a suicide. Leastways not now—too spunky, whatever else you might want to say about her. Just goes to show."

"What do you mean, 'not now'?"

"Well—" He hesitated. "Twenty years ago I might have thought different. She went through some real hard times— that rape case, especially."

"Rape case?"

"Haven't heard about that yet, huh? Well, no harm in telling you. The year the Institute opened there were quite a few servicemen passing through Burlington because of Vietnam, and some of them used to get into a little trouble; mostly drunk and disorderly, or joy-riding in some citizen's car— nothing real serious. But there were a couple of nasty incidents. One of them involved Judith. She was real good-looking then, had a nice little shape, wasn't so skinny, like she got later. It was common knowledge that she and Moore-Gann were carrying on, and I can tell you she wasn't thought of too highly in the town. Girls were supposed to have morals in those days, and if you want my opinion they were a lot better off because of it. Anyway, Judith went to a bar down by the waterfront one night by herself—some said she'd had an argument with her boyfriend and wanted to get even, pick some feller up, others said that wasn't true. She drank some beer and danced with a bunch of marines that happened to be in the bar, and around midnight she left to walk home. Usually a girl could walk home alone and be perfectly safe—and there's plenty of places in Vermont where that's still true.

"But not that night. There were different versions of what happened, but as near as I can tell, four of those boys got in a car and drove up the road ahead of her and then ambushed her in a patch of woods she had to walk through. Raped her at knifepoint, beat her and left her in a ditch." He shook his head. "It was a bad business. There was a trial, but the men were acquitted. After that I heard Moore-Gann wouldn't have anything to do with her. Or the pregnancy. Understandable, in a way."

"You think so?"

"I don't say it was right. Just understandable. Not to Judith, of course—looks like she didn't understand at all, looks like she killed him because of it, twenty years later when she finally got the chance."

I shook my head. "Twenty years is a long time, Eaken. How come those guys were acquitted?"

He shrugged. "Like I said, things were different back then. She had a bad reputation, there was a lot of patriotic feeling, plenty of hawks in Burlington, and the defense lawyer played on it. The men said she'd led them on, she'd asked for it, she'd teased them. Stuff like that. The jury bought it. After the trial she left town, and when she came back a year later she had a baby with her."

"And a story about having married a soldier who'd died in Vietnam."

"That's right. That's how it was. People acted like they believed it, if you know what I mean. Sort of live and let live, and she kept to herself. Maybe the townsfolk felt guilty because of the acquittal. Maybe they should have. In my opinion it was a miscarriage of justice, but—things were different then."

"Yeah. Better, you said. Better for women."

"For the ones that played by the rules, sure. Judith didn't. Well, you can see where it got her."

I stood up. "I'd like to go now. That okay with you?"

"Yep. No reason to keep you, according to the doctor she died around one A.M. and you didn't get here until six–seven hours later. Though I don't see why you're in a hurry, you don't have to do any more detecting." He grinned. "Looks to me like this case is over."

# TWENTY-FIVE

Back at the Institute I parked beside the big spruce. As I got out of the microbus I saw a figure bent over a shovel near the manure-filled trench in which Jordan had been planting shrubs on Friday. He was back! I hurried toward him, but as I got closer I saw that it was not Jordan but somebody else, a heavily built man dressed in dirty work clothes. He wore thick leather boots that laced up the ankle, and with these he now began stomping the ground down solidly around the roots of a bush.

I said, "Hi."

His head swiveled and he gave me an incurious stare. The skin of his face was darkened in streaky patches, as if the unwashed grime of months or years had worked its way into his pores, and I could see that he'd lost most of his front teeth and hadn't bothered to have them replaced. Their absence puckered the skin around his lips and gave him the expression of an old man, though he couldn't have been more than forty and looked to be in good shape.

I said, "Have you seen Jordan around anywhere?"

A dark gob of chewing tobacco sailed past me and landed in the trench. "Nope." He picked up the shovel.

"Well, do you have any idea where he might be?"

"Nope."

"You the new gardener?"

"Nope." He tossed a shovelful of manure into the trench.

I could see I'd better ask him questions that couldn't be answered yes or no, especially no. "What's your name?"

"Bill."

"And what do you do around here, if you don't mind my asking?"

"I'm the caretaker." Three whole words, that was encouraging.

"I'm looking for Jordan. It's really kind of important. Nobody seems to have seen him for several days and he hasn't gone home. Where do you think he could be?"

Bill shook his head and wiped the back of his hand against his chin, depositing a new smudge of dirt that blended into the layers that were already there. "Dunno. Took himself off, left ten bushes sitting in the air. Good thing we had that rain yesterday or I don't know." He shook his head again and grumbled, "Not rightly my work. Can't just let 'em die though, can I? Cost good money."

"You're right, Jordan shouldn't have left them like that," I commiserated. "I'll tell him you said so when I find him. Where do you suppose he is?"

Bill shrugged. "Hiding in the woods, maybe."

"Why would he want to do that?"

"Dunno." He tapped his forehead with his finger. "Hard to figure that boy."

"I bet you know these woods pretty well yourself. Are you saying you wouldn't know where to find him if you were to look for him?"

"Maybe yes, maybe no."

I took out my wallet and removed a ten. "How about giving it a try?"

Another gob of tobacco flew past me. "Mister, I got my work to do. He'll come out when he's good and ready." I took out a twenty and Bill stretched out a dirty hand. The twenty vanished into his pocket. "Won't give no guarantees," he said. "Could be you're wasting your money."

I stepped back just in time to avoid a shovelful of manure.

Up at the administration building there was nobody around—no physicists cruising the bulletin boards, no Gerald at his desk. No Judith down the hall at hers, that was for damned sure. And when I'd parked the car I hadn't seen the usual groups of physicists talking theory on the lawn. Where was everyone?

I looked at my watch. The police were bound to arrive at the Institute any minute, and they'd want to search Judith's office; I figured I might as well beat them to the punch. I slipped down the hall and into the room where I'd talked to her only the day before.

Her desk, I soon learned, was just as bare of personal papers as the one in her bedroom had been. There were letters, but all of them concerned Institute business. Finding nothing of interest, I moved on to the metal file cabinet by the window, not feeling particularly hopeful and not discovering anything of interest until I opened the bottom drawer. It was only half full, and at the back of the drawer, under a crocheted shawl, I found an empty bottle of Digoxin with Saul Sachs's name on the label.

I left the bottle where I'd found it. Either Judith had killed Moore-Gann—or else the murderer was making sure to be very thorough.

I left Judith's office, wondering what to do next. If Jordan was holed up somewhere in the woods I knew I wouldn't find him, I'd never been an Eagle Scout; maybe Bill would have better luck.

I had a nasty feeling that our employment in this case was likely to terminate at any moment. Last night Sabina had said she knew who the murderer was; if in fact she did I wished she'd tell me, so that together we could try to dig up some evidence. Otherwise, I felt certain all the physicists, including our client, would be only too glad to see the case closed, with the guilty party not only a nonphysicist whom no one had liked but, even better, a corpse. What could be neater? There would be no trial, no testimony, no embarrassing revelations. . . .

If Judith wasn't the murderer, who was? Probably not Jean-Paul Brocchiu, who had spent the night in jail; it was hard to believe there were two killers roaming the Institute.

I emerged into the reception hall and found Gerald at his

desk. He looked up as I approached, saying "Oh, it's you, Vic. I thought everyone was at Theresa's talk."

"Is that where they've gone?"

"Yes. Over in the barn. Aren't you going? It's supposed to be terribly historic." He made a grimace. "The plan was for this to be our Nobel laureate day, you know, Moore-Gann in the morning and Sachs in the afternoon, both the same day so nobody could get insulted. It makes for kind of a heavy day but sometimes these great brains can be incredibly childish. Take the word of one who knows."

"Maybe I'll go hear Theresa's talk," I said. "The end of it, anyway. By the way, have you seen Jordan lately?"

"No, I have not," he said with emphasis. "Not a hair of his gorgeous red head, and Brad's in an awful snit about it. Jordan was supposed to transplant some roses for us and he hasn't showed up. So you'll have to ask Judith—lucky you." He frowned. "That is, when she shows up. She *should* be here, but she hasn't come and she hasn't called. Maybe it runs in the family—though it's not really like her." He sounded perplexed.

"I don't think she could make it." I headed for the door.

Behind me, Gerald said, "You saw her? You talked to her?"

"I saw her," I replied as I left the building.

I reached the barn at twenty of twelve. Theresa's talk was almost over. There was a big crowd—not just physicists but their spouses and children, as well, which I hadn't expected. They sat in the barn's odd assortment of chairs, which had been pulled up into a dense semicircle; all the chairs were filled and behind them people were standing, silent and attentive. The vast, windowless space was dim and—despite the fire that burned in the fireplace—cold and damp, as if the rawness of yesterday's rain had soaked into the walls and floor.

Theresa stood beneath the unforgiving glare of a spotlight that was fastened to the roof. Her tall, limber, hiker's frame seemed to have grown gaunt overnight, and there were harsh shadows in the sockets of her eyes and under her nose and chin. She was speaking rapidly, in a clear, resonant voice that echoed against the bare walls. Sometimes she gestured with a piece of chalk, sometimes scrawled a few symbols on the blackboard that stood behind her. As she talked she walked back and forth behind a wooden podium where papers were spread out. She didn't look at them; she was lecturing extemporaneously and seemed totally absorbed in her performance.

I found a spot in the back, with the standees. Theresa was saying "And although it is true that the unified gauge theory approach to the interactions of quarks and leptons has had much success, climaxed by the discovery of the predicted $W$ and $Z$ bosons at CERN, there are, as you know, still a number of unsatisfactory features . . ."

Her words conveyed nothing to me, but there was no mistaking the air of authority in her presentation, even though—or perhaps because—her tone was almost argumentative. She seemed to be debating some tough and skeptical, if invisible, opponent: not her audience but her dead husband, maybe; or maybe God. She seemed a very different person from the woman in the lonely kitchen the night before.

She was saying ". . . The major conceptual difference between string theories and the field theories is that the fundamental objects are not thought of as pointlike but stringlike; and that vibrations of these strings can be identified with the leptons, quarks, and gauge bosons." She paused to draw two loops and a wiggly line on the blackboard. Then she rubbed out part of an earlier diagram with an impatient swipe of her forearm and wiped off the chalk on her skirt, on which there were already several smudges. "The superstring theories offer the incredibly exciting possibility of constructing for the first time a finite quantum theory of gravity. . . ."

The physicists in her audience were totally absorbed; some were taking notes in the semidarkness.

The barn door opened, screeching as it scraped the cement floor. Gerald, his face pale and shocked, entered with a piece of paper in his hand—a message, I guessed, about Judith's death—and brought it to Florian Gawthrop, who was sitting in the front row next to Saul Sachs. A moment later Florian rose, stooping as he crossed in front of Theresa, and hurried from the barn with Gerald. Theresa's voice wavered and went on: "Unfortunately for mathematical consistency, one requires a ten-dimensional space-time, so one must rely on the idea of compactification to find realistic models, as in the Kaluza-Klein approach . . ."

Twenty minutes later the talk came to an end. There was loud applause and then Saul Sachs rose from his seat in the first row, still clapping, and stood until one by one the others got up, too, and gave Theresa a standing ovation. She flushed, smiling, and shook her head as she leaned against the podium, her body sagging with fatigue. Someone turned up the lights, the applause tapered off, and the audience began to trickle out of the barn while a number of physicists, among them Pesnik and Modzalewski, came up to Theresa to ask questions. Magda rose and I caught her eye, but when I moved in her direction she turned her face away—angry, I figured, because I hadn't kept Jean-Paul from being arrested. Well, he'd soon be free if he wasn't already.

She went up to Theresa and put an arm around her waist, whispering something in the ear of the older woman, who shook her head and smiled, and then turned her attention back to the group of which she was the center. Pesnik was scribbling on the blackboard and talking excitedly as he made a point. Beside him, the big Pole was listening and scratching his head. Magda climbed down from the podium and left the barn. Saul Sachs came up and held out his hand to Theresa, who took it after a brief hesitation.

In the audience, Vita rose and yawned. She swiveled her sleek dark head and looked over her shoulder as if searching for someone. She was wearing black stretch pants and a tight turquoise sweater that matched the strands of Indian beads that cascaded down between her breasts. She caught sight of Bruno and started in his direction. At the same moment, he headed rapidly toward me. I wasn't sure he'd seen her but I thought he had; I wondered if he'd decided to play it safe, and whether Sabina was still mad at him. He took my arm and hustled me out of the barn while I said, "You seem to be in a hurry, Bruno. What'd you think of Theresa's talk?"

We were walking double-time, his hand still on my elbow. "It was superb, Vic. A great talk. I'm glad you were here—could you follow much of it?" He darted a quick look behind us. Apparently whatever he saw reassured him, because he slowed to a normal pace.

I said, "Only that it was about these superstrings everyone's been trying to explain to me, without a whole lot of success."

"She was giving an overview," he said. "Pulling together what physicists in different countries have been doing in the last few years, explaining where they agree and disagree, and where there's a need for future research. It was really a wonderful synthesis of a big, messy, difficult topic—it showed an amazing depth of scholarship. Of course the bulk of the work must have been done by Moore-Gann, it had his touch, but still Theresa's performance was impressive. It'll be interesting to see how her career develops, with Moore-Gann dead. She's certainly a bright woman."

"You think she'll become better known as a physicist in her own right?"

Bruno nodded. "I wouldn't be surprised. You know, people have wondered for years just how much influence she had on his work. She always critiqued his papers before he submitted them for publication, and how much more she did is anybody's guess. After today I think there'll be quite a bit of speculation about that."

We had reached the administration building. I was about to mention Judith's death when he said, "Let's go in for a minute, I need to pick up my mail."

We went upstairs and headed for the mailroom, passing Magda who was holding an airmail envelope with foreign stamps on it. Her head was bent as she carefully tore it open. I said, "Hi," but she didn't look up.

Bruno picked up his mail and stuffed it in the shopping bag he always carried instead of a briefcase. Then he said, "Vic, do you mind if I ask your advice?" He tugged at his beard the way he does when he's worried. "Let's have lunch together."

"You can have my advice any time," I said. "For what it's worth. But I don't think I should go to lunch, I need to talk to Sabina. Something's happened—you haven't heard yet." I told him about Judith's death and Jordan's disappearance as we walked out to the driveway.

He was appalled. "But how horrible, to die like that! The poor woman!" He gave a shudder. "And the boy—what's going to happen to him, with his mother gone? You can say what you like about Judith, at least she was a devoted mother." Bruno could find something to like about a boa constrictor wrapped around his waist.

I filled him in on a few more details. When I mentioned the note, he shook his head. Then he said, "You know, Vic, it's a terrible thing. Terrible, but I can't help being glad it's all over."

There was a note of relief in his tone, and I knew it was the voice of the physics community I'd just heard, the sound of a consensus that would form as soon as the news was generally known. I said, "Sabina doesn't think it's over."

"Sabina," he said nervously. Halfway up the hill we could see Vita coming down, walking between her husband and Pesnik. Bruno grabbed my arm again. "At least come to my office for a few minutes. It's not far, it's in the Chicken House."

"Chicken House?"

"It used to be an old chicken house," he said distractedly as he steered me down a gravel path.

When we got to his office we sat down in a couple of hard wooden chairs in front of a blackboard covered with equations.

"Vic, you're a bachelor," he said. "You've had a lot of experience with women."

"It doesn't necessarily follow, Bruno."

He smiled as if I'd made a joke. Then his face became serious. Behind his glasses, his kind brown eyes were troubled.

194

He sighed. "I don't know how I got into this in the first place," he said, and fell into a gloomy silence.

I said, "Is it Vita?" He nodded, his expression guilty yet relieved that I'd guessed. I said, "Don't tell me there's really something going on between you two."

"Depends how you define 'going on.' You won't mention this to Sabina, will you?"

"God, no. What would be the point?" I studied his short, tubby body, the chalk-smudged pants and baggy tweed jacket, the unevenly trimmed beard, his general air of absentminded dilapidation. I said, "I'm sorry, Bruno, but somehow I can't imagine a torrid love affair between you and Vita Sachs."

"Why not?" he demanded indignantly. There was chalk on his jacket, too. "I went to bed with her, Vic." I could hardly believe my ears and then he added, "Years ago, of course." Years ago was different. "There was a mixup, I went to their house for a physics reception and it turned out I had the wrong night. Saul wasn't home and—one thing led to another, you know how it is. It was just the one time, I didn't feel right about going on with it because I was still married to Babs, even though the marriage was falling apart. I won't go into all that—that's not the point." He leaned forward. "The trouble is, she wants a replay. She wants it *now*."

"Does she." Sabina's intuition had been right as usual—more than she knew, and more than she was going to find out if I could help it; she needed to put her energies into solving this case, not into a domestic crisis. I said, "Bruno, this should be your worst problem. Just tell Vita you're not interested. You're not, are you?"

He shook his head and said with only a trace of regret, "No, no, it's out of the question. I love Sabina, you know that. Anyway she's got ESP, there's no way I could keep her from finding out if there were really something going on. She's already suspicious. And *then*—" He winced at the thought.

"I get the message. By the way, where were you yesterday afternoon? Did you really go to a museum?"

He shook his head, looking guilty. "I'm afraid I didn't tell Sabina the truth, Vic. We started for the museum all right, but we ended up having a picnic on the shores of Lake Champlain. A scenic spot Vita happened to know about. We were alone." He sighed. "At first we talked about Saul, his illness, the problems she's been having with him—she's been through a rough time, Vic. She said he was very edgy about seeing Moore-Gann after all these years and even accused her of intending to have an affair with him. That was when she mentioned that Moore-Gann had made a pass at her when he and Saul were collaborators. She said Saul knew about it. I asked if that was what had caused the breakup and she said it wasn't, that had happened over a year later. 'He never told me why he stopped speaking to Moore-Gann,' she said. 'But you can be sure it wasn't about *me*.' She feels Saul takes her for granted, uses her as a scapegoat. She said, 'Whenever anything bothers him, he takes it out on me.' Then she started to cry. . . ." He fell silent.

"Uh-oh." I could see it coming. "And you, being you, innocently put your arms around her to comfort her."

"How did you know?"

"And as it had once before, one thing led to another."

"It's not what you're thinking," he protested virtuously. "We didn't have sex."

"What did you have?"

"Well—we necked," he admitted. I hadn't heard anybody use that expression since my high-school days. "I guess you could call it heavy petting." He cleared his throat. "I shouldn't have done it, I know that. I have to be honest, I encouraged her. Now she has expectations, and how do I get out of it?"

"Bruno, she set it up—that deserted spot she just 'happened to know' and all that. She's no kid, she likes attention from men. I don't know what kind of arrangement she and Saul have but I'd be willing to bet she's slept around a fair amount. You won't break her heart if you tell her thanks but no thanks."

Bruno shook his head. "You don't understand Vita," he

196

said reproachfully. "She's a vibrant, affectionate woman who's going through a terrible ordeal and she needs warmth, she needs support—"

"She needs sex—"

"That, too. After all, with Saul in the shape he's in—"

"All right, she needs sex, but does it have to be from you?"

"Well—no. I couldn't get involved. Really, Vic, I don't want to." A flicker of panic showed in his eyes. "God, no, I couldn't handle it."

"Then tell her to get lost—in a nice way, naturally, since she's an old friend, not to mention the wife of a Nobel prizewinner."

He shook his head again. "I couldn't! It's not possible. She's too vulnerable now, too—"

"Spare me. The trouble is, you can't say no."

"I don't want to hurt her."

Hoo, boy. "Okay, Bruno, I'll see if I can help. That what you want?"

"Would you?"

"I'll try to get her to let you off the hook."

Relief shone in his eyes. "But in a nice way."

"I already said, in a nice way."

"And whatever you do, don't tell Sabina."

I said, "I don't know why I'm letting you manipulate me into this."

He looked hurt. "If you don't want to—"

"Never mind. I said I'd do it."

# TWENTY-SIX

Sabina had gone home. I found her in the living room, sitting in a chair she'd pulled up to face the window, staring outside. She wasn't reading, she wasn't painting, she wasn't drinking tea, she wasn't doing anything. "Hello, Vic," she said in a depressed voice as I came into the house. She didn't look around.

I sat down on the couch. I knew this mood. "Look," I said. "It's not your fault. You didn't kill Judith. Can I get you a cup of tea?"

"I don't want anything. Vic, if I'd spoken to Captain Eaken yesterday—told him whom I suspected and why . . . . But there's no evidence, none at all. I don't think he'd have believed me. Still—"

"Without evidence?" I shook my head. "He was convinced Jean-Paul was the murderer. Matter of fact, he arrested him last night. So if you have egg on your face you're not the only one."

"There's no comparison. A woman has died."

"A woman everybody detested."

"It's not our business to pass judgments."

"Don't tell me you're getting religion." She didn't reply. "Of course you could have told *me*." She gave a limp wave of the hand as if to dismiss the idea that telling me could have made a difference. "Well, you could have."

We sat in silence for a while. Then she said, "Where is Jordan?"

"Holed up in the woods, probably. That's what the care-taker said and he seems to know him pretty well. I have a

198

hunch Jordan's okay, Sabina. He's done this kind of thing before."

"I hope you're right." She slid down deeper into her chair. I couldn't see her face, just the back of her head; the gray-brown hair she'd fastened into a bun was coming loose, and strands hung down her neck. Automatically she started tucking them up, taking the tortoiseshell hairpins out of the bun and jabbing them back in. "Hey," I said. "One day you're going to give yourself a lobotomy with those things, and I'll be out of a job."

Weakly, she laughed. Then she said fretfully, "How can you say Jordan's okay? His mother's dead."

"He has fifty thousand dollars, or he will when Judith's insurance is processed. Once you've proved her death wasn't a suicide, that is."

She sat up a little straighter. "Yes, but who'll manage it for him? He won't be able to do it himself."

"Sabina, that is not your problem."

"I guess not. But it's sad, nevertheless. Pathetic." She turned her face toward me. "Jordan knows something, Vic."

I said, "Why are you so sure Judith wasn't the killer? Frankly, her death looked like suicide to me: the newspaper stuffed in the cracks, the note—and when I searched her office, I found the missing bottle of Digoxin. It was in a file cabinet."

"Where Judith left it for the police to find any time they cared to look? Please. As for the note, there's not a word about Moore-Gann's death. She could have written it any-time, about anything. You said it was on a torn-off scrap of paper?"

"Yes."

There was a knock on the door.

"See who it is," she said. She stood up and pushed her chair around until it faced the room, which meant she was starting to feel better.

I looked through the curtain that covered the glass pane in the door. "The client," I said. "What do you want to bet we're about to be fired?"

I opened the door. "Hello, Victor," said Florian, and shook my hand, something he hadn't done before. It was the kiss of death, for sure. "Is Sabina—oh, there you are, my dear. Well, good."

"Come in," she said. "Have a seat, Florian. Would you like some tea?"

"No, thank you. Nothing, really. I don't think I need to stay all that long." He sat down on the sofa and I took a chair across the room from him. "Well," he said. A look of uncertainty crossed his distinguished face as he smoothed back his straight blond hair. "It would seem the situation has changed—no doubt you've heard?"

"I found the body," I said. "We've heard."

"Ah, in that case, of course—" He cleared his throat. "Naturally this sad event casts a new light on Moore-Gann's death." He really talked like that. "Poor Judith, it's hard to believe she's gone. I've known her since I was a boy. You can say what you like, she had a tragic, tragic life."

"I suppose most people would call it tragic to be murdered," Sabina replied dryly. "And to be technical, even in the classic sense of the word 'tragedy,' as in a Greek tragedy, I would have to agree with them in this case. Judith's death seems to have been the outcome—inevitable, I suppose"—this thought seemed to cheer her up a little—"of the defects in her own character."

Florian leaned forward and said sharply, "But she wasn't murdered, Sabina, she killed herself. She must have felt remorse over having poisoned the man she'd once loved. Or—" Uncertainty drew his brows together for an instant. "Maybe she was afraid she'd be arrested. We'll never know her exact frame of mind, naturally. But in the broad outlines it seems clear." Briskly he added, "We'll have to find someone to take charge of Jordan, a relative, perhaps—though she'd rather estranged herself from her family. However"—he waggled one long finger for emphasis—"at least there's no longer any danger that some innocent man will suffer for her crime. Did you know Jean-Paul was arrested last night?" We nodded. "A terrible mistake. Thank God they've released him. I never believed one of our Institute participants killed Moore-Gann." He fell silent suddenly, as if he'd wound down. Then he said uncertainly, "Surely you're not serious when you suggest that Judith was murdered?"

"I don't suggest it, I state it."

"And have you any evidence?"

"No evidence that would stand up in court."

He shook his head. "The police are sure it was suicide, and after considering the evidence I must tell you I agree with them. Not that I—and the trustees, of course—don't appreciate your efforts, we're quite prepared to reimburse you for your time. Send us your bill—whatever it is, we won't haggle about it." He gave us a condescending smile and leaned forward as if preparing to rise.

Sabina said, "It's not the money, Florian. Do you simply want to protect the physics community from embarrassment, or are you interested in discovering the truth?"

He stood up and said stiffly, "That remark is uncalled for, in my humble opinion. If you have evidence, let's hear it. If you believe someone other than Judith poisoned Moore-Gann, tell me that person's name."

Sabina said nothing. Slowly she shook her head. "I can't—not yet. I need to continue the investigation. Give me another twenty-four hours."

He turned toward the door, ready to put an end to a conversation he found distasteful. "The police are convinced Judith's death was a suicide."

I said, "They were wrong about Jean-Paul, they could be wrong again."

"Vic," said Sabina. "He's made up his mind."

After Florian had gone, Sabina said, "Let's have that tea now."

I headed for the kitchen and put the kettle on to boil. The phone rang in the living room and I heard Sabina pick it up.

"It's for you, Vic," she called.

I picked up the extension. Betsy Fiorentino of the Boston

Police was on the line. "Hi, Vic," she said. "Is somebody else listening?"

"I am," said Sabina.

"How you been, Sabina?"

"Fine, Betsy, except for today."

"What happened today?"

"We were just canned," I said. "And it smarts. Find anything out?"

"Sort of. You asked me whether Florian Gawthrop has a record. Well, he doesn't. No convictions, no arrest record, not a word on the books regarding any crimes, morals violations, unpaid parking tickets, you name it."

"Well, okay. Thanks anyway, Betsy."

"Wait. That's what's on the *record*—or rather, isn't. But I happened to be talking to a guy named Bert Rincone who's due to retire from the force next year. Been around for quite a while. He has a real good memory."

"And?"

"According to Rincone, Gawthrop was arrested around nineteen-seventy or thereabouts and charged with statutory rape and contributing to the delinquency of a minor. The minor in question was a thirteen-year-old boy named Willie Bennett, who used to frequent a neighborhood that was a known hangout for hustlers of both sexes, especially young ones. Apparently Gawthrop was a regular customer of Willie's for a while—Rincone thinks he was genuinely fond of the boy, at least so Gawthrop claimed after he'd been arrested. Gawthrop said he'd taken the kid under his wing, given him good advice, taken him to the ballgame, et cetera, just like a big brother. Which was true as far as it went, only Rincone says it didn't go far enough. The complaint was brought by Willie's mother and stepfather, who usually didn't seem that concerned about what the kid was into. It was one of those multiproblem families, well known to the department: alcoholic mother, father a drug addict who was chronically unemployed, and lots of kids who got into different kinds of trouble. At least two of Willie's sisters were prostitutes."

I said, "So how come there's nothing on the record?"

"Shortly before the case was supposed to go to court, the complaint was withdrawn. Stepfather stated that Willie had made the whole thing up and there'd never been anything but good advice, ballgames, et cetera. Stepfather was very sorry but how could he have known, and he was going to give Willie a beating he wouldn't forget. Rincone is sure the whole thing was a scam and Gawthrop's father paid them off. It's an old Boston family, nothing flashy, just blue-chip stuff, though Gawthrop the son didn't have that much money at the time since he was only an instructor at Boston University. Of course he's rolling in it now that both his parents are dead."

"That's very interesting," I said. "But I'm surprised there's nothing on the record if the case got as far as you say."

"Rincone was surprised, too. It's one of those little mysteries, Vic."

I asked Betsy a few more questions but she had no more information, except that Willie was currently in jail on a narcotics rap, not his first, in spite of all the good advice he'd received, not to mention the beatings. After that the conversation got personal, and Sabina hung up while Betsy was telling me what the doctor had said about the pros and cons of fertility drugs.

When I'd said good-bye to Betsy, Sabina and I sat in the kitchen and drank Russian tea. She drained her cup in silence and then set it down on the table with a rap. "All right!" she said. I was glad to see her back to normal. "No wonder Florian's so eager to close the case. Judith must have been blackmailing him about his old arrest. It stands to reason. He was vulnerable because he was a teacher, and he became even more so once he'd taken his current position as dean of students. We may never know exactly how she found out; there may have been rumors at the time that reached her somehow, and she decided to put them to use."

"Then the deposits in her checkbook came from Florian."

Sabina nodded. "Must have. Theresa sent her money occasionally, but the amounts you mentioned are too large for that. Where else could the money have come from? Not her family—she was estranged from them, and anyway their circumstances were modest—her father cleaned furnaces for a living."

I said, "Florian certainly acted all broken up about her death, didn't he? What was it he said? 'The poor woman had a tragic, tragic life.' Touching, really, considering that I'd expect him to be dancing in the streets because she was finally off his back. He must have been scared to death that you or the police were going to learn his secret. Maybe he killed Judith himself, even if he had nothing to do with Moore-Gann's death, decided this was his chance to get rid of a long-term threat without being suspected. I really don't see why he'd have wanted to poison either Moore-Gann or Magda."

Sabina rose. "I want you to talk to Florian. As for me, I'm going to approach Saul Sachs and see if I can persuade him to authorize us to continue the investigation. After all, he's on the board of trustees and must be very influential. Also I want to ask him what led to his feud with Moore-Gann—although I think I know."

I looked at my watch. "Saul's giving a lecture this afternoon, you won't be able to talk to him till it's over. Most likely Florian will be there, too."

"In that case we'll go to Saul's talk."

"I'd just as soon skip it if you don't mind, I've had enough physics to last me a while."

"Nonsense. Sachs is world-famous, you can't pass up an opportunity like this. It's good for you to stretch your mind a little."

"Is that an order or a suggestion?"

"You can call it an order if you wish. As your employer I have a valid interest in your continuing education. One day you'll thank me."

"Okay. As long as I don't have to thank you now. By the way, haven't you forgotten something?"

"I don't think so."

"Something you were going to tell me? Like who killed Moore-Gann?"

"I think we'd better wait until you've seen Florian and I've spoken to Saul. Then we'll get together and make a plan."

# TWENTY-SEVEN

We found seats in the barn where Saul was lecturing. There was a fair-sized crowd but it wasn't as big as the one that had turned out to hear Theresa, and this time there were few wives and no kids; Saul might be world-famous but he hadn't been murdered, so naturally there wouldn't be as much general interest in his talk.

Under the spotlight he looked frail, but the force of his intellect and the anger, scorn, whatever it was that seemed to be smoldering just below the surface, were palpable. He was saying "I hate to tell you, but a lot of what you're going to hear at this conference is crap. Trendy crap, which is the worst kind because everybody wants to show he can produce it too. This tends to lead to an epidemic of diarrhea, only after a while the stink starts getting in everybody's nose until some smart guy starts sprinkling lime around. Just in time, usually." He jabbed a forefinger at the audience and glared at them, his eyes red-rimmed, rubbing his big nose with the back of his hand. "I hope you're paying attention. Most of you aren't. That's okay. You'll get yours." He shook his finger at them and there was nervous laughter in the audience. "Let me change the metaphor." Lecturing seemed to energize the sick man. His stooped, skinny body had straightened and he kept shuttling back and forth in front of the blackboard. He stopped and studied it for a while. Not much was written on it even though he only had twenty minutes left to go. "I like to use a lot of metaphors, it gives a talk class," he said, shuffling around to face the audience and managing to give the impression that he'd whirled—or that he'd have whirled if he'd been in better shape. "Physics," he declaimed, "is not acrobatics! What the hell, let's throw in another metaphor. Physics is not tightrope walking! You want to forget that, you think you can get away with it. I say 'Ha!' Out there"—he jabbed his finger in the general direction of the roof—"is *something*. Call it whatever you like, the world, the universe, God, physical law. Everything goes together and there's an innate simplicity, even if we have to knock our brains out to get a hint of it, a glimmer. Don't forget that, while you're crapping around with the eight dimensions and the ten dimensions. Sure they're cute, they're fun, they get your name in the *Physical Review Letters*. But is that what it's all about, physics?"

He left the question hanging in the air. After a minute or so there was scattered laughter in the audience, not a whole lot of it.

I noticed Bruno sitting in the front row next to Vita. So she'd managed to corner him and he'd let her get away with it. I was going to have to speak to him. I shot a glance at Sabina and saw that she was looking in their direction, her expression thoughtful, and I knew I'd better do something soon or she was going to be seriously sidetracked. As soon as Saul's lecture was over I would have a word with Vita, though what I was going to say I had no idea.

Several rows behind Bruno I saw Jean-Paul Brocchiu, turning his head to scan the room; beside him Andrzej Modzalewski pressed a large, restraining hand on his shoulder as if to keep him in his seat. I looked around for Magda but she wasn't in the barn. It seemed odd that she hadn't come to hear Sachs, odder that she wasn't with the Corsican now that the police had released him.

In the first row, Theresa and Florian sat side by side, his arm across the back of her chair. What was it with those two? There was something between them, some kind of a bond, yet if what Betsy Fiorentino had told me was true, Florian's sexual tastes didn't run to women.

Saul was winding up his talk. "That's all I have to say. This could be a record, a physicist shutting up when he still has twenty minutes left. I don't want any questions. You either understand what I've been saying or you don't. If you don't, you're hopeless."

He stopped talking. The audience sat there, shifting uncomfortably in their chairs. The applause was light.

Then they started getting up and heading for the door, looking as glum as a crowd filing out of a movie in which the hero has come to a bad end. Sabina said in my ear, "I'll talk to Sachs now," and went up to where he was standing by the blackboard. He was alone, which wasn't surprising since he'd just told his audience that anybody who wanted to ask him a question was hopeless.

Florian and Theresa passed the row where I was sitting, on their way out with a group of physicists; I heard him say ". . . she's been my secretary since the Institute began. I can scarcely believe it."

"It's hard to imagine the place without her," said Theresa, and there were nods of agreement from the others.

Jean-Paul was hurrying toward them through the crowd, followed by Andrzej. "Madame Moore-Gann," he cried. Theresa turned, but when she saw it was Jean-Paul who had called her name she gave him an expressionless stare without replying. "Madame Moore-Gann, forgive the interruption—" He didn't look any the worse for a night in jail though he was obviously upset, nervously licking his thick red lips and sweating, despite the chill of the barn. Theresa turned her back on him and resumed walking toward the door, and Jean-Paul grabbed her arm, saying "Please—where is Magda?" She didn't exactly shake him off, nothing that crude, but in a second he was standing alone and looking confused. "Where is she?" he pleaded.

"I don't know, Dr. Brocchiu."

"Please—just tell me!"

She began walking again, accompanied by Florian, who said over his shoulder, "Sorry, Jean-Paul. I'm afraid we have no idea. Perhaps she went into town."

"But—"

The group filed out of the barn, leaving Jean-Paul standing

beside Andrzej, frustration written all over his handsome, olive-skinned face.

The big Pole put a hand on his shoulder and rumbled, "We have drink now, eh? Is better, you will see." After a moment Jean-Paul nodded, throwing the other man a sullen but grateful look. They left the barn together.

I stood up, wondering what had become of Magda. True, she could have had some innocuous errand, but it bothered me that no one seemed to know her whereabouts. First Jordan, now Magda. Where was she?

Bruno and Vita were heading in my direction, the many-stranded necklace between her breasts rippling as she walked. He caught my eye and shrugged helplessly, as Vita slipped her hand through his arm. I gave him a quick, stern headshake as I intercepted them, saying "There you are, Bruno. Sabina's been looking for you."

"Oh," he said, swiveling his head from side to side as if expecting her to materialize in front of him. "Where is she?"

"Up front." Vita looked at him and then at me as I went on, "So why don't you—"

"Yes," he said with a grateful look. "You'll excuse me, Vita? My wife—" He extricated his arm and was gone.

Vita raised her eyebrows. "What was that all about?"

I took her by the elbow and steered her from the barn. "Don't you smell nice," I said. "Chanel Number Five? An oldie but a goodie."

"That's the general effect I aim for," she said, throwing back her sleek, dark head and looking up at me with a hint of a smile. "I think at this stage it's the best I can do." I was aware of her breasts in the clinging turquoise sweater; between them, the strands of beads winked in the light.

"I don't know about that, but if it's your aim you certainly succeed," I said. "How about a drink?"

The teasing dark eyes met mine. "You just pushed the right button, sonny. This is the second physics talk I've had to sit through today, and that's two too many. I told Saul I didn't want to but"—she shrugged—"*noblesse oblige* and all that old crap. Anyway it's my last for the rest of the summer, I don't care if they resurrect Einstein and stick him in front of a blackboard. Well?"

"Well what?"

"I asked you before. Bruno—are you his keeper, or what?" She gave a little laugh, her eyes watchful.

"Do you think he needs a keeper?"

Her shoulders moved restlessly under the sweater. "I don't know what he needs. I adore Bruno but sometimes I'd like to kick him—ever feel that way?"

"Maybe once or twice." We were walking down the hill, approaching the administration building, my hand still clasping her elbow. She didn't try to remove it. I said, "What do *you* need, Vita?"

She turned her face in my direction. Taking her time, she looked me up and down. She laughed again. "For starters, I need a drink. Take me away from physics, Vic. Drive me home. Okay? I'll make a pitcher of martinis or something. *Not* Bloody Marys."

"What about Saul?"

"He can drive, for God's sake. He has the car. I'm not his *nursemaid*."

I drove her home.

There was a broad, cushioned windowseat in her living room, overlooking Lake Champlain. I sat down and watched the mist drifting over the lake as she mixed martinis at the bar between the living room and the kitchen. When they were ready she handed me one and sat down beside me in a nest of pillows, tucking her long legs beneath her. "Okay, let's have it," she said, and sipped her drink, her eyes regarding me over her glass. "To what do I owe the honor? Am I a suspect, and you're plying me with liquor to soften me up, or are you warning me off Bruno?"

"Who's plying who with liquor?"

She laughed. She had a young laugh, throaty and bubbling and curiously intimate. "You're cute," she said. "Anybody ever tell you that? Sabina's cute little watchdog. You and Sabina seem really tight. You must like older women." She gave me a speculative look. "How old are you, anyway?"

"I have my driver's license." I told myself it shouldn't be too hard to advise her in a nice way to stay away from Bruno, but I was definitely feeling uncomfortable. There was something about the lady that made me feel more sympathetic toward Bruno's difficulty dealing with her—especially since I *have* been known to be attracted to older women, not that it's hard to figure out why, mother stuff and all that. Knowing why doesn't necessarily change things. I felt attracted to Vita, though it wasn't the kind of attraction that makes me tongue-tied, since wedding bells couldn't possibly be in the offing. I said, "Sabina's my boss, we have a beautiful employer-employee relationship. Period."

She pursed her lips. "Aw shucks, I guessed wrong. Poor Sabina, what a waste."

"Sabina and Bruno are very married." I underlined the "very." "He's a good-hearted guy, he hates to hurt people's feelings. He doesn't know how to say no."

She refilled my glass, singing, *"He's just a boy who can't say No, he's in a terrible fix. . . .* Okay, I get your message." Her singing voice was pleasant but breathy. Shaking her head she said, "You'd never know I could sing once. Yep, as we say in Vermont. I played Nellie in *South Pacific* for almost two years, on the road. Probably the pinnacle of my career, such as it was." Her mouth twisted. "Ah, well. It was fun." She finished her martini and put down her glass on the windowsill. "You were wondering what I need, you said. Right? Well, funny you should ask." She slipped off one of her shoes and raised her foot in the air, arching the instep under which there was a taut black strap from her stretch pants. The foot was slim, tanned, and pretty, the toenails painted blood red. She slid it along my leg, watching me, her flat, dark eyes hungry. "You getting any?" she said.

"You're direct, Vita."

"Are *you*?"

"Not right at the moment, no."

"Well?" Her foot had pushed the jeans up my calf and now her knee came around and clasped my thigh. She leaned against me, warm and soft, and dropped a kiss on the side of my neck as her arms went around me. I kissed her on the lips—not passionately, just experimentally. Her lips melted against mine but she didn't get grabby, which was a plus; just took her time and let herself be kissed. "Vic," she murmured. "You have no idea how long it's been. *Awfully* long. You taste good." If it was kisses she was talking about, it hadn't been that long according to Bruno, only twenty-four hours; but I didn't think it was. I kissed her some more and then got up and poured myself another martini, though I didn't particularly want one. She said, "Aw, what'd you have to go and do that for?" Half pouting, half laughing, she lay back against the pillows and watched me.

I refilled her glass and said, "Vita, you're a lot of woman."
"So?"

I said, "I don't like the feeling I might be interrupted at any moment, it's not conducive."

"By Saul? He won't care. Probably turn him on, if anything *could* turn him on these days, which I doubt. *I* sure can't."

"That's too bad, Vita."

She glanced at me sharply to see if I was being sarcastic, but I wasn't. She lit a cigarette and blew the smoke out through her nostrils in a long stream. "Damn right it's too bad."

"You're an attractive woman. I'm sure you've had plenty of admirers."

"Hey, watch it. Let's not slip into the past tense here, okay?"

"I didn't mean that. And you're very passionate and responsive. Is it true that you were attracted to Hervé Moore-Gann, at one time?"

"Oh? Who told you that?" Abruptly she stubbed her cigarette out in an ashtray.

"Theresa."

"Really? What else did dear Theresa have to say?"

"She said he wasn't interested."

"What! Why, that dried-up old bitch! What did she know about it? His tongue was hanging out, that's how uninterested he was." She grabbed another cigarette and struck a match so hard the head of it flared and flew through the air, landing on the carpet. I stepped on it with the toe of my shoe. "I wasn't having any, thank you very much! I thought he was a creep." She gave an exaggerated shudder. "Came on too strong, you know? Too pushy, too needy, whatever. Like me these days, probably." Her mouth twisted and then she gave an angry laugh. "I don't think Theresa *ever* deigned to have sex with him. I mean, can you imagine her doing it?" She shook her head, her eyes glittering with spite. "I doubt she even went to the bathroom, frankly. *Much* too ladylike, my dear."

"So you say *he* was the one who wanted an affair, not you."

"Don't you think I should know, darling?" She said icily. "I was there. Which Queen Theresa was not." Outside, a car pulled into the driveway. Vita gulped what remained of her drink. "Saul. Oh, God. He must be exhausted after giving that damn talk." She jumped off the windowseat, heading for the door, and I had the feeling she'd forgotten me. The front door opened and Vita called, "Saul?"

"Yeah, yeah."

"I'm coming, Saul."

A moment later I heard the two of them going upstairs, very slowly. I waited, but she didn't reappear, so I left.

# TWENTY-EIGHT

When I got back to the administration building I found Florian upstairs in his office. The door was open and I stood there for a minute, looking inside. He was sitting at a big, colonial-looking desk piled with papers, polishing a pair of rimless reading glasses with a handkerchief. After he'd given them a rub he brought them to his mouth and breathed on them, then polished them some more. He didn't notice me. He polished them a few more times and stuck them on the end of his nose and leaned back in his chair, staring into space and smiling to himself, like a man who has come into money and is thinking about how to spend it.

I entered without knocking, and when he saw me he frowned and picked up a piece of paper as if to give the impression he was working and didn't care to be interrupted. "Ah, Victor. To what do I owe this unexpected pleasure? I'm afraid I should warn you I'm rather busy, but—"

"I came to talk about the case, Florian. That okay with you?"

"The case?" He looked surprised. "But there's really no 'case' any more as far as you and Sabina are concerned, I thought I'd made that clear." He shuffled some papers. "Unless you've brought me your bill. Is that it?" He smiled, though not with his eyes, which were as opaque as gray pebbles. "I suppose that's the most important thing we have to talk about, isn't it? Now that the police are satisfied? If you'll forgive my saying so, I'm not aware that your investigations have been terribly fruitful; but I won't press the point."

"We've learned a few things."

213

"I'll take your word for it, though you haven't seen fit to share them with me." He pushed back his chair. "By the way, I saw you at Saul's lecture and I'm sure you noticed that Jean-Paul has been released without a stain on his character. What a pity if a miscarriage of justice had destroyed such a promising scientific career. Not academic, of course," he added in the condescending tone I'd noticed physics professors used when speaking of physicists employed in private industry. "He's an expert in his own field, so they say—something to do with high-altitude photography. Really quite vital to our country's defense, I believe," he said, leaning over backward to be fair to a guy who hadn't been good enough to land a university job. He stood up and came around the corner of his desk. "Of course, as I told you before, I never believed he killed Moore-Gann. Somehow one simply doesn't expect— shall I say passions of that magnitude?—to erupt among theoretical physicists, though I suppose we're no more exempt from the human frailties than the next fellow." He was beside me now and, touching me lightly on the arm, began to edge me toward the door.

I said, "You mean the kind of frailties that could result in an arrest for impairing the morals of a thirteen-year-old boy?"

Abruptly his hand fell away from my arm. After a moment, in which I could see in his flinty little eyes that he was asking himself how much I knew, he shut the door to the office and sat down again behind his desk. "Just what is it you want?" he said coldly. He took off his glasses. They left a red mark like a bruise across the bridge of his nose.

I said, "Mind if I sit down?"

"Sit, if you wish." Two hollow grooves had appeared below his cheekbones, as if he were sucking nervously on the insides of his cheeks.

I took a seat. "Florian, you haven't been very frank with us, now have you? I asked you why you'd never fired Judith and you said she was indispensable. But that wasn't the real reason. Judith knew about that old arrest of yours in Boston, she'd been blackmailing you for years. Her death was very convenient for you." I leaned forward. "You never believed for a minute she killed herself out of remorse, you know damn well she wasn't the type." He sat there, his handsome face bloodless, his hand clutching the edge of his desk. "Right?"

"I suppose—" He got up and went to the window. His hands were trembling and he pressed them flat on the sill as he looked out. The rain that had been threatening to come down all afternoon was spattering the pane with a rattle like hailstones. "Judith was a bitch," he said finally. His shoulders shifted under his imported cashmere sweater. "But—everything is relative." He turned to me and managed a smile. "She made my life more difficult than it had to be, and extorted quite a bit of money from me, you're right. Fortunately I could afford it." He gave a short, harsh laugh. "I got her her first secretarial job at the University of Vermont—well, my father arranged it, I believe under the impression she was an old girlfriend of mine. One might have thought that would be enough for her—that, and an occasional 'loan'—but nothing was enough for dear Judith. Unfortunately for me she happened to run into one of the few persons who knew of my arrest, a Vermont girl who'd been a secretary at Boston University until she'd been discharged for listening in on people's private telephone conversations." His mouth twisted. "Judith really got her hooks into me after that. But if you're suggesting I killed her, the idea's absurd. If I didn't do it years ago, why now? It's not as if I were suddenly desperate for money." He began to pace the room.

"Somebody killed her."

"It could have been suicide," he insisted stubbornly. "She may have had reasons we don't know about. Perhaps her health was bad. . . ." He spread his hands. "Anyway, how could she have been killed in—that way? I gather there was no sign of a struggle."

"She could have been drugged first, or hit on the head and stunned."

He made a dismissive gesture and leaned forward abruptly. "Victor, does Sabina know about that—other information?" I nodded, and the grooves gouged his cheeks again, his pale eyes shifting as he made rapid mental calculations. "May I ask what the two of you are planning to do about it? The—alleged incident you mentioned was years ago and the complaint was withdrawn—won't you keep it to yourselves? If it comes out, even at this late date, it may damage the Institute, not to mention my career. And what would be gained?"

"I didn't say we were going to make it public."

"But you want something. What? Money?"

I shook my head. "No more than our usual fee, plus expenses. But Sabina would like to keep working on the case."

"Can't you just leave it alone?" he cried. "Judith was a vile woman, everyone detested her, and suicide isn't impossible. . . ."

"She didn't kill herself." I stood up. "Florian, you really surprise me. Doesn't it bother you that someone is wandering around your Institute killing people? Suppose there's another death? Aren't you worried, wouldn't you feel responsible?"

"That won't happen," he said flatly, as if stating a self-evident fact. "No one at the Institute is stupid, of that you can be sure. Now that the police have closed the case, no one would be foolish enough to commit another murder—even if, as you suggest, someone other than Judith killed Moore-Gann. And you've no proof of that, no proof at all."

"You can't guarantee it."

His eyes evaded mine and then with an effort he looked straight at me and firmed his weak lips. "Are you saying that if I let you go on with the investigation you'll keep this . . . other matter to yourselves, but if I refuse you'll make it public?"

I was sorry he'd spelled it out; I'd have preferred to leave the threat tacit, because in fact it was an empty one. Now I had no choice but to say "No. I'm not trying to blackmail you." There are ethics in our profession, though you might not think so. Blackmailing a client is a definite no-no.

Relief brought the color back into his face. He thought for a while and finally shook his head. "Then I don't want you to continue the investigation. I happen to believe Judith killed herself."

I stood up. "I'll tell Sabina what you said."

"And you won't mention that . . . episode to anyone?"

"We'll try not to. Unless it becomes relevant."

"Can't you give me more of an assurance than that?" His lips lost some of their firmness.

I shook my head. "Sorry."

The telephone rang. He went to his desk and picked it up. "Hello? Oh, yes, my dear." He listened; I could hear the crackling of a voice on the other end of the line. His eyebrows drew together in a perplexed line, and he sat down at the desk. "*Where* is she? But what is she doing in Barre?" He was silent while his caller launched into an excited explanation. "Now, Theresa," Florian said. "Just calm down, she's all right. Yes. Yes, of course I'll get her, or arrange for someone to do it. No, not him, I quite understand. No, no. Yes, I promise. Now where exactly is she?" He made notes on a piece of paper. Finally he hung up. "Good heavens, what next?" he said pettishly. "You know, Vic, although nobody seems to think so, there happens to be quite a bit of work involved in running a physics institute. What with all these disruptions, and the police, and now Judith gone—"

I said, "What's happened?"

He sighed. "That was Theresa. Magda's had an accident, her car went off the road. Fortunately she's all right." He shook his head. "These young people drive too fast, they're simply not careful. She's in Barre, of all places."

"Where's Barre?"

"About forty-five miles away, near Montpelier, the state capital." He looked puzzled. "I can't imagine why she'd go to Barre, there's nothing there except granite. They quarry and carve it—for tombstones, you know. Vermont granite seems to be very popular for tombstones. It lasts well, I understand; doesn't become corroded. Well." He sighed again and stood up. "Theresa wants me to go and get her."

"I'll pick Magda up if you're busy."

"Well—I don't know. I suppose—yes, actually that would be a help."

"No problem. Just tell me where she is."

217

He gave me the directions and walked me to the door. "And about that other matter, you and Sabina won't tell anyone. . . ."

"Not if we can help it, Florian."

I left him looking anxiously after me.

It was twilight by the time I reached the Barre–Montpelier Road, one of those tacky, commercial strips you find all over the USA. I was a little disillusioned to discover that Vermont wasn't exempt. Magda was sitting over a cup of coffee in a Pizza Hut and I slid into the booth next to her, saying "Hi." She didn't look good. There was a bruise on her right temple, and the brightness had gone out of her hazel-flecked eyes, as if she was still in shock from the accident. She looked twenty years older and drab, almost ugly. Even the glossiness of her thick dark hair was gone, as if the job of combing out the tangles had become too much for her. I had hardly expected her to be looking her best, yet the change in her appearance shocked me.

"Hello, Vic," she said. "You are good to come and fetch me." Her voice was flat.

"Vic's pickup service, always on call." I put my hand on hers and gave it a squeeze. She didn't appear to notice. I said, "So tell me what happened."

"I had an—accident." She hesitated over the word. "I was driving through the woods on one of those narrow, winding dirt roads—you know? It was muddy and slippery—not easy. The road started going downhill very steeply and I stepped on the brake but it did not work. I pumped it, but the car went more and more fast. . . . I pulled on my parking brake and then there was a curve and the car went off the road and crashed into the woods." She paused, her breath coming in gasps, as if she were reliving the moment of impact. "Fortunately the trees were not big. The car knocked some of them down before it finally stopped. I hit my head." She touched the bruise. "I was unconscious, how long I do not know."

"You should see a doctor."

"I did, the man at the garage took me. People have been very nice." On the table in front of her was a letter in a language that wasn't English, on thin airmail paper that was creased and curling at the edges as if it had been much handled. "The doctor said I do not have concussion."

The waitress came over. I ordered a large deep-dish mushroom pizza with two salad bars on the side, though Magda said all she wanted was coffee. "You should eat," I said.

She shrugged. A spasm of pain crossed her face and she pressed her hand to her side. "A rib is cracked," she said. "The doctor taped it, but it hurts."

We got up and went to the salad bar. I could see that walking was painful for her. When we came back and sat down she said abruptly, "Someone is trying to kill me, Vic." Her eyes met mine with a blank, frozen look. "I'm frightened. Before I was not frightened but now I am. Before, when Moore-Gann died, I did not really believe the poison was meant for me." She swallowed convulsively and closed her eyes. On the table, her hands twisted together. "When the car went off the road there was a big rock, enormous, a boulder—I knew I would smash into it, head on. At the last minute the car swerved a little and I just missed it." Her hands came up and covered her face. "Oh, Vic! I keep seeing it! That boulder—I see it coming toward me." She shuddered, shaking her head. "If I could stop!" She began to cry, deep wrenching sobs. I put my arm around her and held her, reminded for an instant of Bruno and Vita. She stiffened and pulled away, her sobs quieting.

I said, "You're sure it wasn't an accident?"

"I know it was not! The mechanic told me the brakes had been tampered with. I didn't understand exactly how but some connecting rod had been filed partway through so it would break while I was driving." She stared at me over her hands, which she was still holding to her face as if she'd forgotten about them. Her eyelids were swollen and red.

No wonder she was scared! First Moore-Gann, then Judith, now this close call for Magda: I didn't like the sound of it and Sabina wouldn't either. While the police congratulated themselves on closing the case, to the applause of the physics community, a killer was deliberately stalking Magda. It seemed more likely now that the first crime had been aimed at her, too. I said, "Have you notified the police?"

"No! And I do not intend to! Why should I, do you imagine they will protect me?" Her voice was scornful.

"Well—"

"I do not. The police are fools, I do not trust them."

I said, "Do you have any idea who could have tampered with your car, or when it was done?"

"I have been trying to think. Who?" Her eyes met mine, less blank now as she tried to force her mind to work. "I have no idea. But the when, I think I may know. It was probably done between the time Theresa's seminar began at eleven this morning and about one o'clock, when I left the Institute."

"What makes you so sure?"

"Early this morning, before the seminar, I drove into Burlington to buy a few things. There was mist and I was driving fast, almost I ran into a deer on the road. I had to slam down the brake very hard. The car swerved but it stopped in time, and I remember thinking I was fortunate to have good brakes. Wouldn't they have failed at that time if already they were not good?"

"Quite possibly. What time was that?"

"Maybe quarter before eleven—I was afraid I would be late for Theresa's talk, that is why I was driving so fast. I got to the Institute and ran to the barn. I was just on time."

And by then probably everyone was at the seminar—except of course for Gerald, who'd been holding the fort in the administration building and who as far as I was aware had no reason to want to harm Magda. Theresa's talk had ended at noon, and everyone had left the barn; probably Magda's brakes had been tampered with after that. I said, "Where was the car between twelve and one?"

"Parked in the driveway of our cottage. You cannot see it from the rest of the Institute, there are woods around."

Plenty of privacy, in other words, if someone wanted to

jack up a car without being seen. "And where were you between twelve and one?"

"Walking in the woods. I had had some bad news." She
turned her head away abruptly, her hand tightening on the
letter.

"At one o'clock you left the Institute. Why?"

She shrugged. "I wanted to drive. I needed to get away."

"To Barre? Why Barre?"

"I wanted to see the cemetery."

"Cemetery?"

"There is a famous cemetery in this town. I read about it in
a guide for tourists. I went to see it."

Her salad was untouched. I said, "Eat." After a moment she
picked up her fork and ate a slice of beet. I said, "There are
cemeteries all over Vermont. What makes this one so special
that you suddenly had to leave the Institute and go rushing off
to Barre instead of attending Saul Sachs's seminar?"

She shook her head. "It was not like that. I wanted to go
for a ride—anywhere. To be alone. I got on the highway and
drove east, very fast; I did not care where the road led. Then
I saw the name 'Barre' on a sign and remembered the cemetery. It is a place where the stonecutters are buried, the ones
who carve the gravestones, you understand. Some of them
have carved their own, as well, elaborate ones. On an impulse
I decided to go there and I took the next exit. Then after I
visited the cemetery I drove at random, on the small mountain roads that go up where there are no towns. Coming down
I had the accident." A shudder ran through her and she
squeezed her eyes shut and pressed her hands to her eyelids.
"God, when will I stop seeing that boulder?"

"Don't think about it. Go on."

"Afterward I had to walk a long way before I found a telephone. It was not easy." She put her hand to her rib and fell
silent. "That is how it was."

The waitress brought our pizza and I put a slice in front of
Magda and insisted that she eat it. She had eaten some of her

salad and it seemed to have done her good. At least she was a little more animated.

When she'd finished her pizza I tried to give her another piece but she waved it away, saying "No, I cannot eat more. Truly, Vic."

I put it on my plate. "You said you'd had some bad news." Lightly I tapped the letter that lay on the table. "Is this how you heard about it? Was it bad news from home?"

"Yes."

"I'm sorry. What—" I let the sentence trail off.

She grew very still. Then she said in a low voice, without looking at me, "My mother is dead. I think I knew it already. Or maybe I feared it. I had not heard any news in so long a time." She nodded, dry-eyed.

I said, "I'm sorry. Really sorry, Magda. Who wrote you?"

"My old friend Elisaveta. My best friend." She picked up the letter. "She gave it to a man who was going to a conference in Canada so he could mail it to me. She was afraid of the censorship. Elisaveta, too, is in the Solidarity and she must be very careful." She took a deep breath. "Word reached her from people we can trust that my mother died two months ago of pneumonia, in prison. She did not get proper medical care." Angrily she burst out, "It is all so filthy, so horrible! There is nothing I can say, it will not bring her back." Her fists clenched and she shook her head. "There are no words. She was always telling people, 'Go to the doctor' when they were even a little bit sick, she believed in medical science like a religion. I used to laugh at her sometimes. 'Go to the doctor! Go to the doctor!'" Bitterly she said, "Probably they did not even give her antibiotics, such a simple thing. Pigs! Why should she have to die? She was a young woman, only forty-seven."

Magda had received a letter from Poland telling her that her mother had died, and in the next hour, in all probability, someone had tampered with her brakes. Maybe there was no connection, but . . . I said, "Did you tell anyone about the letter? Theresa, maybe?"

She shook her head. "I did not tell Theresa about my

mother. I wanted to, but she had just given her talk and they were taking her out to lunch; for the first time since Moore-Gann died she looked almost happy." She shook her head again. "I will tell her later."

"And did you tell anyone else?"

She seemed to hesitate. "About my mother's death? No—" She stopped speaking and sat with her elbows on the table, her head in her hands. After a while she whispered, as if to herself, "Poor Mama is dead . . . Moore-Gann is dead . . . Jean-Paul has been arrested . . ."

"He's been released," I said gently.

"Released? You are telling the truth?" She began to jump up, and a spasm of pain drew her eyebrows together. She pressed her hand to her ribs. "I must go to him!"

I restrained her. "Listen, Magda, Jean-Paul can wait. We have to talk. You're in danger, serious danger, you said so yourself. I don't think you should go anywhere alone until this case is cleared up. Someone has made two very serious attempts on your life; next time he may succeed."

"I know, but Jean-Paul—"

"Never mind Jean-Paul!" The light had come back into her eyes and she tossed her hair over her shoulder with her old impatient shrug. I persisted. "Maybe the best thing would be for you to leave the conference. Go back to Cambridge. Better yet, visit a friend somewhere and stay for a while."

"I have no friend like that—not in America. Anyway, I do not care to run away and it guarantees nothing, who can say for certain I would be safer? If someone wants to kill me he could follow, yes?"

"Not if nobody knew where you'd gone."

She shook her head firmly. "No. I will stay. I promise to be careful. Now I want to see Jean-Paul. Will you take me to him? My car will not be ready until tomorrow. Please?"

Her stubbornness exasperated me. I said, "Why do you care so much about Jean-Paul? He's a violent, self-centered, infantile guy. He isn't as smart as you, and he compensates by beating you up. A real sweetheart. What do you need him for? Sex? Are you that hard up?"

A dark flush had come into her cheeks. "Well," she said, and bit her lip, giving me an uncertain look as if she wasn't sure whether to be insulted or to justify herself. "You are right," she muttered finally, her eyes evading mine. "I do not need him, I have told him so, and myself, many times. I am not going *back* to him, Vic. Never, no." She shook her head emphatically but still didn't meet my eyes. "I only want to *see* him. To tell him about my mother, to make sure he is all right. . . . Three years we lived together. Even if everything is over between us we are not strangers."

I motioned to the waitress for the check. She brought it over and left it. "Come on," I said to Magda. The words of Captain Eaken came back to me: a "matching kink." It was weird and it bugged me—maybe it was none of my business how Magda chose to live her life, but I'm a frustrated shrink and this woman was so smart, so fiercely self-reliant when it came to her work, that it seemed incredible she could be hooked on a real creep, a guy who was sure to beat her again, sooner or later, if she went back to him.

And if she lived long enough. I said, "Maybe you should ask for police protection, Magda." She shook her head, as I'd pretty much expected. "And there's no way I can convince you to leave the Institute for a while?"

"I am not leaving," she said stubbornly. She added with a start, as if she'd just remembered, "Besides, I am on the program, I have to give three seminars. The first one is tomorrow. I am not fully prepared, I must do some work tonight yet—" She looked at her watch.

"All right, I'll take you back."

"You will take me to Jean-Paul."

I threw some money on the table. "If I do, I'm staying there with you, and afterward I'm going to deliver you to Theresa. I want you to stick to her like a tick until further notice. Don't be alone at any time, stay constantly alert to the possibility that someone might try to harm you. Do you think you can handle that?"

Her eyes met mine. "I can handle it. I will be very careful, I do not want to die. And now you will take me. Otherwise"—her tone hardened—"I will find a car to rent."

"That's not necessary." I stood up. "Come on, let's go."

# TWENTY-NINE

Jean-Paul was staying in a rambling old building on the grounds of the Institute that was known as the Bachelor House and looked as if it might have started life as an inn during the nineteenth century. His room was on the third floor. I accompanied Magda up the broad stairs. The halls were deserted, but there was a murmur of voices from several of the rooms, and through an open door I glimpsed an Indian physicist writing on a blackboard and talking, while a Japanese in a Champlain Valley Physics Institute T-shirt stood next to him, shaking his head as if unconvinced.

Magda, though she didn't complain, was obviously in pain as she climbed the steps, leaning heavily on the polished oak railing; by the time we reached the top her face was gleaming with sweat. I followed her down the hall, staying a few steps behind her until she stopped at one of the doors and knocked. There were footsteps inside and the door was opened by Andrzej Modzalewski. When he saw Magda he took a step backward and his mouth fell open as if the sight of her had stunned him; then a sudden transformation occurred, as if he'd slipped on a mask of drunkenness. His body sagged, his mouth became loose, his eyes leered. "Well!" he boomed. "We have visitor! Lovely lady!" He turned his head and said over his shoulder, "Guess who is here, my friend?" Behind him, Jean-Paul slumped in a chair, a bottle of vodka and a glass in his hands. He was pouring a drink, and the vodka was slopping over the outside of the glass and dripping into his lap. An empty bottle lay on the floor near his feet. He looked up and squinted, trying to focus his eyes.

I came up beside Magda, who gave me a look of mingled distress and exasperation.

Noticing me, Andrzej boomed, "Lovely gentleman, too!" He gave a loud laugh and, leaning forward, draped his arms around my neck. "Welcome, young fellow." I could smell alcohol on his breath, but he wasn't as drunk as he seemed—which was interesting. Even more interesting was the look he'd given Magda. Why had he seemed so shocked, did he have some reason not to expect to see her?

Jean-Paul struggled to his feet. "Magda," he mumbled, and stood blinking and wavering. He stumbled toward us, vodka splashing from his glass.

"Come in," said Andrzej and ducked to one side, grinning foolishly. The room was a mess, the bed unmade, papers scattered on the desk and floor, drawers hanging open as if someone had been hastily rummaging through them.

Magda went to Jean-Paul and took the glass from his hand, crying "Look at you! Why do you do this to yourself?"

"Magda," he said, forming the word with difficulty. "Why didn't you come before?" He laid his head on her shoulder like a child, and his legs wobbled under him.

She put her arms around his waist to support him. "You must go to bed," she said sharply. "Come, I will help you. You are very drunk—you know you should not drink."

"The police released me, I thought you would come." He thrust her arms away and lurched backward. "*You* didn't care!" he said accusingly.

"Jean-Paul, how can you say that?"

I caught a glimpse of a movement out of the corner of my eye and turned my head in time to see Andrzej furtively gathering up some papers that lay on the desk. Flashing me a vacant grin he said, "I go now, I give them privacy, the little—how you say?—loverbirds? Ah, poor Jean-Paul! He was so sad, now he is happy. I take my things, I go." Weaving, he left the room.

Magda said, "Vic—please, would you mind if we—"

"I'll be outside the door," I said, and stepped into the hall. I could hear Andrzej's heavy tread going downstairs, pausing at the second-floor landing as if he were trying to make up his mind whether to go to his room, and then continuing down. I peered over the railing and saw him moving downstairs rapidly and purposefully. He was obviously completely sober. Was he about to leave the building? No, when he reached the first floor he turned down one of the halls and I heard his retreating footsteps echo on the bare wooden planks of the floor. I'd have liked to take a quick look in his room, but I didn't know which one it was. I remembered that room numbers were listed in the Institute packet, and if Jean-Paul wasn't too drunk I could ask him to let me take a look at his. I was about to go back into the room when I heard a sound from the first floor—a mechanical noise, a low hum followed by a click, repeated a number of times; it sounded familiar, but I couldn't place it. Then I heard Andrzej's footsteps returning, and a moment later glimpsed him at the foot of the stairs with papers in his hand, more of them than he'd been carrying before. Of course! The sound I'd heard had been a Xerox machine. I stepped back silently, out of sight, and listened while he climbed to the second floor and walked halfway down the hall. A door opened and closed.

Behind me, in Jean-Paul's room, I heard Magda exclaim, "Don't do that!"

I opened the door. The Corsican was sitting on the edge of the bed holding on to her hand as she stood in front of him, trying to pull away; he was twisting her arm behind her back. She gave him a shove and he collapsed back on the rumpled sheets and she jerked away with a gasp of pain and then pressed both hands to her rib cage. Jean-Paul turned his face into the pillow and began to weep.

I stood in the doorway, watching them. He was too drunk to do any real damage, even though with a cracked rib Magda was an easy target. Her eyes met mine with a look of despair. "Time to go," I said.

She came toward me without a word and Jean-Paul didn't make any move to stop her, just went on snuffling into his pillow. We left the room together and I turned out the light as I closed the door.

I took Magda to Theresa's house, instructing her to spend the night in the older woman's room, which had twin beds. Theresa, once she'd gotten over her shock at learning that the "accident" had been the result of a deliberate attempt to sabotage Magda's car, was clear-eyed and businesslike. She bustled around the kitchen making coffee while Magda and I sat at the table.

"So you think it was done in the hour after my talk ended at noon," Theresa said, placing sugar and cream in front of us.

"It seems likely," I replied. "Did you go home to freshen up or anything before you went out to lunch?"

"No," she said, getting the point immediately. "Too bad, or I might have seen someone. No, I went straight out to lunch with the group."

"Who was in the group?"

"Florian. Saul and Vita Sachs." Magda looked surprised, and Theresa said, "Oh yes, Saul's been very, very friendly since Hervé died, I have no idea why. I could hardly tell him not to come." She brought the coffee to the table and said reproachfully to Magda, "I looked for you everywhere but I couldn't find you. I thought you were coming to lunch with us."

"I know, Theresa. I am sorry. I couldn't, I'd gotten some bad news, I simply had to be alone."

Theresa looked concerned. "Bad news?"

"News of my mother. She is dead, Theresa. She died in prison, of pneumonia."

"Oh, no! Oh, Magda, how terrible! Oh, I'm so sorry, I don't know what to say. My dear, why didn't you tell me right away?" Her hand caressed Magda's hair, pushing it back from the bruised forehead. "My poor girl, what a day you've had." There was something possessive, almost greedy, in the way her hand moved over Magda's face.

Magda didn't seem to mind. "Yes. A horrible day." Briefly she cupped Theresa's hand with her own and laid her cheek against it. "I knew they were taking you out to lunch, I did not want to spoil the celebration— You deserved it, after all you've been through and after that wonderful seminar—"

"Nonsense, you should have told me at once." She slipped her arm around Magda's shoulders.

I said to Theresa, "You were saying you went out to lunch with Florian and the Sachses. Was there anyone else?"

"Half a dozen people." She mentioned some names I didn't know.

"Nobody else? Leo Pesnik, for example, or Andrzej Modzalewski?"

"No." Idly she stroked Magda's hair. "I don't think Pesnik went out to lunch, I saw him sitting under a tree near the administration building, eating a sandwich."

"I saw him there, too," said Magda.

"And Modzalewski?" Both of them shook their heads, saying they hadn't seen him.

Before I left I made a circuit of the house, closing and locking all the windows and checking the doors. The house was old, with loose-fitting frames; the locks would be easy enough to open from outside, if someone was determined to break in. I really didn't think Magda would be in any danger if she shared Theresa's room, but there'd been two attempts on her life and I couldn't be sure, and for a while I considered spending the night in the woods outside to keep an eye on things. I decided against it, finally. There were too many things I needed to talk to Sabina about—Magda's so-called accident and Modzalewski's reaction when he saw her, and his subsequent behavior. I was almost convinced he was the murderer we'd been looking for, though there were loose ends. Motive, for instance. Why should he want to kill Magda? Let's say the big Pole wasn't really a Solidarity hero but an agent who'd been planted by the Soviets in the American physics community. In that case it was understandable that he'd want to get friendly with Jean-Paul, who according to Florian was engaged in important defense work—make copies of some of his papers, even try to recruit him. Maybe Andrzej was afraid Magda knew something that could blow his cover. But if so, why didn't she speak up? And why had Andrzej poisoned Hervé

Moore-Gann?—though probably Magda had been the real target. More puzzling, why would he have killed Judith?

I said good-bye to Magda and Theresa, got in my car, and drove in the direction of the Institute gates. As I passed the administration building I noticed Bill, the caretaker, watering the shrubs he'd planted that morning. That gave me an idea. I parked the car and strolled over.

"Hi, Bill, how you doing?"

"Fair to middling." A gob of chewing tobacco flew past my nose and landed in a clump of weeds. "Looked around in the woods a little like you said, saw that young feller."

"Jordan? You found him? That's great! Where is he?"

Shaking his head, he played a fan of spray up and down a bush I couldn't tell you the name of. "Don't know."

"But you said you saw him."

"Yep." He gestured in the direction of the woods that climbed the hill behind us. "Behind that ridge there's some rocks make a cave near a spring. Good spring, never runs dry. He was holed up there, had some cans of food." He shook his head. "He run off when he seed me. Hard to figure that boy." Bill shrugged. "Probly went fishing, plenty of ponds in Vermont. Could be anywhere. Tell you what I think." I waited. "I think he'll come out when he's good and ready."

Fine. Well, at least I could report to Sabina that Jordan was alive, which was something. "Thanks, Bill. Keep on looking." I took a ten-dollar bill out of my wallet and the little eyes brightened in his beefy face. "I wonder if I could ask you to do another job for me. You know the cottage where Mrs. Moore-Gann lives, the lady whose husband died?"

"Yep. Old farmhouse, used to be the Willis place."

"Could you guard it? Just keep an eye on it and make sure nobody tries to break in?"

"All night?" He looked unenthusiastic.

I took out another ten. "For twenty dollars?"

He thought it over. "I guess so." Twenty seemed to be his regular rate.

I handed him the money and I left.

# THIRTY

I found Bruno playing chess in the living room when I got home. He doesn't need an opponent to play, which is a good thing because it isn't easy for him to find a player of his strength; in this case he was playing over a game he'd clipped from the chess column of *The New York Times*. While he was considering his next move he was eating chocolate chip cookies out of a paper bag. Sabina wasn't around.

"Hi, Bruno," I said. Seeing the cookies made me remember I hadn't had any food since the pizza I'd shared with Magda on the Barre–Montpelier Road, a long time ago.

"Vic!" He darted a look over his shoulder and said in a whisper, "Did you talk to her?"

"Her? Oh, Vita. Yes, we talked." I dipped my hand into the cookies.

"Well? Did you—you know, tell her?"

"To leave you alone?"

"My God, Vic, you didn't say *that?*" His mild brown eyes were appalled.

"No, no, of course not. Don't you trust me? Let me get some milk to go with these."

"Wait—first tell me what she said."

Sabina strolled downstairs in a bathrobe, her hair wrapped in a towel, her skin glowing. "So you're back, Vic. You've been gone a long time." She ignored Bruno, except for helping herself to a cookie from the bag he was still holding. "There were a couple of phone calls. One from Vita Sachs." She cast a casual glance in Bruno's direction, checking his reaction to Vita's name; he looked guilty. Sabina pursed her lips. "She asked you to call her early tomorrow morning, said she had something to tell you. She didn't deign to give me the details." Daintily she nibbled a cookie.

"Wonder what she wants." I thought I knew, actually, and I didn't think it had much to do with the case. "I spent some time with her today, at her house." I gave Sabina a suitably edited description of my visit with Vita, while Bruno listened, pretending to be immersed in his chess game. Not *totally* edited, for I thought that if I let her know things had gotten somewhat physical it might relieve her mind about Bruno.

It worked. "Vita's quite a *femme fatale,* isn't she?" she remarked when I'd finished, looking more relaxed and suppressing a smile. "Bruno, are there any cookies left in that bag?"

"There's one left. You can have it." He handed her the bag, pleased that she'd spoken to him directly.

I said, "I talked to Florian, let him know we knew about his arrest in Boston, but he still doesn't want us to go on with the investigation." I told her in detail about our conversation. "How'd your meeting with Saul go? Do we have a client or don't we?"

She sat down and crossed her legs, tucking her robe around her knees. "We do not. He said he couldn't authorize us to proceed with our investigation until he'd consulted the board of trustees. Technically I suppose that's correct, but I think he could have if he'd wanted to—I got the impression he wasn't eager to reopen the case now that the police have closed it. I pointed out rather forcefully that it set a bad precedent to permit murderers to poison Nobel prizewinners with impunity, and that argument seemed to weigh with him. He didn't actually say no, he promised to poll the board, finally."

"So—no client. That's bad. Maybe I should have taken Magda's travelers' checks after all." I sat down on the couch and put my feet up, while Sabina began to towel her hair. "Do we drop the investigation?"

"Certainly not. I've always felt that as professionals we ought to do some volunteer work on occasion, *pro bono publico.*" If this was true, it was news to me. "Here's an opportunity. I shall take off our expenses on my income tax as a business loss."

"Can you do that?"

"It's illegal, Sabina," said Bruno. "Why don't you face facts, you're just a workaholic."

"You don't know for sure it's illegal," she said. "I shall discuss it with my accountant and in the meantime we'll proceed. You had another call, too, Vic, from Mort Goldman. He's had some second thoughts about Andrzej Modzalewski. On reviewing the file he found a detail that raised a question in his mind."

"Now that's interesting," I said, leaning forward. "What's the detail?"

"When Modzalewski was in prison, he was given a weekend pass to visit his sick father, as we've already heard, and it was on that weekend his friends managed to smuggle him out of the country. However, according to Mort, the father has had Parkinson's disease for a long time—still does, presumably—and there was no indication in the file of any particular crisis in his health at the time Modzalewski was permitted to visit. Mort thought that was odd. He raised the faint possibility that Modzalewski might be an agent. If that were true, he said the imprisonment, though perfectly genuine, could have been arranged as an ingenious part of his cover story."

"That's it!" I said. "And Magda must know something about him that could blow his cover. He's the one we want, Sabina! Wait till you hear." I gave her a full report of the events of the day, including the details of Magda's accident and our visit to Jean-Paul's room in the Bachelor House.

By the time I was finished Sabina was looking perturbed. "I don't understand," she said finally. "This accident of Magda's doesn't make any sense at all. You'd better check with the garage mechanic tomorrow."

"But it does make sense," I said. "Modzalewski's afraid of something she might reveal, something she's forgotten but could remember, or—"

"I suppose it's possible," she admitted. "You could be right. Yet Modzalewski can't have been responsible for either Moore-Gann's death or Judith's, I'm certain of it." She shook her head doubtfully. "Could I be wrong? No, it's not possible, everything fits too well."

Of course she couldn't be wrong. "Everything such as what?" I said hopefully. "If I'm working *pro bono publico,* don't I at least have a right to know what's going on?"

"You're not," she said. "*I* am. *You're* receiving a salary, as usual. Plus an extended vacation in Vermont." She rubbed her hair with the towel, her expression abstracted. After a minute or two of massaging her brain, she announced with an air of decision, "Vic, I want you to go and bring Magda here. I won't feel comfortable until I know she's under my roof. That tobacco-chewing yokel you've been lavishing my good money on doesn't inspire me with me with confidence— though I'm relieved to hear he saw Jordan today, assuming we can believe him. I don't fully understand what's going on, but there's no doubt that Magda's in danger. Let's not have a repetition of the Judith incident. Get her."

I couldn't believe she was serious. "It's ten o'clock at night," I said. "What if she won't come? The woman is exhausted. She just found out her mother died, her car crashed, she has a cracked rib. If she has any sense at all she'll have taken a couple of pain pills and gone to bed."

Bruno shook his head. "I don't think so. She's giving a seminar tomorrow afternoon, she's probably up preparing her talk. This must be the first chance she's had all day."

"I agree," said Sabina. "Victor, go and get her. She can sleep in your room and you can have the couch."

I went. I fully expected Magda, not to mention Theresa, to tell me to get lost if I barged in on them and announced that Sabina had decided Magda had to spend the night at our house; therefore I decided it would be better to take it in stages. I would start by telling Magda that Sabina needed to question her about the accident, which I knew Magda was very concerned about. Once I got Magda to come with me to Burlington, the rest would be up to Sabina.

234

I was prepared to deal with objections from Theresa, but I hadn't anticipated that Florian would be there, too. The two of them were sitting in the study in a pair of rocking chairs by the fire, while Magda worked at the desk. A peaceful scene. As soon as I explained why I had come, Theresa shook her head.

"This young lady's not going anywhere tonight," she stated firmly. "She's had quite enough for one day." She turned toward Magda, who was marking places in a book with slips of paper. "Magda, surely this can wait until tomorrow."

Magda looked up, saying "But if it's important—"

"You said you had to work on your paper. *I* don't even think you should do that, *I* think you should get some sleep. Work in the morning, get up early. Your seminar isn't until the afternoon."

"I work better at night," Magda said wearily. "I'm not a morning person."

"You'll make yourself sick." Theresa sighed and turned toward me. "Really, Vic, this is quite unreasonable."

Florian cleared his throat. "Don't get upset, my dear. There's no reason at all why Magda should go." He gave me a stern look. "Young man, the case is closed, it's no longer your affair. As far as Magda's accident is concerned, she drives too fast—you do, Magda, you're not used to these mountain roads."

"But the mechanic said—" she objected.

"I know, I know." He waved the objection away. "Unfortunately, auto mechanics are far from infallible, as we all learn over the years, to our sorrow."

Magda threw her pencil down on the desk and said, "Someone tried to *kill* me, Dr. Gawthrop! You make it sound like nothing!"

Good for Magda! I said, "The case isn't closed as far as we're concerned, Florian."

"Oh? And may I ask who your client is? Or are you simply sticking your noses in where you don't belong?" He turned to Theresa, saying "The trustees are quite satisfied with the way the police have handled matters. Wayne Eaken's a competent officer, I've known him since I was a boy."

"Really," said Theresa. "How interesting, Florian. I never knew that, how did you meet him?"

"Actually it was in Sunday School, one summer when I was quite small. I'm afraid he wasn't one of the better pupils."

Evidently they'd decided to ignore me and hope I'd go away. I said, raising my voice, "Magda's my client, she asked me to represent her."

Theresa looked appalled. "Magda, is this true?"

Magda looked at each of us in turn and then, her eyes meeting mine, she nodded. "Yes, I did ask him." She rose. "I'll come, Vic, if you think it's that important. But I hope it won't take long, I've still got work to do."

"Bring your work along, maybe you can read in the car." That was something I'd been worrying about. I didn't see how even Sabina could get her to spend the night apart from the materials she was using to prepare her seminar.

She gave me a sharp glance and then murmured, "I'll just put these things in my briefcase."

Theresa stood up, squaring her shoulders and pushing the hair back out of her eyes. "Magda, this is absolutely ridiculous. You need rest, sleep, you've had all kinds of shocks today—physical *and* emotional. I forbid you to go."

"You forbid me, Theresa?" Magda's chin rose.

The two women stared into each other's eyes for a long moment until finally Theresa looked away. "Go," she said bitterly. "Go with him if you want to. You will anyway, you want to go." Florian laid his hand on her arm but she seemed unaware of him.

Once we reached Sabina and Bruno's house, it didn't take much persuasion to convince Magda to stay the night. "Yes, I will feel safer here," she agreed. "There are more people, and nobody knows where I am. But what about Theresa?"

"Vic will call her," Sabina said.

"What I mean is, will *she* be safe?"

"She will be quite safe."

I went in the other room and called Theresa, telling her not to expect Magda that night. "Don't tell anyone where she is; Florian shouldn't tell anyone either. It's for her own protection."

She hung up on me without saying a word. You'd have thought Magda was still a teenager and I had plans to impair her morals. Shaking my head, I went back into the living room.

Sabina was saying, "How well did you know Andrzej Modzalewski in Poland?"

"Not well at all." Magda was holding a cup of tea and looking pale but composed. When she saw me she said, "What did she say?"

"Never mind about Theresa," said Sabina. "Just answer my questions."

Magda went on. "Modzalewski came once to give a guest lecture at the the University of Varsovie when I was a student. Afterward I spoke to him and he promised to send me a preprint of an article he was preparing."

"And did he?"

"Yes. It arrived a few weeks later."

"Was there a personal note with it?"

"No. Only on the cover he had written 'Compliments of A. Modzalewski.' I thought it was nice that he did not forget."

"And did you have any other contact with him?"

She shook her head. "None."

Sabina leaned forward. "This is very important, so think hard before you answer. Can you imagine any possible reason, any reason whatsoever, why Modzalewski should want to kill you?"

Magda drew in her breath. "So," she said after a moment. "You think he is the one." Slowly her expression grew stern, almost fierce, and then she gave a quick, decisive nod. "Yes, I see. Yes, of course. I have been stupid, stupid."

Sabina said, "You've remembered something. What?"

"The letter from Elisaveta. Vic told you about it?" Sabina nodded. "There was something in it I did not mention to you, Vic." She threw me an apologetic glance. "According to

237

Elisaveta, my mother had a visitor a few days before she was arrested—a gentleman from Wroclaw who happened to be passing through the town where we lived. She was very happy to see him, although she did not know him, because"—for a moment her voice broke—"he brought her news of me. He had seen an article of mine in an international journal, and he gave her a copy. Kind of him, was it not?" There was sudden venom in her tone. "Now Elisaveta tells me that certain comrades believe he was the one, that so-kind gentleman from Wroclaw, who betrayed her to the authorities! She must have trusted him, told him something." Her right hand tightened into a fist. "The day he came to our house there was a young girl helping my mother with the press. This girl saw the man but did not learn his name."

"Do you have any idea who it might have been?"

"I do, yes. Now. After I read the letter I showed it to Modzalewski, I asked him if knew who the man could have been."

"Aha."

There was a silence.

Magda said, "Yes, I see it now, of course. *He* was the visitor from Wroclaw. He is not really in Solidarity, he is a spy of the government. He killed my mother—now he tries to kill me."

Sabina nodded. "He thought you would learn that he had been the visitor from Wroclaw. So while you were walking in the woods, thinking about your mother, he tampered with the brakes on your car. He was afraid you would give him away."

"And he was correct," she said firmly. "Who should I tell? The police?"

"No, don't, not yet. There still isn't any real evidence, though I'm quite sure you're right; perhaps tomorrow we can find some. In the meantime, Vic will alert a friend of his who works for the CIA."

"Good. If there is anything I can do to help catch him—"

Sabina nodded. "You can, simply by giving your seminar tomorrow. Most likely Modzalewski will attend, and we'll search his room while he's out. I have reason to believe we'll find something useful."

"I was stupid to show him that letter," Magda said bitterly. "Like my poor mother, I suspected nothing."

"Naturally; his cover was first-rate. He's a genuine physicist—not outstanding, but he's done respectable work, I understand. Once he reached this country he actually became famous as a hero of the Solidarity movement, thanks to the article in the *Washington Post,* which was widely reprinted. Why shouldn't you have thought he was genuine? He certainly knows most of the physicists in Wroclaw—there can't be that many—and it was reasonable to ask his opinion about which of them might have betrayed your mother." Leaning forward, Sabina patted the young woman's hand. "It's not your fault; don't blame yourself."

"But if it was Modzalewski who tried to kill me, does that mean he also murdered Hervé and Judith? Because I do not see why he would want to."

"I don't think he did," said Sabina.

"Who was it, then?"

"Until there is evidence, I would rather not say." She glanced at her watch and rose. "Time for bed. Come with me and I'll show you your room. I think I can find a nightgown that will fit you."

"Thank you," Magda said. She stood up, swaying slightly. "I think I am too tired to work on my talk, I will have to do it in the morning."

They went upstairs.

Bruno said in a low, reproachful tone, "So that's how you convinced Vita I couldn't get involved with her—you got involved with her yourself!"

"A human sacrifice," I declared, placing my hand on my heart. "Just kidding. I wouldn't exactly say we're *involved,* Bruno."

"I don't know what else you'd call it. You fooled around, if Saul hadn't come home who knows what else would have happened?" He sounded disgruntled.

"Some gratitude. Listen, don't ask me to get you out of any more tight spots."

"I'm not ungrateful, Vic. I don't want Vita to be hurt. That's all."

"Bruno, you're full of it. You're jealous." Sabina's footsteps were heard on the stairs.

"I am not." Rising to his feet, he swept his chess pieces into their box, folded the board, and went upstairs in a dignified manner only slightly marred by the fact that a large strip of masking tape had attached itself to the seat of his pants.

"She's all set for the night," Sabina said briskly, as she came into the living room. "I want you to stay with her tomorrow morning, then drive her to the Institute after lunch and continue to guard her until Modzalewski is under arrest."

"You know what this means, don't you?"

"What?"

"Another physics talk. I swore Sachs's was the last I was ever going to sit through."

"Nonsense, it's good for your general culture."

"And where will you be?"

"I'll take a look around in Modzalewski's room if he attends the morning seminar. Bruno can come with me and guard the door. Also I want to have a word with Bill, the caretaker, about Jordan's whereabouts. Maybe I can get him to be a little more specific about where the boy might be hiding."

"Good luck. Bill's not the chatty type."

# THIRTY-ONE

Usually I was the first one awake, but when I opened my eyes the next morning after a restless night on the living-room couch I heard the clink of china in the kitchen. I got up and went in. Magda was sitting at the table in a negligée of Sabina's, stirring a cup of instant coffee with one hand while she jotted something down in a notebook with the other. She looked quite fetching.

"Morning," I said, peeking over her shoulder at a page full of wiggly lines and mathematical formulas. "Bringing your diary up to date?"

"Diary? I prepare my seminar."

"I know, I know." I'd forgotten she had no sense of humor. "Would you like some real coffee? I'm going to make a pot."

"Thank you, no, this is quite fine. Do you have aspirin?"

"Sure. Rib hurting?"

She nodded, her eyes on the page, and made a note. "The doctor gave me pills for pain but they are at Theresa's house." I went upstairs for the aspirin and brought down the bottle. She took two of the pills. I tried a couple of conversational openings but she wasn't in the mood to chat; after a while she took her notebook and her cold coffee and went to her room. *My* room.

It was now almost seven o'clock—too early, I figured, to disturb Vita even though her message had said to call her early in the morning; eight o'clock struck me as reasonable. Looking for a way to pass the time, I picked up *The Good Soldier*, which was lying where Sabina had left it when she'd finished it. It didn't look like a page-turner to me and it was far from short; still, Sabina claimed it had told her who the murderer was, so I decided to tackle it. After settling down near the telephone I began to read. I was expecting a call from Mort Goldman. I'd finally caught him very late last night at his apartment in Crystal City; he'd been out dancing at a Mexican cantina in Adams Morgan in the line of duty, trying to pick up a lead on whoever it was that had fire-bombed the car of the Mexican ambassador. All he'd managed to pick up, finally, was a fetching señorita who'd entered the country illegally from the Dominican Republic.

As soon as I told him about Modzalewski he became businesslike. I gave him the details and he said he'd fly up to Burlington in the morning. "Normally, what we prefer to do in a situation like this," he said, "where we're dealing with a known agent, is watch him and track down his contacts while we feed him false information. In this case, I don't know. You say he wants to kill the Tenofska woman?"

"Definitely."

"And he's apt to try again?"

"Probably. Sabina thinks so, she's got me baby-sitting the girl full time."

"Hm. Well, I suppose if he's planning to kill her we'll have to step in." He sounded regretful. "Are you sure she's really first-rate as a physicist?"

"Now, Mort. Didn't you learn anything in that ethics course you took at Maryland?"

"I got a C," he said. "Listen, I'll call you from the airport, after we've rented a car."

*The Good Soldier* is a very strange book. First of all, it has nothing to do with war, just in case the title misled you as it did me. Secondly—well, never mind. I don't want to spoil it for you if you ever decide to read it.

I'll be honest, I didn't read it, I skimmed it. Once when I was between jobs I invested in a course in speedreading at the Evelyn Woods School of Reading Dynamics. Sabina strongly disapproved of this when I told her about it, remarking that subjecting a good book to such treatment was "like freeze-drying a fine Colombian coffee—all the essential oils are lost."

She was right in a way, skimming a book I got maybe a tenth of it, maybe less; but sometimes that fraction came in handy and I had a notion this might be one of the times. I'd covered almost fifty pages by the time eight o'clock rolled around and I laid the book aside to call Vita. Magda hadn't reappeared, there was no sign yet of Sabina and Bruno, and I still didn't know who the murderer was.

Vita picked up the phone. "Hi," I said. "This is Vic. I got your message."

"Hello," she said. "I've been expecting your call." Her voice was pitched low, or maybe it was just husky in the morning—all those cigarettes? Whatever the reason, it was sexy.

"You're an early riser. I'm surprised."

She gave her throaty little laugh. "Always have been, darling. Why? Did you imagine me wallowing in my silken sheets till all hours?"

"Sounds like fun."

"Sweetie, can you drop over this morning? I'd like to talk to you about something."

"Sorry, I'm afraid I can't. Duty before pleasure." I made my voice regretful; it wasn't hard. "Why don't you tell me what it's about?"

"Uh-uh, not on the phone. You *really* can't come over?"

"Cross my heart."

"Then I'll come to you. Where are you?"

"At Sabina and Bruno's place in Burlington."

She hesitated. "Are they there?"

"Yes, but they're going to the Institute for the first seminar. Come over then, if you like."

"That sounds all right. But I don't understand why you have to stay there, Vic."

"I just do."

"Well. You're being very mysterious, I'm quite intrigued. See you later."

She hung up and I went back to *The Good Soldier*.

Sabina and Bruno appeared eventually, looking as if there'd been a big reconciliation scene during the night. I was gratified, because first of all I'd helped make it happen and secondly I expected that Sabina would now buckle down to work. Even when I mentioned that Vita would be coming over later, Sabina just kept on smiling gently while Bruno ate his oatmeal without a sign of a guilty look.

They left for the Institute around nine-thirty. I brought Magda a fresh cup of coffee, which she accepted with a reluctant "thank you" as if she'd rather not have been interrupted, and then I returned to *The Good Soldier,* wondering when Mort was going to call. I read for a while, then called the airport and asked about flights from Washington. There was one arriving at noon that had good connections, and I figured that was the one he would take. I read some more. The book wasn't bad—in fact, if I'd been in a different mood I'd probably have liked it—but it was slow and I kept feeling restless. I wanted to do something, I wanted *action;* frankly, I was finding it a bore to baby-sit.

There was a knock on the door. Cautiously I peered outside, but it was only Vita. I let her in.

"Vic, darling," she said, and kissed me, engulfing me in a cloud of Chanel Number Five, a perfume I've always liked.

We sat down on the living-room sofa. She was wearing a sleeveless white tennis dress with a pleated skirt barely long enough to cover the matching shorts underneath, which I caught a glimpse of as she sat down. After crossing her long, tanned legs, she began to bob her sandaled foot with its scarlet toenails up and down, up and down as if impatient or nervous; though the rest of her looked sleek and relaxed as she leaned back and gave me a flirtatious little smile. I thought I knew why she'd come and I hadn't decided how to handle it, just figured I'd see how things went and let nature take its course; but it turned out I was wrong, there really was something she wanted to tell me.

"I've been thinking, since those questions you asked me," she began.

"Which questions?"

"*You* know. About whether I'd had an affair with Moore-Gann. About dear Theresa's remark that I ran after her precious husband." She lit a cigarette and blew out the smoke in an impatient puff. "Her precious husband! If you want to know the truth, they had the sickest marriage of anyone I've ever known."

"What do you mean by sick?"

"Sexually sick." She jiggled her foot.

"Really? How would you know?"

"How do you think? Hervé told me. In bed." She shrugged. "So we went to bed together a few times over the years, more than a few times, actually. It was no big deal. We were never what I'd consider lovers, I didn't really like the guy. He was just a little Brooklyn Jew-boy on the make."

I didn't care for that comment. "Saul's Jewish."

"Saul's different. Never mind about Saul, I didn't come here to discuss him. I just thought if darling Theresa's telling tales about me I can tell a few tales about her. That's fair, isn't it?"

"Why'd you go to bed with Moore-Gann if you didn't like him?"

She shrugged. "Why does anybody do anything? I don't know, it just seemed like the thing to do at the time, don't ask me why. I need attention and Saul's always been pretty wrapped up in physics, maybe that was it. Maybe I was between jobs—I don't really remember. Saul didn't know about me and Hervé, at least I don't think he did, but Theresa did because Hervé told her." She quirked her eyebrows. "Can you imagine? But that was part of their screwed-up relationship. It made me furious. I wasn't crazy about having her look at me in that smug, superior way of hers, like 'I know what you're doing, you dirty girl.' Crap like that. Who needed it? We saw a lot of them in those days, we were always being invited to the same parties." She laughed. "Not anymore, of course." She stubbed out her cigarette and took another one from her purse.

I said, "You smoke too much."

"Don't you start, too." She lit the cigarette and shook out

the match. "But Hervé found his squeaky-clean Theresa in bed one day with another man. Oh, my God, was he upset! Otherwise I don't think he'd ever have told me what he did."

"Namely?"

She shot me an ironic look. "You ready?"

"I think I can handle it, I don't shock easily."

"Oh, yeah? Well, how about this. According to Hervé, his marriage was never consummated."

"What?" Whatever I'd expected, this hadn't been it.

She leaned back with a triumphant little smile. "You heard me. Sick, huh?"

"Well, it's certainly unusual. Do you think it's true?"

Her foot jiggled and for a moment she looked uncertain. "It's what he *said,* I know it's hard to believe." Then she shrugged. "Sure I believe it, he went into a lot of medical details. She just couldn't, you know, loosen up—it was like she didn't have an opening or something. I mean she did, but he could never penetrate her or she wouldn't let him, he didn't seem too sure about that. They went to doctors but apparently it didn't help. So—some lovely marriage, right?"

"Why didn't they get a divorce?"

"Oh, he didn't want one. Neither did she, I suppose. Who knows, maybe they enjoyed making each other miserable. The only time they came close to divorcing was when he found her with the other man, and that was years ago."

"Who was the man?"

"Who do you think? Who's her laughing cavalier? Don't tell me you haven't noticed."

"You mean Florian?"

She nodded. "Yes, my dear, it was Florian, the great macho lover. Actually, I wouldn't be surprised if they got married some time. He still has a thing for her, don't ask me what kind of a thing." She laughed. "I imagine they'd probably be quite compatible. The queen and the Virgin Queen—he's queer, you know. Another wonderful, healthy relationship, right?" She shook her head. "According to Theresa—this is what Hervé said—she only went to bed with Florian because she was trying to help straighten him out—that's a joke, isn't

246

it, talk about the blind leading the blind? Maybe she was trying to straighten herself out. She *claimed* they never actually made it together. So—" She shrugged. "Finally Hervé forgave her."

I said, "How sure are you that Saul didn't know about your relationship with Moore-Gann?"

"I'm sure."

"He must have known. He's no fool and you're pretty obvious, Vita." The Jew-boy remark still irked me. "I think that's what caused the feud between him and Moore-Gann."

Her eyes flashed angrily. "Who are you calling obvious, sonny? Watch your mouth. Anyway, you happen to be way off track. What do *you* know about it?" Angrily she stubbed out her cigarette. "They didn't break up their collaboration over little me, that I can guarantee."

"You underestimate yourself."

"Listen, smart-ass—that's what you are, you know, you think you're so smart, so young, so good-looking—you don't know what the hell you're talking about." There was viciousness in her tone. She hesitated, then plunged on. "For your information, Saul found out that a lot of the work Hervé did on their Nobel prize collaboration was based on someone else's ideas." She sat back, regarding me with her flat dark eyes, her foot jiggling furiously. "Probably I shouldn't have told you that."

"Were the ideas Pesnik's?"

She shook her head. "No. And that's all I'm going to say about it."

I said, "That's fine with me, I don't believe you anyway."

"What?"

"I don't believe you. If anything like that had happened, the person whose ideas were stolen would have raised an enormous stink—I mean, why wouldn't he? And that never happened, Vita." I looked at her as if daring her to convince me.

"You jerk," she said, rising and smoothing the pleats of her miniskirt with one rapid motion. "You asshole. They were

247

Theresa's ideas. You think she was going to blow the whistle on her husband?" She glared at me.

There were footsteps on the stairs, and a moment later Magda came into the room, still wearing Sabina's negligee. "Vic," she said. "Do you have the aspirin?"

Vita looked at her and then at me. Snatching up her bag from the couch, she said with an angry laugh, "Business before pleasure, I think you said? Bye-bye, Vic, it's been real."

She swept out—that was the only word for it—and the front door slammed behind her.

Magda said awkwardly, "I am sorry if I interrupt."

"It's fine, Magda, just fine. Don't give it a thought. You'll find the aspirins in the kitchen."

She took them and went back upstairs, and I resumed reading *The Good Soldier*. The book began to grip me—maybe because of the way certain aspects of it reminded me of things Vita had said. I kept slowing down to a normal reading pace and had to remind myself to speed-read, or it would take me a couple of days to finish it. I raced through the pages.

Shortly before noon Sabina appeared, wearing a satisfied smile and carrying a large manila envelope. She kicked off her high heeled shoes. "Been doing a little reading, Vic?"

"I found the passage," I said.

"And?"

"I know who did it, and why. But how the hell do we prove it? I don't think *The Good Soldier* would be acceptable as evidence."

"Unfortunately not. At any rate, I'm glad you saw the parallel, once you read the book. I was afraid your abominable method of so-called reading might make you miss it."

"It's not just the book," I said, and told her in detail about Vita's visit.

She listened, massaging her toes and moaning at intervals, "I've been on my feet all morning." When I was finished she said, "Well done, Vic. You handled her beautifully."

"Thanks." I was pleased; Sabina doesn't throw praise around. "What's in the envelope, if you don't mind my asking?"

"Not at all." She pulled a sheet of paper that looked like a Xerox copy out of the envelope, and handed it to me, suppressing a smile.

I looked at it. The sheet was covered with notations in script, but I couldn't read them. "What's this? Polish?"

"I presume so. Maybe we'll ask Magda to translate it. Here's something interesting."

She pulled out a sheaf of eight or ten pages, stapled together—another photocopy. Even upside down I could see the big black CLASSIFIED stamp across the top. I took it from her. The letterhead said "Allied Techtronics, Inc.," with an address in Boston, and under that, "Theory Division." It was a memo addressed to Jean-Paul Brocchiu entitled "New Ideas in Surveillance Detection: A Critique." I said, "Nice. You found these in Modzalewski's room?"

She nodded. "The originals. I made copies. When I'd finished my search I left everything exactly as I found it, so I don't think he should suspect that we're on to him. Any word from Mort?"

The telephone rang. "That might be him."

It was. "Hi, Vic," said Mort. "Just wanted to let you know we're here. What'd you say was the name of the police chief—Eakins?"

"Eaken. Do you have to go through him?"

"It's best, Vic. We can't make arrests, you know. You don't like him?"

"It's mutual. He's a hayseed. How was your flight?"

"Terrible. Awful."

"Oh, too bad," I said. "Turbulence?"

"Diarrhea. I think I got food poisoning last night at the cantina. Do you happen to know a good doctor?"

"Sorry, I'm afraid not. I know where the hospital is."

"Better tell me, just in case." I told him where it was and he wrote it down.

Sabina said, "Let me talk to him." I handed her the phone. "Mort? Sabina. Listen, I took a quick peek at the room of the gentleman in question and I've got some papers here— Yes. Yes, they look good. There are some classified documents he

249

got from the Corsican." She paused while Mort said something. "Why did he bring them with him to Vermont? *I* don't know, that's *your* department. Also there are several pages of notes in Polish. All right if I get Miss Tenofska to translate them?" There was a pause, during which she covered the receiver with her hand and mouthed to me, "He'd rather we didn't." Finally she said, "All right. Certainly, I quite understand. I'll give them to you at the Institute, meet me at the afternoon seminar. In the barn—ask anyone. Sorry to hear you're under the weather. Have you tried Kaopectate?" She paused and then repeated in a louder voice, "Kaopectate." She spelled it for him. "Oh, you're familiar with it. Well, good. Get some immediately, it'll work wonders. See you later." She hung up and turned to me, her eyes bright, rubbing her hands together. "Things are moving, Vic. Oh, I forgot to tell you, I took a shirt from Modzalewski's room. A flannel shirt of a particularly horrible green, I found it at the bottom of his laundry basket; I believe he was wearing it yesterday. It's stained with earth and what look like grease marks. Here it is." She opened her shoulder bag and, wrinkling her nose, drew out the shirt. It was fairly pungent. "When you take Magda to the Institute, leave a few minutes early so she can show you exactly where her car was parked at the time she thinks it was tampered with. Take a few soil samples. Then when she's finished her seminar you can drive her to Barre to pick up her car. Have a little talk with the mechanic, and take a sample of grease from the car. Make sure it's the old grease, of course; nothing that's just been put in."

"I think I can handle that," I said.

Sabina rose. "And now I'm going to make us a pot of tea." She headed for the kitchen. "Russian tea would be appropriate, under the circumstances." She glanced at her watch. "Twelve-thirty. We've got just under an hour before we have to leave for the Institute, time enough to make a plan. In a way this is a very frustrating case, because although we know who the murderer is, there's no evidence that would hold up in court. I really think we'll have to set a trap, Vic—don't you? I can't see any alternative."

250

# THIRTY-TWO

Rain fell late that afternoon. I knew I was going to be spending my evening hiding in the bushes so I kept hoping the weather would improve. Finally the sky cleared, except for patchy clouds that kept blowing across the moon, making the night bright one minute and dark the next. There was mist on the ground in the low places.

I found a nice big shrub under the kitchen window of the Moore-Ganns' cottage and did my best to get comfortable. It wasn't easy. Already the cold was creeping through my windbreaker, and every time I moved I got a shower. The window above my head was open a crack at the bottom and I could hear Sabina's voice. Silently I raised myself until I saw her, standing near the table and unbuttoning her coat. Theresa was standing next to her, looking somewhat stiff and formal, and saying "I was just making coffee, would you like some?" She went to the stove, where a coffeepot was steaming.

"Thank you, that would be lovely." Sabina sat down, slipping her arms out of the sleeves of her coat and draping it over the back of her chair. She crossed her legs, and the light gleamed along her nylon stockings and the thin, patent-leather heels of her pumps.

Theresa brought the coffeepot to the table. "Is it true that Andrzej Modzalewski has been arrested as a spy? That's what Magda told me. She said he was the one who tampered with her brakes—it all sounds so extraordinary! Really, I hardly know what to think. Yesterday when Magda said someone had tried to kill her, I thought it must be her imagination, I couldn't imagine who would want to do that."

"Someone does," Sabina said. "Or did."

"Oh, I'm sorry!" cried Theresa. "I've made your cup too full, now there's coffee in your saucer. Let me get you a new one."

Sabina picked up her cup and blotted the saucer with a napkin. "It's all right, don't bother."

"You're sure?" Theresa sat down. She stirred cream into her coffee. "They say you were the one who told the CIA about Modzalewski. Is that true?"

"Vic and I, yes."

"How clever of you to figure out what he was up to! I heard he managed to recruit Jean-Paul Brocchiu, too. Now *that* doesn't surprise me," she said with satisfaction. "I never cared for him. Well—in a sense that's one bright spot in the whole sorry mess. Magda will finally have to face the facts about that man. I've tried and *tried* to open her eyes but—" She shook her head. "We all have to learn through experience. The poor girl's terribly upset." She sipped her coffee. "When I think what she's been through in the last few days . . ."

"It hasn't been an easy time for you either," Sabina murmured.

"No. That's true. But these things are harder on the young, they haven't learned to rise above them." She leaned across the table toward her guest. "Sabina, I think I owe you an apology—and Victor, too. I admit it upset me last night when he came and whisked Magda away like that without an explanation, and then called to say she wasn't coming home. I understand why now; you didn't want her spending the night where Modzalewski would be able to find her. Still, I think Victor ought to have seen fit to enlighten me a little—and Florian, since he was here." Her tone was reproachful. "Perhaps you should mention that to Victor. I think he fancies himself a bit of a lone wolf, but his judgment could be better at times. Of course, he's young." She gave a little laugh. "He could have trusted us. Someone like Modzalewski is a disgrace to the physics community. We'd naturally want to see him caught. We wouldn't have breathed a word." She waited, but Sabina said nothing. "I suppose Victor meant well." Theresa's skin looked gray as ashes. "There's one thing I still don't understand."

"What's that?"

"Why can't Magda come home? She told me you insisted that she spend another night at your place." Her voice was plaintive. "Modzalewski's in custody, surely you don't think she's still in danger." She leaned forward, her eyes on Sabina's face.

"Maybe not."

"Maybe? But who else would want to harm her?"

"Someone has killed two people, Theresa. I wouldn't want her to be the third—nor would you, presumably."

"Of course not! What's that remark supposed to mean?" Sabina didn't answer. The two women sat in silence. Finally Theresa remarked, "Every night there's a party in the barn, and everybody goes but me. I feel rather like Cinderella. Not that I'd want to go." She sipped her coffee. "I suppose they need to unwind at the end of the day, talk informally—you can't blame them." She sighed. "Florian thinks it wouldn't hurt for me to go over to the barn. Of course *he* has to be there to represent the Institute, or so he says." She propped her elbows on the table and rested her chin on her hands. "Do *you* think I should go? I'll be here until the end of the summer. . . ." Sabina didn't answer. "Sometimes I worry too much about what people might think. In my position one's not supposed to go to parties, festivities, it's not expected, is it? . . ." Her voice trailed off uncertainly. "I'm Moore-Gann's widow, that's how people see me, just as they used to see me as Moore-Gann's wife. And I was, of course. I mean, what else was I?" She fell silent and sipped her coffee. "Actually in a way these aren't exactly parties. You could think of them as an extension of the work of the Institute; people talk a lot of physics—it's useful, really." She set down her cup. "I know it's petty of me to feel left out. I've always prided myself on being able to occupy my time constructively, it's something I had to learn because Hervé traveled so much. Well, I don't know why I'm bothering you with all this."

"You're not bothering me."

Theresa gave a rueful little smile. "You're a good listener, Sabina. Maybe I want to confide in you because you're not a conventional sort of woman."

"And are *you,* Theresa?"

"I?" Theresa gave a brief laugh. "Oh, profoundly, I would say. Far too much. Would you like some brandy?"

"No, thank you."

"I'll have a drop." Theresa went to the counter, where a bottle of cognac was standing. I wondered how many brandies she'd had before Sabina got there. She poured herself a small, cautious shot, as if that was all she thought she should have though she wanted more. "Hervé used to accuse me of being too conventional; sometimes he called me 'Madam Prim.' It was sort of a joke between us. He said he couldn't call me 'Miss Prim' because I was married. I wish I'd been able to give him more . . . affection—be more open and, well, free, but when you're raised a certain way, taught certain things are right and others wrong, you can't just throw it off." She leaned forward. "I really did try. I even saw an analyst a few times. My goodness, I've never told anyone *that* before! It didn't help, I'm just as repressed as ever. 'Repressed'—that's a dirty word nowadays." She gave a little titter and poured more brandy into her glass. "What a funny world we live in. Really, Sabina, I wish you'd tell me what you think—*should* I go to the barn in the evenings?"

"Theresa, that's not what I came to talk about."

"Of course not. Well, what was that? I've been wondering. Is it about Hervé's death? Florian said you weren't satisfied that Judith poisoned him and then killed herself." Carefully she placed her unfinished drink on the counter. "I don't understand why not. The police think so."

"Do you?"

"Oh, yes." She added after a moment, "I admit the idea that Hervé was murdered because of something that happened twenty years ago seems a bit fantastic, but what other explanation can there be? Judith left a suicide note, after all."

"It wasn't very convincing."

"You don't think so? Why not?"

"It didn't say one word about your husband's death. It was just a couple of phrases—angry, perversely proud phrases. It was a fake—probably torn off the bottom of an old letter by the real murderer."

"That's an interesting theory."

"Judith used to write to you sometimes, didn't she, Theresa? Because you sent her money."

"Now why do you ask me that?" Theresa's tone was almost plaintive. She folded her arms and leaned back against the counter.

"Because certain things puzzle me—for instance, things you've said that don't seem to be true. I thought perhaps if I asked you face to face for an explanation—"

"I appreciate that, Sabina. I hate it when people go behind my back." Theresa's voice was pleasant. "What exactly did you want to ask me about?"

"Remember that piece of paper Vic showed you? The one with the passage on it from *The Good Soldier*."

"Oh, yes."

Her first slip. She should have said she didn't know where the passage came from; that's what she'd told me.

"You told Vic your husband found it in his packet when he arrived." Sabina shook her head. "The paper was very unusual, very distinctive. *Your* paper—wasn't it? As a matter of fact there's someone who's prepared to swear she once received a note from you on the same type of paper." This wasn't true, but it was a gamble we'd decided to take.

A flush crept up Theresa's neck. "So what?" she said sharply. "It's just a coincidence."

Sabina shook her head. "You're a scientist, Theresa. Would you like to calculate the probabilities? A sheet of very unusual paper, *your* paper, containing a quotation from a book that happens at this very moment to be on a shelf in your study, is mysteriously found in your husband's packet when he arrives at the Institute—according to you. You lied. Why?"

Theresa stiffened and her eyes were defiant as she declared, "Improbable is not the same as impossible. Judith did kill my husband, she did commit suicide. Why, the police found the empty Digoxin bottle in her office!"

Another slip, a bad one this time. That was a detail the police had so far kept to themselves. Sabina said sharply, "How do you know? The police never said any such thing."

"They did, they must have. What I mean is, they said so to me, I'm not just anybody, I'm the widow—"

"Well, we'll ask them if they did."

Theresa's head jerked. Abruptly she strode toward the window through which I was peering. I ducked down out of sight and heard her voice directly above me a moment later. "There's a draft from this window," she said, and slammed it shut. I didn't think she'd seen me but I wasn't sure, and I shrank back under the bush as close to the ground as possible, holding my breath. I could still hear the murmur of voices but without being able to make out any words. Nervously my hand strayed to the gun in my shoulder holster. It was hard to know what to do next; it seemed a poor idea to try looking in the window at this point, but a worse one to leave Sabina alone in the house with Theresa when I had no way of knowing what was going on.

I told myself Sabina was perfectly safe. She was too cagy to let Theresa get behind her, and at my insistence she was carrying a pistol in the pocket of her skirt, though all she'd wanted to take was the miniature tape recorder, claiming a gun was unnecessary because I would be there to back her up.

"Yeah, and what if I keel over from a heart attack?" I'd objected.

"You're too young," she'd said; but she'd gotten the point.

Suddenly I realized that I couldn't hear the voices any more. Had the two women left the kitchen? There was only one thing to do, though it meant deviating from our plan: I would have to go in after Sabina, doing my best to remain undiscovered.

Silently I crawled away from the house between the shrubs until I came to a tree; then I stood up and peered cautiously around the trunk in the direction of the kitchen window. The room was empty. I took a couple of steps across the lawn toward the front door.

Behind me there was a faint rustle in the grass. I froze, my muscles tensing, and grabbed for my gun but I was too late—an arm came out of the darkness and yoked me powerfully across the throat. I jerked my right knee forward and kicked backward, aiming for my attacker's groin while I pried with my fingers underneath the arm that was cutting off my breath. He blocked my kick with his leg and gave me a punch on the side of my neck that made me dizzy. I stumbled and fell to my knees with him on top of me. We wrestled around in the grass, trading kicks and punches while I attempted to reach my gun. He was a big, husky guy and he knew how to fight. I could hear him grunting as he kept trying to pin me to the ground while I kept rolling away, never getting far enough to pull out my gun. Then I felt cold metal pressing against my neck below the ear while he said, "Okay, feller, put your hands up, this here's a shotgun."

I caught the gleam of the barrel in the moonlight and sat up cautiously, raising my arms above my head. There was a familiar, pungent smell. After a moment I recognized it as manure. I peered at my attacker. "Say, aren't you Bill?"

"Yep." The shotgun wavered. "Mind telling me who *you* are?"

"Vic Newman," I said, in as confident a voice as I could muster with half the breath knocked out of me. "Don't you remember me, Bill?"

"Don't know nobody by that name."

Where the hell were Sabina and Theresa? I started to get up but Bill gave me a shove with the muzzle of the shotgun. "Stay put," he said. "Now, what do you think you're up to, prowling around Mrs. Moore-Gann's house?"

"Bill, I'm the guy who asked you to guard this place, for God's sake. I gave you twenty dollars. But that was supposed to be last night—not tonight."

"Just last night?" He lowered the shotgun.

I stood up. Waves of dizziness sloshed back and forth in my brain for a long minute. I grabbed for a tree and held on until things settled down. "I'm going in the house," I said. "You better stay here and detain anyone who comes out. That includes Mrs. Moore-Gann—especially Mrs. Moore-Gann."

"I can't stop *her*. She lives here, she can come and go however she wants."

Giving up on him, I turned and stumbled toward the front porch. After mounting the steps, I let myself in through the unlatched door and paused in the hallway to listen; there was no sound anywhere. I searched the downstairs rooms. There were lights, but no sign of Sabina or Theresa. Where had they gone?

Moving more quickly, I went upstairs. The second floor was dark and the silence was absolute, the silence of a deserted house. I checked the rooms and again found no one. As I was leaving the last room, a flicker of light outside caught my eye. I went to the window. Below me, light spilled out of a rear window onto what seemed to be a path leading toward the woods. After a moment I saw the flicker of light again. Someone was walking in the woods with a flashlight.

I clattered down the stairs and ran out the back door, where I found myself on the path I'd seen from above. There was no sign of Bill. The moon came out and I began to sprint down the path toward the woods, the grass wet and slippery beneath my feet; the ground sloped downward, and after taking a tumble I was forced to slow down to a walk. Once I was in the woods, the crowding trees shut out the moonlight and I picked my way in darkness between the rocks and the tree roots. Once I glimpsed a light up ahead.

Finally the trees started thinning out. I was coming to the edge of the woods. It was misty there. The fog eddied between the trunks of the trees, thicker in some places and thinner in others. But when I reached the end of the woods and stepped out onto grass, I found myself in a dense fog. I could hear the sound of water lapping, and realized the path I'd been following had led me to the pond, though I couldn't see it because of the mist that hung over the water. I couldn't tell which way Sabina and Theresa had turned, left or right; for a moment I felt close to panic. If anything happened to Sabina . . .

I turned to the right, with some vague idea that this would lead me toward the wooden bridge over the spillway. Soon the fog thinned out a little, and I caught glimpses of the reeds at the edge of the water. A *plop!* startled me, but it was only a fish jumping.

Then, faintly, I heard another sound: voices, floating through the air from somewhere up ahead. At least I was moving in the right direction. I began to run, my footfalls silent on the short, dense turf. After sprinting for a minute or two I ran into something and crashed to the ground, my shoe striking wood with a solid *thunk!* that echoed in the silence. I'd fallen over the bench where I'd sat with Magda.

The voices had stopped but soon I heard them again, coming from the bridge. I picked myself up and ran as fast as I could in that direction. After a moment of total silence there were scuffling noises. Suddenly I heard Sabina scream "Vic!" I raced toward the sound of her voice, my heart thudding wildly, and then there was a heavy splash, as if a body had fallen into the water. A moment later footsteps retreated.

I reached the bridge. It was deserted. Below, under the billowing mist, the surface of the water was calm and still. I shouted "Sabina!" but there was no reply.

I called again and then dove off the bridge into the water. The shock as the cold hit me was intense. I opened my eyes underwater but I could see nothing at all in the blackness as I swam down to the bottom and then to one side and the other, my arms extended and groping, until I had to shoot up to the surface for air. I dove again and again found nothing, fighting the powerful current that kept pulling me toward the dam and the spillway. The next time I rose to the surface there were searchlights on the shore. I thought I heard Bill's voice. "Over here!" I yelled, and dove again. This time I surrendered to the current, letting it carry me until I was spreadeagled against the slimy concrete of the dam. My breath almost gone, I kicked my way down the face of the dam, my arms outstretched—and there she was! I felt a shoulder . . . a neck . . . an ear . . . I grabbed her by the hair and pulled her up to the surface. She came like a dead thing, passively drifting.

# THIRTY-THREE

At two o'clock the following afternoon I carried chairs into Sabina's hospital room. Saul Sachs was there, as well as Florian and Magda; Captain Eaken hadn't arrived yet. Sabina had invited them, over the objections of her doctor, so she could explain what had happened the night before, and why.

She was sitting up in bed. Around her head there was a large bandage, concealing the wound Theresa's alpenstock had made. "I don't see why I can't go home," she was saying to Bruno, who sat beside her bed. "After all, what's a little headache?"

"It's only another twenty-four hours," he said in a soothing voice, patting her hand. "You have a slight concussion, it's better if they keep an eye on you."

She made a face, then started to cough. I knew she'd been coughing up blood and her doctor was concerned about it. "It's a good thing you pulled her out when you did and started mouth-to-mouth," he'd told me. "A little longer and we'd have had a much more serious situation on our hands. As it is, she should be all right in a day or two. A strong constitution."

Sabina's coughing fit tapered off and she took a sip of water from the cup Bruno handed her. She'd gotten ready to receive her guests by having him bring her a lace-trimmed bed jacket from Burlington; she was wearing it now. She'd also managed to requisition from some unknown source a handmade quilt to drape over her knees.

Footsteps were heard in the hall, and Captain Eaken strode into the room. He came up to the bedside and surveyed

Sabina with a bemused expression in his cool gray eyes. "Well, you don't look too bad," he said finally, folding his arms. "Maybe next time you decide to jump in a pond you'll give us a call first." He glanced in my direction. "That goes for you, too."

"I didn't jump, I was pushed," Sabina said with dignity. "Please sit down, Captain Eaken." He took a chair, and Sabina looked around at the group. "Now that everyone's here, let's get started. I'm sure you're all aware that Theresa Moore-Gann has been arrested for the murder of her husband and Judith."

"Poor Theresa!" Florian sighed.

"Poor Theresa my Aunt Tillie, Flor," Eaken said impatiently. "She killed two people. Three, pretty near."

"But why?" said Florian. "I can't understand what made her do such a thing."

Eaken looked uncomfortable. "Well—that's a tough question." He threw a hopeful glance at Sabina.

"It is in a sense," she agreed. "Because Theresa's character is quite complex. However, her motive for murder had a classical simplicity, even though unforeseen events complicated the situation quite a bit." She settled back more comfortably against the pillows. "Originally, when I was asked by Florian to investigate the case, I assumed that the key to the murder was to be found in the character of the dead man; the obvious first question was 'Who had a motive for killing Hervé Moore-Gann? And there were a number of possible candidates: professional colleagues he'd injured, for he'd been a cold and ruthless—though brilliant—man; women with whom he'd had affairs—especially Judith, by whom he'd apparently had a child he refused to acknowledge. A jealous wife, perhaps—though Theresa didn't seem high on the list, since she had apparently accepted his infidelities for years, even decades. Possibly, too, there could be a political angle; he'd become very involved in governmental matters.

"However, one thing that troubled me from the start was that Moore-Gann didn't drink. He'd given up alcohol a year earlier, when he'd become preoccupied with physical fitness, and this was common knowledge. Why should anyone who knew him well enough to have a motive for murder choose such an unlikely means?

"The answer to this question soon became apparent. Magda Tenofska informed Vic that the poisoned Bloody Mary was, in fact, hers. Jean-Paul had made it and handed it to her—though she didn't want another drink, and she'd simply set it down on a table next to where she was standing, and left it there. Some time later, after the dramatic encounter between the two Nobel laureates, Moore-Gann had told her he needed a drink and she gave him hers.

"As soon as I heard this, I realized that Magda had been the intended victim. A slight element of uncertainty remained—it was theoretically possible that the murderer had somehow skillfully managed to poison the drink while Moore-Gann was holding it in his hand—but this seemed unlikely, especially since he drank it fairly quickly. It was Magda, then, who should have died. But why—who wanted her dead?

"The answer seemed to be Jean-Paul, her former lover, even though what he really appeared to want was to resume their relationship. She still cared for him, and although she hadn't lived with him for a number of months it was possible she might go back to him eventually. Vic got that impression, and it was obviously something Theresa feared very much; in that case, shouldn't Jean-Paul, too, be sufficiently aware of it, not to have given up hope completely? So it seemed to me. On the other hand, Jean-Paul is a violent, impulsive, vengeful person—perhaps he really *was* the poisoner. The police, of course, thought so and arrested him eventually; though they released him the next day, after Judith's death.

"If Jean-Paul hadn't tried to kill Magda, who had? No one else seemed to have a motive. Had she been Moore-Gann's mistress, could Theresa, despite appearances, really be a murderously jealous wife? Maybe—yet if there were two things everyone agreed on, they seemed to be, first, that Magda was far too ambitious to risk ruining her reputation as a physicist by having an affair with her mentor, and, second, that

Theresa adored the girl and had virtually adopted her as a daughter.

"That left Andrzej Modzalewski. I wondered if the two of them could have had some connection in Poland that nobody knew about. There was the Solidarity link—Magda's mother was in jail and Andrzej, too, had been imprisoned. I resolved to make some inquiries of a contact in the CIA and to keep an eye on Andrzej. And eventually there did turn out to be a connection, though Magda was totally unaware of it. It was Andrzej who'd betrayed her mother to the authorities." Sabina looked around at her audience. "By now you all know he's been arrested as a spy."

Saul Sachs shook his head in disgust. "Andrzej! Boy, the phone calls I made and wires I pulled to find that son of a gun a job! It wasn't easy, he's not that good." He shrugged. "You win some, you lose some." Leaning toward Magda, he patted her hands, which were clasped rigidly together in her lap. "Too bad about your mother, kid. I heard. Really rotten."

"Thank you."

"If there's anything I can do—"

"There may be," said Sabina. "She's having visa problems. Why don't you discuss that later. I think we have to move on." She took a drink of water. "Modzalewski *did* try to kill Magda, by sabotaging her car; but that was only a couple of days ago. He knew she'd received news from Poland that would enable her, once she put two and two together, to unmask him as a spy. None of this, however, was related to the murder of Moore-Gann; it was merely a complicating element, a side issue.

"To sum up, these were some of the factors I was considering. There were others"—she glanced at Florian—"which I needn't go into; they're not really relevant.

"And then a new element entered the case: a piece of paper with a curious paragraph typed on it, which Vic found in the study of the Moore-Gann cottage. As soon as he showed it to me, I felt intuitively that it would prove to be important. Yet it didn't seem on the face of it to *mean* anything. I have a copy here, let me read it to you." She took out her glasses and put them on.

> "It is almost too terrible, the picture of that judgment, as it appears to me sometimes, at nights. It is probably the suggestion of some picture that I have seen somewhere. But upon an immense plain, suspended in mid-air, I seem to see three figures, two of them clasped close in an intense embrace, and one intolerably solitary. It is in black and white, my picture of that judgment, an etching, perhaps; only I cannot tell an etching from a photographic reproduction. And the immense plain is the hand of God, stretching out for miles and miles, with great spaces above it and below it."

The faces of her audience were puzzled. She handed me the paper and I passed it around the room so anyone who wanted to could study it. She said, "It doesn't convey anything to you? It didn't to me either, at first; yet there was something about it that teased me, a memory I couldn't quite grasp. At first I thought I might have seen somewhere the picture it was describing, but then Captain Eaken made the very intelligent comment that it sounded like something in a book." Eaken stirred in his chair, looking gratified. "I knew at once that he was right. The passage came from a book I must have read at one time, which was why it seemed so familiar. And as I studied it I found myself wondering more and more about the triangular relationship it referred to, from which one of the members had evidently been ejected, to be left 'intolerably solitary.' Had one of the three people in the Moore-Ganns' house identified so strongly with that solitary figure that he or she had copied out the passage, with its tone of torment and despair?

"I didn't know, but I thought it was strange when Theresa told Vic her husband had found the paper in his packet when he'd picked it up. Vic had noticed a number of novels in the Moore-Gann study, as well as the physics books one would have expected to find; among the novels was Ford Madox Ford's *The Good Soldier,* one of the masterpieces of English fiction. As soon as I recalled that fact, I realized that the style of the passage reminded me of that book. I'd read it so long ago that I barely remembered it, I'm ashamed to say. I was able to obtain a copy at the public library, and when I reread it I located the passage in question.

"It seemed to me an unlikely coincidence that the quotation would simply have 'appeared' in Moore-Gann's packet, when the book the quotation came from was right in his study and obviously belonged to a member of his household. Theresa had told a lie—a rather stupid lie. The reason became clear to me as I reread the book, for it told me it was *she* who had poisoned Moore-Gann—and why she had done so. Unfortunately *The Good Soldier* wasn't evidence—at least not the kind that would stand up in court. And a major problem with this case has been that there was little or no solid evidence to be found. I was convinced Theresa was the murderer, but I couldn't prove it."

Magda suddenly interrupted. "I do not understand," she said agitatedly, as if she hadn't really been following what Sabina had been saying. Of all the people in the room, she seemed the most shaken, and no wonder. In one week she'd lost everyone she was closest to: her mother; Jean-Paul, who'd been taken into custody late yesterday afternoon and charged with passing classified documents to Modzalewski; and both the Moore-Ganns. There was a note that was close to hysteria in her voice as she demanded, "Why should Theresa want to kill Hervé when he meant everything to her?"

"She didn't want to kill him," said Sabina, and paused. "Actually, she was trying to kill *you*."

"Theresa kill Magda?" said Florian in disbelief. "Nonsense, she adored her!" He shook his head vigorously. Saul, too, looked skeptical, and Eaken seemed totally confused.

Magda jumped up. "No, you are wrong! There must be some other explanation. Theresa loved me, she needed me! She leaned on me—even more so after Moore-Gann died! No, it is impossible. I would have known if she had hated me enough to want to kill me. I would have felt it, here." She laid her hand on her heart.

"Please sit down. I never said she hated you," said Sabina.

"As a matter of fact she didn't. It's true she depended on you, perhaps even loved you. Yet she *did* try to poison you, Magda. Moore-Gann's death was a mistake. She said it was, to Vic, on two occasions—once in the hospital and again when he was driving her home after her husband had died. Both times she meant it literally. It had never occurred to her that he could possibly end up drinking the poisoned Bloody Mary she'd intended for you, since he no longer drank alcohol. The way the whole thing turned out was really quite ironic."

"But why, why, why—"

"Why did she want to kill you? I'll come to that in a minute. Certainly there's no doubt she was attached to you. She told me last night when we were walking to the pond that she'd always wanted a child, desperately. You filled that void in her life, and it was truly an enormous one. Moore-Gann never gave her much emotionally, everyone who knew him seems to agree that he was a cold, selfish, ambitious man. Nevertheless, her life revolved around him completely, until you came along. For years she'd overlooked his infidelities and sacrificed her own career—exactly how much that sacrifice entailed, nobody knew." She turned to Saul Sachs. "Except for you. You knew, didn't you?"

Saul's frail body was huddled in an armchair, one leg crossed over the other, the bones of his knees sharp through the cloth of his trousers, one hairy, wasted ankle visible above a crumpled sock. After a moment he said, "Yeah, I guess that's right." He looked around the room, his high forehead wrinkling under the sparse, wispy hairs that fringed his narrow skull. "I'm not crazy about conferences in hospitals. Let's make this short and sweet, okay?"

"We can try," said Sabina. She turned her head to survey the rest of us. "Everybody in the physics world of course knew about the feud between Hervé Moore-Gann and Saul Sachs, two preeminent physicists who'd known each other since boyhood, who were very different kinds of people but who found that intellectually they made a remarkable team."

Saul nodded. "That's probably a fair statement. Most of

the ideas were mine. Not all, of course. But Harvey was a brilliant calculator—much better than me. He had a fantastic ability to translate physical ideas into mathematical formulations, and he was a nitpicker *par excellence.* You couldn't fault his calculations; when he produced a result you knew it was right.''

Sabina went on, "In other words, you complemented each other superbly. And of course for a while the collaboration went well—so well that you won the Nobel prize. Then suddenly everything changed—you stopped speaking to Moore-Gann, you refuse even to appear at conferences where he would be present. Everyone in the physics world wondered why, but nobody really knew.'' She leaned toward Saul. "I think what happened is that you'd discovered that some of the ideas in the work you'd won the prize for, ideas that Moore-Gann had contributed, were actually not his but Theresa's.''

He stared at her in amazement. "How the hell did you figure that out?''

"My God!'' Magda said in an appalled voice. "My God, he did that? And Theresa let him?''

"She sure did, doll,'' said Saul. "I'd have given her credit if I'd known—but I didn't find out until later. Leo Pesnik once asked me to read through a file of old letters a bunch of physicists had written him, including Harvey and Theresa. He wanted my advice on whether to sue Harvey for plagiarism. I told him not to, because he couldn't prove it and he stood to lose more than he would gain, even though what he claimed was probably true.'' He waved his hand. "But that's a side issue. I looked through the file and guess what I found? A couple of letters from Theresa to Leo, dating back before her marriage when she was still actively engaged in research. I read them and my hair stood on end. Back then I had hair.'' He paused. "Right there in her handwriting was the germ of a major idea Harvey had presented to me as his. I thought I'd *plotz.* Right away I went to see her. Guess what she told me? I should keep quiet. If I made a stink, she'd say I was nuts. Not that the whole thing wasn't true—she admitted it was. Harvey'd helped himself to her ideas as if they were his property and in fact he was still doing it. I wouldn't be surprised if quite a few of the ideas he claimed as his were basically hers—maybe most of them, even. What really floored me was that *she* seemed to think this craziness was reasonable, just because they were married; I think she was worried that Moore-Gann would leave her if she objected." He held out his hands, palms up, and shrugged. "What could I do? I told her the whole thing was ridiculous, preposterous, criminal even. The son of a bitch had no right to steal her ideas. And he sure had no right to foist them off on me and taint *my* work! But under the circumstances there was nothing I could do. So that's what I did—nothing. I can't honestly say I was dying to tell the world. There's such a thing as guilt by association." He sighed. "I confronted Harvey and he denied everything, lied in my face. I let him know what I thought of him, and after that I had nothing more to do with him." He fell silent, his head dropping back against the cushion of his chair.

Sabina, whose eyes had been fastened intently on Saul, now looked around the room. "There's no way we can be sure whether Moore-Gann would really have divorced Theresa, as she may have believed, if she'd refused to allow him to use her ideas. Their marriage was certainly a strange one, there wasn't much of what most people would consider love, and certainly no sexual passion. Theresa talked to me quite openly last night—no doubt once she'd decided she had to kill me she felt it didn't matter what she said—and she told me, when I asked her, that her marriage to Moore-Gann had never been fully consummated. She apparently suffered, and I'm sure 'suffered' is the right word, from a pathological aversion to sex that was the real reason for her childlessness—not infertility, as she let people assume."

"It seems incredible," muttered Bruno. "They were married for twenty years."

"Unconsummated marriages are not unheard of," said Sabina, who'd sent me to the library of the University of Vermont that very morning to bring her an article on the subject. "In fact, they're less rare than one might think. From what

Theresa told me, I'm pretty sure she had a condition called vaginismus, in which the vagina goes into such a severe, involuntary spasm, usually for psychological reasons, that penetration is impossible. Eventually she and her husband seem to have adjusted to it, in a way. Moore-Gann satisfied his sexual needs outside the marriage, and Theresa knew this and put up with it.

"Probably the real basis of the marriage was intellectual compatibility. On that plane I suspect it was satisfactory to both of them, at least at first, despite his exploitation of her work—which she permitted. Perhaps she felt it was the price she had to pay for having a husband, like other women, in spite of her handicap. As time went on, though, the lack of emotional sustenance in the marriage took a heavy toll on her, though at the same time she was totally and desperately dependent on her husband; he defined her whole world, her whole identity. If that's a definition of love—it wouldn't be mine, but—" She shrugged. "She loved him.

"Which brings us to the part Magda played in the lives of the Moore-Ganns, and it also brings us back to *The Good Soldier*." By this time the sheet of paper that had been making the circuit of the room was lying on Sabina's bed again, and she picked it up. "Quite simply, Magda's arrival on the scene stirred up such powerful feelings in both of them that the bizarre and fragile equilibrium of their marriage just . . . collapsed.

"Obviously it must have unnerved Theresa when Vic suddenly showed her the passage from the novel, a passage she herself had copied out because it was deeply meaningful to her. I suppose she lied because she had to say *something*. She was well aware of the revealing parallels between the plot and her own marriage." Sabina lay back for a moment against the pillows, blinking as if her head was hurting. Then she resumed.

"In *The Good Soldier* there's a couple named Ashburnham—Captain Edward Ashburnham, the 'Good Soldier' of the title, and his wife, Leonora. They appear to have a happy, though childless, marriage, but in reality he's had a series of affairs and is no longer even on speaking terms with his wife, except when other people are present. The two of them have a ward named Nancy who has lived with them since childhood and whom both of them, especially the wife, love as if she were their own child. However, when Nancy reaches nineteen or so, the husband falls desperately in love with her. The wife learns of it and feels utterly betrayed, all the characters are torn between conflicting loyalties and desires, and the story has a tragic ending." Sabina looked around the room at her audience, who were listening with great concentration.

"Certain similarities to the lives of the Moore-Ganns, especially after Magda came to live with them, are obvious; others are less so. According to Magda, Moore-Gann had made advances to her soon after she came to work with him in a postdoctoral position, and she had turned him down in no uncertain terms. What he had in mind at that time, I believe, was merely a brief sexual liaison, such as he'd often had in the past with other women. He told his wife about his attraction to Magda, as was his custom. Perhaps he enjoyed boasting about his exploits, not that he'd been very successful in this instance, perhaps he just appreciated having an accepting listener in whom he could confide anything and everything. Or perhaps he blamed Theresa for his affairs because of her sexual inadequacy, and wanted to hurt her by telling her about his women. Theresa admitted to me last night that she found it painful to hear about them, even though she didn't object. Naturally it pained her; she loved him.

"In any case, I'm sure Theresa was glad to hear that she had nothing to fear from Magda, whom at that time she scarcely knew. I'm sure it never occurred to her that as her husband continued to work with the young woman he would find himself, like the Good Soldier, falling wildly in love—in Moore-Gann's case, probably for the first time in his life. At least, nobody who knew him ever mentioned that he'd had a real love affair, despite all his philandering.

"This love of Moore-Gann's for Magda probably took him completely by surprise and caused him to suffer in a way he hadn't known was possible—as he hinted to Saul Sachs when the two of them finally shook hands for the first time in many years. I think he'd come to feel he couldn't live without Magda, and that he desperately wanted to share with her every aspect of his life. The disparity in their ages must have tormented him, and I believe that explains his sudden craze for physical fitness; he jogged, he exercised, he gave up alcohol, as if these things could make him young again. He fantasized about marrying her.

"Yet at the same time he felt bound to Theresa, who had shared his life for so long and contributed so enormously to his work—far more than was right or ethical, as he was well aware and as he knew his colleagues would feel if they ever found out. They would react the way Sachs had. He was afraid that if he divorced her she would make public the fact that he had taken credit for ideas that were really hers.

"He was trapped in a terrible dilemma. For months he did nothing, perhaps hoping his infatuation would pass; but then he returned from a trip and found that Magda was actually living in his house. Now he saw her day and night, and his love for her must have grown even stronger.

"I don't think Theresa suspected anything. She seems to have been more preoccupied with Magda than with her husband. In a way, you could say she fell in love with Magda, too—at least, she became fascinated by her to the point of obsession, as if she was trying to pour out the frustrated maternal longings of a lifetime all at once. The fact that Magda, like herself at that age, was a talented physicist made it easy for her to identify with her and vicariously enjoy her professional accomplishments, as if Magda had really been her daughter. And at first Magda was grateful, which encouraged Theresa's fantasies, for Magda was bruised in body and spirit and missed her own mother, whom she had left behind in Poland. But as she became stronger, she was often irritated by Theresa's overprotectiveness. Theresa felt her pulling away and clung even harder.

"Finally, I believe—probably not long before they were all to leave for Vermont—Moore-Gann must have made another of his 'confessions' to his wife—only this time telling her he was passionately in love with Magda and was determined to marry her. It's the only thing that can possibly explain what happened subsequently—though when I asked Theresa last night if her husband had ever asked her for a divorce, she vehemently denied it. I think she simply couldn't bring herself to admit it.

"Moore-Gann knew he was shortly to be named as an ambassador, and perhaps he felt that afterward the opinions of the scientific community would be less important in his life, even if Theresa were to publicly accuse him. Or perhaps he had such a desperate need to grasp at this last chance for happiness that he simply didn't care about the consequences."

"But I never said I would marry him!" cried Magda. "He never asked me, why should he have believed I would marry him if he got a divorce?"

"Obviously because of your visa situation," Sabina replied. "The two of you had often discussed the possibility that you might marry an American to solve your problems with the immigration authorities."

"Oh, my God!" said Magda. "But I never thought—"

"Moore-Gann must have been convinced that once he was free you *would* marry him, that you would be unable to resist the prestige that went with his position. Of course, we'll never know now whether he was right." There was a silence, in which Magda began to weep.

Sabina went steadily on. "How would all this have affected Theresa? Quite simply, she was devastated—maybe even temporarily insane; I suppose her lawyers may decide to offer that defense in court. Just when she felt she had the family she'd always wanted, and was happier than she'd been in years, she suddenly found she was about to lose everything: her home, her husband, her status as wife of one of the luminaries of the scientific world, and also—Magda. She was tormented by thoughts of the two of them"—Sabina read from the quotation, which she was still holding in her hand—"'Clasped close in an intense embrace,' while she would be

272

the 'intolerably solitary' one. And she hated to be alone, even though she liked to boast of how self-sufficient she was.

"She must have brooded, becoming more and more angry and bitter. Moore-Gann had used her—her life, her work, her ideas—and now when she was no longer young he intended to discard her, leaving her with nothing. She who had met kings and presidents, who had looked forward to becoming the wife of an ambassador. How could she start over, at her age? No. Magda had to die—even though in a way she still loved her. She must have regretted the necessity; I don't believe she really blamed Magda; but with Magda out of the picture, everything would go back to normal, or so she apparently convinced herself." Sabina paused. Magda shuddered, pressing a wadded handkerchief to her lips.

Saul Sachs said, "So she stole my Digoxin and poisoned Magda's Bloody Mary."

"Yes. Probably she saw the bottle when she went looking in the medicine cabinet for mercurochrome to put on Magda's scraped knees after she'd had a fight with Jean-Paul, which Vic broke up. Suddenly, when Theresa saw the digitalis, the idea of poisoning the girl at the cocktail party that night must have occurred to her. We know roughly when the Digoxin was taken, and that time slot would fit. Theresa must have imagined it would be easier to get away with a crime when there were many other people around who might have committed it.

"But somebody happened to see her. Not a very good courtroom witness, unfortunately. It was Jordan. I talked to him yesterday afternoon—Bill, the caretaker, took me in a jeep to the pond where he'd gone fishing; it was quite an exciting ride. Jordan told me he saw a lady put something in Magda's drink while it was standing on the table, and told his mother about it. Judith immediately realized the implications and warned Jordan not to tell anyone, threatening to punish him severely if he did. He was afraid and ran away. Then she tried to blackmail Theresa, whom she'd hated for years for, as she saw it, taking Moore-Gann away from her.

273

"Jordan came home this morning," said Eaken. "I talked to him, and he told me the same thing he told Sabina. We'll see if he identifies Theresa later today—I reckon he will." He shook his head. "I thought he'd be all broke up about his mother's death, but he wasn't. Maybe he didn't really take it in."

Magda said in a low voice, "All that you say, it is logical, it sounds true. Yet, after Moore-Gann died by mistake, why wasn't Theresa hostile toward me? She didn't seem to be; if anything, I had the feeling she wanted me closer than ever. How is that possible?"

"Once Moore-Gann was dead, Magda, you were all she had left. She was determined to hang on to you, to go right on being your American mother and simply forget she'd ever wanted to take your life. She's an intensely pragmatic woman, with a quite remarkable ability to dissociate herself from her own deepest feelings. As she put it, she'd learned how to 'rise above trivial things.' She needed you, Magda—she couldn't bear to feel completely alone—and I think she imagined a role for herself in your life not totally unlike her role with her husband. That is, talking physics with you, participating vicariously in your successes, perhaps even feeding you ideas that you could incorporate in your work, which would tie you closer to her through a mixture of gratitude and guilt."

"I do not need the ideas of another person," Magda said stiffly. "I have my own."

"Naturally," said Sabina. "I'm only speculating about how *she* felt."

Captain Eaken cleared his throat. "Speculating is well and good but we also need evidence. Speaking of which, you'll be glad to know your tape recorder has been dredged out of the pond. They tell me the tape should be playable when they finish drying it out."

"Oh, good," said Sabina. "I was afraid it would be ruined." She turned to the others. "As I said before, a problem with this case was the lack of solid, courtroom evidence. We had a witness, but he was a boy of borderline IQ at best who could easily break down when questioned by a clever lawyer. We had a lie Theresa had told about the source of the paper with the quotation on it, but no way really to prove it wasn't the truth. The case I'd built up rested mostly on deduction and inference, and that wasn't enough.

"That was why I decided to visit her last night, while the other participants in the Institute were socializing in the barn. I took a tape recorder, hoping that if she thought we were alone I could provoke her into saying something incriminating—or if all else failed, into attacking me. I didn't think I'd be in any real danger because Vic and I had agreed that he'd remain nearby at all times.

"We talked for a while in her kitchen, with Vic hidden right outside the window, and I hinted pretty broadly that I knew she was a murderer. After a while she closed the window and suggested we go for a walk, saying she liked to take a walk every night after dinner and hadn't been able to, that evening, because of the rain. I suspected she'd made up her mind by then to kill me, for she was beginning to talk with extraordinary openness about her relationship with her husband. I didn't want to do anything that might make her stop. I agreed, and we started walking toward the pond, on a path that led through the woods. I assumed Vic was right behind me, but in fact he'd run into a snag."

"I sure had," I said, rubbing the side of my neck, which was still sore. "Good old Bill."

"You mean Bill the caretaker?" said Florian.

Sabina nodded. "That's right. The night before he'd agreed to guard the Moore-Ganns' house, where Magda was supposed to be spending the night after her automobile accident. Vic was quite concerned about her safety. So was I—in fact I later told him to bring her to my place as a precaution, and he did. I'm afraid Bill completely slipped our minds. Anyway, we wouldn't have expected to find him there the following night, but Bill apparently thought he was supposed to guard the place until further notice. He mistook Vic for a prowler and detained him for a while. By the time Vic finally figured out where we'd gone and had just about caught up with us,

Theresa managed to hit me on the head with her alpenstock and push me into the pond to drown."

"We found the alpenstock," said Captain Eaken. "We dredged it out of the pond when we went after your tape recorder. You'll be interested to know that the brass knob on top fits a bruise on Judith's head, under her hair. I'd call that solid evidence."

"Wonderful!" Sabina's hand strayed to her head as if she remembered Theresa's alpenstock all too well. "I knew she must have knocked Judith unconscious in some fashion or another; since Judith knew she was a poisoner, she'd certainly have been on her guard against any sort of drug. Poor Theresa! What a shock it must have been when Judith accused her of the murder—as I'm quite sure she did. Blackmail was nothing new for Judith, she'd had other victims. We needn't go into the details, but that was how she'd managed to pay for Jordan's expensive schooling. She worried about him constantly, and her greatest desire was to accumulate a nest egg for his future.

"I think Theresa felt she was above suspicion—the bereaved widow who had no reason to kill her famous husband. Certainly not because of his infidelities, which she'd known about for years. Vic saw her coming out of Judith's office on Sunday afternoon, only a few hours after she and Judith had had a vicious public quarrel, and Theresa told Vic that Judith had been helping her with some secretarial chores.

"That was patently absurd. No, the only reason she would have gone to Judith's office under the circumstances was that she'd had no choice, that Judith had informed her she'd seen her drop the poison into Magda's glass. I'm sure Judith must have claimed she herself had been the witness, not Jordan. She was always very protective of him and wouldn't have been apt to mention him in such a context. Unknowingly, she signed her own death warrant with that lie; if Theresa had been aware a third party was involved, she'd probably have paid the money Judith had demanded. As it was, she *said* she would pay—but that night, while everyone was at the cocktail party, she went to Judith's house and killed her. Theresa is a large, muscular woman who has done a good deal of mountain climbing, and Judith was short and slender; there's no doubt she could have overpowered her in a struggle, hit her over the head, and carried her out to the garage, just as she'd carried Magda to the car the night in Cambridge she took her to the emergency room."

"What about the note?" Eaken objected. "We had it examined by an expert and it was Judith's handwriting, all right."

"Oh, yes, the note."

Sabina took a sip of water from the cup beside her bed. "First of all, I was sure Judith wouldn't have killed herself. The whole focus of her life was her retarded son, and she'd never have left him to fend for himself if she could have helped it. Also it's been my experience that suicides tend to be quiet, depressed types who hold everything inside; people as openly hostile as Judith rarely kill themselves.

"It followed that the so-called suicide note was a fake, even though it *sounded* like Judith and was signed with her name. According to Vic, who saw it, it was written on a torn-off strip of paper; most likely it had come from the bottom of a letter she'd written to someone. Theresa, presumably—by then I was sure she was the murderer.

"I'd heard that Theresa sent Judith money on occasion for Jordan. Why she did so I'm not sure, but she let people know about it—she mentioned it last night to me. Did the thought that others admired her for her supposed generosity and her ability to rise above things that would have bothered other women gratify her ego? Perhaps. Or this may have been her way of punishing Moore-Gann for his infidelities, by reminding him every now and then of the existence of the retarded boy he'd tried to forget about completely.

"Actually she wasn't all that generous to Judith; recently for Jordan's birthday she sent her a five-dollar bill, which Judith considered an insult. Judith being Judith, she didn't hesitate to express her anger; she let me know that she'd written Theresa a letter—I'm sure it must have been scathing—and left it in her packet. Finding this letter probably gave

Theresa the idea for the lie she told about the passage from *The Good Soldier,* as a matter of fact.

"Once she'd decided to kill Judith, she carefully tore the last few lines off the letter and left them in the garage, next to Judith's unconscious body."

Sabina stopped speaking and for a moment her eyelids drooped tiredly. Bruno leaned toward her and said, "Maybe you shouldn't—" He groped for her hand.

A moment later an elderly nurse with tight brassy curls, her bust immobilized beneath a starched uniform, marched through the door, taking in the number of visitors with one scandalized glance. "This patient is supposed to rest," she stated firmly. "Besides, visitors are restricted to two per patient at all times."

Captain Eaken rose and pulled down the tunic of his uniform. "This is a police matter, ma'am," he said in an official voice. "We have permission from the nursing station to hold this meeting."

The nurse drew herself up and tossed her head. "Maybe so, on the last shift. I wouldn't care to speak for *them.* But this is *my* shift, and I'm responsible for the condition of the patients in this ward. All of you will have to leave. Now."

"But I'm all right," murmured Sabina.

The nurse produced a thermometer and thrust it under Sabina's tongue. "We'll see about that."

Everyone stood up and got ready to go. Eaken came over to Sabina's bedside. "I have to admit it all kind of hangs together," he said. "Let's see what's on that tape of yours when we get it dried out." He extended his hand. "It's been interesting meeting you, Mrs. Herschel."

"My name's Sabina Swift," she mumbled around the thermometer.

"No talking, please!" the nurse said sharply.

Bruno said, "May I stay? I'm her husband."

"And I'm her son," I added winningly.

The nurse's glance fell with favor on Bruno, whose teddy-bear looks are irresistible to certain women, and with suspicion on me. I did my best to look filial. After a moment she said reluctantly, "*You* two can stay."

278

The others filed out.

The nurse took Sabina's blood pressure and pulse, and made notes in a chart. Then she left the room, saying "Five minutes."

Sabina's eyes drooped and then she opened them to direct a quizzical blue stare in my direction. "Son, huh?"

"Just a technicality, don't worry about it," I said. "I've got one question. How come you let Theresa get behind you with her alpenstock?"

"I caught my heel in a loose plank on that damned bridge," she replied, looking embarrassed.

"I figured it was something like that. Here," I said. "I brought you a present." I handed her a box wrapped in tissue paper.

"A present?" She loves presents, she's like a kid with them. She reached weakly for the box and then said, "Bruno, would you open it for me?"

He took it and tore the paper off. Then he removed the cover and held the box so she could look inside. After a moment she said disgustedly, "You call that a present?"

"This present will change your life, I guarantee you'll love it." I took out a pair of running shoes. "Just try them, that's all I ask. The next time we set a trap for a murderer you'll be able to wear them and you won't have to worry about catching your heel in a hole. And I won't have to rescue you."

"Well, if it was too much trouble—"

"I didn't say that." I handed her one shoe. It was navy blue with a double red stripe near the heel, and red laces. Sharp. "You're going to experience comfort such as you've never imagined, Sabina. You'll see, you'll thank me."

She held the shoe in her hand and examined it critically. "You know," she said finally, "it's actually not bad-looking."

I smiled.

Her eyes closed and the shoe dropped on the blanket as the nurse stuck her head around the door. "Okay," she said in a voice that meant business. "That's it, everybody out."

Bruno and I stepped meekly past her iron bust, and I turned and called, "Bye, Mom," to Sabina. She was already asleep and didn't hear me. Probably just as well.